PRAISE FOR
FAMILY PORTRAIT

"All families have secrets and are made up of quirky personalities. It's almost like sitting on the outside looking in as Braun's characters reveal the patchwork of their personalities in her latest novel, **Family Portrait**. A great read."

Elizabeth Conte, award-winning author of
Finding Jane, The Chosen Mistress, and *Life of Her*

The Guest Book Trilogy
The Maidservant in Cabin Number One

"The descriptive narration and historical setting are flawless. Chrysteen Braun details every scene so the reader can experience everything that Ruth Ann feels. The little historical tidbits add such depth to the overall story. There are big world events (World War One, etc.) that are poignantly described, which had me whipping through the pages.

"If you're looking for a book that will transport you to a different time period, pick up *The Maidservant in Cabin Number One: The Beginning.* It's quite lovely. 5 Stars."

Nancy Light, *N.N. Light Bookhaven*

The Guest Book Trilogy
The Man in Cabin Number Five

"Masterfully written. An entertaining work that will keep the reader hooked until the end. Congratulations on an exceptional book."
Readers' Favorite

"An engaging drama with a strong cast and a final surprise."
Kirkus Review

The Guest Book Trilogy
The Girls in Cabin Number Three

"With themes of love, family, friendship, new beginnings, and the complexity of life, readers will get hooked from the very beginning."
San Francisco Book Review

The Guest Book Trilogy
The Starlet in Cabin Number Seven

"[The Starlet in Cabin Number Seven] feels like catching up with old friends as the narrative amiably revisits the highlights of Lake Arrowhead... A light and engaging read, with an enticing mountain setting."

Kirkus Review

The Guest Book Series
Dear Noah, The Conclusion

"Dear Noah is a story of love's timeless power, no matter a person's age. The descriptive and emotional narration makes Dear Noah a poignant and emotive read. The characters draw you in as the story unfolds. Chrysteen Braun's writing makes readers feel like part of the story. Dear Noah is an unforgettable read."

Nancy Light, N.N. Light Bookhhaven

"Chrysteen, you owe me a box of Kleenex!! I just finished Dear Noah, and I read it in one day as I could not put it down—LOVED it and can't wait to read your next book."

Deanne Dillenbeck, an avid fan.

The Guest Book Series
When The Daffodils Bloom, Charlotte's Story

"A compelling work of women's fiction. Chrysteen Braun does a mind-blowing job of building the characters and making them lifelike, loveable and loathsome."

Kate Osborn, former editor, *Mountain News, Lake Arrowhead.*

Also by Chrysteen Braun

The Guest Book Series
Love, Friendships, and New Beginnings...with a touch of mystery
(can all be read as standalones)

The Man in Cabin Number Five, Book One
The Girls in Cabin Number Three, Book Two
The Starlet in Cabin Number Seven, Book Three
The Maidservant in Cabin Number One,
The Beginning, Book Four
Dear Noah, The Conclusion, Book Five
When The Daffodils Bloom, Charlotte's Story, Book Six

FAMILY PORTRAIT

BASED ON A TRUE STORY

CHRYSTEEN BRAUN

Editing, design, and distribution by Bublish.

PART ONE

Panos Family Tree

Yia'Yia (yī'ya)

<u>Kate</u>	<u>Cynthia</u>	<u>Stavros</u>
Married	*Married*	*Married*
Tasso, Nick	Eddie	Eleni, Julia, Kelli, Jane
Children	*Children*	*Children*
Alex, Vaso	Kaylee, Eddie Jr.	Emma, Sophie

PREFACE

2025

By the time my father died in 2011, my relationship with my brother was nonexistent. And then four years later, when my mother passed away, the frayed thread that held us together finally snapped. There was so much anger and resentment between us, we never spoke again.

I've waited over ten years to write this story, and now that everyone is gone, I finally have the freedom to do so. We were all so multifaceted, imperfect and fragmented, but that's what makes up a family, isn't it?

Equally, if this was to be a true story, I had to be willing to talk about some of the things I did when I was younger that I'd never spoken of: not because they were unforgivable, but because I wasn't sure anyone would understand the girl I was back then versus the woman I became.

So, for better or worse.

In my case, better.

I've left nothing out.

But first, I want you to meet my family—to have them tell you their own stories—so that you'll know them not just from my point of view, but from theirs as well.

1980

My name is Vasiliki, but I go by Vaso.

And if this were the beginning of a movie, in the background, while the credits were rolling, the members of my family would be making an attempt to assemble on my grandmother's front porch for a portrait. The patient photographer would be doing his best to organize us by family. But he would be contending with someone who didn't want to follow the dictates of hierarchy. That would be my uncle. Even though he was the youngest of the siblings, he was the only surviving male—and the only college graduate, and the only pompous attorney, and the most married and divorced—*did I say all that aloud?*—he wanted to stand closest to my grandmother with his family in front of him, right in the middle of us all.

"Psst!"

Yia´ Yia's whisper was barely audible as she tapped his shoulder. But I heard it. And so did Stavros. "Stand where he tells us," she said.

His face immediately turned beet red, and he glanced about to see if anyone else had heard her. Then he gathered his current wife, Kelli, and his daughters, Emma and Sophie, and moved to stand next to my mother, who was already in place with my father and brother.

I could see Uncle Eddie's mother, Bessie, awkwardly waiting to find out where she would stand, since she technically wasn't part of our family; and then my Aunt Cynthia made room for her to stand next to her on Yia´ Yia's right.

The standing arrangement was supposed to be much like our family tree:

My grandmother

My parents, Kate & Nick, with my older brother, his then-wife and children, and me, Vaso, with my family	My aunt Cynthia, with her husband, their children and their families	My uncle Stavros with his current wife and his children

That's the way it should have been; my mother was the eldest, my aunt in the middle and my uncle, the youngest.

"Enough!" Yia´ Yia finally said, impatiently tapping her cane on the porch step. She didn't use her matriarchal influence on us often, but when she did, we came to attention and responded accordingly. In other words, we all fell into place.

It was a perfect day for the photo, although it meant the photographer stood facing the sun in the heat of the afternoon, and we were testing his good nature. He pulled a small towel out of his bag and wiped his forehead before he called us to final attention.

In a few clicks, he was done.

Finally, the director would call, "Cut!"

Afterward, Aunt Cynthia stood smoking one of her skinny cigars and said, "You know, this will be the last photograph of all of us together."

In my mind I said, "This is also the *first* photograph we've ever taken," and "Can you please put that awful thing out?" But I didn't.

Then she added, "I read the coffee grounds with Mother this morning, and soon, some will no longer be with us."

My cousin Kaylee heard this dire prediction, and we caught each other's eyes. I thought what Aunt Cynthia said was troubling. It made sense though, since Bessie was in her eighties, my grandmother was in her late seventies, and her three children were in their fifties. But my aunt was known for saying what she thought, and my older brother especially adored her. After all, they were both kindred spirits.

In other words, they were both rebels.

Aunt Cynthia had predicted our fate accurately, for soon everything changed. A year later, Bessie died, and then, years later, Uncle Eddie died of prostate cancer. My uncle Stavros, my brother, and my cousin Kaylee got divorced, and to make up for those we lost, my other cousin, who already had four children, had twins.

My mother and grandmother had had their portraits framed, and even though my uncle and brother remarried, for years, my mother hung hers in the hallway amid other family pictures, and my grandmother kept hers on a table in the living room. It was there until she died almost twenty years later. I put mine in a drawer with other photographs and memorabilia, and I had no idea what everyone else did with theirs.

CHAPTER ONE

EFFIMIA (YIÁ YIA)

I've been different ages over my lifetime, depending on current events; when we sailed to America from Greece in 1912, my mother said I was ten. When I needed to find a job to help support my family, I became sixteen.

For hundreds of years, records of births, baptisms, and deaths were kept in the village churches. It wasn't so long ago, on one of my visits back home, that I searched my family's records in our small church in the central Greek town of Karpenisi, where we were from, and I discovered I was born in 1898.

I've had eight children; four died in childbirth, one lived to the age of five, and three grew into adults and lived full, if not complicated, lives. One of my daughters died last year, and I think most of me died with her. I haven't been able to find much of a reason to live since then, for she was the one who needed me most.

Where we lived in Greece, farming was a way of life, but it was difficult because of the rocky land and limited good soil. Each family had small plots where they raised goats for milk and cheese, and sheep for wool and meat. Our olive trees provided enough olives for us both to marinate them and make them into 'Greek olives' plus make our own olive oil. If we had more than we needed for ourselves, we'd sell the finished product at our local market or trade with our neighbors for their apricots, peaches and figs, which were always so sweet tasting and delicious. Our grapevines provided us with enough grapes to make our wine.

In our outside ovens, we cooked all our meals and baked Koulourakia (koo-loo-RA´-key-a), a hand-braided hard cookie, which is still my favorite dessert. My next favorite is a twice-baked crunchy biscuit called Paximathia (pox´-e-ma´-th-a), also known as Greek Biscotti.

Our two-room house was made with stacked stones gathered from the land, and we had no glass windows. Our floors were dirt, covered with multiple layers of rugs, and since our roads were also dirt, dust always found its way into everything. I had outside chores, like cleaning the ovens every week, but unfortunately, dusting inside was something I had to do each day. I eventually learned to put a cloth over my mouth and nose so I wouldn't sneeze so much or taste the dirt.

Retaining walls made from dry-stacked stones with no mortar were used for terracing our gardens and building boundary walls along some of our roads. Many years later, when I returned home and traveled to other parts of old Europe, I realized that almost every country used the same construction techniques. For what other materials did they have access to?

My father used to call me his little katsika (cot-si´-ka) which was the name we called the babies of our goats. Female goats always stayed cute, but the male goats grew really long beards, and when they would urinate, it would spray into them. Needless to say, they were very smelly. I also used the rag over my nose and mouth when I had to help my father clean their pens.

Sheep, on the other hand, were not as offensive, and one day after I watched a lamb being born, I wanted to name it and keep it as a pet.

My mother tried to discourage me by saying, "You know the lamb will grow up and we will use its milk. We'll shave it and sell its wool. And we might need to kill it to eat its meat. We can never think of our animals as pets."

But I was undeterred, and once I discovered it was a female, I called her Pan, the Greek word for nature. Thankfully, my parents never slaughtered Pan, but one day they *did* trade her to a farmer, telling me he had more land for her to roam around on.

"She'll miss you," my mother said, holding me close, "but she'll have new friends and will be happy with more room to wander."

My eyes filled, and I tried very hard not to cry in front of her. But the minute I turned to walk away, the tears fell, and I wiped them from my eyes with the sleeve of my blouse. I knew Pan would be better off, and it was much more comforting to think she went to a new home, rather than have her end up in our oven for a meal!

Our school was in the village to the east of us, and ten of us crowded into one room. As girls, we were only expected to learn to read and write, but our teacher also taught us arithmetic. I actually loved learning, for I knew an education would allow me a chance at a better future. I loved my parents and our town, but I didn't want to be stuck there forever.

Because our school schedule was based on preparing and harvesting our land, we sometimes were out of school for several weeks at a time, so we could help work the land and care for the animals. As soon as my chores were done, I'd run to my friend Thalia's house, or we'd meet at our well, and then we'd climb to the highest point in the village. The warm Mediterranean climate was hottest during the summer, and we'd be sweating by the time we got to our destination. We could see what we thought was the coast and would imagine what it would be like to meet a handsome sailor and travel to other parts of the world. We were such dreamers when we were young.

During those free afternoons, we often sat with our knees pulled up to our chins and the sunlight glistened off the pale hairs that grew on our legs. In no time, the hair would turn dark, as it also would under our arms. My mother said it was a sign we were turning into women. Thalia was blonder than I was, for her grandparents had come from the north where over the centuries, cultures of Greeks and far away Scandinavians had mixed and married.

It was our tradition to be promised in an arranged marriage when we came of age. The most pleasant hope was to marry someone of our own age, or someone we'd grown up with. But we could also end up marrying men in their thirties who'd lost their wives and had children that needed to be cared for. Other, more distasteful matches were with men almost three times our age, either because they lived in a more remote village with no young women, or they'd never married because they'd had to care for their land and parents. To a young girl, this made any hope of romance seem impossible.

Many times we'd overheard the village women talk. "We'll never see that one again," they'd say when a local girl from our village left to marry a man from another town. "Once she's stuck taking care of a new family, she'll never have time to be free until her husband dies."

Because of the dirt roads, travel between towns was difficult, and my mother often told me she hoped I'd be betrothed to someone from our own town, so that we'd be able to see each other often. There were three such young men in our village, so I had high hopes it would turn out to be one of them.

However, I'd recently seen an older man who was a second cousin to my father stop by our home, when my parents thought I wasn't there. His name was Yanni, or Greek for John, and he spoke of his wish to possibly take me as his wife. His trousers were soiled where he undid his pants, and his dirty white shirtsleeves were rolled to his elbows. He had never married and was ready to settle down. I held my breath as I listened to them talk.

"It's too soon for us to make any plans for Effimia," I heard my mother say to my father. In a Greek family, the father is supposed to be the one who makes the decisions, but often it's the wife who makes her feelings known, and then they do what she thinks is best.

"I see," the man said as he stood and gathered his things. "I'll come back when she is older then." With that, he bowed his head slightly and left.

I'd made myself dizzy with worry as I listened in, and as I let my breath out, I felt like I was going to faint. Instead, I leaned my head against the cool rock of our bedroom wall and tried to calm myself.

My mother never spoke to me about Yanni, and I knew I needed to wait until the right time to bring up the dreams *I* had for a husband. Even at the young age of ten, I was determined I'd never marry that man or anyone else I didn't care for.

Marriage must have been in the air, for not long after Yanni's visit, Thalia and I met at our spot on the hill.

"Oh, Effie," she said, trying to hold back tears.

We'd braided each other's hair to keep the wind from blowing it in our faces, but she wiped at the wisps that had blown into her mouth, anyway.

"I heard my parents talking, and I will die if I have to marry my second cousin Dimitri. He smells and his mother—she treats him like a baby."

"At least he would be better than some old man with hair in his ears. No matter who my parents choose for me, I'll never marry anyone," I said confidently. "I want to travel and see the world."

"I wish I had your courage," Thalia said, leaning her head on my shoulder. It was warm out, and I could smell the sweat in her hair.

"I'm sure everything will work out for us," I said. Then I had a great idea. "You could come with me. We'll run away together," I said, taking her hand.

In my heart, I wasn't sure who my parents were planning on me marrying, but I knew I would do anything I had to, to keep from being with someone I didn't love.

Thalia just sighed and ran her free hand under her runny nose.

Every year, we celebrated two major events in our village. One was Easter, a tradition we took very seriously and even brought with us to America.

We all knew that Jesus died on the cross. By the end of the forty days of Lent, with its prayers and fasting, we could hardly wait to taste the foods we'd been without and kick off the celebration. The Saturday before Easter, just before midnight, the church would go completely dark. When the candles were lit again the next morning, we chanted "Christos Anesti," Christ Is Risen. And the reply was "Alithinos Anesti," Yes, He Is Risen.

I didn't know it then, but Greek Easter, as we later referred to it, was based on the Julian calendar, and usually fell on a different date than the traditional western "American" Easter, which is based on the Gregorian calendar.

We roasted the traditional meal of lamb because, according to the Apostle John, Jesus was the Lamb of God. He died on the cross as a sacrifice for our sins, and eating lamb honored this belief. (However, if lamb wasn't available in certain parts of the country, the people would eat goat meat instead).

We baked traditional sweet Easter bread, called tsoureki (sou-rek´-i) usually with a red-dyed egg in the center. Some ingredients used in this bread were not to be used during Lent, such as sugar, butter, and eggs.

We dyed hard-boiled eggs in red dye, which signified Jesus' blood in the tomb. By adding vinegar to the dye, it kept the eggs from turning pink, or pale. Then we'd wipe them with olive oil to give them a shine. When the meal was over, we each chose what we hoped was the toughest egg and tapped them tip to tip. The last uncracked egg won the game and, with it, a year of good luck.

There was always a main dining table for adults only and a children's table for the young ones. We could hardly wait to grow old enough to sit at the adult table where you would be included not only in the egg cracking but also in the adult conversations.

As the eventual matriarch of our family in America, Greek Easter celebrations were a tradition I insisted we carry on even if it meant I did all the cooking. I knew it was the one time of year my family would gather to celebrate. As I grew older, I accepted that when I was gone, the tradition would likely fade with me. With each new generation of our American-born children, a little more of it slipped away.

The second most wonderful event was the annual Greek festival. Since our town was too small for its own celebration, we rode our donkeys into a larger town about ten miles away. The church there was much larger, and there was room enough for the festival and everyone who came. The women of the church sold roasted chickens and lamb, tasty rice, and Greek salad as their major fundraiser. Hundreds of cookies and desserts were set up on tables around the dining hall. Outside, vendors set up tables under tents so they could sell their handmade jewelry, bags of almonds and pistachios, crosses and icons, and handmade clothing.

Musicians played dance music, and throughout the day there were performances by young dancers dressed up in traditional garb. Young boys dressed as Evzones (ev´-zones)—elite Greek soldiers—and the girls wore off-white dresses and red embroidered vests. Their hair was covered in festively tied scarves that coordinated with their outfits.

Even though the festivals were held during the hottest month of the year, we ate and danced all day. If we had enough money left over, we brought home cookies and something else I loved, galaktoboureko (gal-a-to-bū´-tico) a traditional Greek custard made with a crispy phyllo pastry shell. After the festival ended, and once we returned home, even though it was late at night, we ate the rest of the galaktoboureko, knowing it would spoil by morning.

CHAPTER TWO

EFFIMIA

By 1912, the tensions that would soon lead to World War I were already building, and my parents feared Greece might be drawn into the war. They began making plans for us to go to Canada, where my mother's cousins lived. We would have to leave everything we'd known behind, but the good news was that any talk of my marriage plans would be put on hold.

We told our village we were leaving because our family in Canada needed us. My father was afraid that if we told them the truth, rumors about the war would spread and frighten everyone. He also feared that if more people wanted to leave, we might not get to go ourselves. He sold our land, our animals, and our household furnishings. This provided us with enough money to pay for passage and give us a fresh beginning in what was to be our new homeland.

I was allowed to bring one suitcase, and after packing my clothes, I didn't have much room left for my treasures. I only had room for my collection of bird feathers and my smallest of seashells from a trip we'd taken to the coast the previous year. My mother was bringing our family photos, our silver censer (incense burner), the painted icons from both my grandmothers, her copper teakettle, and the mortar and pestle that had been handed down for generations.

Both my grandfathers had already died, but I still had my grandmothers. While they were only in their fifties, they were both bent over from calcium deficiencies and walked with canes. They decided they were too old to make the trip to North America and start over, so they stayed behind. They still wore black, the traditional widow's clothing;

black scarves covering their hair, black dresses, stockings, and shoes. Whether they were hauling water from the well, working in their gardens, or caring for the animals, widowed Greek women dressed in black, unless they were still of an age to marry again.

The next time Thalia and I climbed the rocks to our favorite spot, I carried a fabric bag over my shoulder, and by the time I got there, I could feel the sweat trickling down my back.

"I will leave you my rock collection, and these shells." I said, handing her the bag. I knew very little about Canada, but I shared what my mother had told me. "We will stay in a brick building with my cousins. There are cars, and factories, and tall buildings where everyone lives."

"But what will I do without you?" she cried as she unwrapped her new treasures.

"We can write," I answered as cheerfully as I could. "I can send you letters when we get there."

"I will probably have to marry Dimitri unless some miracle happens. Who will you marry?"

"I don't know," I thought, encouraged by all the possibilities. "Maybe there will be more choices there."

I'd thought to bring a mantili (a handkerchief), and I handed it to her to wipe her face and nose. I felt bad for her, with no future here. And I felt guilty I was so excited about all the new opportunities I dreamed were ahead of me.

I wanted no tearful goodbyes when we left, so on the day we set out, I made Thalia promise she wouldn't come to see us off. As we rode out of town, it would be the last time I would see the widow women pumping water and the old men with their Greek fishermen's hats sitting on benches under one of the large olive trees. I'd miss seeing the village cats rub against their legs, begging either for food or to be petted.

As our donkey strained to pull us with all our belongings, I was hoping my father had done a good job packing our cart. I was also hoping we'd have no accidents before we got into port, so we could sell the cart and our faithful donkey Elia (il´-e-a) (Olive). As we passed the last corner before the open road, I couldn't help but turn to see if Thalia had come against my wish to say goodbye. But for once, she'd listened to me, and she was nowhere to be seen. I sighed with disappointment.

We'd been best friends forever, and I never envisioned my life without her. I'd accepted the idea of our move, and I was eagerly looking forward to our new adventure, but I was troubled for her and her family. I'd promised my father I wouldn't tell her what he knew about the future. I couldn't tell her about a possible war, and I felt terribly guilty.

"I know I'll be back for a visit," I'd said.

But when that would be, I did not know.

The truth was, I would not see Thalia for many years.

CHAPTER THREE

EFFIMIA

Anything beyond steerage was far beyond our means, so we sailed in the cheapest quarters, along with everyone else like us. And even at that, it was almost a quarter of what money we had. Because we could save money if I traveled as a child, my mother bound my budding breasts and we passed me off as being only ten years old. I was at first insulted that I could be considered so young; however, when my mother gave me the evil eye, I knew I wouldn't be able to fight her on this matter. Somehow, throughout the voyage, she maintained the deception, but I was constantly afraid someone would see my wrapped breasts and report us.

The lower deck was all that most immigrants could afford, and the conditions were deplorable. We were actually placed in the cargo hold, where there was never enough light or air. We were considered lucky because we traveled as a family and we slept in the center section of the ship. There, when the sea was rough, we were bounced around the least. They used the family area as a separation from the other passengers. Fabric partitions were set up, and single male travelers stayed on one side of us, and women with or without children were on the other.

As we soon discovered, traveling in steerage was nothing like traveling in first or second class, where food was plentiful. We had a dining area where tables and benches were set up and, in twenty-minute increments, they served us lukewarm soup, soggy boiled potatoes, stale bread, and stringy beef or some type of fish. We ate in shifts, and if we missed our designated time, we went without a meal. There was no choice but to leave our possessions unattended while we ate, and after our first meal, other passengers in our group complained that some of their things had gone missing. After that, we all decided that the group with a different seating schedule would watch out for our property, and we would do the same for them.

My mother had packed some fruit, bread, and hard cheese that wouldn't turn rancid, and while we tried to ration our portions, other passengers managed to help themselves to our food when we weren't looking. Rats got into what was left, and we ran out only days after we set sail.

Over a hundred of us were crammed into our living space, and once passengers started getting seasick, there wasn't enough clean air to breathe. We used buckets of saltwater to wash ourselves and our clothes and the floors. Almost from that first day, we too got seasick, but my mother and I pulled out of it quicker than my father did. We tried to get up on to the deck where the cool salty sea water sprayed our faces bringing temporary relief from the stifling heat down below but most times it was impossible for us to find any room up there since that's where everyone else wanted to be.

Sleeping accommodations were metal beds stacked on top of each other, with a six foot long straw mattress covered by a sheet of fabric. We each received blankets; however, they weren't big enough to cover us, and they gave us no clean bedding for the entire trip. We had two and a half feet from the bottom of the bed frame to the bed on top of us, and in this space we had to find the room to sleep plus keep any personal belongings we'd brought with us. Again, we made sure someone was always keeping watch, for we couldn't bring everything with us every time we went for meals or used the toilets.

Soon, people began coughing, and my father was one of them. He'd never been ill in his life, but the prolonged seasickness had so weakened him, he didn't even want to go have meals. We could tell he was losing weight, and then thankfully, by the second week, he started feeling much better.

"Dóxa sto Theó," my mother said. "Praise be to God."

Our washrooms were only about ten feet by seven feet! At least there were sinks, but it was impossible to keep the men from using the women's area, and if someone was sick, the entire room smelled disgusting. That was also where passengers with lice tried to wash them from their hair, often to no avail.

There was no privacy, and try as we might, there was absolutely nothing that could be done to guarantee someone wasn't watching us when we changed our clothing. I had started my monthly bleeding at least six months before we left Karpenisi, and I'd brought rags to use between my legs. None of the women paid any attention to me as I changed them and rinsed them out, but it was impossible to keep the men from looking my way. I went to my mother and asked if she would start accompanying me and keep watch when I needed to take care of my woman's duties.

Men who had been waiting for the opportunity attacked several women. I'd never heard men speak so crudely before, and even when their words weren't in Greek, I understood enough to know what they were saying. Women screamed, and children cried. At first I tried to cover my ears, but that didn't help, and eventually I just did my best to block it all out.

The other thing I had to block out was listening to husbands and wives doing their private business! I couldn't believe they could actually do that when there were so many people around to hear them.

"If you and Papa ever do that, I will never speak to you again," I told my mother harshly. We had both been listening to a neighbor while my father just snored. "It's worse than listening to the animals mate," I added, then rolled over to face the opposite direction.

Our quarters were only cleaned three times while we were on board, which meant everyone had to gather their belongings and make their way to the decks so the deckhands could pour buckets of water onto the floors. This always seemed to create additional chaos, for when some people returned to their areas, they "forgot" where they originally slept and tried to take different beds.

If there wasn't enough money to pay for passage for an entire family, sometimes only the men would make the trip to the new country to find work—and eventually they hoped to send for their wives and children after they'd established themselves. I later learned that a lot of families never reunited, for it sometimes took years to save enough money, and some men just stayed. Sometimes, husbands would even return to Greece defeated. Or, as in one case with a family I'd met once we got to Chicago, the mother died while the father was in America, and the children were just left behind to be raised by aunts and grandmothers. My mother reminded me over the years that no matter our hardships, we were lucky to have stayed together for as long as we did.

There was no proper hospital for steerage—only for first and second-class passengers. There was, however, a doctor, but since seasickness was the primary ailment, he wouldn't treat us. Mostly, we were cared for by sympathetic fellow passengers, unless death was inevitable. Then, that person would be removed from the area and relocated to somewhere else where no one saw them again.

Almost halfway through our voyage, my parents discovered there could have been another option for passage; for a little more money, we could have stayed in rooms with only sixteen berths and enough space for hand baggage. There were hooks for clothing, electric lights, partition walls that allowed air ventilation, and even a washstand. While still oppressive, it had to be a lot better than how we were living. However, by the time my parents found out about it, there were no more berths available, so we had to make do and stay where we were.

It was forty-five days in all until we reached our destination, the port of Halifax. And where I once sat on the rocks looking out at the horizon with Thalia, wishing I could travel the world, I prayed I'd never have to travel by ship or see the ocean again.

We were supposed to be vaccinated before arriving, but some people told my mother they'd never received an immunization at all. Passenger lists were rare, so there was no way to prove that someone boarded the ship, arrived in port, or died along the way! None of us spoke English; otherwise, we would have understood what the crews said as we disembarked: "Here we are, letting the invasion continue and selling out our country piece by piece."

CHAPTER FOUR

EFFIMIA

A Greek-speaking porter on the dock told us about a small boarding house where we could stay the night until we boarded the train the next day. We had to pay someone to load and bring all our things, but it was better than leaving sleeping at the station.

There were six other people also staying in the house, so there was a lot of activity. The good news was there was a bathroom down the hall, and the best news was it had hot water. I stayed with my parents in our one room, and while it was cramped, it was a great improvement over the accommodations we'd just left. They served dinner to all the guests at the same time. We sat around a large table and watched as bowls and platters of odd-looking food were set down in the center, eventually to be passed around.

I was starving, so I would have eaten almost anything. I could recognize vegetables, cabbage and potatoes, but the meat looked funny and pale.

"It's been boiled," my mother said when I hesitated serving myself.

I took a small portion, then a tiny bite, and after tasting it, when the plate came around again, I had another piece. It was the first time any of us had eaten corned beef. I recognized it in our breakfast the next morning, diced and fried with potatoes and made into what they called hash.

Around noon the next day, we boarded a train that would take us to Montreal, where our relatives lived. The train traveled through the vast countryside, stopping at small towns constantly picking up and dropping off passengers.

Along the way, roadside houses were set up to feed those who were hungry, so on one stop we got off and had a dinner much like the one in the house we stayed in. Because it was very expensive to eat on the train, we bought some fruit, cheese and bread to tide us over for our morning meal. We had another day of travel before we got to our destination, and again we stopped at a place where we could share a meal for dinner.

I was eager to see our relatives when they greeted us at the station in Montreal, and we were disappointed that no one my parents recognized was there. Once we realized they would not have known exactly when we'd be arriving, we showed a driver with a horse-drawn cart the address. Thankfully, he knew where we wanted to go, and he took us directly there.

The streets were lined with three-and four-story stone and red brick buildings built right next to each other. The sheer number of them amazed me. I watched as women hung laundry from clotheslines outside most of the windows. I'd never seen so many people in one place, and I couldn't believe cars, horse-drawn carriages and trolley cars shared the same street.

As we unloaded the cart in front of a building, two young children who didn't recognize us asked my father who we were, and then rushed inside. By the time we had neatly stacked our belongings, my mother's cousin, Theia (aunt) stood on their porch stoop drying her hands on her apron, then wiped perspiration from her forehead.

"*Ela*," she cried out. "*Ela thoh* (eh´-lah-tho). Come here!" she called both in Greek and in English.

Everyone grabbed something, and we made our way up the steps, then up two flights of stairs to their apartment. Almost before we could set our things down, she pulled first my father, then my mother, to her. She was crying by the time she got to me, and she hugged me so tightly I could hardly breathe.

"I can't believe you're here!"

She held me at arm's length, and then hugged me again.

"How did you grow so much since I last saw you?" she asked in Greek. "Are you hungry? Are you thirsty?"

Once she released me, I looked around the apartment and I was amazed to see it had wood flooring, windows with glass, a kitchen, and a bedroom.

What my father saw was entirely different. He said, "You don't have room for us, Katrina. We don't want to be a burden to you."

"Stop now, do you hear me? There is always room for our family. And once you get a job, you can find your own place. But for now, you will stay here. Aristos will be pleased to have you here to help with his work."

I pulled at my mother's sweater and asked, "What does Theios Aristos do?"

"He is a cobbler. He makes shoes for everyone."

"Oh," I said, watching my little cousins hiding behind my aunt's dress.

It seemed my father would learn to be a cobbler.

Since my aunt, uncle and three children shared the one bedroom, we would have to stay in the living room. We attempted to stack our belongings as best we could and only unpacked our clothing, which we put in baskets so they would be easy to access.

I hadn't seen my older cousin, but waited to ask about her until we finally sat and had some coffee.

"Where's Lexi?" I asked.

"She'll be home any minute now," my aunt said. "She's gone to the market for me . . ." Tilting her head in thought, she added, "I hope we have enough to make a nice dinner for tonight. We might have to get a few more things."

"If we do," I offered, "I'll go with her."

"Wonderful," my aunt said, patting my hand.

My aunt and uncle had lived in the village next to ours in Greece, and we'd made it a point to see each other as often as we could. I was trying to remember how long it had been since they'd left for Canada, and when Lexi came home, I couldn't believe how beautiful she'd become. She was only one year older than me, but her figure was full, and her long brown hair was braided and wrapped into a bun at the nape of her neck.

Lexi took one look at us and rushed in for hugs. For the entire trip, I'd thought about how sad I was to have left Thalia behind, but when Lexi got to me, she hugged me extra hard, and I knew she could help fill the void within me.

The women started cleaning vegetables and preparing a lamb roast for dinner, and the moment my uncle came home, he and my father found a space in the living room so they could talk.

Even though our stomachs were full, we slept fitfully that first night; my parents shared the sofa, each resting their heads at the opposite ends, and I slept on the floor. Hopefully, we'd be able to find a mattress for me.

It was agreed my father would become my uncle's apprentice, and the next morning after breakfast, the two of them went to work. Because we needed money, my father found a part-time job sweeping and cleaning for one of the local Greek store owners. Women traditionally didn't work outside the home, but my mother also found work, cleaning and cooking in a small taverna. After all, there was only me to take care of, and I was no longer a child—plus the extra money would help us get on our feet faster. She could also bring home any leftovers, so that meant she could contribute to the household meals.

When we first got there, my aunt's landlord was sympathetic to our situation, but after a few months, he wanted to talk to her about charging more rent because there were more people staying in the apartment.

My father had earned enough money by then that we could afford to pay the additional rent and still save.

"It's our way of taking another step towards re-establishing ourselves in our new country," my father said while counting out the rent. "I will not live dependent on anyone. I never have, and I never will."

CHAPTER FIVE

EFFIMIA

For the rest of the summer, we sweltered in the crowded apartment, and when fall arrived, the cooler weather was a relief. But then my father started coughing like he had on the ship. We attributed it to the long hours he worked and the little sleep he got when he came home, and thankfully, after about a month, the cough went away.

We attended the local Greek church on Sundays, and the Greek families who had also settled in Montreal chipped in to hire a teacher who could help us learn English. We'd quickly learned that immigrants who didn't try to better themselves were treated worse than those who did. Plus, if you knew English, you could apply for non-Greek jobs. It expanded your horizons. Everyone but my father and uncle went to classes.

After a couple more months, Lexi and I decided it was time we also looked for work, and we eventually found a factory that needed seamstresses. At first, our parents weren't happy, and they didn't want to accept our financial contributions to the household, but eventually they came to agree it would be a good thing. We could help pay for our keep, and better than that, we could set aside some money for ourselves.

"I still have a dream to travel," I told Lexi in English. "But not on a ship unless it's first class!"

"But how will you do that?" she asked.

"I will save my money, and one day, I will go to America."

She was crestfallen. "But how can you leave your family? And how can you leave me?"

"You can come with me," I said.

It was only a year ago that I told Thalia she could travel with me, too. How quickly the time had passed. Although I'd written several times, I had only heard from her once since we left, and I wondered how she was doing. Was she going to be stuck marrying Dimitri?

Thankfully, there had been no talk of any marriage for me yet, but I was growing older, and I was certain that even here, in this new country, many of the old traditions would be upheld.

When we had no chores or work to do, Lexi and I would often sit outside on the steps to our building and watch people walk by. I was still thinking about traditions when I asked, "Have your parents talked to you about who you will marry?"

"Not a lot yet. Here, it's not much like it was back home. First, there aren't enough single Greek men to go around, and second, if I work, I can continue to help support the family. They would lose that if I married. I would have to stay at home and have children. *And take care of my mother-in-law*." She made a face and then laughed.

I was relieved to think I had more time to experience life before I had to marry.

When the apartment next door became available, we finally moved into our own place. But as the winter cold bore down on us, my father started looking more tired than usual. His bones ached and his back hurt—he still had his second job, and we all attributed his ailments to that and to the weather. It had never been this cold in Greece. When his cough came back and he started producing spatters of blood on his handkerchief, we made him see a doctor, who confirmed he had tuberculosis. Since no one else here had any symptoms, we told the doctor about my father coughing while on the ship.

"Most likely, that's when he contracted it," the doctor said. "The good news is there are vitamins we can try. They might help," he said, more to himself than to us. "We can try that and see," he continued. "In the meantime, he needs to rest. You need to make sure your husband, *and* father, continues to cover his mouth every time he coughs.

"If it were warm, we could have him sit in the sun, which has proven to be a very effective treatment in itself. There are even places where patients can go to rest and be in good weather, but nothing like that is available here. We'll try this and see what happens," he continued.

Of course, my father hated that he wasn't able to go to work, and I think that made his recovery even slower. With my mother's work, and my seamstress job, we had enough money to pay our rent, but the longer it took my father to get well, the tighter the finances grew.

By summer, my father was well enough to go back to working as a cobbler, but he'd lost his other job.

"This is not how I thought we'd live when we came here," I heard him say to my mother.

"No, it's not," she replied with encouragement, "but you're back on your feet now and something better is going to come along for us. For now, let me and Effie do our part to help out."

With his jaw firmly set in resignation, and a shake of his head, he took his hat from its hook and said, "I'll look for more work today." Then he left.

Once my father found another part-time job, we felt almost immediate financial relief. Back then, our rent was twenty dollars per month, bread was six cents a loaf, a dozen eggs were thirty-four cents, and milk was fifteen cents for two quarts. Meat was about twenty-three cents a pound, so we made sure to make our meals stretch as far as possible and we learned to waste nothing.

In a few months, I was able to start setting aside my savings again. I'd gladly used it when we needed it, and I would do it again if I needed to.

By the time I was seventeen, more Greek immigrants had arrived in Montreal, which meant several things. More people were given the opportunity to have a better life, more eligible Greek men filled our growing community (which meant of course that the subject of my future marriage would most likely come up), but most of all, more people crowded into the already small apartments their relatives lived in, and more people needed jobs. On the other hand, the more people who came to live there, the more services the cities needed, so more jobs were created out of necessity.

The factory where I worked hired a few more girls, and I was promoted. I trained them to sew buttonholes quickly and efficiently. My raise was minimal, only a few cents more, but I didn't complain, for it meant I could add more each week to my savings envelope.

I'd never lost sight of traveling to America, and once my savings grew to be what I thought was enough, I started talking about my plans with Lexi, and then my mother.

CHAPTER SIX

THE DAY OF THE PORTRAIT, 1980
VASO

We were running late even before we left to pick up the girls, and then we had to wait for them to finish dressing. Steven had gone to their front door, but when no one answered, he opened it and stuck his head in.

"C'mon, girls," he called out.

Holly and Tara lived with their mother. We'd only been married a couple of years, but since the girls were now my family too, I wanted them to be included in our portrait. While they were the only stepchildren in the photograph, we weren't the only ones with mixed families. My uncle Stavros was there with his third wife, and my cousin Kaylee was there with her second husband.

"C'mon," Steven called again, and as he got back to our car, the girls stepped outside and closed the front door behind them.

"You girls look very pretty," I said, turning to them in the back seat.

We were driving our 'new to us' 1975 dark blue four-door Mercedes sedan. Steven loved buying and selling cars and had come across a deal he couldn't pass up, hoping to drive it a while before he found something else he liked better. And I liked the way I felt driving that car. Not that I felt I deserved it, or was better than anyone else, but I felt special in it. We were only about a mile from my grandmother's house when we stopped at a red light, and I looked at my watch.

"I'm sure we're not the only ones who'll be late," I said wistfully as I put my hand on Steven's thigh. We suddenly heard brakes squeal and tires screech. Then we felt a jarring thud as the car behind us plowed into our rear end. My clip-on earrings flew off my ears and landed on the dashboard.

I quickly checked on the girls.

"*Great*," Steven said, putting the car into park and getting out.

"Are you two okay?" I asked them at the same time.

I waited in the car but could tell the young girl in the Volkswagen behind us was still in her car, and she'd started crying.

When Steven finally got back into our car, he said, "She's okay. She'd just picked her cat up from the vet, and he went between her legs. She's fine. Are you guys okay?"

"Did you get her information?" I asked.

"Our bumper has a minor dent in it, but the front end of her VW is pretty bad. She wants to pay for the repairs and not turn it over to her insurance company. Says her parents are going to kill her."

Eventually, we were back on our way, and as we pulled up, my uncle made a big deal about looking at his watch.

"Sorry we're late," Steven said to Yia´ Yia once we got out of the car. "We just got rear-ended."

"Oh, dear. Are you all okay?" my mother asked.

"We're fine," I said.

"What about your new car?" my father asked.

"It's fine. Just the bumper, but the poor girl who ran into us had damage," Steven answered, then gave him a blow by blow of what had happened.

"Where do you want us?" I asked, to no one in particular.

"I think we should be on this side," my uncle Stavros said, attempting to direct traffic.

"The photographer wants us to stand according to our age, like a family tree," my Aunt Cynthia said crossly.

"You mean all the old folks in the back?" I joked.

"I'd like to stand in front of Mother," Uncle Stavros said.

"*You're such a child*," my aunt said.

"*Okay*," my mother said, trying to speak over everyone, "let's do it the way the photographer suggests. He knows best."

"*Enough*," Yia´ Yia said, striking her cane loudly on the porch.

We paused, then wordlessly shuffled ourselves into new positions, all under the watchful eye of the neighbor across the street, who sat smoking on her porch and taking in the show. When we were finally in place, the photographer sighed.

"We need to get this show on the road, kids, before we lose more natural daylight," he said.

My Aunt Cynthia ground out her cigarette in the ashtray sitting next to her, and she pulled her shoulders back to accentuate her bust line. It reminded me of one of my father's famous jokes.

"Mirror, mirror on the wall, who's the fairest of them all? You are," he'd say to my mother, trying to give her a kiss on the cheek. "But your sister has bigger knockers."

Cynthia definitely made the best of her height and figure. She wore her dark eyebrows thick before it was fashionable, and red lipstick was her trademark. She was the kind of woman who could walk into a room and men would stop what they were doing and stare. She liked it, and so did my Uncle Eddie.

"Who's the lucky one in this deal?" he'd ask, basking in the attention.

"Of course, you are, darling," my aunt would answer coyly.

She and my grandmother were one of the few women who could still wear a knit dress and get away with it.

I used to call us the bun women. Yia´ Yia wore hers pulled back at the nape of her neck, my mother wore hers loosely on top of her head, and my Aunt Cynthia wore hers tightly pulled back at the nape of her head. When I wore my hair in a bun, like it was that day, I wore it to the side, above my right ear.

My mother was more petite than Aunt Cynthia, shorter, and also a natural beauty. She could get away with wearing no makeup other than lipstick. My grandmother was like that too. It gave me hope for when I grew older.

It seemed to take us more time to get ourselves in place than it did to take the photographs, and within minutes, we were finished.

My cousin's young children ran off to play while Yia´ Yia, my mother and Stavros' wife Kelli, finished preparing a leg of lamb for dinner. I realized it was the first time in ages we'd all been together for a meal, and there was only room for the two oldest grandchildren, Alex and Kaylee, and their spouses at the adult table. Steven and I sat at the intermediate table with our girls, Alex's children, and Stavros' girls. Eddie Jr. and his wife sat with their young children on the other side of the living room at their own crowded table.

I knew Yia´ Yia was in seventh heaven to have her family together, and Stavros stood to give a toast.

"To our family."

"To our family," we all echoed as we lifted our glasses.

CHAPTER SEVEN

CYNTHIA

Kynthia, in Greek, was another name for Artemis, the goddess of the moon and hunting. In mythology, she had a twin brother, Apollo.

I'm not sure if my mother knew that story when she named me; I think it was more because it was a Greek name that could be translated into English. In those days, speaking the English language and being Westernized were more important to her than maintaining our heritage; it made her feel more like an American.

I was always the one who wanted to do things differently. When we were young, I didn't want to sit next to my sister Kate at the dinner table; I wanted to sit next to my mother. But it was Kate and my brother Michael who always flanked her. In the family hierarchy, the older children sat next to their parents. But when Stavros was born, he sat next to my mother in his high chair, and I was pushed to the end of the table. If I didn't get my way, Mother tried to make me behave by giving me her famous look, the evil eye, but I wasn't afraid of it, or of her. If my father were home, he would pound the table and try to silence me. The jolt of his hand hitting the table *would* silence me, but only for a moment.

I was spoiled. When I didn't want to clear the table, Kate did it for me. And when I didn't want to cut the potatoes for dinner, Kate did it just to keep me from whining.

When Michael got sick, I was old enough to know better, but I still pouted and stomped my feet with jealousy.

"Akatonomastos," (a-ka-to-ono-mas´-tos) my mother would call to me. 'He who must not be named' meaning I was acting like the devil.

When I was older, I realized just how badly I'd behaved before Michael died, but it was too late. I remember my father not talking to me for months, and my mother barely tolerating me. It was only Kate who held me when I cried.

Stavros, being the baby of the family, and now the only male child, soon seemed to get all the attention. If he got on my nerves, I'd walk by him and pinch him. Of course, this just made him cry, but I didn't care.

It was during the Great Depression, which I didn't understand, and I resented our parents worked seven days a week in their store, just to keep food on our table. Often if customers couldn't afford to pay their bill, my parents would never send them away, but would instead keep a journal of who owed what, telling them they could pay them once they were back on their feet.

Around the age of nine, my parents put me to work in the store after school—a job I quickly grew to dislike. I remember once knocking over a crate of onions by accident. They rolled across the floor in every direction, and since Kate wasn't there, I had to collect them myself and sweep up the mess.

Stavros rarely had to work, claiming he was studying, and when he turned twelve, he began talking to my parents about his education and future. My mother still clung to him; after all, he was her only son. My father argued it was time to teach him discipline, and when my mother finally agreed, they sent him to the military academy in Signal Hill.

"It's a reform school," I said to him one afternoon.

"It's definitely not," he replied in that righteous tone of his. "It provides young men with an educational environment if they're seeking greater achievement. It grooms us for leadership."

"Did you read that and memorize it?" I asked sarcastically.

Stavros hadn't lost his ability to totally irritate me! And they chose him to succeed instead of me or Kate. He was a male child, and he was expected to make something of himself and support a family, where we were here to get married and take care of our families.

With Stavros now at school, Kate and I had to work at the store even more. Fat old Greek women, always dressed in black from head to toe, and with hair growing out from their chins, came into the store regularly, and it was all I could do to keep from giggling when I saw them coming. If my mother or father saw them first, they quickly sent me to the back room to do something more important, but I knew it was to keep me from embarrassing them.

As my sister Kate and I grew older, sometimes these women would come in with either their unmarried sons or young nephews directly from Greece to introduce them to us. I think the only thing Kate ever agreed with me on was that there was no way she was ever going to marry someone who'd been selected for her.

"In my day," our mother would say, "our parents arranged our marriages."

One day, when I was around fifteen, an older man came into the store and tried to catch my eye. I could tell he was interested in me, so I pretended I hadn't seen him and went into the storeroom. Later, when I told my mother about him, she shared the story about herself and Yanni back in the old country.

"So you escaped him when you came here?" I asked. "Then why do you let those women come in and talk to you about marriage for us?"

"I am guilty," Mother said. "I left home as soon as I could and eventually met your father. He was my choice. That's really what we want for you girls. We just don't want to make any oceans."

"You mean waves," I said. "Thank God."

"One day, you'll find someone to marry," she said.

Never, is what I thought. That was until I met Eddie.

Once I turned sixteen, Mother would let Kate and me take the bus to the beach, and on our way we'd walk past an amusement park called the Pike. Although I dared her, Kate was never brave enough to stop there, but it always looked so tempting. And the more our parents told us to stay away from there, the more I wanted to explore it. I'd heard that was where the sailors went when they came to shore, and I was always a sucker for uniforms.

I eventually talked Kate into going to the Pike, but she wouldn't go in.

"I'll wait outside," she said.

"Suit yourself," I said, leaving her with my beach bag.

I met Eddie while standing in line for a snow cone, of all things. He cut in front of the sailor behind me, and just when I'd ordered lime flavor, he said, "Oh, I'd get cherry. It's the sweetest. Just like you must be." And then he winked at me.

I should have been insulted, but he was so cute, I couldn't help but laugh at him.

"If only you knew," I replied. I turned to the vendor and said, "I'll take the cherry instead."

"I knew it!" Eddie said to a buddy standing to the side.

When I turned to see who he was talking to, the top of my cone fell off.

"Oh, damn!" I said, pouting.

He stepped up to the stand and said, "Mister, did you see what just happened? Can you give the lady another one?"

The snow cone vendor frowned but begrudgingly gave me a new one. I would have sworn it was not as generous a serving as my first one!

Eddie reached up to get it and handed it to me. "Here you go, Doll."

Again, I should have been insulted, but I loved that nickname. Doll.

"I was here once when they filmed an Abbott and Costello movie," Eddie said as we started walking. "I could never work making movies. I wouldn't have the patience."

Maybe so, but I thought he was handsome enough to be a movie star.

Two months later, we were married—I became Mrs. William Edward Landon III, and from then on I called him William.

Although my parents weren't pleased I'd married a man whom I barely knew, they were more concerned that he wasn't Greek.

"I don't recall them ever giving us restrictions," I told Vaso.

"I think it was just implied," she said, rolling her eyes.

Not long after that, I realized I was going to have a baby.

Being the kind of man he was, William told my parents he would be baptized in the church and remarry me.

I was pregnant with Kaylee the first time I lost my balance and fell. I was at our store on 7th Street when I turned too quickly to greet a customer and I knocked over the display of cantaloupes I'd just finished setting up. Pop was more concerned about bruising the melons than he was with me, for he rushed to pick them up while a middle-aged man came to my rescue.

"Cynthia," he scolded. "You need to watch where you're going!"

I quickly dusted myself off and gave off the impression I wasn't hurt, when in fact, I'd hit my ribs on the end of the platform. I didn't tell William about my clumsiness, for fear he'd agree with my father, and instead nursed my wounded pride in silence for a few days until I was back to my old self.

As I carried Kaylee in my womb, I grew increasingly tired, and if I'd been on my feet a lot, there were days when I could barely walk the two blocks from the store back to the house. I'd often sit on the porch of my parent's house and catch my breath before dragging myself home. William was out of the Navy by then and had taken a job as an apprentice meat cutter in the new grocery store. It wasn't unusual for him to come home after a long day to find me lying on the couch.

"I'm just too tired to cook," I'd said. "I hope you brought dinner home."

"Well, I did just that, my love, and I'll do the cooking tonight."

Eventually, the weariness of the pregnancy began fading, and I had a sudden urge to start cooking again. I had Mother sit down with me, and I made a recipe book of all the delicious foods she'd made for us over the years. William was delighted.

The second time I fell was after Kaylee was born, and I lost my balance when I went to pick her up. I didn't think much of it, and when I was stiff and sore after that, I chalked it up to pulling muscles in my fall.

Over the next few years, one of my mother's widow friends who lived down the street offered to watch Kaylee so I could work more hours at the store. Mostly I unpacked and displayed boxes of fruits and vegetables, and sometimes by the end of the day my muscles were stiff or tingling. I attributed it to overexertion, and once I could put Kaylee down for the night, I'd soak in a warm tub before we went to bed.

Three years later, I was pregnant again. Just as I had with Kaylee for the first few months, I felt off balance, but I began to feel better as time passed. Eventually, William Edward Landon IV was born, and even though he technically wasn't a junior, we called him that. As he grew, I noticed I'd developed a slight tremor. I pushed aside any thoughts of something being wrong with me until William noticed I kept dropping Eddie's bottle.

"You should go to the doctor," he said.

"I'm just tired. I'm due to see him in a couple of months anyway, and I'll let him know then."

But when I went in, I didn't mention any of it, because I thought I'd been fine. I believed that if I didn't think about it, I couldn't have anything wrong with me.

A couple of years later, I started getting headaches. My doctor did some tests, but couldn't find anything unusual in my blood work.

We stayed in the duplex my parents owned until we could save enough money to buy a three-bedroom, one-bathroom house of our own in East Long Beach. By then, William was in charge of the meat department for a large grocery store, and he was making enough money so that I could quit working at my parents' store. Since we still had only had one car, it made sense.

Part of me welcomed the change, and not having to be on my feet all day made a big difference in how I felt. But another part of me felt guilty that my parents would now have to pay more to hire someone else to work in my place.

When I complained to William about being by myself while the children were at school, he took it upon himself to solve the problem. One afternoon, he brought home two Boxer puppies with adorable flat faces. We'd never had pets growing up, so I was unsure how to care for them, but William insisted they were going to be great company.

"They're good watchdogs and they're great with kids," he said, handing me one who insisted on licking me.

I named them Blanche (after *A Streetcar Named Desire*) and Richard (after Richard Burton). It turned out William was right; the dogs were patient and protective, and we loved them.

The children blossomed in their new school, and I made friends with several neighbor ladies, rotating from house to house for afternoon coffee. For the most part, I felt good, and it seemed everything about my life had fallen into place.

CHAPTER EIGHT

CYNTHIA

It was several years later that I began having anxiety attacks so severe I couldn't go outside the house by myself. I was still plagued with fatigue, and my balance and co-ordination skills were growing more troublesome. Doctors diagnosed me with a disease called multiple sclerosis, or MS, which affects the brain and the central nervous system, controlling everything we do.

Our lives were knocked sideways. Back then, my doctor recommended we move to a warm, dry climate to slow down the degenerating process, so we found the warmest weather we could while remaining in California. William quit his job at the market, and we sold our house. I'd never heard of Imperial Valley before, nor the small town of Holtville, both near the Mexican border, but that's where we moved, lock, stock and barrel.

We hoped it would provide the help I needed.

We bought a farmhouse on acreage, and William quickly took to farming. I envied him his new passion—for I had nothing. He gave me vitamin B-12 shots every day, and I swam in the town pool, which I admitted helped reduce my fatigue and lessened the stress on my joints. I was told I'd be in a wheelchair by the time I was thirty-five. But I refused to accept this prediction—after all, I was only in my late twenties.

Initially, I hated it in the Valley. The heat exhausted me, and dear sweet William kept reassuring me I'd soon begin to feel better. I hated to see his eyes so filled with hope, positive I would eventually share his optimism.

"You'll get better, my love. Just give it time."

He meant well, but I knew how I felt.

I eventually learned to welcome the warm, dry temperature, often closing my eyes and letting it sink deeper, absorbing me, almost wrapping around me like an embrace. And after several months, I actually began to feel better.

But I was still almost four hours away from my mother and sister, and phone calls between us seemed to make me more homesick. When we hung up, I'd stare at the phone, and the silence that followed was deafening. I'd always thought I never needed my parents, or anyone else for that matter, but I would now close my eyes, wishing I could hold on to them longer. I would keep a brave face when I spoke, but the moment we hung up, I sank back down into despair.

My father had been gone for some time by then, so every few months, my mother would make the long drive down and stay with me for a few weeks at a time. She'd knit while I smoked and played solitaire. Each afternoon, Mother made elleniko kafé, from finely ground coffee beans, almost like a powder, in her special briki, a small, long-handled copper pot. The rich, strong, creamy-textured coffee, served in small demitasse cups, was a beloved tradition back in Greece, but it was a drink one had to grow a liking to. And when we finished our coffee, Mother tilted our cups upside down onto the saucer so that she could eventually read the grounds.

It was considered bad luck to read your own fortune, so she only read mine. Airplanes or animals like camels suggested journeys; hearts, rings or initials could point to romance, while figures like a cat could mean fighting with loved ones or solitude. Shapes like an arrow or cage could indicate unhappiness, depression or bad news; a bag or an egg could signify wealth and success, and a bell might suggest good news or visitors.

My mother, with her simple expressions like a raised eyebrow or a nod, always swiftly filtered out any unpleasant thoughts.

She'd say, "It looks like you'll find peace and balance in your life." Or, "You'll have a long and fulfilling life."

I knew her predictions weren't true, but I'd smile and nod back.

When it was time for her to get back to Long Beach, almost the moment she drove away, my anxiety returned, and I blamed the constant buzzing of the cicadas for most of it. That's when I started drinking. At first, I was unable to drown the constant noise out, but as with the heat, I grew accustomed to it, and eventually found the sound hypnotizing. Whiskey on the rocks was my drink of choice. That, cigarettes and playing Johnny Mathis albums helped me pass the time.

During the summers, Kate would drive Alex and Vaso down, and it was so obvious Alex felt instantly at home in the open spaces—the back roads, the fields stretching out in every direction. He loved the small town, the early mornings, and working with William. The dirtier he got, the more he loved it.

But I could tell the lifestyle made Vaso uncomfortable. She was the type of child who wasn't drawn to nature, or to roughing it. It was like she watched and observed, and I could tell she felt like a guest, always polite and willing to help. One year, when Kaylee bleached Vaso's hair, I thought Kate would kill me, but she just chalked it up to Vaso having an adventure.

Alex would have stayed forever. Vaso could hardly wait to get home.

I knew Nick loved Alex, and I had to give him a lot of credit for taking on another man's child when he married Kate. Not all men can open their hearts to a child that wasn't their blood. And I never saw Nick show favoritism between the two children. Given how I was naturally more drawn to Alex than to Vaso, I could understand how difficult that might have been for him. Even though Alex was complicated, he was just easier to love. Vaso was more of a homebody, and was pampered by both Kate *and* Nick.

Just before Alex turned sixteen, Kate called. "I need your help," she said. "Can he come down for the summer? He loves you and Eddie, and maybe you can talk some sense into him. He's talking about quitting school, and he needs to go somewhere he can get his head on straight— somewhere where there is structure he respects. We're not giving up on him . . . we just don't think we can do this part alone anymore. "

I told her Alex was always welcome, and the day after school was out, Kate drove him down.

Even Kate said later, the change in him was immediate. The moment his suitcase hit the floor, it was as if a weight had lifted with it. His shoulders relaxed, and something in his expression softened. The tension he'd been carrying seemed to fall away. This place felt exactly like where he was meant to be. Not forever, maybe, but for now it was enough.

That summer, William worked Alex hard. Eddie Jr., constantly underfoot, followed the two of them around, and even though he was probably more of a hindrance than a help, he wouldn't give up until William gave him things to do. The transformation was subtle, but unmistakable. Not forever, maybe, but for now. For right now, it was enough.

About three weeks before the summer was over, Alex told me he'd found the wedding photographs of his mother and Nick at their reception. I'd seen them, and there was no denying he'd discovered their secret. I was out of line when I asked him if he wanted to stay with us and finish high school, but when he jumped at the offer, I knew it was the right thing to do.

I called Kate, and while I knew the decision didn't come easily for her or Nick, they agreed he could stay.

"Anything to keep him in school. And kids always listen to someone who isn't their parent. I know he idolizes you and Eddie. I can't thank you enough, Cynthia."

Two years later, he graduated and moved back up to Long Beach.

Kaylee and Eddie Jr. were on their own when William was first diagnosed with prostate cancer. An overwhelming sense of dread overpowered me. On the outside, for him and the children, I wore a mask of optimism. But inside, I knew he was not going to beat it. Years ago, I'd predicted we'd lose some of those who posed in the family portrait, and when his mother died, I thought that would be it for a while. Even though it had been years, I never thought the next loss would be him.

Eventually, when he could no longer work the farm, he found someone to lease the land and take over. There weren't a lot of treatments back then, and his cancer spread to his bladder and lymph nodes.

I watched him wither away, and before he died, he said, "You'll need to sell the farm and move into town when I'm gone."

"I don't want to think about it," I answered. "Who will give me my shots?"

"Well, you'll need to. The kids aren't here, and you'll need a neighbor to look in on you."

And when he finally left me, I did what I needed to do. I listed the farm and bought a house in town. My sister Kate and a friend came to help me pack, and after the sale, a few of the workers moved me into my new place.

As it turned out, I lasted longer than I wanted to without William. I'd always prided myself on being pragmatic, and almost ten years later, when I acknowledged I could no longer live by myself, I did what I had to do. I was going to sell the house. My brother, Stavros, now a big attorney, read through the offer, and after almost laughing at the paltry amount it was worth, acted as though he'd saved the day by asking the realtor to pay for some random repairs in a counteroffer. My sister Kate and my nephew Alex came down and helped me pack, and Alex drove me back up to Long Beach to live with Mother.

As much as I didn't want to think it was getting close to my time, I was giving up. My children had no idea how ill I'd been. My daughter lived in Idaho with her abusive husband. I never liked him, but your children don't heed your advice when you give it to them. You can't tell them what to do. My son, who now had eight children, was going through a divorce and lived in Hawaii.

William was gone, and I had nothing left. I sat court at Mother's dining room table, drinking and smoking my cigarillos. Once a week, Kate did our shopping for I was no longer able to walk with any measure of steadiness, and often, I didn't even make it to the damned bathroom before I peed myself.

My niece Vaso began stopping by too. Sometimes she and Mother would play gin rummy while Kate wrote checks and did Mother's banking. Kate was like that; she took on the responsibility of making sure my bills were paid too and deposited the proceeds of the sale of my house into a high-interest CD. My brother would stop by periodically, but his visits were short and annoying. He still had a way of getting on my nerves—even more now with that holier than thou attitude of his. I was only sixty-two, and I felt every inch of it. Each day, I grew angrier with the world for letting me live so long. I tried to keep my temper in check, yet I found it difficult to control my little outbursts; often I'd have bouts of blurred vision or dizziness, and my headaches returned with a vengeance. Mother and Kate forgave me for my sudden fits of anger, sometimes leading to tears, but Vaso didn't understand when I barked orders to anyone who was close to fill my drink. She would look at me as if I were a stranger, and to her, I probably was.

Most days, battling my demons left me on edge, and soon, patience was nowhere to be found. It was on a Saturday afternoon when I handed her my empty glass I said, "Isn't there any way to get a drink around here?"

Before she even spoke, her cheeks flamed, and I could tell something was coming.

"No wonder no one wants to come visit you," she said, almost petulantly.

For a moment, I pictured her as a young child again, absolutely adored by her father, and the favorite one, no matter how much he tried to hide it. Even with the weight she'd put on, she was a lovely young woman. And she was right; she was the only one besides my sister who came to visit me and Mother.

I quickly realized she didn't understand the severity of my condition—or she never would have said anything like that. Forgiveness came easily. How could I blame her for something she didn't even realize?

A week later, I went into the hospital, and never left.

I was sixty-two.

CHAPTER NINE

MY MEMORIES OF AUNT CYNTHIA, WILLIAM EDWARD BRIDGES III AND HOLTVILLE

I called him Uncle Eddie; my brother called him either Uncle Eddie or Uncle Ed; my parents and grandmother referred to him as Eddie, and my Aunt Cynthia called him William. Their grandchildren called him Papa and her Grammy. I don't think I've known anyone else with that many monikers. Somehow, we all kept it straight.

The story went that Aunt Cynthia met Uncle Eddie at the Pike in Long Beach. In 1945, it was still a popular destination for tourists and servicemen. It opened in 1902 on the shoreline south of Ocean Boulevard, and it was famous for the Cyclone Racer roller coaster built on pilings out over the water. There were arcades, bumper cars, a ride called Laff in the Dark, and food stands with corn dogs, cotton candy, popcorn, hot nuts and snow cones tucked in between a variety of rides and souvenir shops. I knew this because it was still a place your parents warned you against when *I* was growing up.

Uncle Eddie was a sailor, and I knew this was where sailors came when they were in port and wanted to have a good time. Eddie said they stored their uniforms in an area set up with lockers so they could change into their civvies and avoid being heckled and beaten up. They visited the tattoo parlors, bars, and the motion picture theater. They rode the carousel and swam at the bathhouse. And of course they picked up girls.

Over the years, the Pike's reputation got worse as gambling, seedy dives, and peep shows proliferated and crime increased. Parents definitely didn't want their children roaming around. In 1979, the Long Beach city council voted against renewing the land leases, and the Pike was demolished.

Uncle Eddie once told a story about the sideshows and a performer called Cobra Woman. At her last show, her rattlesnake killed her during her "kiss of death" routine when, within just seconds, she was bitten twice in the face. She died at Seaside Hospital, where my brother was later born, and during her autopsy they discovered she was really a man. Sometimes I wondered if he made stories like that up to freak me out.

When my aunt was diagnosed with MS, they moved down to Holtville—just outside of El Centro—and they bought a small wood-framed house on several acres. It was painted white, and a large wooden swing hung from the rafters of the porch. It could get to a hundred and ten degrees or more during the summer, but the hot, dry climate was what they said my aunt needed. Alex loved it. I think it was the freedom of the outdoors that attracted him.

Although they had a swamp cooler, each bedroom had a window air conditioner, which in some ways negated the purpose of moving to the warm temperature, but it was the only way anyone could tolerate the heat. They raised alfalfa, and Uncle Eddie had an old beat-up tractor and other harvesting equipment. Once his own fields were taken care of, he picked up extra work from farmers whose land stretched much farther than his.

I was around ten when they moved away, and while we didn't see them often when they lived in Long Beach, I missed my cousins. Kaylee, who had always been my idol, was two years older than I was, and Eddie IV—who we called Eddie Jr.—was two years my junior.

Any time I went down there, Johnny Mathis' records were constantly playing, and Aunt Cynthia would either dance and sway to his music or sit on their couch holding one of her funny slender cigarettes in one hand and a drink in the other.

"They used to tell me I'd be in a wheelchair by the time I turned thirty-five," she'd remind me.

When Uncle Eddie came in after working, if the music was still on, he'd take Aunt Cynthia in his arms and they'd dance until Kaylee and I would serve dinner. My cousin Kaylee would roll her eyes with embarrassment, but I thought it was so romantic—even *I* could tell he still loved her madly. No matter where I am or what I'm doing, to this day, any old Johnny Mathis tune brings back that picture of the two of them moving together, lost in the music. An unexpected wave of wistfulness and melancholy washes over me, and a door to the past unlocks. I still can't help but think about the life changes they made in order to keep her disease at bay.

Each year, when summer rolled around, I would always count the days until I could go down to the valley and visit them, even though I hated the heat. Once I got there, I was always homesick and could hardly wait to get back home. I never told Kaylee how I felt, because I didn't want her to think I was a homebody and a baby, for I always looked up to her. Every morning, when we finally got out of bed, I'd sit and watch her while she applied her makeup, and then she'd do mine. I would never be allowed to wear it once I returned home, but after she finished with me, when I looked at myself in her mirror, I felt beautiful.

"I'm going to go to beauty school," she said.

She was fairer than I was, and when I was around twelve, she told me her mother let her bleach her light brown hair.

That summer she said, "Let's do your hair."

Thinking it would turn blonde, we started applying peroxide to my dark brown hair, but within a few days, my hair was bright orange.

"Oh dear god," Aunt Cynthia said when she saw it. "Your mother's going to kill me."

My mother didn't kill me, but for weeks after I came home, she made me keep it that way until she thought I learned my lesson. Just before school started, she finally took me to a beauty salon to have it dyed back to my original brown color. I never tried to change my hair color again.

Another summer when we were bored, we hiked down the road, took our shoes off, and waded in a ditch. When we got back to Kaylee's house, I discovered I had a cut on the bottom of my foot between two toes. I showed Uncle Eddie, who treated me with disinfectant, and told me I'd probably need a tetanus shot.

"I just happen to have one here," he said, pulling out one of Aunt Cynthia's syringes.

My stomach lurched and my eyebrows shot up, and then he laughed.

"Nah," he finally said, "if there's anything in there, it'll come to the surface by itself. I was just pulling your foot. I mean leg."

I worried about that cut for days, but just like he'd said, any dirt inside made its way to the surface of my foot and in no time you couldn't even tell I'd cut it.

Before my brother Alex moved down there, letters would arrive every so often, signed by "Prunella Prunewhip." They were always postmarked from Long Beach, though neither of us knew who was really sending them. Each time one came, my heart sank, because Alex would rush off to his room, slam the door, and read it in private. I was still young enough that such things could reduce me to tears.

"How come he gets letters and I don't?" I once asked my mother. She knew the truth, of course, though I realize now how much it must have hurt her to hear me ask. She would hug me close, and though I can't remember the exact words she used, I always found comfort in her arms.

The letters stopped when Alex turned sixteen. Eventually I learned it had been Aunt Cynthia writing them all along. I never said anything to her, but I carried a quiet resentment—that she had chosen Alex and never stopped to think how it made me feel to be left out.

It was around that time that Alex moved down to the Valley.

When I was fourteen, my parents and I went down for his high school graduation. He was almost eighteen, and he'd lived down there for the last two years. I never knew why, other than my parents wanted him to finish high school, and sending him down to *The Valley*, seemed the best way. At the time, I was so wrapped up in my self-centered teenage years, I hardly even noticed he wasn't home, and I loved being an "only child."

That's when he and my aunt and uncle grew closer. Many years later, when the pieces of the puzzle started fitting into place, it made sense why Aunt Cynthia cared more for Alex than she did for me. In their minds, he was the underdog, and I was the princess. He was the rebel, and I was still the princess.

Everyone was so proud of Alex that day, and you could tell by the look on his face that the accolades made him feel proud of himself, too. It surprised me when my parents said I could drive separately to the ceremony with my cousin Kaylee and her boyfriend Johnny. We were late leaving the house, and we hadn't given ourselves enough time to pick up their friend Lew and drive the additional twenty minutes back, so Johnny was stressing.

"Your parents are going to kill me," he said to Kaylee.

"They'll be fine," she said, turning to look at Lew and me sitting in the back seat of the 1960 Chevy Impala.

I'd never met Lew before, but he was the most handsome man I'd ever seen. He was twenty to my fourteen, and dressed in a cowboy shirt, jeans and boots. I wanted to close my eyes and breathe in his aftershave, but I was afraid he'd see me and I would have died of embarrassment. I've always been a romantic, thinking someone could fall in love with me if I just dreamed it, and I knew I was the perfect girl for him. Of course, I had no idea what I'd do if he even wanted to kiss me.

Once we got to the school, Lew held the front seat forward so I could get out, and then closed the car door behind me. *How romantic*, I thought. We walked side by side behind Kaylee and Johnny, and I pictured Lew taking my hand in his—and then my bubble burst.

"Christ, the ceremony's already started!" Johnny said, panicking and stopping us all.

Kaylee shrugged her shoulders and said, "Let's just forget about going! No one will ever know we weren't there."

Johnny looked at her like she was crazy, and there was no way I was going to let on I was scared, too. I'd never done anything like that, and if my parents found out, they would have killed me.

"No one will know," Kaylee repeated.

Johnny looked at Lew and then back at Kaylee. "I guess you're right. If not, we're in really deep shit!" He took her hand and led the way back to his car. "We'll be home when everyone gets there and we can agree what a nice ceremony it was."

Kaylee gave me a look that said, 'Shut up. We're going to have a ball.'

We went to an out-of-town diner so no one would recognize us and had hamburgers and sodas. I wanted the afternoon to go on forever, but eventually, we had to head back home.

We pulled it off. No one had a clue we hadn't been there. Why would they?

Though I dreamed of it, Lew never fell in love with me. A year later, I heard he'd been killed when his truck went off the road and into a ditch on the dark outskirts of town.

Kaylee and I drifted out of touch for a time, and the following year she and Johnny were in a terrible car accident. Kaylee's head went through the windshield, and it was a miracle she didn't lose her sight. She avoided a coma or brain damage, and after two weeks she was released from the hospital. The doctors repaired what they could of her eyelids, but for the rest of her life, scar tissue remained above her eyes and across the bridge between her brows.

The next thing I heard, Kaylee was pregnant. I'd always envied her having a boyfriend who loved her like Johnny did, but for reasons she never shared, they never married. They had a baby and named her Katrina.

Several years later, when Kaylee moved back up to Long Beach to stay with Yia´ Yia for a while, I saw her more frequently. But by then, though, too many years had passed, and we were living totally different lives. She had a baby, and I was in my last year of high school.

She used to talk about things we did as kids, but more often than not, I'd say, "I don't remember that."

"You're kidding me. I wonder if you have teenage senility."

"Hilarious."

"Well, do you remember when we missed Alex's graduation?"

"I wish I didn't," I said.

CHAPTER TEN

VASO

I didn't know until after the fact that Uncle Eddie was undergoing treatment for prostate cancer. Back then, there weren't a lot of treatment options, and he chose the less invasive one called prostate seed implantation. It didn't work. In 1986, at the age of sixty-one, he died. They cremated him in his Levi's and his favorite belt buckle, cowboy shirt and boots.

Cynthia, as I later called her, stayed down in The Valley for a number of years, and then eventually moved back to Long Beach to stay with my grandmother.

On Saturdays, my mother would visit her at Yia´ Yia's, and I started joining them when I could. I couldn't help but notice Cynthia was slurring her words more frequently, and I attributed it to the constant glass of whiskey she kept at the dining room table where she sat. On more than one occasion, I witnessed her barking orders to my grandmother to get her another drink, or to help her get to the bathroom.

Yia´ Yia took her outbursts in stride and said nothing, at least not while I was there. But one afternoon, after my mother had already left, Cynthia said to me, "Go get me another drink! What kind of place is this, anyway?"

My grandmother was cooking in the kitchen, and while I filled Cynthia's empty glass, I asked, "Why do you let her talk to you that way? She's acting like a spoiled child."

"She's not well," was all that my grandmother said. "Be kind to her."

Here was my grandmother, in her late eighties, taking care of a daughter who wasn't the least bit grateful, and I wanted her to acknowledge it. Annoyed, I took Cynthia's drink back into the dining room, and set it down on the table. Her ashtray was full of offensive cigarette butts, and I picked it up to empty it.

"Well, it's about time!" my aunt said.

I've always hoped I never looked at her with the disdain I felt when the words came tumbling from my mouth. "You're drinking too much."

The silence that stretched between us was heavy. Her face stayed completely still, almost as if she hadn't heard me; but I knew she had. And when she had no reply, I let her have it again.

"And you're so grumpy, no wonder no one wants to visit you."

I stood there, frozen, after I realized what I'd just said. Cynthia still said nothing, but she pursed her lips as if deep in thought, possibly trying to come up with some biting retort. I turned toward the doorway to see if my grandmother was on her way out to see what was going on, but she was still busy in the kitchen.

I closed my eyes and sighed deeply, hoping I could stop the images replaying in my mind, and I didn't know what to say. Cynthia still sat there, just looking at me, her lips now tucked in, and I realized her lack of words was worse than anything she could have said to me.

Like a coward, I gathered my things and left, and I didn't go back to see her again. And as it turned out, those were the last words I ever spoke to her.

When my mother told me Cynthia had developed brain cancer and was in the hospital dying, all I could think about was how awful I'd been to her that day. And now I wondered what she must have thought of me? I was appalled at my behavior. I'd said dreadful things to her, and there was never going to be any way to make amends. I was almost sick to my stomach.

"I'd like to see her," I said, hoping to tell my aunt I was sorry.

"No, I don't think you should. I don't want you to remember her as she is now."

My mother always respected other people's privacy, and while I understood, I still thought I should go.

"I wouldn't want anyone to see me that way if it were me," she said.

I didn't have the heart or the courage to tell her what I'd said to Cynthia, and I wanted to at least tell my aunt goodbye.

I'd learned a life lesson. You never know what's going on in another person's life until sometimes it's too late. I never should have judged her for being so rude, and I should have been able to see there was something more going on with her than just her drinking.

Against my mother's wishes, I should have gone to see my aunt in the hospital.

CHAPTER ELEVEN

STAVROS

I wasn't always an arrogant, cynical, narcissistic prick, as my third wife, Kelli, called me when she divorced me. I just grew into that guy. Well, maybe I was most of the adjectives she used to describe me, but I didn't get there overnight. No one really does. I was arrogant and cynical, for you see, I was an attorney. And a very good one, if I may say so myself.

Suspecting I'd been unfaithful, which was my middle name, she'd followed me one evening to my latest girlfriend's home, and unfortunately she could see into the bedroom window. Just as I was in the middle of an exceptional climax to our copulation, she broke the window and took a photo of me, ass in the air.

My mother named me Stavros—which means "cross," because she prayed I would live—and my middle name was Tomaso—because I was a twin to a brother who died at birth. I didn't know this until one day my mother shared with the three of us—Kate, Cynthia and me—her remaining children, that she'd given birth to eight children. First, a set of twins, then a single child, all stillborn, then Katherine, Michael, who died when he was around five, Cynthia and then myself, and my twin.

Because I was the only surviving male, I always felt as if the world was heaped on my shoulders, like I was Atlas. If we were still in Greece, our parents wouldn't expect any of us children to go to college; we'd help work the land and tend the animals. But I was the only one left to carry on our family name.

We originally lived in Los Angeles, where my father had a fruit cart, but by the time I was ready for school, we'd moved into a duplex in Long Beach which my parents purchased with their koumbara (koom-ba´-rra) my godparents. My father opened a market around the corner, and that's where the three of us went every day after school. Kate helped customers and made change. I swept and restocked the baskets of fruit, and Cynthia mostly stood around, knocking over displays and looking pretty.

In the beginning, I thought I was being punished when my parents sent me to the Southern California Military Academy in Signal Hill. I was in fifth grade. To the outside world, it was thought of as a place where troubled boys went because they were unruly. However, they were noted for their use of military discipline, and it was an environment that stressed very high educational standards and taught the discipline it would take to become a strong leader—it was too bad they didn't accept girls, for my sister Cynthia could have certainly benefited from a firm hand.

Because it only went to ninth grade, I enrolled at Wilson High School the year Kate was graduating. I played football and dated girls and, after joining a debate team, decided I wanted to become an attorney. I figured I'd be good at it, and I assumed the good ones made a lot of money.

Fulfilling my dream of getting my law degree from prestigious Stanford University was one of my greatest accomplishments. Part of my strategy was cultivating friendships with students from affluent families—a process that came naturally to me. I quickly learned the value and its many benefits. Throughout my lifetime, those friends opened doors and enriched the lifestyle I'd only dreamed of. Early on, this did sometimes pose a problem if I found myself in a position of not having the budget to match them.

A perfect example was one time we were to sail on my friend's family yacht to Catalina Island. I knew I'd need a new pair of swim trunks, for mine were old, and I was certain we'd be mingling with ladies I'd want to impress. My sister Kate was working as a bookkeeper by then, and when I told her about the weekend trip, she sent me enough money for the swimsuit and a pair of deck shoes whose style would become one of my lifelong mainstays.

"You need a spot of cash?" my friend Doug asked before we left. He'd reached into his pocket and brought out what, to me, was a wad of money.

"No, I'm good," I said awkwardly, tossing my head back. But he'd met my family one spring break, and I knew he was aware my financial situation didn't equal his. One thing about Doug, and something I'd never forget, was that he never made me feel any less of a person because we were from two different stations in life.

"It's not my fault my parents have money," he'd said when he footed the bill for something. "You'll have to meet them. They'll love you. After all," he laughed, "you're a Greek god."

Because Doug belonged to a fraternity, I thought I should join too. I knew there would be pledging and hazing, but I never expected it to be so belittling. How did these men think they could ever be my friends afterwards when they acted so above me? I was obviously very naïve, and I had to decide what price I was willing to pay in order to belong.

"You'll be glad you did it," Doug said, encouraging me to roll with the punches. "We all had to do it."

So I shaved my legs, put on a stuffed bra, dressed up as a woman, and went to classes for a day.

"Mr. Panos," my law professor acknowledged as I tried to sneak into class. "You're looking especially lovely today."

The entire class laughed, and I was mortified. I straightened my shoulders and tilted my head, feigning indifference—although I could feel my face redden.

"If you want to play, you have to pay, I guess."

I went on to cleaning toilets in the frat house, and a dozen other things I can't even recall, and eventually Hell Week was finally over.

I met my first wife, Eleni, at Stanford. I won't say I *never* intended to marry, but it certainly wasn't in my overall plan at that point in my life. My parents loved her, for she came from a respectable Greek family in New York, and I knew they always hoped their children would marry traditionally.

The problem was that she was pregnant, and I didn't love her. I was a 'man about campus', and she was the wholesome type, and I was certain she wasn't seeing anyone but me. We did the whole Greek wedding at St. Sophia's in Los Angeles. Her parents flew out along with brothers and sisters, and even though it was just our immediate families, Greek weddings could be quite a spectacle, and ours was impressive.

I'd just started an internship with a well-known Long Beach law group, and I knew in my heart I could never focus and be happy unless I figured out what to do about my marriage. Every day was a reminder I'd been trapped into a marriage I never wanted, and I felt suffocated.

About a month later, I was graced with a favorable outcome of my predicament. Eleni's pregnancy ended in a miscarriage, and I had a perfect out; I just had to figure out the timing. In the meantime, my life was miserable, and the only thing I could think of was to make hers miserable, too.

I deliberately did things I knew would get under her skin, acting in ways that would drive her crazy—like leaving my clothes on the floor next to my side of the bed and leaving the toilet seat up so if she had to go to the bathroom in the middle of the night, she'd fall into the cold water. I interrupted her long stories and moved things just to watch her nudge them back to where she'd left them. The worst was that after I started arguments over mundane things, I'd smile and say something like, "Whatever you think is best."

Even I had to admit I was being childish and petty. It was ridiculous, really, and I should have had the courage to tell her I wanted out, but I didn't. I was a jerk. In past relationships, I'd usually just leave, but I couldn't do that now.

I reached out to a few of the gals I had dated before the wedding— they were surprised to hear from me—and they welcomed me back into their beds. When Eleni heard me on the phone with one of them, she confronted me, and I confirmed her suspicions.

"I think we made a mistake," I finally said honestly.

"I knew you weren't being faithful, and *I* made the mistake of thinking we could make a life together even after the miscarriage," she replied. "I'll be going back to New York. I can be with my family, and you can be free to live the life you'd rather have here."

Our marriage was annulled.

Julia, wife number two, worked at the accounting firm next to my law office. I'd seen her a couple of times in the hallway before I introduced myself. She was beautiful, with a conservative hairdo, large brown eyes, and a great figure. And the good thing was, she wasn't wearing a wedding ring—not that *that* ever kept me away.

When she spoke, I could tell she wasn't from around here.

"Georgia," she told me when I asked.

"Well, I declare," I said, trying to be funny, "a Georgia peach."

She blushed, and I knew she was going to be my next wife. I'd been working for my mentor for several years then, and I was feeling some pressure from him to marry again and settle down, although from what I'd heard, I understood he'd been quite a playboy in his heyday, too.

"It'll be good for your image," he said.

On our first date, Julia shared that she had a small child, a daughter named Emma. I tried to keep my surprise to myself; I hadn't thought to ask her if she'd been married before, nor had I thought about marrying someone with a readymade family. But throughout the evening, the softness of her voice drew me in, along with the polite way she continually thanked our waitress. And even better, she seemed to be genuinely interested in what I had to say.

I thought about asking her if she wanted to go back to my apartment, which *I* really wanted to do, but for the first time, I think *ever*, I didn't want to spoil our evening with a premature advance. She wasn't an immature college student *or* a party person, and I respected that about her.

Her parents were divorced, and she had no brothers or sisters. Her mother still lived in Georgia, and her father lived out here; in fact, she'd been staying with him since her divorce, until she could save enough money to find her own place.

Again I was surprised, and this time it showed, for she said, "I know; it kind of puts a damper on dating." Then she blushed again. "Daddy says it'll keep the men I date respectable."

I replied, "Well, I have to agree; he's right."

We both laughed.

We dated for about three months, and then we were married. Emma was a beautiful little girl, about two years old, and I fell in love with her instantly. She was gentle and cheerful, and I wasn't sure where that heartless bastard inside me had disappeared. I decided I wanted to adopt her if we could get her father to relinquish his rights to her. It turned out he didn't fight our request, and as soon as all the paperwork was processed, Emma Panos became mine.

My mother loved both my girls. Julia called her Mom and Emma called her Yia´ Yia. Mother bought a house in North Long Beach, and Julia, Emma, and I moved into the front house in Belmont Heights .

Nothing escaped the nosy neighbor across the street. She had a son the same age as Emma, and before we were even settled, she brought him to the front door, asking if the children could play. (Years later, she still lived across the street and sat on her front porch watching us when we all assembled for our family portrait.)

We had another child, and when it turned out to be a girl, Mother asked if we could name her Sophia. At first I was surprised, and I could tell from her expression that it was obvious. I knew it was a name she'd given one of her stillborn daughters, and honestly, it gave me the creeps.

I changed the name to Sophie, and ran it by Julia, but I never told her about my sister, only that it was a name Mother had asked me about.

"I love it," she said.

"What about Sophie?" I asked Mother.

"That would be perfect."

CHAPTER TWELVE

STAVROS

I was content and happy for about five years until little things started niggling at me. Julia's southern drawl had begun to wear on my nerves, and she was always so soft-spoken and polite, even when something made her upset.

"That isn't how I was raised," she would answer when I encouraged her to respond to something more aggressively.

She'd been a good wife to me, and no matter what I needed, she was always there. I think that's what the problem was. I was growing tired of *nice nice* and I needed some spice in my life. How had that *jerk* slithered back in?

I'd never had a problem finding women when I wanted them. If I were at a restaurant or at a bank, I flirted. Rarely was I rebuffed. That was probably one of the major reasons I became so pompous.

History has a way of repeating itself, especially with me, and I found I was leaving telltale signs of my infidelity around our bedroom and the house. If Julia asked me about something she found, I'd make something up, and she would just reply, "Oh, okay."

I sometimes just wanted to shake her by the shoulders and shout, "Say *shit*, or *Godamnit*, for God's sake! Do something besides being nice to everyone. Don't you get pissed off at anything?"

I loved my children, but I was growing weary of leading a second life, lying about where I was going and who I was meeting. I decided I had two ways to handle this. One was to humiliate Julia and make her divorce me, or be a man and tell her I was unhappy. At first, I couldn't decide.

I chose to be a man about it.

"I'll make sure you and the kids have a nice home to live in, and I'll take care of the paperwork at the office," I said. I knocked the wind right out of her. She reached for a nearby chair and sat. How could she not have been aware of my unhappiness?

Not long after that, my mentor suddenly died of a heart attack, and it knocked me off balance. Of course, I'd grieved when I lost my father years before, but this was more devastating for me. I'd had in him a friend who would praise me for the good job I was doing, and then toughen me up by showing me how I could have done better. My father worked hard to provide for his family, and I missed him. But the law firm had also been my family.

I swore off marriage again. I was no good at it, and I probably never would be. I'd been made a full partner in the law firm the year before, and now, for the next several years, I focused on my practice. Julia and the children moved down to San Diego, where her father now lived, so I knew they were taken care of. I missed my children greatly, but rarely took the time to go see them. When Julia remarried, I was happy for her. She deserved a good life and a husband who would put her first. I knew that wasn't ever going to be me.

Not long after that, when Emma and Sophie came up to spend a weekend with me, they inadvertently let it slip they were going to have a new brother or sister. All I said to them was, "Congratulations."

One thing I'd observed with men like me—men who wanted everything but then were never truly happy—was that I was territorial. I was prepared for Julia to live her own life, but I wasn't prepared for the fact that she would have another child. She named him Michael, and every time I thought of him, my mind went straight to the large framed photo of my older brother that hung in my mother's bedroom. From the time I was a child until this day, I swore when I looked at that image, his eyes followed me everywhere I went.

Once their brother was old enough, the girls began asking if he could join them when they came up for Christmas. I would have looked like an asshole if I had said no, especially since my mother and sister Kate embraced all children with open arms. They almost had to, considering the stepchildren now included within our family unit. Unlike me, Kate made sure to recognize them and have presents or, as they grew older, a card with money for them.

I continued to date and spent many hours with women in my bed. However, I wasn't always careful about contraception, and I fathered another child. My first response was to pay for an abortion; I'd had clients who'd done the same. But when she said she wanted to keep the child, I knew there was nothing I could do but wait it out. Being intimate with a woman who could be carrying my child, and one that I didn't want, was out of the question. So I didn't see her again until the baby was born.

Being the cynic that I am, I did verify I was indeed the father before I assumed any responsibility. And because I was still sexually energetic, to eliminate the possibility of another miscalculation, I scheduled a vasectomy.

The child was never introduced to my family, but he was well taken care of.

In my law practice, I specialized in corporate law, and I was meticulous and very good at what I did. Over the fifty years I had my practice, I also handled the personal affairs of my corporate clients and saw just about everything people could do and try to get away with. I saw greed among family members, heirs cheating siblings out of their inheritances because of technicalities, and families that were broken apart by hurt feelings and misunderstandings. Entire estates were sometimes lost to pay for attorney fees and accountant's charges just to make sure that everyone got their fair share—and in the end, no one got anything.

Throughout the years, I maintained several friends from Stanford, and stood by silently as their children never worked for what they received. I handled their legal affairs and trusts. I watched as their wives took them to the cleaners, not that some of them hadn't had it coming, and I made sure that my college mate Doug's family trust was protected when he married Beth, who already had two children. With my own history of divorce and property settlements, I knew I would accumulate no vast fortunes, but I did make sure my children would be provided for when I died.

When my father died in the early 1950s, life was simple; everything he had went to my mother. Before *she* died, we'd sold all her property except for the house on Loma, and we set up an investment account. It was Mother's wish that her children would inherit whatever she had left, which technically meant it was just Kate and me, since by then our sister

Cynthia was no longer with us. (I'd already handled her estate when she died and divided it between her two children.)

Kate's brother-in-law, her husband Nick's brother George, lived in the back house with his wife, and Mother had made it clear she wanted him to be able to stay there until he died if she passed away before him. After her death, we rented the front house out until George died of a heart attack. Neither Kate nor I wanted to deal with finding a new tenant in the back, so we left it vacant, and when the couple in the front eventually left, we sold the house.

Kate suggested we give a third of what we had to Cynthia's two children, but I argued that that wasn't what Mother had requested. I didn't share that I had planned to use my full share to buy a new car.

"Don't be so selfish," Kate admonished. "Mother didn't expect to outlive Cynthia, and if you won't do it, I'll give them part of my share."

I almost said, *"You wouldn't,"* but I knew she would. Kate was definitely cut from a different cloth than I was. She and Nick did well for themselves—I knew they worked hard for what they had, but her holier than thou attitude still annoyed me sometimes.

"You're being petulant. And it's not becoming," she said.

"Fine," I acquiesced. "I'll write the checks and close the bank account tomorrow."

I was always the family's go-to person for legal matters, and sometimes it annoyed me. I processed my niece Vaso's first divorce and then assisted her first husband with his divorce to his third wife. Of course, I could never share his ridiculous escapades with her. Ha! Look who was calling the kettle black? The only difference between him and me was that I was privy to his foolishness, and he was not to mine!

When Alex's wife divorced him, I handled that. When Kaylee divorced Bruce, I took care of that.

I didn't charge anyone for my services, and that annoyed me too. However, if they had gone to someone else to handle their problems, I would have been just as annoyed; how does that make sense? There was no pleasing me.

In my practice, I created leases, assisted with the sale of properties, and put the fear of God into many who needed it. I successfully defended a client who had been accused of a hit and run; he was ultimately found not guilty. And I won a much-deserved settlement for a client's son, who had been misdiagnosed when he entered the hospital with an undetermined illness and ultimately left as a quadriplegic.

I also handled the arrangements my sister Kate and her husband made when she married Nick.

I was a keeper of many secrets.

CHAPTER THIRTEEN

STAVROS

Now, my third wife was another big mistake. Everything was going along fine the way it was until I met her. If I ever had a trophy wife, Kelli was it. By this time, I was almost sixty, and I should have learned my lesson. But she was absolutely gorgeous. Blonde hair, green eyes, with a figure that would take your breath away. She was intelligent, a great conversationalist, could keep up with my terrible jokes, and if I admitted it, she made me feel young and virile again. Plus, she didn't need me.

Of course, she'd been married before with those good looks—but she'd never had children. She was a very successful real estate broker, and I met her while I was looking for a condo by the water. She wasn't scheduled to sit at the open house I went to, but her assistant had an emergency, so there she was, walking me around, pointing out all the amenities. But I wasn't really paying attention—I think I would have bought the place even if I'd hated it.

We dated for several months, and then she agreed to marry me. My friend Doug told me afterwards that I would have had enough time before the service to change my mind, but even he admitted I was smitten.

Nick and Kate had a home in the desert, and that's where we tied the knot. Kelli wore an off-white suit and looked like a million bucks.

Everyone was drinking champagne, and as I worked the crowd, I stood behind two women who were whispering.

"I wonder how long *this* one's going to last," and then they giggled conspirationally.

At first, it incensed me that someone who felt this way would actually attend my wedding, but then it hit me like a ton of bricks. I looked at

Kelli, flashing her diamond wedding rings, and said, "*Fuck,*" as the wind rushed out of me.

The two women turned to look at me, and they both turned beet red.

They were right.

I never should have married her.

Kate had invited us to stay with them at the house after the wedding, but I'd reserved a suite at one of the large hotels in town; I can't even recall the name of it now. I continued to drink once we checked in, and I ended up passing out in one of the chairs by the window. I woke in the early morning and barely made it to the bathroom before I proceeded to throw up.

Of course, this woke Kelli, who rushed to my side, and as she used a damp washcloth to clean my face, I pushed her hand away. I didn't want her to see me this way, for I hadn't been this sick since college.

Once I was back in bed, she brought a cool washcloth and sat by me. As she dabbed at my face, I didn't want to look at her. She was still beautiful, even without her makeup, but I had brought her into my world, and I knew I'd eventually break her heart.

I continued with my marriage charade for three years. My biggest problem was that my mother adored her, and likewise. Everyone in my family loved her! The more I pondered how I'd end my marriage, the more I started having periods where I was unable to perform in bed. This had never been a problem for me in the past; in fact, my overactive libido had gotten me into trouble more times than I could count.

I was back to choices, and I had two of them; one was to contact my urologist, and the other was to contact an old girlfriend and test the water. I chose the girlfriend.

Unfortunately, this was also at the time my mother wanted to have our family portrait taken, and there was no way I'd be able to tell Kelli she couldn't be in the photograph. And when I heard my sister Cynthia predict this would be the last time we were all together, there was nothing I could do but show up and say "cheese."

CHAPTER FOURTEEN

STAVROS

I thought back to my first girlfriend from high school, Sally, and how lucky we had been back then that she never got pregnant, when my ex-wife Julia called to break the news that our youngest daughter Sophie was pregnant.

"Are you sure?" I asked stupidly. "Christ!"

I think I was more upset because I had to hear it from Julia instead of from my daughter, but once I reconciled in my mind that the likelihood of that happening was me being thickheaded, my thoughts went back to where they needed to be.

"How long have you known?" I asked.

"A few days."

"And you're just telling me *now*?" I knew I was sounding condescending, but I couldn't help it. I was angry and frightened. "And what about *the boy*? How old is he? This *could* be statutory rape, you know."

When the line went silent, I thought maybe she'd hung up on me.

"*Are you there*?" I snapped.

"Yes, I'm here. I'm just waiting for you to calm down a little."

"How can I calm down when this could ruin her life?"

"She's almost sixteen, Stavros. And to answer your other question, he's seventeen."

"Like that makes it any better. *Shit*. What are we going to do about it? They can't get married at this age. And she should just. . ."

"Just *what*?"

I'd heard *over my dead body*, and the panic in her voice, but I said a little more calmly. "She should just get rid of the baby." There, I'd said it.

Julia didn't speak immediately. "I don't think she's decided yet."

"*Julia, they're too young.*"

"Don't you think I know that? They're confused. At least the worst is over."

"What do you mean by that?"

"Having to tell everyone. . ."

I sighed loudly.

"I need to talk to Sophie. Should I come down there?"

"I don't think she wants to talk to you right now. And I agree, especially if you're so upset."

"*Upset?* What do you expect?"

But Julia was right.

"You won't be hard on her, will you? She already feels bad enough."

"I don't know. I need to think."

I hung up.

The next day, I made a few calls, and a week later, for all anyone knew, Sophie had been accepted at a boarding school in Massachusetts.

CHAPTER FIFTEEN

CHILDHOOD AND MY MEMORIES OF UNCLE STAVROS

When Uncle Eddie's mother, Bessie, passed away. I'd forgotten she'd even been in the photo. I never knew much about her life, except that Eddie was her only child, and when her husband died, she'd never remarried. Kaylee had once told a story about her great-grandfather, Edward Bridges, who came from a family of bridge builders in England. The story went, the first Edward Bridges came to America as a young man after being caught with another man's wife, but with Kaylee, I could never be certain. I do recall that Bessie was a sweet woman who adored her grandchildren, Kaylee and Eddie Jr. She had a soft voice, a cheerful smile, and a warm hug for everyone whenever we saw her.

Stavros's comment when he heard the news was that it was too bad, but she really wasn't a member of the family.

I grew up in a three-bedroom, one-bath home in Wrigley Heights—a safe working-class neighborhood in Long Beach—and the P.E. (formally known as the Pacific Electric Railway Company Red Car) ran right behind our house.

My brother walked me to school until I was in second grade, and I never told my mother that along the way he'd join up with other friends and run ahead of me, only periodically looking back to see if I was still there. At first, I was frightened to walk under the train tracks by myself, thinking someone might lurk there, hoping to kidnap me. And no matter how many times Alex hid ahead in the bushes and jumped out at me, I fell for it. When I cried and told him I'd tell on him, he and his friend would laugh at me.

"*Baby*," they'd called out, running up the hill towards the gates of the schoolyard.

Further up the sidewalk, there was an old metal bell mounted on a brick pediment at the main entrance to the school. My father was a house painter, and at the beginning of one school year, my entire class got to watch him paint it. We all oohed and aahed, and just when I thought he'd never seen me, he turned and gave me a wink, and I knew I was the luckiest kid in the class.

Our school was built right in the middle of the old-money neighborhoods of Los Cerritos and Virginia Country Club, and my father had built a solid reputation painting some of the most beautiful homes I'd ever seen. Sometimes I'd get to go with him when he had to give estimates, and while he reminded me to wait in the van, the minute he went inside a house, I'd climb out and quietly close the door behind me. I'd just stand there, and take in all the details of the houses and the manicured front yards before me. I'd never felt we were poor, but I certainly could see how rich these other people were.

My mother was a bookkeeper and a carhop at a local drive-in. On Saturdays, she'd take Alex and me with her on her bookkeeping job if my father had to work. One of her customers lived on the beach, so we always came prepared to swim. Alex brought his handmade fishing pole and practiced casting his line into the waves, but I knew we were too close to the shore for him to catch anything. He kept at it until something struck me in the mouth and I started crying. Alex took one look at me, and his face turned white. His fishhook had nicked my lip.

I finally stopped crying, and promised I wouldn't run up to the house, but wait until my mother was finished with her work to show her.

"Oh, dear," she said quickly, assessing the damage. "You'll be okay," she promised.

The next day, however, the right side of my lip had swollen to twice its normal size, and it felt as though there was a bump in it. A few days later, we had an appointment with our family doctor, who said I'd need surgery to remove what had become an infection.

The nurse covered my face with a white paper sheet, leaving just a cutout for my mouth as the doctor injected something to numb my lip.

Although I didn't feel a thing, I cried out when I saw blood spurt onto the paper. I remember my mother and the nurse holding my arms down so I wouldn't move again, and then he was done.

When I got home, I thought my father was going to cry when he saw me.

"Oh, my *koukouch*," he said, wrapping me in his arms. "Are you all right?"

When my mother still worked as a carhop at Merle's Drive-In, sometimes my father would take us there for a hamburger. All the waitresses dressed up in red and white uniforms and skated when they waited on customers. When my father started his own painting business, she eventually quit the drive-in, and worked from the dining room table for him and her one bookkeeping client named Marie Wright. In those days, most mothers still stayed home with their children, but mine knew it would take the two of them if they wanted to get ahead.

An older woman named Helen Dunnigan came in to care for us— Alex hated it, but I loved it. She was there for us when I came home from school, and would make dinners that my parents could later warm up. My mother handled the grocery shopping and always made sure to buy extra for Helen to take home to her husband.

I never knew if it was coincidence or not, but Helen was also a piano teacher, and since my mother loved playing the piano, she hoped I'd love it too. Of all the music I could have chosen, I wanted to play Tchaikovsky's Piano Concerto No. 1, and I practiced the introduction for years. But my heart really wasn't in it. I never mastered the keys, and although every page of my music book sparked with gold stars, it was just a gesture from my teacher, pretending along with me. Finally, with my mother's blessings, the lessons stopped.

No matter how many hours my mother worked during the weekend, she always made some type of roast for Sunday dinner. There was comfort in the routine—the smells from the kitchen, and the clatter of pots and pans and dishes. Sundays were the only times when both my parents were in one place at the same time. We waited to be called to the table, and when I was very young, if I was bored, I'd sit on the arm of my father's chair while he was reading the Press-Telegram newspaper. I'd thump the paper, startling him, and I thought that was the funniest thing ever did. I'd wait to tear off any bandage to show him a cut or scratch, and I could tell that while he wanted to be grumpy with me, he'd kiss his finger and put it on my knee or elbow—wherever my injury was. Then he went back to reading his paper. I'd thump it again until he called out to my mother to make me stop.

"Let your father be," she'd call back.

As I grew older, my attention turned to other things that interested me, but even if I was in the middle of something, when my mother called, I came to the table. Alex would sit there and sulk, his mind still in the garage where he kept his snakes and projects always in various stages of repair. *I* wanted to talk about whatever my parents wanted to talk about, and Alex wanted to talk about how he fed his snake a mouse, or how an engine part needed to be rebuilt.

With a theatrical sigh, I'd roll my eyes. My parents would act like they were interested in what he had to say for a few minutes, and when they could find a pause in his dissertation, they'd steer the conversation back to something more interesting to them and me. Alex would just shrug.

My father always asked us how our week went, and I'd quickly learned to make a list of interesting things to tell him, even if I made them up, so he would spend more time with me.

I was his princess, and I knew it.

Alex had nothing to talk about, and it was obvious he resented having to stop what he was doing to wash the grease from his hands just to spend an hour of his precious daylight away from his current passion. He always had a way of turning everything sour.

On the Sundays when Uncle Stavros stopped by, it was worse. For some reason, when he came to dinner, he felt he had the right to tell Alex and me what was acceptable at the dining room table.

"Sit up straight."

If we came to the table in bare feet, he'd ask, "Where are your shoes?"

If, God forbid, he heard the fork hit our teeth while we were eating, he'd say, "Please don't clink your teeth with the fork. And lay your fork down gently on your plate."

"Pass the food to the left. And to the adults first."

"Would you take my plate when you get up?"

"Did you ask to leave the table?"

"Who set the table? The knife goes on the right and the fork goes on the left."

On more than one occasion, he said to me, "Don't you think you've put a lot of food on your plate?"

"Stavros," my mother always said, but he disregarded her.

"Well, she's maturing, and she needs to watch what she eats."

"She's fine," my father would say, imploring my mother to back him up.

If Alex came to the table after working in the garage, he'd said, "Why are you wearing that awful t-shirt?" Or "Why are you still in a dirty shirt?" And "You still have grease under your fingernails. Did you wash your hands?"

At least once during the meal, we'd look at my mother and father, who would roll their eyes, and Alex and I would crack up.

One weekend, when he agreed to watch us while my parents were away, he was on the phone all day talking to a girl or lying on the couch watching a movie. He locked me out of the house, and when I had to go to the bathroom, he wouldn't let me in. Alex was out in the garage working on his bike, and when I told him, all he said was, "So what?" *He* didn't care; he could pee in a bush if he needed to.

"Let me in!" I finally screamed as I pounded on the back door. "If I wet my pants, I'm telling my mother!"

When Stavros finally opened the door, I yelled, "Don't you ever do that to me again! This is my house, not yours."

"Be quiet," he said, going back to the phone. "And go back outside when you're done."

That night, a girl showed up at the house, and she and Stavros went into my parent's bedroom. As he closed the door, he said to me, "If you say a word about this, you'll have hell to pay."

They were in there for hours, and finally I heard them laughing when she left around midnight.

He smoked silly brown cigarettes and blew smoke in my face when my parents weren't looking, and he had a way of making me feel like he thought he was superior to me. When I asked Alex about it, he said, "I don't give a shit what he thinks. He's just being Stavros."

When he first brought a date to Sunday dinner, I'll admit, I was captivated. How could someone like him have such a pretty girlfriend?

Of course, she was about half my size and wore makeup. She smelled good, and her blonde hair bounced as she talked with my parents. Even Alex behaved.

After that, if he brought a date to dinner, it was always someone new, and while I tried to be polite and cheerful, I stopped wasting my time getting to know them and I didn't bother trying to remember their names. The way they flirted with him and the way he acted like he was God's gift made me crazy.

He had an annoying habit of closing his eyes while he was thinking about what he wanted to say. When I asked him one time why he did that, he answered, "Because attorneys need to think before they speak, and it's easier for me to concentrate that way."

That made sense, but it still drove me nuts. Plus, he wasn't even an attorney yet. He'd talk about what *this* person did or what *that* person did, and he used these stories to boost his opinion of himself. He also developed an annoying habit of saying, "Ahh. . ." in a long, drawn-out manner before he said something. I don't know how my parents tolerated him, and one time after he'd left, I heard my father say, "I think he lives beyond his means, Kate."

My mother only said, "I know."

When I was around ten, Stavros married Julia, a stunning woman who reminded me of a blonde Jacqueline Kennedy. She had a beautiful two-year-old golden-haired daughter, who suddenly became Emma Panos. In those days, no one spoke of adoptions—children suddenly and miraculously belonged to someone else. I'd never known anyone who'd been adopted, so after giving it a lot of thought, I finally asked my mother about it.

She said, "Emma is now Stavros' daughter, and it's something to tuck in the back of your mind, and not speak about again."

I did just that, and two years later, he and Julia had their own baby, a girl with dark hair and dark eyes, and they named her Sophie.

As time went on, I saw him mostly on holidays. After his third divorce, he came with his children for Christmas dinner. Before long, he began bringing not just his children, but a girlfriend as well.

No one ever spoke about Sophie being adopted, and even as an adult, I wondered if she knew. She looked so much different from her younger sister . . . had anyone ever told her?

There were a few kind things Uncle Stavros did for me once I became an adult; he wrote me a reference letter for a college application I'd made, and, on his own, he verified my first husband's divorce was final before I married him. Eight years later, he handled our divorce when we parted ways. When Stavros learned I was marrying again, he wanted me to have Steven sign a prenuptial agreement; I'd never heard of such a ridiculous idea, and I declined. How do you ask the man you're about to marry to sign something so offensive?

"I'll do whatever you want," Steven said when I told him about the idea, although he was just as surprised as I was.

"I'm not going to do it," I said, still insulted my uncle would have even mentioned it.

"If this marriage lasts, you have your inheritance to think of," Stavros said point-blank. "It needs to remain your property."

I never thought my *first* marriage would end, and I didn't plan for this one to end either. I didn't know what lay ahead of me when my parents eventually passed away, and as it worked out, I would have amended the prenup, anyway.

Before our marriage, I knew Stavros had verified that Steven's divorce had been handled satisfactorily, because he told me he'd done so just before our wedding.

His vote of confidence in us felt unsettling. Only years later did I understand that his cynicism came from years of being worn down by people.

I wondered if Stavros had mellowed with age, when one time, he surprised us by asking Steven for an opinion about a car. He was handling a divorce for a client who wanted to pay him with a 1955 T-Bird. Being a car enthusiast, Steven jumped at the chance to go look at it with him. Once he agreed it was a good trade, Stavros had the car towed to a friend's dealership, where they began the restoration.

My husband was also a gun collector, and when Stavros discovered that, he told Steven about his college friend, who collected vintage Browning rifles. Steven asked about seeing it, and I was amazed Stavros arranged it.

"His collection spanned generations, and every wall was lined with polished wood racks. It looked like an armory and museum combined," Steven said afterward. "I was blown away."

Both times I asked him if Stavros had treated him civilly, and he said, "Of course. Besides, I don't take him too seriously, anyway."

Good for him, I thought. Steven could be sensitive sometimes, which was something I loved about him.

Sometimes, if we went out to dinner to celebrate something with my parents, Stavros would join us. The evening would always start out well, and I began asking him questions about some of the cases he'd handled over the years. Surprisingly, he met my questions head-on, and without naming names, he offered answers freely, and more than once he caught me off guard. His openness was a little disarming. I realized there was a human side to him, after all.

But once he started drinking, he changed. He never missed an opportunity to flirt with an attractive waitress, and most of them took his flirtation in stride. Sometimes they'd even blush, but one evening he'd had too much to drink and he actually touched our waitress's arm and asked if he could call her. She politely refused him.

We were all embarrassed, and I don't recall ever seeing my mother so infuriated with him. My father held her arm when she looked like she was going to reach across our table and strangle him. It was the only time I'd seen her pull away from my father, and surprised, I looked at Steven. He shrugged.

"Stop it," was all she said.

My uncle casually sat back in the booth and took a drink. "It doesn't hurt to ask," he said, shrugging his shoulders.

"Why does he always act that way?" I asked as my father drove the four of us home.

There was only silence before my mother finally said, "I hope he's okay to drive." It was obvious she was still annoyed, but now she was concerned.

"What an ass," I said.

It was surprising how many people I met who knew Stavros, especially if they were attorneys. They would look at me as if they were sizing me up before they acknowledged knowing him.

"Yes, I know Stavros," they'd say with hesitation.

"Unfortunately, he's my uncle. Please don't hold it against me," I'd said, breaking the ice. Then we'd laugh.

He was the type of attorney who could be a total asshole; he came on strong, but if you needed help and wanted someone on your side, he was the one to call.

I occasionally wondered if he was aware of what people thought of him, but then I also wondered if he would even care.

CHAPTER SIXTEEN

VASO
FAMILY PHOTOS AND
MY PARENTS

When I was younger, I used to pull our family photos out of the boxes where my mother stored them in the bottom cabinet of a bookcase. They were in no particular order, so sometimes I'd dump them all out before I'd go through them. I always thought the photo of Alex tied to a clothesline was interesting. It was as if he were on a leash while my mother hung our laundry. He seemed happy enough, and my mother told me once she did this to keep him from running around the backyard or darting out into the street since there was no front fence then. The date on the photograph was 1947, so he would have been two. I came along in 1949. One of my favorite photos of us was the one of me with my parents on the front porch of a house we lived in on Henderson Street. According to the photograph, I would have been nine months old and my parents both squatted behind us; I was on my father's knee, and, in his underwear, Alex stood leaning one leg against my mother.

I loved looking at the photographs of my parents on their wedding day. My mother, Kate, was so beautiful. She was slender and wore a simple white wedding dress, and her hair was bobbed just above her shoulders. She wore clips in her hair rather than a veil, and my father, Nick, wore a suit.

One day, with photos strewn everywhere, I asked her why she didn't have a fairy tale wedding like I'd always envisioned. She reminded me they didn't have a lot of money back then.

"We needed to save what money we had, so that we could buy a house for you children to grow up in. And in those days, most weddings were modest, with a small reception and family members cooked the wedding meal. I'm sure when you grow up and get married, you'll have quite a celebration," she said as she touched my cheek.

I loved it when my mother smiled. She was the one I went to when I woke with a bad dream, or if I needed to be assured there were no monsters under my bed. No matter what, she assuaged my fears.

That day, she left me with the box of photos, but she quietly closed their wedding album and instead of putting it back, took it with her.

Also in the box were photos of Alex in his Boy Scout uniform, and me with my Bluebird troop. Several of the pictures were from a birthday party I didn't remember, but a group of young girls were gathered around a wooden table, sitting on benches and watching me as I blew out the candles on my cake. As in most of my younger photos, my hair was cut short, just a little longer than if I were a boy. I had naturally curly hair, and I hated it when my mother had to brush the tangles out. She hated dealing with *me*, so, always being practical, she kept it short and manageable.

My father didn't care for my hairdo because I'd overheard him tell my mother, "Little girls are supposed to have long curly hair."

"Then *you* can try to brush it. She's miserable, and so am I for making her cry," my mother replied.

He never said anything to me about it. I was his katsika (cot-see-ka), his baby goat. I was his princess, and he always told me I looked beautiful no matter what.

I always felt my brother Alex and I were too far apart in years to be really close—there was only a four - year difference, but as children, we had nothing in common. The age difference didn't keep me from trying to mimic what he was doing, but rarely was I successful. Mostly I was frustrated, and as we grew older, I realized envy played a part in it.

Sometimes, when he *would* acquiesce to my pleading and play with me, it was something like tetherball. Because he was taller and stronger than me, he'd hit the ball so hard it would come around and smash me in the face. Or if we played hide and seek, he'd totally disappear and I'd search for him, to no avail. He always tripped me up if we played *Mother May I,* or *Simon Says,* and when he'd let me play marbles with him, he gave me the ugly ones. Naturally, he was a better shot than I was, and I always used more force and shot *my* marbles out of the circle.

I went through a stage of idolizing Alex. I was never really interested in any of the things he did, but I'd often pretend he actually invited me in to see what he was working on. Even *I* thought he was handsome, and he knew how to do so many things. He was my Wally Cleaver on *Leave it to Beaver.*

There was something about my brother that attracted the neighborhood boys, too, for unlike me, he never had to try to make friends. Of course, when I was old enough to rationalize it, I knew why all the boys were in awe of him; he could tear apart and customize his bike, or anything else he set his mind to, and when he was old enough, he always had a motorcycle or a car in various stages of disrepair in the driveway. When he started keeping snakes and tarantulas, my mother made him keep them out in the garage. If the garage door was open, Alex was there, and so were his followers.

Of course, no one ever noticed me, and I could see why. I was dorky-looking with my short hair, and I hadn't even started shaving my legs yet. But that didn't keep me from going out there where the washer was and doing laundry without being asked, or asking if anyone wanted some lemonade.

"Beat it," Alex would say.

By then, my mother no longer worked at the dining room table, but in the new family room off the back of the house. It had knotty pine paneling, an open-beamed ceiling and plenty of windows. On one wall there was a fully stocked bar with bar stools where they entertained their customers, and on the opposite wall was a fireplace surrounded by built-in bookcases. There was room for four desks, plus a sofa and a couple of chairs.

Instead of playing dolls, I'd set up a TV tray next to my mother's desk with an extra adding machine, pencils, and paper. She'd patiently stop what she was doing if I wanted to sit at my 'desk' and work, too. She'd read off random numbers so I could add them up. By the time I was twelve, I knew how to use a ten-key adding machine by touch, and I typed ninety words a minute.

Helen Dunnigan was no longer looking after me, and once I'd outgrown the TV tray, I'd sit in one of the chairs in front of my mother's desk and tell her about my day. She always made time to talk to me, and yet I felt my life was an open book when there were other people in the office. I likened it to being a movie star living a life that was shared with the world.

By the time I was a teenager, they had remodeled my bedroom to include a wall of built-in cabinets with a long Formica countertop and a mirror four feet high by eight feet long. It was my new dressing table and desk, and I had my own phone. We had two telephone lines, and during the day, whoever was in the office would answer them. Tired of coming to tell me I had a call, my parents set up a buzzer in my room, so if someone called for me, they could buzz me. For my sixteenth birthday, my parents bought me an antique-style European phone, which I still have.

My father became a general contractor specializing in insurance restoration. Clients were insurance adjusters who would stop by on their way home from work to have a drink, for everyone loved my dad. He had a great personality, an uncanny business sense, and a natural way of entertaining people—he was the one who brought in the business. My mother was the behind-the-scenes person who made all his ideas and plans work.

For Christmas one year, my parents wanted to do something different, so they hung a Christmas tree upside down from the ceiling in the office. It was a big hit, and it became such a part of the room, they didn't get around to taking it down until March or April of the next year. It's amazing the house didn't burn down because by then the tree was obviously totally dead and brown. They tried wrapping it in a sheet of plastic before they unscrewed it from the beam, but for months after they took it down, we found pine needles in everything.

They'd also have cocktail parties a couple times a year, and they set tables up on the patio where everyone could sit and eat. My father would marinate and barbecue lamb *souvlaki*—Greek shish kabobs—which everyone loved, and he'd be sure to cook enough for Alex and me to snack on for the next few days.

I was the one in charge of hosing down the patio and getting it ready, and maybe that's where my love of watering first took root. I think it also came from watching my father, who often picked up the hose when he needed a quiet break from the day's worries. Up until I married and left home, if I grew restless, I'd pass the time outside watering the planters and trees, then wash the dust and leaves off the patio and driveway.

When I was in the fifth grade, I started private school. Alex had started the previous year in order to advance his learning skills, and I went because I was jealous he got to go. I remember many evenings when my mother would sit with Alex at our maple dining room table, going over his homework and spelling words; it was like pulling teeth with him. After about an hour of impatiently waiting for my turn, they would finally finish, and I'd bring my papers to the table and spread them out.

"This looks pretty good," I recall my mother saying as she looked over a story I'd written. "You should do well with this. Now, where are your spelling words?"

The difference between me and Alex was that he'd get most of his words wrong, and I'd get most of mine right. My mother and I would finish in minutes, and I'd be miserable afterward. I didn't want to pretend to be dumb just to prolong the uninterrupted time I got to spend with her, but more than once, the thought had entered my mind.

If my father wasn't home out giving estimates, my mother would sit at our upright piano and play. There was something about the way her fingernails made a clicking sound as her fingers hit the keys. I loved listening to her, and while she never said anything to me, I was certain she still wished I had fallen in love with the keys the way she had.

The year I turned twelve has been forever etched in my mind. My April birthday fell during Spring Break, and my parents had just bought a second home in Palm Springs. Alex and I each got to invite two friends, and my mother drove us down for the week. On the way into town, we shopped for enough food to feed an army: hamburger meat, hotdogs, chips and cookies. My father was going to join us for the weekend, so my mother also bought steak for them.

We got to choose bedrooms, and Alex and his friends chose what we referred to as the maid's quarters—a small bedroom and bath off the pool. Even though it was the smallest of the five bedrooms, it gave them the most privacy to mess around and stay up all night.

We stayed on the other side of the house, where the larger bedrooms were, but at the opposite end of where my parents would stay. The first thing we did when we got there, after helping my mother unload all the groceries, was to unpack our suitcases and claim our areas of the bathroom counter. Then, after making a huge production of shaving our legs and armpits, we changed into our bathing suits and headed for the pool.

There were plenty of pool toys, two bicycles built for two, and an adult three-wheeled bike. My girlfriends wanted to be where the boys were, but I wanted to explore the neighborhood and see if we could spot any movie stars. The house was in an older part of Palm Springs called Deepwell Estates, where Ava Gabor, Loretta Young and William Holden once had homes.

During the day, my mother would drop us off downtown, and we'd shop at all the stores. At night after barbecuing dinner, we'd all sit around the fire pit and roast s'mores while the boys told scary stories.

Alex's friends were almost sixteen, and while they made a show of telling us girls to buzz off more than once, I caught them eyeing my girlfriends in their swimsuits. One night, while everyone slept, I woke as the door to our bedroom opened, and the boys sneaked into our room. I pretended to be asleep, but watched as they stood by our beds and muffled their laughter. Alex slugged one of them to be quiet. Eventually, they left and snickered again as they closed the door.

They were jackasses, and I was going to tell my mother in the morning. But the next day when I gave Alex the evil eye, a half smile crossed his face as if daring me to tell on them. I never did; it would have just ruined our trip.

Over the next few months, Alex kept to himself, meaning he didn't talk to me unless he had to, and I was fine with that. I actually forgot he'd been such a jerk in Palm Springs.

Then, one Saturday night during the Christmas holidays, my parents decided to go to a party. Even though it wouldn't be long until I was thirteen, they told Alex he needed to stay home with me.

"You can have a friend over if you promise not to get into trouble," my mother said to him.

I insisted I was old enough to stay by myself. Plus, Alex had been moody again for the last month or so, and he hadn't spoken a word to me. I thought it would be fun to stay up late and watch something on television, plus I knew Alex wanted to go out with his friends. When my parents insisted he stay home, he stormed into his room and slammed the door like a child.

My mother kissed me goodnight, and when she hugged me, I remember closing my eyes as I inhaled the familiar fragrance of her lipstick and cologne. I told her I would wait up for them before I went to sleep.

Not long after they left, his friend Richard Bice came over, and within minutes, I could smell cigarette smoke coming from Alex's bedroom.

"You're going to be in trouble," I yelled.

My parents had outgrown the home office the previous year and had purchased a building where there was more office space and plenty of parking. They'd turned the den into a big family room with a mishmash of furniture: two sofa beds, tables and chairs, and a big old television set. It was a perfect place to have parties or just hang out with our friends.

I heard Alex and Richard giggling like girls as they walked past my bedroom and into the family room. I was sure they were going to watch a stupid movie I would've despised, and I knew if I asked if I could tag along, they'd send me on my way. Instead, I chose to read in bed, nestled under a blanket on one of the corner beds in my room. I quickly got tired of hearing the TV blasting, so I got up and closed the door to the family room.

Around nine, I got up to check the refrigerator to see if there was anything worth munching on, and eventually found the Tupperware container my grandmother had filled with freshly baked cookies. I wrapped a handful in a paper towel, and making my way back to my bedroom, I noticed how quiet it had become. I closed my door, and just as I climbed back under my covers, Alex called out to me from the family room.

"Vaso!" he yelled.

I could hear their laughter, and I thought if I pretended I didn't, he'd go away.

"Vaaaa-soooo," he called again, this time almost singing it.

I was certain they were going to ask me to get them something to eat, and when I stepped into the family room, the air was thick with the smell of cigarette smoke, sweaty teenage boys and dirty clothes. Both Alex and Richard were sitting next to each other in the sofa's pull-out bed, their chests bare. Their blanket was pulled up just past their waists, concealing what I was to discover was the secret below.

Alex was the first to throw off the cover, and Richard followed a moment later. What I saw were two naked boys—hairy legs sprawled out, their erections exposed and unashamed. I'd never been afraid of my brother before, but I stood there frozen, staring at them both. Aside from colored textbook diagrams of the male body, I'd never actually seen a man naked. I turned to my brother, hoping for some kind of reassurance that I wasn't making this up.

"Come here," he said.

I was confused, disgusted, and paralyzed at the same time.

His voice was absolutely emotionless when he said, "Vaso, come here."

Then all I recall was that I was sitting on top of my brother.

You'd think I would've remembered more—the specifics, at least. What happened after that moment? How far did it go? How far did they go? How did I get out of that room, and back into mine, back into the world where nothing had happened? And the question that haunted me most was, why didn't I say a word to my parents? Why didn't I scream, cry, or even whisper the truth?

But what I did remember was their odor. It was foul and sickening.

That night, I found blood in my underwear, and my stomach churned at the discovery. I couldn't sleep for fear Alex would come to me, and when my parents finally returned, I pretended to be asleep when my mother opened my door to check in on me. I was sure she'd be able to smell me even from my doorway.

I was petrified. For weeks, I'd lay awake at night wondering what I'd do if I got pregnant. I was only twelve and had no clue about anything anatomical. I hadn't even started my period yet.

Eventually, I found a way to compartmentalize, which was a trait I've carried with me my entire life. I could set certain things aside and keep them separate from the rest of my emotions. Like being angry with someone but still wanting them to accept you, or feeling torn about doing the right thing but protecting someone you cared about. Or finding guilt with something someone has done, but treating an isolated incident without prejudice.

And especially with Alex, keeping my guard up and being drawn to him with a pull I couldn't explain, even when my instincts screamed otherwise.

It was a busy party season for my parents that year, and two other times when my parents went out, I begged them to let Alex go out and leave me at home. But that was not to be the case. Both times, when it was time to go to bed, I'd close my door and pray. Alex would stand outside my doorway whispering my name. And each time he did, I lay still in my bed, pretending to be asleep. If he came in, my plan was to scream bloody murder and kick him in the face. But both times, he eventually gave up and went away.

Sometime between Christmas and New Year's, my first period arrived, and to my relief, it felt like a milestone I'd been waiting for. My mother and I never had a birds and bees conversation, for she knew I'd learned about the body in my health class. So, she gave me a little Hallmark calendar, the kind with twelve months printed on the back, and told me to circle the dates so I could keep track and plan ahead. Embarrassed, I tucked it away in my top makeup drawer but used it.

After that, every time I saw Alex, I couldn't get the images of him, Richard, and their hairy legs out of my mind. It was difficult to explain, but I wasn't frightened of him; I'm not sure what I felt. For the next few months, I took no chances and when I closed the door to my bedroom, I propped my dressing chair up under my doorknob like I'd seen people do in the movies, just to make sure he didn't come in unannounced.

I would sometimes see him in the garage, working on something, or taking care of his wildlife creatures, but I'd never venture in like I used to do. And even when he closed the door to his bedroom, I'd quickly pass by, hoping he wouldn't hear me.

Thankfully, his interest in me waned, and I attributed it to the fact he started going out with girls his own age. I was grateful when he was invited to parties, and I'd have the evening to myself, although I'd usually spend it in my bedroom. But after that one night with Richard, he rarely spoke to me—or to my parents—and it was as though he didn't live with us anymore.

I knew he was there because I'd hear him make a sandwich for dinner, almost as if he purposely avoided having meals together as a family, eliminating any possibility of having conversations with my parents.

I'm not sure what became of Richard Bice. I never saw him at the house again. That was the year my parents took Alex out of school, and he went down to the Valley to stay with Aunt Cynthia and Uncle Eddie. And life for me went back to normal.

I hated to admit it, but I had never been so happy. I became an only child, and I didn't think about my brother for almost two years.

CHAPTER SEVENTEEN

VASO

Still in private school, I flourished. I studied Latin, Spanish and French, and even though I'd mastered the typewriter when I was younger, I took a class in typing and I loved it. I hadn't intended to show off, but I could type faster than anyone in my class, and throughout the time I was there, I won pins for typing seventy, eighty and even ninety words per minute.

My school was at Tenth and Pine Avenue. Shoe stores and dress shops, along with Long Beach's finest department stores, Buffum's and Walker's, and the famous J.J. Newberry five and dime store, were down the street. I loved shopping, and because my mother didn't have time to shop with me, if something caught my eye, I'd tell the cashier I wanted to charge it to her account, and they'd look up the number. I also learned how to put purchases on layaway and make weekly payments with my allowance.

I had everything I wanted; parents who loved me, their undivided attention when they were home, clothes and shoes. I was doing well in school; my teachers highly regarded me, and I got straight A's.

When I was fourteen, Alex, who was by then eighteen, graduated from high school, and moved back home. He came back even more handsome than when he left. I didn't see the young man who did what he did to me; instead, I envied him when he talked about all the girls he'd dated and all the friends he had down in TheValley. If I were hard-pressed, I'd have had to say I still didn't have many friends *or* a boyfriend.

And I became discontented.

When he did talk to me, Alex used to tell me stupid stories he swore were true.

One was about a Highway Patrol officer who pulled him over, and when he approached the car with his ticket book out, Alex rolled down the car window and said, "I'll have a hamburger, French fries and a shake." The other one was about another time he was pulled over, and when the officer came up to the car, Alex asked if he was selling tickets to the Highway Patrolman's Ball. The officer said, "Highway Patrolmen don't have balls."

That summer, we traveled to Europe. We went with another family—a good friend of my father's from the North Long Beach Lions Club. Bud made our itinerary and took care of all the travel arrangements, which included sailing to Portugal on a gigantic ocean liner.

At first, I was surprised my parents put me in the same cabin as my brother, but from their perspective, there was no reason not to. They didn't know what he'd done. Somehow, though, I saw him differently now. Whatever fear or hesitation I might've felt—I'd managed to tuck it away, almost as if it didn't belong to me anymore.

However, for good measure, after our first meal, I pocketed one of the serving forks from the dining room, and I went to bed with it every night just as a precaution. I was prepared to tell him to 'fuck off' if he ever came near me—but he never did.

It turned out he had other things to do; he sneaked out of the room and partied every night and then slept until noon the next day.

On that voyage, I learned to sing *Hava Nagila* and the Spanish song *Sabor, a Mí*. I tasted shrimp cocktail for the first time, and I learned how to run my fingertip around the rim of a wine glass to tell if it was crystal. On a beach in Italy, I fell in love with a young Italian boy named Franco Marinello, who professed his love for me by breaking a long, slender rock he found on a rocky beach.

We shopped at bazaars in Morocco, and I bought brass candlesticks and a brass box. My mother insisted I buy a gold charm from everywhere we went, and when we returned home, she had a jeweler attach them to a beautiful gold and pearl bracelet.

I didn't have a care in the world.

About three months after we returned home, Alex announced his girlfriend Jean was pregnant.

CHAPTER EIGHTEEN

ALEX

I would have been happy to have been born when the Wild West was still wild, and law and order was an eye for an eye. Or if it had to be in the 21st century, then I could have been happy if I'd been dropped into deeply forested mountains to survive on my own.

I am balding, with very curly salt and pepper hair that I wear pulled back, braided in a ponytail that runs down my back. Because my beard is also very curly, it always looks scraggly, and I've been told it looks unkempt. That's a big word for me; I'll have to look it up someday to find out exactly what it means.

One time at Target, while the wife shopped, I sat on the ledge of the flower bed drinking a cup of Starbucks. Someone walking by thought I was a beggar and put a tip in my cup. I looked in there and cracked up. I guess my bib overalls and the motorcycle chain hanging from my pocket make me look like a bum.

At my dad's funeral, my sister asked me if her husband could take me shopping to get a pair of pants and a shirt—but I said, "I'm fine the way I am. It's how Dad remembered me."

That's the way I roll.

My mother said I was born angry. I took to her breast, but she said I stiffened when she or anyone wanted to hold me. I learned to say "No" before I said Mama. Of course, I don't remember this.

What I *do* remember is that I've always bucked society.

I hated going to school and was constantly bored. My parents sent me to a private school when I was fourteen, hoping the change of scenery and the small class size would open my mind to a higher education. I'm not sure what it was about school that turned me off. I didn't have dyslexia or vision or hearing problems. I think I just couldn't sit still.

Private school didn't work. All it did was cost them more money when my sister Vaso was jealous and actually *wanted* to go to school there. Of course, she excelled at that place. I think she took three languages and actually enjoyed going on the field trips—like to the county fair and to that old people's hospital for Christmas, where they brought purse-sized tissues and made pipe cleaner deer. She was a little princess, but I could tell she had a streak of me in her when some girl pissed her off and she hauled off and slapped her one.

I can't complain about my childhood; my parents let me do just about anything I wanted to do. I had this thing for bugs, and had tarantulas, worms, ant farms, and grasshoppers. Once I graduated to rats and snakes that also ate the grasshoppers, the rules changed, and I had to move everything out to the garage. That was cool. Then no one would come in and *bug* me, get it?—unless they had to do laundry.

I started stuffing animals I'd caught, like squirrels and one of my snakes, and at one time I thought I wanted to become a vet or taxidermist. Once I found out you had to go to school to learn to do either, my interest in both vanished.

I had taken apart just about everything I owned and put it back together again; bicycles, motorcycles, tools, a car or two—if anything needed fixing, I was the guy to do it. I also ended up with a lot of unfinished projects going on at one time, and this was a trait that followed me throughout my life.

I hated the Viet Cong and was ready to go over there and kill those fuckin' commies, so I enlisted in the Air Force when I was eighteen. I was stationed in Oahu, and that's where my daughter Chloe was born. Somehow, they thought I was better suited to work on airplanes than fight, which pissed me off. But you do what the service tells you to do or you end up in the stockade. And that definitely was not an option I wanted to consider.

When I got out of the service, we bought our first house in Long Beach. We had our second kid soon after. I worked for my parents in the construction business, and I knew I'd found my calling; I worked under another lead carpenter and had to take orders and do grunt work, but I became one of their best carpenters. I loved knocking things down and rebuilding them. I bought a Harley and spent a year re-doing it so I could ride it back and forth to work. I knew my folks gave me a lot of leeway, but I pulled my own weight. By the time our third kid was born, I had so many remodeling projects going at the house, I couldn't decide which one to work on. So I finished none.

We went to my parents' on Sundays to have dinner with them and my sister Vaso. Her first husband was my dad's age, and he somehow ended up working for the company, too. My mother would cook a big dinner and each week, I had hopes we'd be able to finish a meal without having some kind of argument, but it seemed that that never happened. We always talked about the business. Either my dad was upset about something an employee did and Vaso or I would defend them, or I talked about bureaucrats and we'd get going on politics. Somehow, the conversation always circled back to whatever home project I'd abandoned, and my dad liked to joke, "With the way you leave things half-done, it's a wonder you had three kids."

My poor mother would just sit there and shake her head.

One night when we were leaving, I said to Vaso, "I don't know how you do it, working in the office with them every day."

I hated fighting with my father, but I was growing restless. I was tired of all the bureaucracy of day-to-day life, of all the taxes I had to pay, of having to conform to all the rules, the price of gas. You name it; I hated it. I loved my wife and kids, but at the same time, I wanted to escape. I started thinking about moving somewhere where no one else lived, where I had land to build what I wanted, and where I could do what I wanted to do. I was ready to move away, but since I still needed my job, I settled on moving east, to Orange County, where I found an acre of land in a neighborhood that was still zoned for horses and farm animals.

The biggest problem wasn't packing everything up; it was completing the unfinished projects I had started around the house. My wife, Jean, made a list of everything we needed to do to get the house ready to sell, and by the time I was done, I wondered why I hadn't finished them while we were still in the house and could enjoy them.

Life was good. There were houses on one side of me, but there were acres and acres of vacant land on the other side, and every time I'd look out at that land, I'd imagine I was out somewhere in the countryside. It reminded me a little of Uncle Eddie's land before it got replanted; pure, wonderful dirt.

Traffic to work and back was a bitch, but I was happy out there on my acre. I built a barn where I stored the hay for my horses and a cow, and then I built a large pen where I could raise a couple of pigs. We had chickens, cats and dogs, and I kept my snakes and mice out in the garage. For about five years I was livin' the life. And then we got a notice that a housing development was going in on the vacant land next door!

For the first time ever, I went to city council meetings and tried with all my might to fight those houses. But I seemed to be the only one who hated the idea. It was "progress," they all said. We won two things, though; the zoning for animals in our neighborhood was grandfathered in, and the new homes had to be single story so our neighbors wouldn't be looking down onto our properties.

Every day, I'd come home to see they'd made a little more "progress" with the grading for roads, then curbs and utilities. Then came the concrete slabs, the framing and the roofs. For a while, it looked like a ghost town, but I knew they were doing the rough plumbing and electrical. And then eventually, the houses were finished.

I lasted another five years loving my property but hating the way everything had changed, and I started growing restless again. I bought 20 acres of land in northern California, in a podunk town called Hayfork, where I could build a house and raise pigs. I'd be free of all the traffic and government idiots once and for all.

Jean was perfectly happy where we were, in a home filled with unfinished remodeling projects we had going on. The kids were settled in school, and Jean had just started a part-time office job at the junior high school. But I eventually got my way, and Jean sold our house for an exorbitant price to my sister, who was inheriting step kids and needed more bedrooms. I figured she could finish most of my projects, since she was going to redecorate, anyway.

I took most of our stuff to the dump since we wouldn't have a place to store anything while I built the house up north, and I told Jean we could buy all new when I was finished. I found the spot where I would build, then took my camper shell off my truck and that's where the five of us lived for over a year while I built a two-seater outhouse, a sauna for our showers, and then started on the framework for the house. I was building to code, and I figured no one was going to be around to see what I was doing. What I didn't count on was having to deal with the kind of people I hated the most—the building department and county officials who wanted me to get permits to finish building it! I had to kiss their asses if I didn't want to tear down over half of the framing.

Once the framework was done and the plywood walls were up, we could sleep there and still have access to the camper with the stove. I was in hog heaven, so to speak, because I also found time to fence off some of my land to build pens for the pigs I'd bought.

The kids adapted well enough to country life, although I quickly realized there wasn't much to do up there but drink and do drugs. Since we were in the middle of all the illegal marijuana growers in the forest, even I, who was wrapped up in my own world, noticed the inevitable yet subtle changes in all the kids up there. Jean was tired of roughing it and complained relentlessly about everything she'd given up to follow me, and when our oldest daughter graduated from high school, she gave me an ultimatum to either finish the house within the year or she was going to move. And it'd be at my expense.

By this time, we'd both started drinking pretty heavily, and at first I thought when she was clearheaded, she'd change her mind. She made me sign a contract to do what she wanted, or I'd have to buy her a house over in Shasta where she and the other two kids could enjoy all the amenities life had to offer.

I had a firm belief that when my kids turned eighteen, they were on their own. And when I handed my oldest daughter, Chloe, a couple of black trash bags and said, "Here you go. Make your way in life," Jean was even more pissed at me. Not to let the second daughter, Alexandria, off the hook, when she turned eighteen, I also gave her the plastic bags and expected her to move out.

Things were moving along, albeit slowly, when our boy Nik was in his senior year, and then one day, when everyone was off doing their own thing, there was an electrical short and the house caught on fire. We'd just put the carpet in and had our new furniture delivered. Thankfully, none of the cats or dogs were trapped inside, but the firefighters later told me that because all my ammunition kept going off, they didn't get close enough to the house to even try to put the fire out.

It ended up that Jean got her new house in the city, and Nik and I stayed on our land and moved back into the camper shell. I still had the outhouse and sauna, so all was not lost—but part of my spirit died. For a long while, I didn't even try to clear the ashes and start rebuilding.

Nik stayed with me to finish high school, and before he graduated, he had a head-on collision with a tree, which gave him a noticeable scar on his forehead. Plus, he was arrested for a DUI.

Jean bailed him out, and none of us talked for about six months.

His excuse to me was, "Well, you got a DUI too."

"Bullshit," I thought. I hadn't been drinking when I got mine. I was so drunk I couldn't drive, so I pulled off the road to sleep it off. A sheriff drove by and checked on me. Once he discovered I wasn't dead, he arrested me.

CHAPTER NINETEEN

ALEX

Jean and I got divorced not long after that. The three kids had moved in with her, and then I found out she'd been sleeping with my best friend, John. I had a meat counter at the little grocery store in town by then, and I couldn't believe he could come in to work every day and look me in the eye and act like nothing was going on the whole time. The kids said nothing about him either, like, that he'd been staying at the house with them.

I was pissed.

"Get the fuck out of my sight," I told him.

Since he stayed in the city with Jean, I never saw him again. They eventually broke up, and about a year later, I heard he had died in a car accident. He'd probably been drinking or doing drugs like everyone else up there.

Business at the meat counter was not great, so in order to earn more money, I started a portable slaughtering business, killing not only pigs, but cows and sheep. My folks bought me a new truck, so I rigged my old Chevy pickup with equipment heavy enough to hang a carcass after I shot it in the head. Because I was the only one up there doing that, I stayed really busy. I brought everything to the meat market, where I had a walk-in. And I had a sign on my counter that said, "Alex's meat can't be beat."

I hung bull testicles, bear baculum (penis bones) and deer antlers on the outside wall where my sign was. I always cracked up when I told people what the baculum was.

I ended up building a fifteen by fifteen room off the camper so I'd have a little more space to get around in. That was my living room, TV room and bedroom. I eventually planned to build a kitchen, but in the meantime, I still cooked in the camper. I kept a couple of cats and the three dogs, so I had plenty of company at night. Once it got dark, you couldn't let them out, or they'd have a hell of a time defending themselves against mountain lions or bears.

I met my second wife, Linda, at a livestock auction. Actually, I'd seen her in town, and we'd nodded in recognition of each other after a few times. She was different from anyone I'd been interested in before. She wore no makeup, didn't shave her armpits or legs, was on the heavy side and wore her long hair braided. She was definitely a country girl.

She was perfectly happy living in my one room with the camper shell attached, and she had a gentle way of eventually encouraging me to build on another room where she could sew. She mispronounced words like 'ax' instead of ask, and 'libary' instead of library. But I felt that was part of her charm. She didn't mind the outhouse or the sauna, and I knew I'd met my soulmate in her.

Jean and my kids hated Linda, which made me like her even more. When we decided to get married, my parents came up with my sister and brother-in-law. We had our ceremony in the forest. It was still warm at the beginning of fall, and Linda wore an off-white cotton dress. She decided to wear her long hair down, and she added a ring of flowers on her head like a flower child. She was beautiful.

I watched as my parents pretended to like her—they did all the right things, like telling me they were happy for me. I knew that part to be true. But I also saw that they were uncomfortable being out in the forest during the ceremony, standing on the uneven forest floor, and my dad swatted at flies that were determined to annoy him.

They'd only met Linda once when we came down for a weekend. I could tell the laugh that made *me* smile made them and my sister almost cringe. But I didn't care. And Linda was never aware of the judgment they were passing on her. Or at least if she was, she never said anything to me. I think she truly cared for my parents and thought they cared for her, too. At least she did until after my parents were both gone, when Vaso told her they'd only tolerated her.

CHAPTER TWENTY

ALEX

I think I was almost sixteen when my cousin Kaylee was up visiting my grandmother, and she showed me photographs she'd found of my parent's wedding. I'd seen them before at our house, in a small album my mother kept in her bedroom. "I've seen them," I said as I passed through the dining room where she sat.

"No, I don't think you've seen *this* one," she said, being a smartass. She placed them on the table.

My mother was beautiful in her wedding dress, and my father was so proud of his new wife. There were pictures of them standing on the steps of the church, and then of both my sets of grandparents in Yia´ Yia's living room on Loma Avenue. My dad's stepmother looked happy for him, although I always thought of her as a bitch, knowing how she treated him when he was young. There were gifts on the floor, and my parents sat opening them, and then one photo jumped out at me. There I was, standing by my father as he helped my mother untie a ribbon from a white-wrapped box.

I was too surprised to do anything but sit at the table next to Kaylee. I felt the heat rising up inside me as I tried to digest what I'd just seen. By the look on her face, Kaylee was expecting my response. I felt my stomach drop, and I instantly went cold. It felt like my blood had stopped flowing. I was unable to control the adrenaline rush.

"See," was all she said.

Somehow, I pulled myself together and said, "See what?"

I couldn't think of a reasonable explanation for why I was standing there in that photo. It looked like I was around two, but I was no good at telling a kid's age. I'd heard of people having two wedding ceremonies; one at the courthouse and then one in the church to make the family happy. That's what my Aunt Cynthia said she and Uncle Ed did. They did it to make Yia´ Yia and Papou happy.

I was sure that's what my parents did.

It had to be.

My heart was still racing, but I thought I was the master of indifference, so I said to her, "Fuck off." And I walked out of the room.

The color of my world changed for me that day.

I saw my parents differently now. My mother was still my mother, smelling flowery when they went out, playing the piano in the living room, cooking dinner. And I tried to look at my dad as still being my dad. But I didn't see my curly hair in either of them, and my cheekbones were more pronounced than my father's. I'd started growing hair on my body, and mine was darker and curlier than his, too. I tried to use logic; we were all different. Even I knew two children born to the same parents could be totally different.

But as hard as I tried to make it all work in my mind, I couldn't. I tried to think of a hundred reasons for me being in that photograph. My mind raced; Aunt Cynthia and Uncle Eddie knew. Yia´ Yia knew, and so did Stavros.

And then I blew it. I didn't say anything to anyone because I really didn't know what to say, and I didn't know anything for sure. I tried to think back to anything my dad did to treat me differently than he did Vaso. Aside from her being a girl and his princess, I couldn't think of anything off the top of my head. But he was the one I chose to blame.

A few days later, my parents asked me to watch my sister, and I called her into the den where Richard Bice and I were in the pullout bed watching the television. That's when I decided to pay my dad back.

CHAPTER TWENTY ONE

VASO

Alex was still eighteen when he joined the Air Force. He and Jean, who was only seventeen, told everyone they got pregnant on purpose so they could be together wherever he was stationed. When he told my parents, I watched my sweet mother's expression twist into the smile she rarely wore—the one when she was furious. Her lips parted just enough to show her gritted teeth. I'd only seen it a few times, and I saw it now when she talked about Alex and her soon to be daughter-in-law. When she told me, I could see the disappointment in her eyes. I didn't understand her disapproval, but what did I know?

I thought Jean was pretty cool; she was three years older than me and seemed so worldly. She was blonde and had a big bouffant hairdo. It was so long ago; I don't even remember the ceremony, but years later, I came across their wedding photo. They looked happy standing on the steps of a wedding chapel in Long Beach and being pelted with rice.

My parents and I flew to Oahu when their daughter was born, then again when she was about two and a half years old. That's always been my favorite age for children, and Chloe was the cutest little girl I'd ever seen. For years, I kept a photo of her in my wallet. She was standing on the balcony of their apartment, and she gave us a backward wave—that of a child who hadn't quite mastered the art of waving yet.

President Kennedy was assassinated on my father's birthday, November 22, 1963. When the school announced it was going to close because of the shooting, I was among the students who ran from the building in mass hysteria. We ended up a couple of blocks away before looking at each other, wondering what we were even doing. In silence, we made our way back to the school, gathered our things, and left.

I took the bus home that afternoon and sat in front of the television with my parents that night. They hadn't voted for him, but they were speechless nonetheless. We watched in silence as Jacqueline Kennedy leaned over the president in the back seat of their car, tending to her husband. Had she known he was going to die? How was it that something like that could even happen in America?

By ninth grade, none of us brought lunch anymore. We'd line up at the little catering truck that rolled into the schoolyard each day. One afternoon, in the chaos of the crowd, someone bumped into me, and I accidentally knocked Sherrie Howard's orange drink, spilling some onto her white shirt. The way she looked at me—you'd think I'd done it on purpose. But I hadn't. I barely even knew her. She and her friends hardly ever spoke to me.

She was livid. Without saying a word, she hurled the rest of her drink in my face.

I wiped myself off as calmly as I could, then turned and walked toward the girls' bathroom. Sherrie followed, still shouting, still fuming.

I don't know what came over me, but I wasn't going to stand there and take it. So I did the only thing I could think of—I slapped her. Hard. Her head snapped to the side like in one of those slow-motion movie fights, and for a few seconds, we both just stood there.

My heart was racing. *Holy shit. I'm really going to get it now.*

But I didn't flinch. I looked her dead in the eye and said, "And if you tell anyone, you'll regret it."

I could see it—the rage still rising inside her. She turned to face me, and for a second, I thought it was on. We were really going to fight. And even though my confidence was slipping, I didn't let it show. I gave her a tight little smile and walked out like I wasn't scared at all.

I found an empty classroom, slipped inside, and leaned against the door, trying to steady my breath. My thoughts spiraled. If she told the principal, I'd be in serious trouble—maybe even expelled. My parents would be furious. Worse, they'd be humiliated. Even if I were just defending myself, they'd never understand.

As I stood there, heart still pounding, something settled in. Something inside me was shifting. It wasn't just about the slap. It wasn't even about Sherrie. It hit me then—I was changing. I wasn't the same girl I used to be. I took a deep breath, opened the door, and stepped back into the hallway.

I could stand up for myself. And I just had.

I was growing bored. Even though I'd pleaded with my parents to let me go to private school, I now thought I was missing out on life by not attending a public school. There were no boys I was interested in, and I had no friends to speak of. Students attending my school came from all over town, so there were no slumber parties or get-togethers outside of class. I was by myself when I walked to the bus stop, and no one on the bus was someone I would want to be friends with.

I thought if I were in a new environment, things would be different. I finally convinced my parents that I should be allowed to go back into the public school system. I think they finally relented so they wouldn't have to hear me complain all the time.

I changed schools, and it turned out to be one of the worst decisions I ever made.

CHAPTER TWENTY TWO

VASO

During that summer, my mother drove me to Jordan High School in North Long Beach to register for tenth grade. Groups of girls giggled and chatted among themselves, and only a few students nodded at me when we passed them.

Even though I thought I didn't have friends at my private school, when September came around and I had a huge campus to navigate and multiple classes to jockey, I realized I'd left a sheltered lifestyle for a freedom I wasn't sure I was ready for. I don't know what I expected. I hadn't grown up with any of these kids, so I knew no one. And accordingly, no one came up and talked to me.

My certainty about being tough and taking care of myself after my encounter with Sherrie Howard the year before vanished. I quickly realized I'd left one disappointment for another.

It didn't take long to see I wasn't like the girls who were popular and belonged in the socialite sororities. I didn't look like them or act like them. Eventually, I made one friend in my English class. I'd met Spanish-speaking kids, and even a black girl at my new school, but I'd never met someone who was half Filipino and half white. She was quite pretty with her thick dark hair and almost black eyes. Her name was Demaris, and I thought even her name was fascinating. Her parents were divorced, and she lived with her mother and grandmother in a neighborhood not far from the school.

She knew a few other girls who didn't quite fit the mold—girls who didn't wear all the trendy clothes or bother with painted nails. They mentioned a sorority that was recruiting, and she encouraged me to give it a shot. Somehow, I ended up getting an invitation to pledge.

What followed was six weeks of pure chaos. We weren't supposed to shave our legs, but I did—every single day—until the last week. Makeup was off-limits, and we had to wear our hair in curlers anytime we stepped out in public. We wore mismatched outfits to school and ridiculous costumes on trips to the mall. It was embarrassing and hilarious, and strangely fun.

One Saturday night during pledging, a loud knock shook our front door. A group of pledges stormed into my room—they were there to kidnap me. My parents were in on the plan, of course. My mother had even made sure I was wearing something "presentable" to bed and had quietly placed her bathrobe at the foot of my bed before saying goodnight. Only then did it click.

What they didn't know was that we weren't going to a sorority event—we were going to a party. That night, I met my first boyfriend. His name was Richard Kline. He had short, curly blond hair, blue eyes, and drove a '62 lowered Chevy Impala with a record player in it. He was a senior at Poly High, near downtown Long Beach, but he lived in Bixby Knolls and had friends at Jordan. When he offered me a cigarette, I took it just to seem cool. I pretended to inhale, and later, when he offered again, I casually declined.

We each had a beer, and when he took my hand, we danced to a slow song. I froze when he leaned in to kiss me. I'd never kissed anyone before, and I panicked—half worried about what the others would think, half stunned by how natural it felt. His kiss tasted like beer and cigarettes, and it surprised me—how heady, how thrilling it was.

I knew some of the girls dated older guys, and a few of them drank and smoked pot. I hadn't done either, and when I glanced around, everyone else seemed lost in their own little worlds, doing the same. We danced again. Then he leaned in and whispered, "There are too many people in here," and led me out to his car. The cool air hit my skin like a reset.

I slid in close beside him, and we kissed again. And when he asked if he could see me sometime, I already knew I was in love.

My parents agreed to a date—he even came by to meet them before. I had a midnight curfew, and I was home right on time. We saw each other a few more times before my parents suddenly said I couldn't see him anymore. No real explanation. No room for argument.

"I hate you!" I shouted, storming to my room. The door slammed behind me, and the tears came fast and hot. I called Richard the moment I could breathe again, only to start crying all over.

I didn't speak to my parents for days. Their minds were made up.

But so was mine.

No one was going to decide for me who I could love. That was the moment I crossed the line—from good daughter to quiet rebel—and stepped into my first act of defiance.

I saw Richard for over six months behind their backs. I'd tell my mother I was going to a friend's house or to the soda shop after school. Sometimes he'd pick me up from school and we'd cruise for a while, or go have a hamburger where all my sorority sisters were with their boyfriends. Sometimes we hung out at his house. I'll never forget the day his mother unexpectedly came home when we were making out on the sofa. I'd worn black nylons that day and had snagged them on something, so there was a large hole in one leg. His mother took one look at me and gave Richard a look I'll never forget. I was sure to her I looked like a tramp.

Not long after that, he disappeared from my life. Just like that. He stopped coming by the school, didn't call, and never returned my messages. I was frantic, imagining the worst. What if something had happened to him? Then another thought hit me—what if my parents had found him and told him to stay away?

But they acted the same, going about their lives as usual. And I couldn't exactly go to them for help—not with this. The only person I could talk to was Demaris. She tried to comfort me, but nothing could quiet the constant thoughts running through my head. Had I done something wrong? How could he just vanish without a word?

I was heartbroken. Every afternoon, I scanned the crowds as I left campus, hoping to spot him. And every night, I lay in bed, replaying everything in my mind, wondering where he went—and why. I started to believe I wasn't enough for him. Maybe I had never been.

Watching my friends with their boyfriends only made it worse. I'd become the third wheel, the odd one out. I didn't belong with them anymore, either. If I could just understand why he left, I told myself, maybe it wouldn't hurt so much.

Then, that summer, the North Long Beach Lions Club held its annual Labor Day Fair at Houghton Park next door to the school, and my father told me about the Queen competition. It wasn't a beauty contest, but rather the winner would be the girl who sold the most tickets for the raffle. I was up for the challenge, and he introduced me to the ticket master. I signed up for a hundred tickets, and then soon realized I could sell tickets to all of my father's business associates and subcontractors. I sent everyone a book of ten tickets, along with a self-addressed stamped envelope and a letter asking for their help in winning the contest.

I went to any Lions Club function I could to promote ticket sales, and I was somehow invited to a luncheon where the newspaper took my photo with Senator George Deukmejian—who eventually became California's governor.

Contestants earned a small amount of money for each ticket sold, and with that cash, I purchased more tickets. Because we processed so many tickets, we used rubber stamps in both my name and my father's name. On the last day of the fair, I waited nervously for them to announce the Queen, and draw the winning tickets for either a 1966 Chevrolet Chevelle, a trip to Hawaii, or one hundred dollars. I thought for certain I'd win the contest, for I'd dedicated myself and I knew I'd sold over a thousand tickets. It was almost as if I couldn't lose. To keep the butterflies at bay, I played carnival games, and ate two hamburgers, and kept an eye on the other contestants.

The stage was decorated with red, white, and blue for the Labor Day holiday, and I tried to act nonchalant as I stood there, waiting. My parents were standing in the audience, and my mother waved to me when I looked over at them. A loose banner caught my attention as a warm breeze blew it off to the side.

The announcer finally climbed up onto the podium and tapped the microphone.

"Testing. Testing."

"Ladies and gentlemen, gather around. This is the event we've been waiting for all summer. We have three lovely ladies, all vying for Lions Club Queen, and we've finally verified the count of the tickets they've sold."

He waved to us and said, "Ladies, will you come on stage?"

You know how in movies, there's always a happily ever after when the underdog who's struggled the most to win a race or contest wins against all odds? I prayed for that to happen to me as I joined the other two girls who started giggling. We stood there fidgeting, and I hadn't thought about what I'd do if I lost. Then it happened. When he called out the name of the new queen, my worst nightmare came true. It was one of those moments when you think to yourself, 'How the hell did I get here and what in god's name made me think I could pull off winning anything as prestigious as this. I looked out over the crowd, and I wished the floor would open up and I would disappear.

I didn't win the contest.

My mother's hand went to her mouth in shock.

The audience cheered, and of course the winner cried tears of joy as I stood there and watched someone else steal my glory.

Somehow I made it back to my parents, my eyes burning, and every muscle tense as I fought to keep my composure. Miraculously, I held back my tears, and it was the hardest thing I had ever had to do.

On the stage, someone was talking about announcing the winners of the drawing, and all I could think of doing was running away.

And then I heard the name. The winner of the new car was Nick Pappas! My father won the car.

CHAPTER TWENTY THREE

VASO

My parents as much as admitted that there was no way to be certain if the winning ticket was actually one they bought, or if it was one we stamped with the money I reinvested. Either way, I became the proud owner of a new Chevelle, and I don't know how I slept that night.

After persuading my parents to let me return to public school, receiving that car seemed like another victory—but in hindsight, it was a mistake. It relieved them of the responsibility of transporting me, sparing my mother and her bookkeeper from shuttle duties, especially on rainy days. At the time, it felt like a ticket to independence, but looking back, it merely offered the illusion of freedom.

Now, I was bursting with this newfound independence, and overnight, I became more popular. I'd pick up my friends and take them to school, or we'd cruise around the park after our last class. I could drive into the Park's Texaco gas station and buy us cigarettes, and it didn't matter then if I had a boyfriend or not.

In my junior year, I grew tired of my stripped-down Chevelle, and I sold it to buy a 1963 Buick Riviera. It was silver with a black leather interior, and before I even made the first car payment, I lowered it and replaced the original mufflers with Glasspacks. I wanted that sound; the rumble and vroom that the guys who had lowered Impalas had. Record players were all the rage then, so with my Christmas money that year, I had one installed. My allowance paid for my car payment, insurance, gas, and cigarettes.

I loved my car, and I now had plenty of friends.

Even though I was bored with school, my teachers loved me, and I could do no wrong. One of them recommended me to work in the school office, and I jumped at the chance. I could type and answer phones from years of being in my parent's office, and I got along with everyone.

The following summer, I'm not sure where we got the pot, but someone had an apartment, and we spent our days smoking it. We'd listen to the Doors playing loudly on the record player, and that's when I met John. He lived next door to where we'd hang out, and one day he caught me as I walked in with some friends.

"What are you doing here?" he asked.

"What does it look like?" I answered.

"You look smarter than these losers," he said.

His eyes were almost turquoise. And he was handsome in a pretty way.

"Come with me," he said, gently taking my hand.

Mesmerized, I followed him to his apartment.

John was the first man I made love to. He was mature, experienced, and gentle, especially when he discovered I was still a virgin. He told me he'd just gotten out of prison, but nothing about him frightened me.

"I was in a fight," he explained. "Everyone was drunk, and this guy hit me. When I hit him back, he fell and hit his head on the bar rail, and ultimately died. I was going to be married, but my fiancé called the wedding off when I went in."

I'd never heard such a heartbreaking story, and my heart went out to him. He encouraged me to quit smoking pot, and we were together for about six weeks. Part of me hoped something would come of us, but I knew I'd never be able to tell my parents about his past. And then one afternoon, he told me he was leaving for an out-of-town job offer. I wasn't sure what I felt for him; I didn't think it was love. But deep down, I knew this was good for him. I wished him the very best. He'd been a positive influence on me—I hadn't smoked pot in all the time we were together.

Mothers seem to have a second sense about them, and while we still never talked about sex and its ramifications, one day when I came home from school, I found my current menstrual calendar open on my desk. Next to it was a note that my mother had made an appointment with our family doctor, and I went on the pill.

I can't even remember now, how I met Tanya. It was the first time I'd known anyone whose mother was gay. We went to her house once, and she took me to her mother's nightstand, where she kept all her paraphernalia. I'd never seen anything like that. When I finally met her mom, she looked like anyone else, and I could never tell if she wondered if I knew about her or not. Or if she even cared.

Tanya's boyfriend was a drummer in a band, and they smoked a lot of pot. We'd sometimes take some amphetamines, and I'd let Nick drive my car to Hollywood, where we'd cruise Sunset Boulevard and freak out about how the streetlights had purple rings around them. I'd make up my eyes with black eyeliner with wings that made me feel like I had cat eyes. I had to walk with my eyes half closed so people would see the total effect.

We started smoking with a group of their friends, and one night I smoked so much pot, I blacked out. I had visions of my head rolling from one side to the other, and I remember saying, "Wow, man," when I came to. I asked the person sitting next to me if I'd really done that or just imagined it.

"No, man. You did that," he said. "What a trip."

Tanya's boyfriend, Nick, knew a guy who'd just gotten out of prison, and one night after smoking, Nick asked me if I'd have sympathy sex with him. I thought about John and how not everyone who went to jail was bad, so I agreed.

This guy looked like a gangbanger though, with a craggy face, long hair and tattoos, and the minute I saw him I flashed back to my brother. I froze, but then Nick nudged me.

"C'mon," he said. "He's okay."

I should have walked away, but I didn't. In the few seconds it took for me to go ahead, I should not have cared what Tanya and Nick thought of me and that if they had any respect for me, they never would have put me in this position. Like with my brother Alex, I wasn't afraid, I just felt empty. I never thought I'd do anything as low as that.

After that, I decided I needed to smoke a lot less.

When fall semester started, I went back to working in the school office.

I'd never been to a prom, and that May, my parents said I should go. I still didn't have a boyfriend, so I invited one of my so-called friends to go with me. I bought a dress and my own corsage, which should have sent up a red flag, but he promised he'd pick me up on time. When the night came, my mother took a photo of me all dressed up for the dance, but as the clock ticked by, I realized my loser friend was going to be a no-show.

I could add this to my wall of shame; I'd been stood up for my own senior prom.

I was too proud to cry, so I just changed my clothes and headed out for the night. I ended up in a bar that didn't ask questions. I'd always looked older than I was, and the dives I went to didn't care, anyway. At midnight, I called it a night. When I went outside to get in my car, a thick fog had rolled in, making it almost impossible to see five feet in front of me. I was so drunk, I later counted my lucky stars I made it home without killing me or someone else on the road.

When one of my sorority sisters dared me to ditch school, she said her boyfriend's sister was gone during the day, so we had a perfect place to hang out. Some of the others smoked pot, and some took downers, but I was trying to draw the line somewhere, and I didn't do either. I began to wonder why I was even there. Was it just for the thrill of doing something I could get into trouble for? Why did my good judgment constantly fail me?

We skipped school for ten days before the sister finally called the office. I'll never forget the look of disappointment on the staff's faces when I got caught. They pulled out all the notes I'd forged with my mother's name, and the principal called me into his office. I could tell I'd thrown him a curveball, and he didn't have to spell out how much I'd let him down.

"Return to your classes," he said, barely masking his disappointment.

I dreaded going home that day. I knew I'd disappointed my parents, and not for the first time. I warmed something up for dinner, and when they came home from the office, my father just looked at me sitting at the table, and said, "When will you stop?"

Shrugging my shoulders would have seemed disrespectful, so I just sat there, unsure of what to do. It seemed I was still caught in a pattern of self-destruction, and I didn't know why or how to change it.

"You can drive to school and back," my father said. "But that's it. And that's only because your mother and I have a business to run, and, frankly, we don't want to see you."

He'd never spoken to me with such contempt, and if I'd had the courage to look him in the face, I know I would have seen how the disappointment in me had drained him.

I spent the entire weekend holed up in my room, except to make myself something to eat or use the bathroom. I gave my overflowing closet drawers a much-needed purging, bagging up unwanted clothes and shoes for donation. I cleared out my vanity and desk, discarding outdated makeup, jewelry, and hair accessories into a box. I polished my countertop and cleaned my mirror, and when I was finished, I vacuumed. My room hadn't had such a thorough cleaning in years.

I deliberately avoided my parents. I couldn't bear to put them in the position of dealing with me. Deep down, I knew I was spiraling out of control, but I had no idea how to stop it. To make matters worse, I was certain that returning to school on Monday would mean facing expulsion.

I spent extra time getting ready for school on Monday morning, hoping my appearance might make the right impression on the principal, but the minutes dragged into hours and I sat through my classes throughout the day without a word from him. My stomach churned and my heart skipped a beat every time one of my teachers looked at me, expecting they knew what I'd done and wondering if they knew what my punishment was going to be.

That night, my mother made hamburger patties for dinner, and I pushed my food around on my plate, unable to eat. A few times, she gave me a tenuous smile, and knowing how to read her, I could see the sadness in her eyes.

On Tuesday, I got the summons, and I felt the weight of the world on my shoulders as I made my way to the office. When I walked in, the air felt thick with unspoken tension, and instead of the administrative manager greeting me with a cheerful smile, her mouth was tight and grim. I'd let everyone down.

"Sit," Mr. Peterson said as I stood in his doorway. "I've been giving this a lot of thought."

He opened my folder, and I could feel a trickle of sweat roll down my back.

"I've looked at your grades, and it looks like you've accumulated enough credits to graduate early," he said, closing the file.

His smile was glum.

"I've spoken with your parents, and I'm sure you're aware of how they feel about the direction you're heading. We think you have what it takes to make something of your life, and they've agreed for you to graduate in January instead of waiting until June. You can start community college and get ahead a little bit."

He let out a heavy sigh.

"It's obvious you need a new environment."

My parents weren't oblivious to the stupid things I had been doing the last few years—how many times I'd come home either drunk and smelling like smoke, or with red eyes from smoking marijuana. And I thanked god they never knew the extent of choices I'd made and how far they'd gone awry. They just didn't know how to fix me. I knew I was hurting not only myself, but them, too. By this time, I knew they were getting close to giving up on me.

My classes ended in December, and in January, I officially graduated. There was no pomp and circumstance. The day I graduated was just like any other day, except I didn't even go to school. The plan was that I would start community college and then go back in June and walk with my friends. I'd already looked over the schedule of the new semester's classes, and since I had no idea what I wanted to do, I started where everyone else does; General Ed. I enrolled in English and math to start.

But two new problems presented themselves; one was that there were several weeks before the new semester started, so I was bored. I stayed out late and slept until noon, and then I worked a few hours every afternoon in my parents' office to while away the hours.

My second problem was that in college, no one cared if you attended classes and no one got on your case if you didn't do your homework. My classes were filled with students of all ages and backgrounds, and I had no friends to walk me through it all. When I realized I was on my own, I thought I was getting away with murder if I didn't go to my classes.

I'd cruise around the high school looking for my friends, and I spent more time hanging out with them until I finally concluded I was a lost soul. Two months later, I dropped out of college.

Even though I wanted to move on, I just couldn't figure out how to do that.

In June, we rented my cap and gown, and my mother took another photo of me in our entryway. I told my parents I'd meet them at school and left to pick up one of my girlfriends. After cruising around the school a couple of times, I abandoned the idea of standing in line to get my diploma, and as we drove around the last time, I saw my parents and my grandmother get out of their car. I'd missed my brother's graduation years before, so I wasn't familiar with the inner workings of it all, and I figured no one would notice I wasn't there. We went back to my house, opened my graduation presents and left a note that said, "Thanks for the gifts!"

We went back to that dive bar and drank beer.

Well, they noticed I wasn't there. What I hadn't realized was that the only way you were acknowledged was if you handed them your name on a slip of paper as you walked up to the stage for your diploma. So my clever little plan to slip by unnoticed didn't work after all.

I had just humiliated my parents beyond words. I wasn't sure how I'd gotten to be such an inconsiderate, self-absorbed, miserable shit. The worst part was that my parents never said a word to me, and it made me realize just how much I'd hurt them.

They didn't need to tell me I'd become pathetic.

Plus, I was letting my so-called friends influence me and continue to drag me down.

CHAPTER TWENTY FOUR

VASO

I'd worn my parents down. If breaking their spirits had been my goal, then I'd won—but it didn't feel like I'd won anything. Being grounded, losing my car—none of it touched the part of me that was unraveling. I was on a path I couldn't seem to get off of, even though I had no good reason to be on it in the first place. I had a safe home, a warm bed, and parents who truly loved me. I wasn't mistreated or overlooked, and I had more than so many others. Still, it wasn't enough.

We never talked about what I was doing or why, and even if we did, I wouldn't have had any answers. But I could see the quiet defeat in their eyes, the way hope faded from their faces a little more each day. We moved around each other carefully, like we were all afraid of what might happen if we said too much.

They stopped asking where I was going, or when I'd be home. I felt a pull both to leave home and to isolate myself in my room because of their silence.

I think they kept telling themselves it was just a phase—that I'd grow out of it—that their daughter was still in there somewhere.

And then, just when I thought I'd burned every last bridge, they offered me something I never expected—one last, undeserved chance. And for the first time in a long time, I had no words; just a sharp ache in my chest, the kind that comes when someone believes in you more than you believe in yourself.

They'd sent my brother away when they thought *he* was heading down the wrong path, and they decided sending me away too was the solution. Chapman College in Orange was offering a four-month college at sea program. It wasn't punishment; it was far too generous for that. It cost a small fortune, and I knew it was less about discipline and more about desperation—one last effort to lift me out of whatever darkness I'd wrapped myself in.

My mother took me shopping for clothes that wouldn't wrinkle in a suitcase, and we packed two footlockers full of essentials—cartons of cigarettes, bottles of shampoo and hairspray, and stacks of music and books. It was a strange kind of sendoff; part exile, and part gift. Roughly nine hundred students boarded the ship in New York, bound for a semester-long voyage around the world that would eventually bring us back to California. Not everyone on board was running from something; but I was.

I'd fallen in with my so-called friends; the kind of people who didn't ask questions or expect anything from me. It was easy being accepted by them; no effort, no risk. But I knew they were lost, and deep down, I knew I had become lost with them. I wanted something different, something more. I just didn't know how to reach for it. Not yet.

Before we set sail, my mother arranged for me to meet a girl who was also going on the trip, so I'd have a familiar face on board. However, once on board, we never became friends, and it wasn't the first time I wondered if I was just unlikeable to normal people.

My father's parting words to me were, "You've broken our hearts. If you don't come back a different person, don't come back."

I knew in my heart this was my last chance to turn my life around.

Ship life was incredible. There were classes during the day and dances or entertainment at night if we were at sea. With all the sailing we did, we passed through many time zones, and it didn't take me long to realize I wasn't acclimating well. I ended up having a difficult time sleeping at night and attending classes during the day. So—I ended up sleeping during the day, and being up all night. Attending classes gradually came to a stop.

Even though it was small, I was lucky to have a cabin to myself. It was inside, with no view of our surroundings, but it gave me the luxury of spreading out, and I didn't have to share my space. Because it was pitch black when I turned out my lights at night, I got in the habit of sleeping with my door open to the hallway. One night, I'd fallen asleep as usual when suddenly I awoke to a man hovering over me. His hand covered my mouth as I screamed.

He rushed out of my cabin, and once the panic subsided, I locked the door behind him. But that night, sleep never came, not even with the light on. My mind wouldn't stop replaying the image of my brother, Alex, standing in my doorway quietly calling my name. I hated that he lingered in my thoughts, even now. Back then, I saw him as nothing more than a clueless sixteen-year-old, but his presence stayed with me throughout the night.

I'd always hated the dark, but after that, I started closing my door before bed, depending on the thin strip of light coming through underneath the door. I remember wishing I'd packed a nightlight—something small to push back the shadows.

My mother had thought ahead to pack a cassette player, and I listened to tapes of Jefferson Airplane and memorized the song *White Rabbit*. Part of me was still my old self, but another, more mature part of me was open to being introduced to new things. I'd always appreciated the music my parents listened to—Frank Sinatra, Dean Martin and Louis Prima, and I also loved more current music like that of Isaac Hayes, Nancy Wilson and Jack Jones.

I read classics from the ship's library and spent afternoons on deck reading *To Kill a Mockingbird, The Spy Who Came in From The Cold, The Godfather,* and *The Agony and the Ecstasy,* and I read a lot of my Rod McKuen poetry. I even tried my hand at writing down my own thoughts.

While I was away, my mother was my anchor and my tower of strength, and she somehow found the time in her busy schedule to write to me every day. In each port, while some students got either one letter or none at all, I had six or seven. She wrote about the most mundane things, like how our Yorkshire Terrier, Tax, missed me, and how he surprised the new mailman who had to learn to hand him his junk mail the minute he came through the office door. She sent me Polaroid photos of the office after they had a flood; they were drying out all the wet paperwork. Mundane or not, I loved it all. My father would sometimes add a note and say something like, "Keep your grades up. Miss you, Dad. XOXO"

I couldn't help but think how disappointed he'd be with me when he learned I had abandoned my studies.

The faculty and staff constantly reminded us they would tolerate no drugs or alcohol on board, and if they caught a student using them, they'd be given an incomplete and sent home. That warning and my newly adopted mantra of my father telling me to come back a different person kept me on the straight and narrow, at least in the beginning.

Before we landed in our first port, Portugal, they cautioned us about pick pocketing and they especially urged the girls to be alert and cautious of all the young men who would be interested in meeting us. As we got on the buses to take us into town, several young men in cars waved as they followed us. When our bus stopped, they were waiting, and two of them called out to me. I actually thought it was romantic. They seemed eager to give me and another girl a personal tour, but only I agreed to go with them.

I had a wonderful day. They were genuinely interested in showing me the sights, and they took me to a sidewalk café and an outdoor market where I bargained for treasures. In Spain, it was the same; young men greeted our bus and offered to drive us around. I went to bazaars in Morocco, and in South Africa, I met some older men who took me water skiing in the harbor—and afterward we went to a wonderful restaurant for dinner that I never would have known about had I not met them. While we'd been warned about men, none that I met had intentions other than showing me the sights.

In Bombay, India, I met a young man named Narain Manglani as we disembarked. He took me to his home, where his mother squatted on the floor and cooked a meal using pots on a clay stove. After dinner, he pointed to their 'bathroom', which was a hole in the ground with a ceramic edging. I told him I'd wait until I could find a hotel. On the streets, I saw poverty everywhere, and when a blind child came up to me asking for money, my heart broke. He told me not to give any money, that some mothers purposely maimed their children so they could become better beggars.

As night fell, he asked if I wanted to go to the park and smoke hash with him. I didn't even know where I was, let alone what I was putting into my body. I followed without hesitation, never once considering my safety. Anything could have happened—rape, arrest, worse—and I wouldn't have seen it coming. I'd told myself I was searching for something on this trip. . . Freedom maybe, or wisdom, but clearly, I hadn't found either.

Years later, I watched the movie *Midnight Express*, which was a gut-wrenching story about a young man who escaped from a Turkish prison after trying to smuggle hash into the U.S.

I've never forgotten that, in all my naivety, that could have been me.

I truly believed that no matter what I did, nothing bad would happen to me. And indeed, someone had been watching out for me.

CHAPTER TWENTY FIVE

VASO

I had warned my mother I was bringing home more souvenirs than our car could hold, so she'd written back that Alex would bring his pickup truck to pick me up at the dock. Once I disembarked, I stood there surrounded by my two footlockers, a camphor chest from Malaysia, an African drum and numerous boxes, and waited as other students with far less were being picked up. Eventually, I saw my mother's Rambler pull into the parking area.

I was always so embarrassed that my parents drove Ramblers, but that was their company car, and whenever I'd said something about them, my father would say, "Yeah, it's rough when you have five of them."

My mother laughed at the sight of me, and the sound of her laughter wrapped around me and filled me with love, thankfulness, and an ache I couldn't name.

"You weren't kidding when you said you brought home a lot," she said, hugging me tightly. "I'm so glad you're home, honey."

"Why'd you get all this shit?" Alex said, obviously annoyed with me.

I gave him no thought as I helped him load up the truck.

I could hardly wait to unpack everything and show my mother what I'd bought: brass accents from bazaars, wooden African masks and carved statues from stalls in Kenya and Mombasa. I brought home a sari from India, a kimono from Japan, and in Portugal and Spain I found beautiful unframed hand-colored prints and carved statues of Don Quixote.

We'd docked in so many ports across the world, each one revealing a different but similar story of struggle and resilience. In Africa, we met families whose lives were rooted in hardship—some of them doing well by local standards, yet still living on bare dirt floors. It broke my heart to see how many of them relied solely on the small income they made selling handmade goods to passengers like us; people who would come and go without truly understanding what they were leaving behind.

The journey opened my eyes in ways I hadn't expected. I was genuinely grateful to return home, to see my parents again, and to stand on American ground. All along the way, I kept my father's words close, repeating the same quiet prayer over and over, "God, please make me a better person." I knew standing there with my mother, my actions didn't always reflect that wish, but I'd felt something inside me had shifted. I believed I was changing, and more than anything, I wanted my parents to see that, too.

I was grateful to be home. It instilled in me a new appreciation for everything I had.

Perhaps that had been the idea?

Once we got home, Alex and I brought everything into the family room. I was exhausted, but I wanted to unpack. I set everything out on the bar so I could marvel at it all, and then I headed for bed. The next day I called a couple of my friends to tell them I was home and then went to the taco place where I'd worked before I left. I got my old job back, and they wanted me to start the next day.

Three of my friends came by in the morning, before I had to leave for work. I finished getting ready to go, and when they said they wanted to hang out and watch TV, I left them in the house; after all, what could go wrong? I'd known them for years.

"Just lock everything up," I said, closing the front door. "You need to be gone by the time my parents get home."

About an hour after I got to work, my boss took me aside and said, "I don't think this is the job for you," and he let me go.

It seems I still filled the taco shells with too much meat, and I dropped a large order when I was getting ready to hand it to the customer through the window. I knew filling tacos wasn't going to be a forever job, but it was something I could do to prove I was headed in the right direction.

How was I going to tell my parents?

When I got home, the house was empty—everyone had already left, which was a relief. I wasn't ready to talk about losing my job, and all

I wanted was to be alone. I headed to my room to take off my uniform, but for some reason, I glanced across the hall into my parents' bedroom. That's when I saw it—the wardrobe doors were wide open, and their dresser drawers were pulled out and emptied onto their bed. It took a few seconds for it to register, then it hit me like a punch to the gut. My stomach turned ice cold. How could I have been so blind? And so stupid?

My mind was spinning. How was I supposed to explain *this*? I could lie and say someone had broken in. The thought crossed my mind for only a few seconds, but I knew I'd never be able to pull it off. I couldn't look my parents in the eye and pretend.

My hands were shaking, and rage was burning through me. I couldn't wrap my head around it. How could this have happened? How could my so-called friends cross a line so personal, so violating, without a second thought? I felt exposed, blindsided, and humiliated all at once.

Worried they might've gone through my things too, I checked my wardrobe, my desk, and my makeup drawers—anything they could've rummaged through. Nothing seemed missing. Even the things I'd brought home from my trip looked untouched. Still, the violation hung heavy in the air, and the shame settled deep in my chest.

My head pounded with the humiliation of it all and the understanding of my parent's disappointment in me, again. Realizing I was an idiot, I couldn't stop the tears from slipping down my cheeks. These people weren't my friends, and they never had been.

I called the police, and then I called my mother.

CHAPTER TWENTY SIX

MY FATHER, NICK

It took my father, Theo, years to save enough money to come to America. Like everyone else, he dreamed about doing more than growing food and tending goats in their remote village in Greece. America promised a better way of life with opportunities for everyone. My parents came through Ellis Island and made their way to stay with a Greek family in Ohio, and that's where my brother and I were born.

When I was nine months old, my mother grew ill with tuberculosis, and when she realized there was no cure for her, she wanted to go back to Greece to be buried with her family. We returned to her hometown, and when she died, they buried her in the small church graveyard where her mother and father would one day be laid to rest.

We traveled back to my father's hometown and lived with his family until he had enough money to come back to the States. However, he only had enough to bring my older brother George with him. He left me to stay with my grandmother, my Yia' Yia.

I was around four when I understood I had a father and a brother. My grandmother and aunt took care of me, and when my grandmother tried to explain that one day my father would send for me, I had a hard time understanding what she was trying to tell me. Of course, when I was older, all the pieces fit together, and each time we received a letter from my father, I hoped it would be the one that enclosed the money for my passage to America.

We had no electricity, and we got our water from the well in town. Once filled, the buckets were too heavy for me to carry, so my grandmother bought two smaller buckets from a vendor in the market, which, when filled, were a perfect weight for me.

Yia´ Yia and I raised the goats and sheep after my grandfather, Papou, died. The goats provided milk for drinking and for making cheese. We killed sheep twice a year; once for our Easter celebration, and once after we sheared them. We sold their wool to traders who came through town. We also had chickens, and I'd watch as my grandmother skillfully killed and prepared them for cooking. Like everyone else in the village, we lived off what we needed and sold or traded the rest, making sure nothing went to waste.

I wore the same pair of pants until the hems were frayed and several inches above my ankles. When that pair needed to be washed, I'd have to run around in my underwear until they dried. The soles of my shoes made a flapping noise when I walked, for there was no one in town who could repair them for me. But I really didn't care, because I knew no different. Of course, when I finally went to America, I realized just how poor we'd been.

I pestered local farmers to let me help them earn extra money, but they paid me in food. Eventually, I asked my grandmother to make some of her jam with the fruit they gave me. Because we didn't have jars to put it in, I'd sit in the town square and sell a slice of bread with the jam on it. Eventually, people started bringing their own containers that could be filled and reused, and with the extra money I earned, I bought bottles for us to use. I charged a little more for them but gave the customers a refund when they returned the bottle.

Once we started making money, I gave most of it to my grandmother, but set aside a little for myself. I thought I was so clever in hiding it, but it didn't take long for her to discover my hiding place while she was cleaning our two-room house.

"You're a very smart boy, Nico," she said to me while I waited for her to scold me. "Save your money, for one day when you go to America, you'll need it."

In my father's letters, he told us he painted bridges and smokestacks, moving from city to city following the work. Eventually, he settled in Michigan, and when I was nine, we finally got the letter I'd been waiting for; the one with the money for my fare to sail to America. At first I was very excited, but the only world I'd known was with my grandmother and aunt, and the thought of being by myself on a ship terrified me. I hadn't seen my father and brother since I was a baby, so I didn't even know them.

I was too old to cry, so I had to force those tears to stop, but try as I might, they still came.

"My handsome Nico," my grandmother said. "This is what we've been waiting for. This is your chance to better yourself in a country where you can be anything you want to be."

My grandmother sat next to me on my straw mattress. "It's okay to be afraid now, but you'll see what an opportunity this is for you, and you'll be strong."

I wasn't totally convinced, but I wiped my eyes and decided I would not let her see me cry again.

"But what do we do with the jam business?" I asked.

"Your cousin Athena can take over for you." Then she whispered conspirationally, "Of course she's not as good a salesperson as you are, but you are the one who got the business started, and I'm sure she'll do just fine. You're such a smart boy and. . ." but she didn't finish her sentence. She got up, and as she walked away, I could see her hand go to her face, and I was sure she was wiping her own tears away.

I stayed with the other single men while we were on the ship. Everyone was getting seasick, and the smell was overwhelming. I tried to go on to the upper deck for fresh air whenever I could, but I was always dragged by my ear back down into steerage.

It took me a week to figure out how I could get out of there, and the next time I went on deck, a sailor came towards me. I didn't speak English, but I tried to pantomime that I could cook or wash the decks; anything to get me out of the crowded deck down below. I thought he finally understood what I was trying to say, but when he grabbed me by the arm, I thought he was going to drag me back down below. Instead, we found the captain of the ship, and after he talked with him for a few minutes, I knew I'd have a job doing something. It turned out to be washing dishes and mopping the upper deck, and I eventually got to stay with the crew. Even their cramped quarters were a great improvement over the hellhole I was in before.

Eventually, we sailed into the New York Harbor and past the Statue of Liberty. It was an incredible sight, but I did not know its meaning until one day my father explained it to me. I had to go through Ellis

Island like the rest of the passengers, but my American birth certificate sped up my process. I wore my name on a card hung around my neck, and that's how my father found me when he came to meet the ship.

He didn't know what to do with me first—hug me or hold me at arm's length just to look at me. He ended up doing both. He pulled his handkerchief out of his pants pocket and wiped his eyes.

"These are tears of joy, my son," he said to me in Greek. "I can't believe you're finally here!"

I followed him with my one suitcase, and although there were already many cars on the streets by then, we took a horse-drawn wagon to a nearby hotel where we spent the night. The next morning, we boarded a train to Detroit, and my new life in America began.

My father had re-married but hadn't mentioned it in any of his letters, so I was shocked to see a strange woman and three extra children in the apartment when we arrived. I was introduced first to my brother George, who sat slouched on a chair, the glumness impossible to miss. The next two boys were my stepbrothers, and the young girl was my half sister.

"Now that you've seen your brother," my new stepmother said, poking George, "you need to get back to work. We've already lost money because your father had to pay for the train tickets and take off work to go get Nico."

When she turned her back, I saw the hatred on George's face. My father saw this also and shook his head as a warning not to aggravate the situation.

"And you, my new son, will call me Mother. After all, that is what I am now, your new mother."

"Ioseph," she said to her one son, "get back to your studies. And your sister and I will start dinner. Nico, when you've rested overnight, you will go out tomorrow with George and help him sell his peanuts."

And that was that. *Mother* had spoken. I watched as my father took a deep breath and left.

It was common within the Greek community for widows to seek husbands who could care for them and their children. Widowers did the same, looking for women who could help raise *their* children. The idea itself was sound, but it was obvious my father was not a happy man. As I grew to know her more, I wondered if my stepmother had put on her best face until she caught my father—then she showed her true colors.

"As soon as I figure it out," my brother George whispered to me that night, "I'm out of here. She is such a bitch, and our father never stands up for himself. I hate it here."

I took English lessons at our church, and I caught on quickly. I started grade school too, but I was older than anyone else in my class, and I hadn't learned enough English to understand what children were saying to me. All I knew was they were teasing me because I was a foreigner.

One day, when a couple of boys wouldn't let up, I grabbed one of them. Because I was twice his size, I pulled him up to my face and said in Greek, "I'm going to kill you." I knew he had no idea what I'd said, but it did the trick, and he and his friends left me alone after that. I was amazed at my new power.

Things changed when I began selling the peanuts.

I used to call myself the "Peanut Vendor" for when I wasn't in school, my stepmother filled bags with peanuts, and I stood on a street corner to sell them. It didn't matter what the weather was like; I couldn't come home until I'd sold everything.

Since she didn't give me lunch, like she did with her children, I was constantly hungry. I'd stare into the windows of the little shops that sold food, and every time the front door would open, the smells from within made me even hungrier.

Then I had an idea—what if I ate one bag of peanuts? Surely no one would figure it out. But when I got home, my stepmother counted my money and realized I was short one bag! She clapped me in the face and warned me if I ever came home short again, my father would hear about it.

"If I had something to eat, I wouldn't have had to eat the peanuts!" I cried, but to no avail.

So the next day, when I was hungry, I came up with a better idea. I'd take two peanuts out of each bag and eat those. The bags would feel the same, and no one would notice.

And no one did!

Once, a gentleman gave me a penny tip, and I bought myself some candy. I quickly realized the foolishness of my ways, because the candy was quickly gone and so was the penny. The next time I got a tip, I bought a piece of candy and sold it for two cents. Then I bought two candies and ate one and sold the other. I did that until I figured out I could double my money if I didn't eat a candy, and then once I had some money tucked away, I could eat as much candy as I wanted.

However, when my father figured out what I'd been doing, he boxed me in the ears and told me that any money I made had to go to the family. All that did was make me figure out a way to keep doing what I was doing and not get caught!

George had already quit school when he was sixteen, so I did the same. I started painting with my father and brother. Because my stepmother knew exactly how much money we made, it was impossible to pigeonhole any of it for myself.

My stepbrothers were never put out to work, and although I understood they were good students working towards college, it caused a lot of resentment between us. I knew they felt guilty for the way my brother and I were treated, but they never stood up for us.

At Christmastime, there wasn't enough money to go around, so my older brother got a used pair of work boots, my half brothers got new everyday shoes, our little sister got a new dress *plus* shoes, and I got new soles for *my* shoes.

My brother George hated our stepmother and our little sister, who was the vassilopoula (va-si-lo-poo´-la), or princess.

"I've had enough," he said one morning, and that's when he took off. We didn't see him for about six months. Eventually, when he made his way back home, my stepmother told him, "If you didn't like it here before, then you're not welcome here now. Things were just fine when you were gone."

George left us again and went to live with another family my father knew so they could both paint. When there wasn't enough work for me, I got a part-time job at one of the large hotels in downtown Detroit. I worked first as a busboy, cleaning and setting tables in the main dining room, and then alternated doing that and taking the room service orders up to the rooms at the top. It didn't take me long to figure out who was staying in those rooms—gangsters and hookers.

"Keep your mouth shut," one of them said to me as I was setting up a table in his room. I kept my eyes down and never uttered a word.

If there weren't room service deliveries, I worked the elevator. Again, I was told to keep my mouth shut as I brought girls up to the top.

One day I saw a girl I knew, and when she saw me, her face turned red as a beet. I gave her a quick smile, and lowered my head, and off she went to take care of her business.

I still had an accent then, and one of the bodyguards told me to lose it, and I could probably go somewhere. I was interested in losing the accent, but I wasn't interested in going anywhere with those kinds of people. I could imagine them killing people or beating them half to death if they were caught stealing or even suspected of doing anything wrong.

I met an Italian guy named Ernie, who'd started at the hotel just before me. We became quick friends, and he was someone I could talk to about my home life. His pop was still around, and his ma was a great cook. Sometimes she'd make us a big pot of spaghetti and meatballs after work, and I thought I'd died and gone to heaven. I was always hungry, for I never had enough to eat.

The best thing about working with the Mob was that I got to earn extra pocket money. I'd turn my hourly pay over to *Mother*, but I kept the tips I made. The worst thing about working there was that I saw things I didn't like. Like the girls I took up in the elevator—I knew what they were doing. I didn't care about the illegal booze, and I never wanted to know any details about anyone who got killed. I wanted it that way. I didn't care about the gambling—hell, I loved it myself, but I could only afford the neighborhood dice games, not the real stuff.

"You need to be careful," my father said to me one day. "If you get in too deep, you'll never get out."

When he said that, it scared the hell out of me and Ernie. We weren't so dumb; we'd figured that out. But we also hadn't thought about an exit plan.

I was always thankful when the painting work picked up so I could get back to doing something honest, but I had to admit I made some pretty good money when I worked at the hotel. That's where I learned to set a table, and which forks to use with which part of the meal. The rule was, 'warm plates for warm food, and cold plates for cold food.'

My brother George had moved to California by then, and he kept writing about how well he was doing. "There's plenty of work for all of us out here," he wrote.

One day, my father decided.

"We're moving to California," he said.

My stepmother said something that closely translated into "over my dead body," and I was so proud of my father when he answered, "Suit yourself."

I had my exit plan. I never told anyone, not even Ernie, we were moving. One day, I just didn't show up. I figured I didn't know enough for them to find me, and I was right.

We were all crammed into a two-bedroom apartment in a tall brick building in Los Angeles with no working elevator, and we quickly found there wasn't enough work for the three of us downtown.

"Let's move to Long Beach," I suggested. "It's near the ocean, and there are shipyards down there. Surely there's something for us there."

My father liked the idea, and even though my stepmother complained about having to pack everything up again, we moved. By this time, her two sons were in college, so they stayed in Los Angeles. We found a small house with a yard, and the first thing my sister wanted was a dog.

"Yes," my stepmother told her.

"No," my father said, for once stepping up. "We'll think about it later once we're all working. And we need the money right now so we can buy a different car—I need something I can put my tools in."

"Plus, we have two young men in college now," she reminded my father.

On our first weekend there, we packed a lunch and took the bus down to the beach. I later swore the sunshine worked its wonders on my stepmother, for she cheerfully unfolded the blanket and set out our lunch. By the time we were ready to go home, however, her mood had turned sour, for she was now sunburned and complaining.

"I don't know why I ever married her," my father said to me in English when she wasn't within earshot. "It was the worst mistake I've ever made."

I'd noticed the stress my father was constantly under before, and now I truly felt sorry for him.

CHAPTER TWENTY SEVEN

NICK

My brother George and I both received our induction papers within a week of each other. Mine was from the Air Force, and his was from the Army.

"You must serve your country," my father said.

"How will we manage without their income?" my stepmother asked.

"I'll send some pay home," I offered.

"Yeah, me too," George added, although I was certain he never would.

Boot camp for me was Lackland, Texas, where no matter what the season was, the humidity wore me out. They gave me an aptitude test, and although I had no experience, they felt I'd best serve the country by becoming an airplane mechanic.

I was stationed at Ellsworth Air Force Base about ten miles northeast of Rapid City, South Dakota, and although there were plenty of rules, for the first time in my life, I felt free. I learned to smoke, and there were plenty of bars where we could drink and raise hell. I'd been kicked out of one when some guy picked a fight with me. All I did was punch him back, but that was the only part the bartender saw.

"Out, buddy," he said, hitching his thumb towards the door. "And if you know what's good for you, you'll never walk through that door again."

I had no problem finding another bar, and it turned out, there were plenty of women to choose from.

Even though I was of slight build, I thought I was hot stuff. I had a buddy take a photo of me flexing my muscles with only my work pants and hat on. I sent it home and thought everyone would get a kick out of it. My half-sister loved it. My stepmother thought was aselges (a-sel-gēs), lewd, and my father thought she was overreacting.

(Kate ended up with it before we were married, and I think it's still somewhere in one of her memory drawers.)

Sturgis and Deadwood were our weekend hangouts, and we quickly learned which bars drew women to us if we dressed in our uniforms. In others, it was clear the minute we walked through the door—men in the service weren't welcome. In either case, in no time, I had a different woman on my arm every weekend. (I used to tease Alex when he took his motorcycle to the Sturgis Motorcycle Rally that he shouldn't date any of the girls in town—they could have been his sister! He laughed, but I was serious.)

I took my work seriously, but I took my partying even more so.

If I was interested in more than a one-night-stand, I'd take a girl to the movies, or go bowling. And dancing was right up my alley. I thought I was a regular Fred Astaire. And then afterward, it was time for romance. If anyone started getting too serious, I quit calling and laid low for a while. I wasn't going to let anyone tie me down.

If we were really looking for trouble, we'd set up illegal card and dice games, and there were a couple of backroom bookies if we wanted to do some serious betting. Lost pay, IOUs or worse—owing the wrong people—could land you in serious trouble. One guy we hung out with had the crap beat out of him when he couldn't make a payment on his loan. To make matters worse, he almost got thrown into the brig for it.

We all knew how to hot-wire a vehicle, and some nights we'd borrow a car and go joyriding, steal road signs, and crash town dances. But whatever we did, we all knew that breaking curfew could mean demotion, or KP duty. There were plenty of mornings when we were still drunk, showed up for breakfast and morning formation.

I wrote home with some money, but I knew my stepmother would read everything I wrote, so most of the time, I wrote about the weather, or having milkshakes in the diner. Anything to make it sound like I was staying out of trouble.

My sister was the one who wrote back, and sometimes my father would add a quick note at the end, reminding me to behave and be careful. I always felt bad for him, knowing he'd never had the chance to do anything adventurous back in Greece, and especially once he came to

America. It was always work, work, and then more work, just to support his family. I swore my life would never be like that.

George and I both got out of the service around the same time. I never had to go fight, although I was ready if they called me. I was eager to get back home, although I didn't have any plans. My father was still painting in the harbor, and I thought that was just as good a place as any to work until I figured out something better. George never saw action either, but when he came home, he'd changed. He drank whiskey and smoked—obviously traits he'd picked up while he was away.

He met a girl in Long Beach and fell head over heels for her. She was not Greek, so they got married in a small chapel and had a reception in the attached hall afterwards. My father, stepmother, and I chipped in and bought them pots and pans, and I heard my stepmother scoff every time they opened a gift.

"Stop it, please," I finally said.

I'd never talked back to her, and she turned her head in surprise. Her face tightened into a scowl, and she gave me and then my father what we called the evil eye.

"Katse, (cot-say) be quiet," he said in Greek. And she turned as red as her lipstick.

She didn't speak to either of us for the rest of the day, which was fine with me.

A few of my buddies relocated to Long Beach, and we'd spend our free time at the beach, where there were always girls, or we'd go to The Pike and go on rides like kids. We picked up girls at the skating rink or go dancing in bars—I went on a couple of dates, but I was never serious about anyone. I loved my freedom too much.

And then in 1947 I met Kate. I'd gone to the beach with a couple of friends, and there, under an enormous umbrella, sat this gorgeous young woman with dark brown hair. Her legs were crossed at her ankles, and she was leaning back on both arms.

"You go on ahead," I told the guys as I stopped to introduce myself.

There was room for two on her blanket, and it was obvious someone had already been sitting there, so I first needed to make sure there wasn't a husband lurking around somewhere.

"Sit," Kate said, shielding her eyes with her hand. "My sister is in the water."

So far, so good, I thought. We spent hours just talking, and I learned everything I needed to know about her; she was Greek, she'd been married before and had a young son, she lived at home with her parents, but had two jobs, and she was available for dinner that evening.

From the beginning, Kate made it clear she had a son to raise, and I took that as it was intended. If I wasn't interested in stepping up and making him mine, then I was wasting her time. When she told me about her first husband, I knew he was a lout, and I also knew if he ever came back to the States, I'd take care of him.

She was nothing like any girl I'd been with, and I knew from the start she wasn't the kind of girl who'd sleep with someone before marriage. I loved her, and I wanted her to know that—and I respected her too much to ever cross that line.

I loved Kate's spunk. And I quickly took to her son Alex. I hadn't planned on becoming an instant father, but I could tell by the look in his young eyes when he held my hand, that I was the man that could help raise him. In only a few months, we were married in the Greek Church in Long Beach, and I knew she would be the love of my life until the day I died.

Kate's brother Stavros helped me adopt Alex, and it was one of the happiest days of my life. That was until I heard the best news ever; Kate told me she was pregnant. I wondered how a poor Greek boy like me had gotten so lucky!

Vaso, as we decided to call her, was the most beautiful baby I'd ever seen. I always thought parents, especially fathers, acted silly when they showed off their children, but now I understood. I'd never seen a newborn baby, and I instantly fell in love with her and her pouty mouth. And then it struck me—how was I to take care of my new family?

My father lived long enough to see her turn two and a half. He was only in his late fifties, but he looked years older. He'd had a tough life, and working outside had weathered his skin and stiffened him with arthritis.

I have a photo I've kept of him when he visited San Juan Capistrano, where the swallows are famous for returning every year. He was sitting at a stone fountain, and a swallow landed on his head. He always thought that brought him good luck, but it didn't.

When he died from a stroke in 1951, he left very little money, so a few years later, my stepmother moved out of their small one-bedroom duplex in Long Beach. Although I never respected her, I knew I had a responsibility to my father, so I chipped in to help care for her. She alternated living with her three children until her death about twelve years later.

She wanted to be buried next to my father in Long Beach, so I paid my portion of the funeral. No matter our past, it was a solemn day, for it was the end of my former life. On the way to the cemetery, we were two cars behind in the procession, and as we passed through an intersection, a car coming from the right ran into the side of the hearse. The chauffeur got out and checked to make sure the coffin hadn't shifted, and as we waited for him to exchange information with the other driver, I recalled when the children were young and we'd visit my parents in that old one-bedroom house. She'd ask us to set up a crib for Vaso in the bedroom while we talked in the living room. One time when my half-sister came down from Northern California with her children, we set up the crib in the bedroom as expected, however her children, who were about the same ages as Alex and Vaso, were allowed to play in the living room while we visited.

My father just sat there, because he didn't know what to do. There was no anger, no defense, just that heavy stillness when she did something he hated. I understood his reluctance to start an argument with her, but Kate was furious.

I was lost in those thoughts when Kate nudged me to start the car again.

I had always worked two jobs; one painting at the harbor with my father and the other painting for people I'd met over the years. One day, while at the paint store, I saw that a painting contractor had posted a help wanted card to the bulletin board. My father was working less and less, and I needed a way to help support him and my family. I didn't have enough customers to work for myself full time, so I applied and got the job. Between Kate and me working two full-time jobs, the door to our future opened up.

During the day, I worked for Al White, and on the weekends, I continued to take on side jobs. Mr. White knew I had my own customers, and instead of discouraging me from doing side work, he encouraged me to build my business more. I never did extra jobs for his customers, pocketing the cash; instead, I'd look around while I was working and I'd recommend future projects we could do. I learned how to quote prices, and I increased Al's business almost overnight.

Al was my mentor. He introduced me to a world I'd never known—people who were successful. The majority of his customers either came from wealth or they were self-made men. Through him, I joined the Lions Club, and he introduced me to other business owners, some of whom became lifelong friends. One of them, Hank, an insurance agent and realtor, encouraged me to become a licensed general contractor when there was a shortage of contractors after the oil fire incident. He also taught me about owning property, believing that buying property was a path to financial stability and long-term security. Through him, Kate and I bought our first house, and even after Hank died, I remembered his advice and we saved every penny to invest more. Our philosophy was that even if we didn't get rich on the rent we charged, our tenants paid our mortgage, and over time, we could raise rents to show a profit.

That money was then set aside to buy something else.

I eventually hired my brother George so I could still work for Al, and when he was eventually ready to retire, he sold me his business for ten dollars, as a way to thank me for all those years of honest work. By the time George wanted to go out on his own, I had a strong crew of painters.

I continued to believe that in order to succeed in life, you needed to surround yourself by people smarter than you. That wasn't hard for me; I never finished school, and it was only after I began achieving wealth and security that I would share my story with people, turning it into a joke.

Joining Virginia Country Club in the Los Cerritos/Virginia Country Club neighborhood was on my bucket list, and Stavros, who was already a member, sponsored me for membership. It came at a steep price, though. Sixty-five thousand dollars to be exact, but for the first time in my life, I felt I was part of a privileged lifestyle. Of course, I knew my roots, and when other members asked me which college I'd attended, I would tell them I never went past sixth grade.

I was sure it was shocking to many of them, but to spare them the embarrassment of asking such a personal question, I'd say, "I went to the school of hard knocks. Not bad for a poor Greek boy."

I never got ahead by stepping on anyone else's toes. I took advantage of opportunities when they came. Even when someone's misfortune put me in a position to benefit, I made sure to offer them a fair price. I always believed that if I treated people right, things would balance out in the end—maybe I'd break even, maybe I'd be lucky enough to turn a profit, but either way, I could live with myself.

I spent time around men who took pride in scoring a deal by stepping on others, and I couldn't stand it. That kind of cutthroat attitude never sat right with me. I've always believed that what you put out into the world eventually comes back around. I later learned that was called karma.

CHAPTER TWENTY EIGHT

MEMORIES OF MY FATHER, NICK

I always thought my father looked like the actor James Garner. He was handsome and carried himself with the confidence he later admitted he hadn't always had. He never had a formal education, but he was the most street smart person I ever knew. Everyone, including his business competitors, was drawn to his gregarious personality, and he could tell the worst jokes and still make everyone laugh. He was quick to make friends, and could work a room of strangers, turning some of them into lifelong friends. I always understood why my mother loved him.

Maybe it was a secret fantasy, but throughout his lifetime, I often wondered if he'd maintained some kind of connection to the men he'd met in Detroit. He never *acted* like a gangster, but when he reflected on that time in his life, I could tell he'd witnessed things he shouldn't have. To my knowledge, no one from his past ever contacted him, except his old friend Ernie every now and then.

He also had a passion for Las Vegas, and in the early sixties, he became friends with several pit bosses at The Mint Las Vegas and the Sands Hotel and Casino. By the time I was thirteen, I'd sat in the adult audiences and sung along to Louis Prima and Keeley Smith to *"Such a Gigolo"* and *"I Ain't Got Nobody."* I saw Wayne Newton, Sammy Davis Jr., and the *Folies Bergere* by the time I was fourteen.

I was married to my first husband when my parents took me there for my twenty-first birthday. As always with my father, I dressed as his princess in long dresses, wore my flashiest jewelry, did my nails and wore bright red lipstick. The old bosses treated my father like royalty, rolling out the red carpet for him, comping our rooms, meals and shows, and seeing him like that in his glory, filled me with pride.

When the weekend ended, I felt deflated—like the bubble I'd been floating in had suddenly burst. For weeks afterward, I found myself daydreaming about running off to Las Vegas and starting a whole new life. What would I even be? A dancer? The idea was ridiculous, but for some reason, it stuck with me. It was a fantasy—completely unrealistic—but it offered an escape I didn't know I was craving.

The world eventually righted itself, and I found my feet once more on land, my life returning to normal. But my father continued to love Vegas. The craps table was his favorite, and he was uncannily lucky. The few times I found myself back there, I tried to follow his gambling routine, but I wasn't as lucky as he was; he'd bet a hundred dollars and walk away with two. I'd bet twenty, and walk away with nothing.

I remember him having markers, which were, in essence, short term, interest-free lines of credit to use for gambling. He always had the money to pay them back in the event he didn't win enough, but this was how he established credit with the casinos, earning the treatment he got. My father reciprocated by inviting the bosses to stay at their second home in Palm Springs.

For years, my father took his best clients for day trips to Vegas, not only impressing them with his VIP treatment but chalking it up to business entertainment.

If he were really trying to impress someone, he had a go-to trick. He'd casually excuse himself from the table, head over to a house phone, and page himself. By the time he returned to the floor, the operator's voice would echo overhead—"Paging Nick Pappas." He'd act surprised, then excuse himself again, as if some important call was waiting just for him.

Once my mother shared a secret with me: my father established credit at the two hotels he went to, and the first thing he'd do was go to the cashier's cage and write a check for a thousand dollars. Throughout the weekend, he'd win and lose, and the bosses would watch him play. More often than not, he managed to win enough to entertain his clients and come home with the same thousand dollars that would go back into their checking account to cover the check he'd written. Extraordinary would be a word to describe him.

My father was generous with his employees, yet he expected a lot from them in return. Over the years, both he and my mother lent a hand to many people, whether it was helping them get their car fixed or helping them pay their rent. My parents also gave a lot of young people jobs when they needed them. They were always hiring someone's son to work in construction during the summer, even if they didn't need the help. Some of those kids came back years later as adults and thanked them for giving them a start, which made my parents feel appreciated.

I was always my father's vasilopoúla (va-si-lo-poo´-la) princess. He left the discipline to my mother, unless it was something really serious. An exception was one summer when my cousin Kaylee came up from Holtville and stayed with us. The 405 freeway was just being built at the end of our housing tract. We went on an investigative journey and were gone hours longer than we were supposed to be. My father came looking for us, and when he found us, he was so angry with me, he pulled my hair until we got back to our house. I thought I was going to die of embarrassment, for I was certain all our neighbors had seen us. And when we got home, he was still so exasperated with us that when Kaylee and I were washing up in the bathroom, he came in and pushed me so that I fell into her and she ended up in the tub. We couldn't help laughing by this time, and that made him even more upset. He just threw his hands up and walked away. I knew he reacted not so much out of anger, but fear that something could have happened to us out there.

I also remember how hard he worked when I was young. He was still painting houses, "swinging a brush" as he used to say, and slowly building a reputation around Long Beach. He worked for another contractor but took on side work whenever he could. Even after a long day on the job, he'd come home, take a quick shower, we'd eat dinner, and then he'd head out again to meet someone and give them an estimate. Sometimes my mother and I would tag along, waiting in the car while he went inside.

As most young girls do, I placed my father on a pedestal and thought he was not only handsome, but perfect and invincible.

In the mid-seventies, my parents sold their office on Pacific Coast Highway in Long Beach, and bought what used to be the model home and sales office for the Apple Valley Ranchos home tract in Apple Valley, California. The City of Long Beach wouldn't let them keep the old neon sign of a cowboy on his horse, and unfortunately, they ended up tearing it down. They moved the construction company there, and the company had everything we needed. A large showroom for flooring samples, enough offices, parking and space to build ten garages.

We still had Sunday dinners at my parent's house, and more often than not, we ended the meal with some kind of argument. He used to call me 'Crusader Vaso' because I tried to look at things from our employee's point of view when he critiqued something or was trying to figure out ways to save money. Alex was usually the first one to throw down his napkin and leave; he didn't like anything about the business anyway, and he kept talking about how he was going to get out of the rat race we were all so blinded by.

His answer was to move to Orange County, where he could have land and animals. And that gave him the perfect opportunity to start stay- ing away. I wasn't ever sure anyone missed him. The arguments seemed to grow less intense, which was a relief for everyone.

My thirtieth birthday ended in the worst argument I ever had with my father. We were celebrating at The Velvet Turtle in Bixby Knolls. By then, I was married to Steven, who had already joined the business, though he tried to stay neutral as the tension at the table quietly escalated.

My father began criticizing me, implying I was not paying close enough attention to our installers, and claiming no one was properly tracking the materials leaving the warehouse. I felt blindsided—caught off guard and deeply hurt. I trusted our crews, and I believed I was doing everything I could to handle things the right way. But the more we argued, the more heated it became, until I couldn't take it anymore. I broke down in tears, got up, and walked out of the restaurant.

Steven followed, trying to comfort me. I remember choking out the words, "I just hope my father lives long enough for us to stop all this fighting."

Not long after that, my father shared a story with me—about one of his favorite painters, named Jimmy. By that time, my father had about ten men working for him, and each of them could order materials for their jobs. The invoices were assigned to specific projects, and eventually Abby, my mother's bookkeeper, noticed something odd. Based on the size of the jobs, she thought far too much material was being ordered.

Quietly, one of the other painters confided in my dad—he'd regu- larly seen unopened cans of paint sitting in the back of Jimmy's truck when he left at the end of the day. The next morning, when he checked the storage shed, the paint had never been returned to stock. At first, my father didn't want to believe it; he'd trusted Jimmy, so he didn't act right away. But after hearing another rumor, he realized he couldn't ignore it any longer.

One morning, he drove to Jimmy's house unannounced. The moment Jimmy saw my father, he broke down in tears. He confessed—he had been stealing. Then he opened his garage, and inside were over fifty five-gallon buckets of white paint, stacked and untouched.

I finally understood what he'd been trying to tell me.

My father and I rarely had disagreements at the office, but one day, he got so angry with me, he fired me. He told me to leave. I looked at him for a moment, then thought, 'the hell with you,' and left. I didn't come in to work for a few days, which I knew would put him in a bind, and I tried to figure out how to work this out without either of us losing face. The following Monday, I went back in.

"You can't fire me," I told him. "Slaves have to be sold."

He looked at me like I'd lost my mind, and then when it sunk in, he laughed.

"I'll come back if you buy me a new car. I've seen a Corvette I'd like, and I'll pay for half of it. You can write the rest of it off."

I started back to work that day. We had a truce, and I got my yellow Corvette.

My father was so focused on work that he didn't pick up golf until his late fifties—but once he did, he made up for lost time, racking up trophies and awards. He played in celebrity tournaments alongside football pro Vince Ferragamo and won ten thousand dollars golfing with actor Telly Savalas—he said he considered himself blessed and donated half of it to the Greek Church. He also played with baseball legend Mickey Mantle. Known for being a sore loser, Mantle lost to my father and paid up with an autographed baseball and a one-hundred-dollar bill, scrawled with the message: "To Nick, you lucky Greek fucker."

My father had a pretty good run and celebrated getting three holes in one, and he played almost every day until he started slowing down in his mid-seventies. He went down to playing nine holes and eventually became part of the geriatric "Soup Group," as they called themselves. Every afternoon, a group of friends, who no longer golfed, met in the club dining room for lunch and talked about world affairs and their accomplishments in life.

Because he didn't know how to use a computer, I became his email secretary when his buddies sent over jokes, and I'd respond by sending them ones my friends sent to me.

"Did I get any mail?" my father would ask the minute I came through the front door.

"Yes, you did," I'd respond, and hand him the printed emails.

Before he passed away, my father gave both Mickey Mantle's autographed ball and the one hundred-dollar bill to my husband, Steven.

CHAPTER TWENTY NINE

MY MOTHER KATE

I was almost seven when my younger brother Michael died. He was the most precious boy, with soft curly hair and a chubby angel's face. Even today, when I hear a child's laughter, I think of him, for he was so easy to please and so full of life. My father called him Sonny Boy.

I was the eldest, and I was expected to watch after my sister and brothers. When I look back at it now, I carried a lot of responsibility on my shoulders, but that was the way it was in those days. My father had a little store on 7th Street, around the corner from our house on Loma Avenue, where he sold fresh fruit and vegetables. When he made his daily morning produce pickups, my mother would work the store, and I would stay at home with the children, making sure they had their breakfast. When I was ready to walk to school, I'd knock on our neighbor's door, and she would watch the three of them until my mother returned home about an hour later.

I was organized even as a child. Although my mother was mostly home during the day, she was busy cooking and cleaning, and I took care of wringing the laundry after she washed it, and hanging it out to dry on the clotheslines we had strung up in the backyard. When the clothes were dry, I'd load everything back into the baskets and bring it all inside to fold. I made sure all our playthings were removed from the living room before my father came home from the store, and I dried the dishes after dinner.

Cynthia, Michael, and Stavros were too young to do much. Michael used to try to help me with my chores, but most of the time, he would just get in the way. I wished later I had been kinder to him. By then, Stavros was still a baby, but he was old enough to run around the living room with Cynthia, and if they broke something, they would point to Michael. He just took it in stride.

When she wasn't blaming him for something, Cynthia adored him. He made her laugh, and he'd sit with her for hours if I asked him to while I finished my homework.

I first noticed Michael's shortness of breath a few days before he became really sick. We were all playing outside with some neighborhood children, and Stavros and Cynthia were in a crib so they couldn't get into trouble. When Michael came to dinner, he wasn't very hungry, which I thought was odd. I was surprised no one else at the table heard the slight wheezing sounds he made. Sometimes, if we'd been playing outside when the lawn had just been mowed, all our voices would be raspy, but this was different.

I asked him why he wasn't hungry, and he just shrugged like it didn't matter. He was, however, interested in dessert, so I figured he was all right. Michael and Stavros shared a room, as did Cynthia and me. That night, I heard him coughing, and my mother got up a couple of times to check on him.

The next morning, he didn't want to get out of bed. I didn't really know what someone would look like if they had a fever, but he looked like he didn't feel well and his face was flushed. I was sure my mother had checked on him before she left for the store, but it was the first time I'd ever seen him so lethargic.

"I think Michael doesn't feel good," I told our neighbor when I went to get her.

"I'll check on him," she said, "and when your mother gets home, I'll tell her."

I gathered my books and left for school. When I returned home, Michael's bed had been moved into my parents' room, where he would remain until his death five days later. The doctors said it was pneumonia or maybe influenza. We never knew for sure how he caught it, but whatever it was, it claimed not only my brother's life, but a piece of my parents' lives as well.

They had already lost four children to stillbirth, and when Michael survived, they lit candles in church and prayed with all their hearts he would survive. He was their miracle.

His casket was placed in our living room, and my mother insisted on staying with him through the night. The next day, we brought him to the Greek Orthodox Church in Los Angeles. After the service, just before they closed the casket, my parents and I kissed him goodbye. I'll never forget the waxen feel of his face beneath my lips. . . it's something that's stayed with me ever since.

He was buried in Inglewood Cemetery, and after the casket was placed in the ground and the dirt filled in, we planted flowers to purify the grounds around the site. On the way home, my mother cried silently, constantly wiping her eyes and blowing her nose. My father, however, was stoic as men were expected to be. He showed no emotion but was silent as he held my mother's hand.

When we returned home, many of my mother's friends had cooked a large meal, and we all shared it in Michael's memory.

Life for Cynthia and Stavros returned to normal, but I could see an acute sense of loss in my father. Every day, he seemed to diminish before my eyes. Where he was once full of strong opinions, he was silent. He still went about his business, but the joy was gone from his life.

I could tell my mother also struggled with her loss, for occasionally I'd see her face lift in response to hearing a sound that she thought could be Michael's. Then she'd crumble when she'd realize he wasn't there after all. But she was the one who held us all together.

And Michael's death frightened me. I'd never thought of dying before, and I'd certainly never seen anyone who had died. Sometimes I'd lay awake at night just listening to Cynthia's breathing, or I'd go check on Stavros. And once I was satisfied they were okay, I could go back to sleep.

Mother had a wonderful photo of Michael in his sailor outfit enlarged and hand colored, and she framed it in a tiger-stripe wood frame with a domed bubble glass. It hung in their bedroom under a crucifix. Every time I had to go through their bedroom to get to the back porch, no matter how hard I tried, I'd give him one quick glance, then look down at my feet as I rushed by him. I swore his eyes followed me everywhere I went.

Stavros was only about three, and instead of being distressed about Michael's death, I think he was jealous of the grieving my parents did for him, which made them both less attentive to us all. There were times when I could tell he thought they didn't pay attention to him the way he wanted them to, and he'd have a meltdown. If my father was home, he would grab Stavros by the arm and just look at him. The meltdown stopped. If he did it in front of my mother, she would go to him and bring him onto her lap. She'd rock him, and tell him, "I know, poulaki mou, *my boy*, I know.

Because I was quick with math, English and spelling once they were in school, I helped Cynthia and Stavros with their homework. We all knew how to speak Greek, so that's what we spoke at home, but my parents also spoke English fluently. What was amazing was that my parents spoke with American accents instead of the heavy Greek ones like so many of their friends. And because of this, none of us children had accents either.

By the time I was fourteen, I was helping my father with the bookkeeping for the store. I could tell he was slowing down mentally and physically, although he was only in his early forties. He'd served America in WWI and luckily had escaped any major injuries, but I could tell his body ached after a long day, for he'd make grunting noises when he sat down or got back up out of a chair. I also sometimes wondered if he'd never fully recovered from Michael's death.

"Thank you for helping him," my mother said one afternoon as she sat with me at the dining room table. She'd made herself a cup of Greek coffee and had set it aside to cool. I had papers spread everywhere and was entering numbers onto a lined journal page. "If you haven't noticed, sometimes your father can be stubborn. I'm glad he's letting you help him."

"I actually enjoy it," I said, stopping to watch her now as she sipped from her cup.

"You should learn more. I wish we had enough money for you to go to college."

It was the first time she'd ever talked about this possibility to me. It was always a given that Stavros would be the one to get a better education, so he could provide for his own family one day. Women were still expected to have children and stay home.

"I could look into going to community college," I said. "There are classes I could take, and I think they're not expensive at all."

"Look into it. If you're truly interested, I'll find the money somewhere."

When she took my hand and squeezed it, I realized she understood all that I did to help support our family, and I hoped this was a way I could be compensated.

When I was seventeen, my parents got involved in a plan to build a church in Long Beach. Ten families set up a savings account where they all regularly deposited money. Soon they had saved enough money to look for land to build on.

In the meantime, a third cousin from my mother's side had written asking if my parents could help him come to America. He was twenty-three and had saved almost enough money for the journey over. He wasn't sure what needed to be done, or how long the process would take, but he hoped that if they could start it now, he would have more money by the time his paperwork was finished.

For several nights, I heard my parents talk it over, and they decided they could help him. After all, they'd had the same dreams not so long ago. My mother wrote back and told him he would have a place to stay with us when he came over.

It took almost a year for everything to fall into place, but eventually Tasso boarded a ship sailing to New York. He'd take a train from there, so they expected him to arrive in about three months.

Stavros would have to share his room, which, of course, threw him into a tailspin. He was around fourteen then, and we were all hoping his days at the military academy would have taught him to understand life's trials and to deal with them. But it hadn't registered yet, for he ended up stomping out of the house. Thank goodness my father wasn't there to witness his behavior, or I'm sure he would have yanked Stavros back into the real world.

I was just finishing high school and had purchased my first car, a 1939 Chevy Sedan from our neighbor, when we got word that Tasso was on the train to California. He'd sent a photo of himself so we could identify him, and he was indeed handsome, but I was more interested in finding a job for the summer than I was in having anyone come live with us. Cynthia, on the other hand, swooned. As far as sharing a room went, my father must have convinced Stavros he needed to change his attitude, for they started making room for a second bed again in his bedroom.

On the day Tasso arrived, I worked the store while my parents went to pick him up at the train station. I had no way of knowing what it was like in Greece at that time, but it couldn't be at all like it was here with all the people, the conveniences, and, of course, the cars.

I heard him before I saw him. He was in the dining room and was speaking in Greek with my parents and one of the members of the church committee.

"This is like a dream to me, to be here in America," he said with laughter in his voice. "This must be paradise."

"Kalispera," I said as I joined them.

Everyone turned towards me, and Tasso said, "Good day," back to me in a strong accent. I'll never forget how his dark eyes assessed me, and I thought I saw a glimmer of mischievousness in them. I also think I turned several shades of red.

Everyone started talking at the same time, and then they calmed down. I thought for sure they could see that he was still looking at me. I tried to give him a stern look that said 'stop it', but he just laughed. I looked at my mother, who was boring holes into me, so I turned to go to my bedroom.

I was grateful Cynthia wasn't home yet, and I closed our door and lay on my bed. I needed to get a hold of myself. I'd seen plenty of cute guys at school, but that's it; they were just guys, and I hadn't been interested in them.

But Tasso was a man, and he was more handsome than the photo he'd sent. I'd never been a romantic, but as I lay there, I wondered if he'd been mocking me. Sure, I'd seen in movies where two people who just meet lock eyes, and they fall in love. And then my cynical inner voice said, *'There's no way he was interested in you. He was just teasing you.'*

Eventually, my mother called me to help with dinner, and there was no way I'd be able to escape talking with him. I decided to deliberately avoid him. I wouldn't be rude, but I wouldn't encourage any conversation, either. I made a point of setting this indifferent and cavalier look on my face and made sure Tasso didn't sit opposite me at the table. Cynthia sat next to me and kept pinching me. A couple of times it hurt, and I jumped in my seat. Eventually, I pinched her back as hard as I could.

When she cried out, all my father had to do was look at her, and she hung her head like a petulant child. Tasso was taking it all in, and I could tell he found us amusing.

I'd hoped to escape to the kitchen as soon as the dishes were being cleared, but as I washed them, Tasso insisted on helping me dry them. I thought maybe if I actually talked to him, I'd feel more comfortable.

"Afta," I said in Greek. "So," I continued in English, "what type of work did you do in Greece?"

He started to answer in Greek, then spoke in English too. "I have gone to university to study business. I want to open a restaurant."

"How Greek," I said more sarcastically than I'd intended. "It's what Greeks are known for here. Having restaurants."

He wouldn't have known that, and I was instantly sorry I'd made that comment. He either hadn't noticed my sarcasm or it hadn't fazed him, so he continued.

"I worked in several at home and have ideas for opening one here. If you can do it in Greece, you can do much bigger and better in America, yes?"

I didn't have the slightest idea, but I also didn't want to discourage him right off the bat.

"Sounds reasonable," I ended up saying. I'd washed the last of the dishes and emptied the sink of soapy water. "We're almost done." I finished putting everything away and tossed the damp dish towel in the laundry basket.

"I will want to have a tour of the city," Tasso said, looking around the kitchen rather than at me. Some of his newness had worn off a little, and I wasn't as nervous around him as I had been earlier.

That night, when we were both in our beds, Cynthia wouldn't stop talking about how handsome Tasso was and how exciting it would be to marry someone like him. I wanted to tell her to shut up, but I couldn't, especially when I was having similar thoughts.

I think that night was the first time I'd ever thought about falling in love.

CHAPTER THIRTY

KATE

There were some things I definitely didn't like about Greek men. They usually had enormous noses. No matter what color their hair turned, they always grew dark hair from their ears and nose, and their eyebrows grew like miniature awnings over their eyes. If they had a potbelly, they'd pull their pants up over it and sometimes have to wear suspenders, which made them look roly-poly. They smoked incessantly, and they smelled like garlic. They wore sleeveless t-shirts no matter what the weather was like; if it was cold out, they wore them under their shirts, and if it was hot, that's all they wore. And I didn't like men with accents.

No matter what, I couldn't imagine Tasso turning out to be an old Greek man.

I tried to pretend I wasn't interested in him, and I thought I was doing a reasonable job of acting nonchalant until one day, about three weeks after Tasso arrived, my mother wanted me to sit with her at the dining room table. She had her cup of coffee and seemed lost in thought.

"I've seen the way you look at Tasso," she said bluntly.

I could feel my face flush.

"And I've seen the way he looks at you, too—which could be a problem. I believe in love and romance, of course. Let me tell you the story of how I met your father.

"When I was young, and we were still in Greece, it was assumed I would marry an older man in the next village over from ours. Two things happened; I couldn't stand the thought of someone telling me what to do, and one day, I sneaked over to the village to see if I could find him. Once

I saw him, I knew I would die before I married him. Of course, that was a dramatic way of looking at it, but that's how I felt.

"When my family came to Canada, I thought my parents had forgotten all about marrying me off. Life was so different there, and arranged marriages weren't that important as long as you married someone who was also Greek. We had our own apartment by then, and my cousin wanted to go to Chicago to meet the man her parents thought she should marry. A single woman couldn't travel alone in those days, and I wanted to get away. So I said I'd go with her. We somehow convinced our parents we would be safe, and they went with us to the train station where they watched us board.

"When she met him, my cousin was satisfied with her parent's choice, and because she had no dreams of her own, she thought she could be happy married, raising children, and living in Chicago. But I was restless in Canada, and while I wasn't sure exactly what I thought Chicago would be like, it still wasn't what I'd dreamed about. Like Canada, it was too cold there, and I wanted to go to California.

"Of course, I couldn't go by myself, so I asked my cousin to go with me. Before we left, I wrote my parents a long letter trying to explain my dreams and asking them to understand. When we made it to California, that's when I met your father.

"My cousin wanted to go back home so she could be married, but I decided to stay. Of course, my parents reminded me then that I was promised to someone else in Greece, but I hoped he'd never find me if he still insisted I become his wife."

"I've never thought of you and Papa falling in love," I said then, and I hadn't. I thought certainly there was no time for romance in their lives, with the business, the household, and the three of us children. Plus, I saw them only as they were now, old and tired.

I wasn't sure what my mother's story had to do with me, for I'd never been promised to anyone. While my parents wished all of us would marry Greeks, the arranged marriage tradition wasn't practiced here. Unless of course you couldn't find someone to marry on your own. Then, your parents could look to the old country.

How dreadful!

My mother finally continued. "I know it's only been a short time, but Tasso has expressed interest in you. He's talked to your father about the possibility of his courting you."

I thought I was going to fall off my chair!

"The thought is actually a good one. If he marries an American citizen, then he can stay here and work toward his dreams of one day owning a wonderful restaurant. We were hoping you could pursue your interest in bookkeeping, and you could still do that even if you were married. If this is something you would agree to, then we can continue with making the arrangements. I would have to remind you that you would not have any relations with him in his house until you are married."

I was at a loss for words. First, we'd started the conversation about my mother's life as a young woman and her romance with my father, and now we were talking about me marrying someone I hardly knew.

"If you stay in this house after your wedding, then, of course, we would expect it. We'd have to rearrange Stavros and Cynthia. Oh, don't just sit there with your mouth open. You'll catch bugs," my mother said.

"Your father and I want you to be happy. And we don't want our children to be forced into marriages. Of course, we want you to make the best choices, but we agree they are to be the choices you make, not ours."

Saying I was stunned didn't even come close to describing what I'd just heard. Sure, I'd shown Tasso around a few times, and was always careful to bring either Cynthia, who couldn't stop ogling him, or Stavros, who thought it was cool to ride in my car. I didn't think I'd ever given him any signs I wanted to have a relationship with him, and yet here I was, about to be courted!

A million thoughts raced through my mind.

Did he really want to marry *me*?

What would he do when he discovered I shaved my legs and armpits, unlike the women in Greece?

I couldn't have sex in my parent's house.

And the worst was, what if he decided not to marry me once he got to know me?

I spent the next few nights trying to keep this all a secret from Cynthia, but she could tell something was up. When I finally told her and swore her to secrecy, she cried, "How could he love you and not me?"

I, on the other hand, couldn't stop thinking about anything and everything that could happen, good and bad.

Two days later, I sat with Tasso on the front porch of our home, and he took my hand in his. "I think I could make you happy, Kate. And I could live here in this wonderful country. I could have everything I've dreamed of. I could take over your father's store. I could have a restaurant and a family."

He was so handsome when he smiled, and these were all the things I wished for him. He'd come to America to better himself, and I knew I could be a good partner. With my support, he could have everything he'd dreamed of. And those would become my dreams too.

Before the wedding, my parents purchased a property down the street where we would live. We'd stay in the smaller house in the back, and they could rent out the larger front house. We'd already shopped for some furniture at a secondhand store downtown, and found a couch and living room tables, a bed and a dresser. We needed sheets, and towels and everything for the kitchen.

We were married in the Greek Church in Los Angeles, and after the service, we came back to my parent's home for the reception, where the ladies from the church committee set up food and drinks. Wrapped presents filled a table covered with a white cloth, and my bouquet was put in a vase of water and placed in the center of the table. Normally, if there was dancing, men would pin money on the bride, but because our reception was small, there was no dancing, and a basket for money sat next to my flowers.

What we didn't get as gifts, we got in money, so we had enough to buy almost everything we needed to set up our kitchen. Tasso stayed in our new home the night before our wedding, and that's where I joined him after our reception.

Before our marriage, we'd kissed a little, and I thought I was ready to accept him as my husband, but it embarrassed me to have him see me without my clothes on. Tasso had no problem undressing and standing before me with his anticipation of our evening very obvious. I made him turn the bedroom light off. Even though we had installed window shades, I was certain neighbors could see in if they wanted to be nosy.

My mother had warned me there would be blood on the sheets from losing my virginity, and I was self-conscious about that too. The next morning, I quickly pulled the top sheet up to cover the stains, and as quickly as I could, I took the sheets to my mother and we washed them and hung them out to dry.

I quickly adjusted to married life. My mother had taught me how to keep a calendar so I could prevent pregnancy, and I would write my periods down on the paper I kept in my dresser drawer under my underwear. Because my parents helped us with our rent, I could go to community college and take bookkeeping classes and still have enough time to have two part-time jobs.

In the mornings, Tasso would work off a little of our rent by helping my father in the store, displaying the fruit and vegetables, and because he loved to cook, he started bringing in Greek cookies and pastries that didn't need refrigeration. My father saw that his customers loved the new offerings, and he found a used meat display case that eventually could be cooled with ice and salt if there was interest in items that needed to stay cool, like some custard desserts.

Tasso and my father figured out a fair commission for what they sold, and Tasso started getting his first paycheck. He also found a job at a small Greek restaurant in downtown Long Beach and worked there in the afternoons and evenings. Within a year, we'd saved almost five hundred dollars, and Tasso was dying to look for a restaurant site. We all thought he was a little premature, but we didn't want to discourage him, so when he finally found what he thought was the perfect place, my parents gave us the fifty-dollar deposit, and we rented the building. All he had to buy were tablecloths, napkins, and silverware. We already had pots and pans and some utensils, and between what we had at home, and what my mother gave him, he was set in no time.

He called it The Greek Taverna, and we were all pleasantly surprised at how well he did.

He worked seven days a week, and so did I. After my two jobs, I'd go to the restaurant, and when I was finished with sorting the cash, I'd serve customers. We had hardly any time to spend together, so it surprised me when I managed to get pregnant. My parents were delighted, but Tasso wasn't.

"We don't need a baby now," he said, creasing his brow.

"I thought I was doing a good job keeping track. . ."

"You keep track of when we have sex?"

Now I was getting a little defensive, and I couldn't help but respond with, "You can't just have sex and hope you don't have a baby."

"It didn't work then, did it?"

I suddenly felt drained of all happiness and energy. I knew this was not the best time to have a baby, but I thought we could figure it out. I never thought Tasso would react as he did, and it left no doubt in my mind that this wasn't the news he'd looked forward to.

That night, he didn't come home after he closed the restaurant. I was exhausted and finally went to bed around midnight. When I woke in the morning, he was sleeping on the living room couch, his hair mussed, and he reeked of alcohol.

He didn't speak to me for two days. I was devastated. I couldn't say anything to anyone, especially my parents. They were so excited they were going to be grandparents; it would have crushed them. And I figured if I waited it out, Tasso would realize how much he'd hurt me and everything would be fine. Until now, I couldn't have been happier.

Thankfully, I had very little morning sickness, and I could continue working and taking my classes. But I had to make allowances for being so tired. Tasso finally came around, and while he never apologized for being so hurtful, he pulled me to him one night and we made love. I took this as a sign of a new start, and my outlook changed instantly.

I didn't realize it would change again so soon.

One day, when I wasn't feeling very well, I took a much-needed break and didn't go to either of my jobs. I lay in bed lazily while Tasso got ready to go to work at the restaurant, and he kissed me on the forehead before he left. I didn't think I could, but I went back to sleep and only woke up when I heard our mail being dropped through the slot in our front door.

Eventually I got up, took my shower, gathered the mail and went into the kitchen to warm up leftovers. I was starving. Normally Tasso opened and sorted the mail, so I quickly glanced through it, and set it aside. I eventually went back into the living room, where I dozed again on the sofa. A knock on the door woke me.

"Here's a letter for Tasso," our neighbor up front said.

"Thanks," I said, taking it from him. It was in a woman's handwriting, and I instantly had images of it notifying him that someone had died. Since I'd known him, I'd never seen a letter from his hometown.

"The mailman keeps delivering them to us," our neighbor said as he turned to leave.

Well, of course he did. The letter was addressed to the front house and not ours. I thought about waiting until Tasso got home, but I opened it. I could always call him if it was bad news.

Of course, it was in Greek.

My dearest. I'm so happy the restaurant is doing well. It's what you dreamed about when you wanted to go to America. I know it will still be awhile until you've saved enough money to bring me and the baby over, but there isn't a day that goes by that I don't love you and long to hold you in my arms again...

I quickly scanned the rest and then looked to see who's sent it.

With all my love, Calandra

CHAPTER THIRTY ONE

KATE

I hugged my stomach, as if holding my unborn child was going to fix this. I was so stunned, at first I couldn't even cry. My knees weakened, and I sat silently on the couch while I tried to calm the swirl of the hundreds of thoughts that were going through my mind.

I'd always respected Tasso's privacy, so I'd never gone through any of his personal things, but I figured if there was one letter, there'd be more. I looked in his underwear and sock drawer, then I looked between the box spring and mattress. I went to the closet and saw there were several boxes on the top shelf, so I pulled them down and dumped the contents on our bed. There were only receipts from the restaurant.

I tried to gather my thoughts, but they were still frantically racing, and then I checked the laundry cabinet in the hall. There, tucked behind the first stack of towels, I found them. Twelve letters held together with a rubber band.

Why was he so stupid to keep them? One by one I opened them, and they were more of the same. . .

"When will I see you? The baby is crawling and misses her papa, and your mother is not well."

He had a baby?

Ice raced through my veins, and I could feel it running through my entire body. I'd been made a fool of, and more than that, so had my parents. We took Tasso in and shared our home with him. *I married him and shared his bed.*

Before I could change my mind, I packed all his belongings, including the letters, into boxes and set them outside. I drove to the bank and closed our bank account and put his half of our money in an envelope. I dropped that off at his restaurant, where I told him not to come home.

"Your things are sitting outside on the porch, and you can go to hell."

I didn't care where he ended up. He looked at me like I was crazy, and of course he had no idea what had prompted my actions.

On the second day, my father drove with me to the courthouse in downtown Long Beach, and I filed for a divorce.

Within two days, Tasso was gone from my life.

And here I was, a pregnant and soon to be divorced woman.

I realized then I was not a forgiving person.

During this upheaval, Cynthia announced that she and Eddie wanted to get married. She wasn't eighteen yet, but she and Eddie wanted to marry before he shipped out within the month. My parents liked Eddie well enough, even if he wasn't Greek, so they consented with the condition that Cynthia would finish high school after the wedding. They were married in front of the Justice of the Peace, and I hated the thought of going into the same building where I'd filed for my divorce earlier. But I was her matron of honor, and one of Eddie's shipmates was their best man. We all witnessed the brief ceremony, then Cynthia and Eddie took off on a quick weekend honeymoon to San Diego, where Eddie had a buddy who owned a motel. They wanted to have their wedding shower after they returned, so since there wasn't time to send formal invitations, we called everyone to come help celebrate.

Around thirty people showed up, which filled my parent's living room, and the new couple unwrapped their gifts and opened cards filled with money. Cynthia seemed to be happy with everything they got, and as they'd done before, my mother's friends served the food they'd made.

After we all ate, there was a quick toast, and then guests started leaving. Eddie helped clear the trash, and Cynthia and I brought all the dishes into the kitchen so we could start washing. It was a beautiful day for her, and I was happy for them both.

I packed up some of my personal things and stayed with my parents. They stayed in the back house, at least until Eddie had to leave. It was the first time I'd ever slept in our room without her, and on one hand it was peaceful and comforting to be back at home. I also felt disjointed, like I wasn't sure *where* I belonged.

I ended up moving out of the little house and back into my old bedroom. To be honest, I didn't want to be pregnant and alone. Cynthia came back, and we quickly fell into the old routine of sharing a bedroom again. I could tell she tried not to gloat about her happiness, but it wasn't her fault I was unhappy. Plus, my parents could now get more rent than what Tasso and I were paying, and I was relieved I could be with my mother until I had the baby.

I had loved Tasso, but I was so angry with him, I pushed my emotions away and refused to wallow in my sorrow. We never spoke his name again in our house, and when Alex was born, I gave him my last name. If I had my way, my son would never know his father.

I'd obviously been around when my brothers and sister were babies, but I did not know what it was like to have a baby of my own. *My baby. Alex.* He still wore a bandage where he'd been circumcised, and I worried I'd never adequately kept him dry. I was certain he'd get a rash, so I changed him frequently and added rinsing and washing his diapers to my daily chores.

Alex cried incessantly. If he was hungry, he cried. If he threw up or was wet, he cried. It was as though when he drank from my breast, his nourishment came from the anger I had inside me. He was rigid when I held him, sometimes almost pushing me away

When he would finally give up fighting so hard and nurse, he slept, and he was the sweetest baby ever.

CHAPTER THIRTY TWO

KATE

The summer Alex turned a year and a half old, my sister Cynthia and I took him to the beach for the first time. I packed my car with everything I could think we'd need, and I drove to the Long Beach Pier, where we found a parking space near the restrooms.

A few hours was all either of us could manage with him. He was too young to play in the sand, and I was concerned he'd get sunburned. As we packed everything back up, I said, "Next time, I'll leave Alex at home, and it'll just be the two of us."

That next weekend, our neighbor offered to watch Alex so that Cynthia and I could spend the afternoon basking in the sun. We found the same spot as the weekend before and set up the blanket and umbrella. Cynthia immediately headed towards the water.

I was comfortable sitting by myself, and it wasn't ten minutes later when a man stopped next to me.

"I'm Nick," he said. "Nick Pappas."

"Greek?" I asked.

"It's a dead giveaway, isn't it? The name, right?"

"Unfortunately, yes," I said wryly.

He looked at me with slight confusion.

"I'm Greek too," I finally said.

"Wow, I didn't expect that."

"What, that I'm Greek?"

"No, your reaction."

"Well, it's a long story. And I'll try not to hold it against you."

"Would you like me to leave?" He made a half-hearted attempt to turn and leave.

"No, you're fine."

"Are you with someone?"

"Just my sister."

"Oh, good."

I could tell he was relieved.

"Good," he said again.

I think he was a little nervous. When I turned to find Cynthia, I could see her in the water.

"You might as well sit," I said. "If you'd like to."

He bumped his head on the umbrella and reached out to bring it upright.

"Thanks," he said, not skipping a beat.

I couldn't believe almost an hour had passed before I saw Cynthia heading our way. I hadn't scared him off when I told him about being divorced with a baby; in fact, he asked if I'd be free for dinner that night. I said yes and gave him our address.

"Great," Nick said. "And you can bring the baby if you want."

I was clearly surprised, for he said, "What? I like kids."

"I'll see if my sister can watch him for me," I said.

"Watch who?" Cynthia now asked as she approached us.

"Alex. Nick and I are going to dinner."

"I see," she said, giving Nick the once-over.

"He's Greek," I added.

I'd been so nervous at the prospect of going out on a date that I must have pulled everything I owned out of the closet before I settled on a red dress.

"Well, aren't you something?" Cynthia said, mocking me.

At six on the dot, the doorbell rang, and I called out, "I'll get it."

I didn't want my parents to give him the third degree while he waited for me. The moment I opened the door, our eyes met, and I could feel myself redden. Nick stood there in a black and white shirt and black pants, and he was truly the most handsome man I'd ever seen. He grinned and held out the bouquet of mixed flowers he'd brought.

"Oh," I said, delighted.

"These are for your mother."

He'd barely stepped inside when Alex came running out to me, calling, "Mama, mama." He grabbed hold of my legs, and I thought for sure I was going to fall on him.

"Alex," I scolded.

"Hey buddy," Nick said, his smile broadening.

"This is Nick," I said, introducing him to my parents and Alex. "Here, let me take these flowers. Mother, they're for you. Come in. I'll get a vase."

"Hey, big man," Nick said, touching Alex's hair.

My mother got up and followed me into the kitchen, and I saw my father peer over the newspaper he was pretending to read.

"Ela tho, come in," my father said.

"Kalispera, good evening," Nick said, going to my father and shaking his hand.

"My, he's handsome," my mother said, finding a vase.

When we got ready to leave, I said, "Say goodnight to Nick, Alex." I gathered my sweater and handbag. "We'll be home soon," I said, reassuring him.

"Nice meeting you all," Nick said as he opened the front door.

"That wasn't too bad," I whispered as we walked down the porch steps.

"You look lovely," Nick said.

"You don't look too bad yourself," I said.

We went to an Italian restaurant Nick knew of, and just like that afternoon, the evening flew by. Nick told me about growing up in Greece and about how the family moved wherever they could find work. He told me about being in the service, and how they finally settled in Long Beach. I told him about marrying Tasso and how I wanted to finish taking bookkeeping classes. He was a perfect gentleman, and I could tell right away he was very interested in me. I was surprised he had impeccable table manners, and he told me he'd worked in a hotel back in Detroit. He admitted he hadn't started out looking for a readymade family, and that he wanted one of his own one day.

I told myself I wasn't ready to fall in love again, and yet I knew it would be hard not to with someone like Nick. As we grew more serious, there was no doubt in my mind that he would be a wonderful father to Alex and to any other children we might have. A month after our first date, he asked me to marry him.

The new Greek church in Long Beach was still under construction, and going into Los Angeles was too far away. When I told Nick I didn't want to go to the courthouse where I filed my divorce papers, he came up with the idea of having the wedding in my parents' backyard. Stavros knew a judge who performed the ceremony, and with both our families, there were around thirty of us. Again, the church committee ladies cooked and served at our reception, and we took a lot of photos. I thought little of it at the time, but later when the film was developed, I realized Alex was standing next to us in some of them while we opened gifts. When I made up our wedding album, I thought I had kept those photos out and tucked the rest away in my drawer.

We rented a small house a few miles away from my parents, and that's where we had our daughter, Vaso. One of my favorite photos of us was taken on our porch toward the end of 1949. Nick and I squatted down to be eye level with Alex, who was going to turn five, and Nick held Vaso, who was almost six months old, on his lap. I had on a white dress with black polka dots, a white hat and white earrings. Even then, I knew my children were like night and day, both in temperament and looks.

Vaso was a sweet baby. She loved to be cuddled, and she laughed and smiled constantly. Of course, she was Nick's precious girl. He adored her. But he also loved Alex. As soon as we'd married, he started the adoption process, and soon Alex had his new last name. In those days, things like that became family secrets.

I knew Nick hadn't had the best of childhoods, and he promised me he would always do his best by Alex. I don't think there was a time he didn't treat Alex the same as Vaso, except he would let Alex do things like camping or boating, that he wouldn't consider letting Vaso do.

We both worked several jobs to save enough money to buy a house. In the evenings, I worked at a drive-in. I'd come home at night, and we'd sit on our bed and count my tips. During the day, I worked for several customers doing their books, and somehow I also found time to take another bookkeeping course at the community college. I'll never forget my teacher looking at my hands stained from handling money at the drive-in, and she said, "With hands like those, you'll never amount to anything."

No one had ever said anything like that to me before, and I was crushed. When Nick got home that night, I tried to keep my tears at bay as I told him.

"Let me see those hands," he said, taking them into his. He made a face, then said, "You have the hands of a very successful woman, who has a husband who loves her more than anything. And anyone who tells you differently is just jealous. And stupid! We'll show her."

Somehow I focused on what I was learning from her, but every time I saw that teacher, I wanted to shake her and say, "You have no idea who you're talking to." But of course I didn't.

Not long after that, we bought our first home on Magnolia Avenue in Long Beach. Nick and I had the same work ethic, and over the years, every time we made another step forward, or bought a new piece of property, I'd think back to that jackass of a teacher, and remind myself how dumb I was to have allowed her to hurt my feelings.

Nick worked for several years for a well-known painting contractor and also did side jobs on his own or with his father and brother. It had always been an unpredictable and sometimes turbulent relationship between the three. His father was short-tempered, but his brother was worse, often flying off the hook and accusing them of cheating him, and if he'd been drinking, it was worse.

When their father died, the relationship between the two brothers deteriorated even more. His brother was married to a very sweet woman, and they had three children, but there was never any long-term plan for their future or of them buying a house of their own. They rented for years until his wife developed cancer and died. After that, there was a period where the brothers would often get into arguments on the job, and eventually agreed they could no longer work together.

When Nick went out on his own, I supported him wholeheartedly. He already had a panel truck, and he had *Nick Pappas & Son Painting and Decorating* painted on it. Of course, Alex was way too young to work, but Nick thought it sounded impressive.

I still had two bookkeeping jobs, and Nick encouraged me to stop working at the drive-in, which suited me fine, especially since my shifts were still mostly in the evenings. The wives of our friends and neighbors stayed home to be homemakers, and I never begrudged them for their choices; I knew myself well enough by then that I'd be totally bored at home, and the plans Nick and I had for our future required two incomes.

As soon as we'd saved enough money, we bought a small rental house. Nick's philosophy was that if we could rent it for enough money to pay the house payment, then it was as good as having money in the bank. Sometimes, we ran short of cash if a tenant moved out, but Nick and I saved a lot of money by doing all the work to get the house rented again. We were very conservative landlords, and if we raised the rent at all, it was in very small increments. We looked at our tenants as customers, and in essence, they were. They were our future, and we wanted to keep them happy.

Dinners out were rare, for we both agreed that the only way we'd get ahead was to save as much money as we could so we could buy another rental house. When we *did* go out, it would be to some place very afford-able, and it gave Alex and Vaso the opportunity to learn to behave in public.

In 1951, there was a Union Oil fire in San Pedro, which caused a lot of oil damage to homes and buildings in the surrounding area. By then, we already had two painters working for us, and this was when we officially started doing insurance restoration work. We had a painting license and hired a man with a general contractor's license to expedite running the jobs.

Somehow I made the time to be a Cub Scout and Blue Bird den mother, and I was always home to cook dinner. During the summers, if we entertained, Nick was always our barbecue chef; he made the best teri-yaki steak and Greek Soulavkia (shish kebab). We all loved the leftovers, so we always cooked more than enough to last for a couple of days.

We soon bought another property and had started to show a monthly profit from the first house, which went right into the bank. By this time, we'd added a large room to the back of our house and used it as an office, and our garage became our warehouse for paint Nick bought in bulk. In those days, painters could mix colors, so white was the base color for everything, and the more he bought, the more profitable we became.

CHAPTER THIRTY THREE

KATE

Alex was always the adventurous child. I kept a photo of him tied to the clothesline when he was really young; it was the only way I could keep track of him while I hung our clothes out to dry. I never told anyone that I did that, for fear they'd have thought I was a terrible mother. But if I didn't do that, I was afraid he'd run out into the street, since he'd done it before. And leaving him unattended in the house was never an option. He got into everything. Soon, though, he figured out how to untie the knot holding him, so I had to resort to looping the rope through his belt loop and tying the knot up as high as I could. Of course, I never gave it a thought he could have choked to death if he'd ever got his head caught in the loop!

Once, when we had company, he climbed into the back seat of their car, and they didn't even know he was there until they were a couple of miles away. We couldn't figure out where he'd gone. Other times, he'd hide under the bed, scooting himself as close to the wall as he could, so when we bent to look under there, we wouldn't see him. He'd hide in the closets, or climb up onto a shelf, and would never come out when we called him.

We went on a trip one summer to the redwoods, and he disappeared into the forest for hours. We worried ourselves sick and even called the park ranger to see if they could find him. I just knew they thought we were terrible parents, but how could you tell them your son just liked to run away?

He loved bugs, and snakes, and at one time, he even had tarantulas. It got so I hated going into his bedroom, which was probably why he had all those things. I'd bring his clean laundry in and instead of putting it away, I'd just leave it in stacks on his bed. Once, I swore I felt something touch me from under his bed and I jumped. I couldn't believe I actually looked, and when I saw there was nothing there, I felt silly. But I still kept my distance, and eventually, once we bought a building to house our office, when I couldn't take it any longer, I made him move everything outside into the garage.

As a teenager, he was always dirty with greasy fingernails, and we tried everything to get him to clean them. I bought him hand brushes and Boraxo soap and even his own set of towels so he wouldn't stain our good ones. Nothing seemed to work, and eventually we just got used to it. When Stavros would come for Sunday dinner, he'd always point out Alex's nails, and one time he took me aside and told me I needed to be a stricter parent.

Vaso was a delight. She loved sitting on Nick's lap at night, sucking her thumb and watching whatever he was watching on TV. She was a homebody, like I was. Even as she grew up, if a friend wanted her to spend the night, she didn't want to. One time when she was younger, we pushed her to go to a friend's, and around midnight, her friend's mother called to see if we could come pick her up. She was totally different when someone wanted to spend the night with *her*; she shared her toys and books, and would help me make breakfast in the morning.

Both Nick and I had straight hair, but my two children had curly hair like my father. Vaso hated it when I brushed hers, so I kept her hair short. She detested it—and Nick didn't care for it either—but it made bath time a lot easier. Once she was old enough to wash her own hair, we let it grow out.

Vaso was bright and did well in school, often doing extra credit work just to keep busy. She learned to use the adding machine and typewriter, and even when I was at my busiest, she'd sit at her TV tray desk next to me and pester me to call out numbers she could add up. She loved it when our customers came by the office and she could offer them a soda from the bar we'd built. When she came home from school, she'd always sit in the chair in front of my desk and tell me everything she did that day. She was a chatterbox, and somehow, I learned to listen to her and do my work at the same time.

When Alex turned sixteen, something dramatically changed in him. We'd witnessed the gradual changes that came with being a teenage boy, like arguing with us about everything we suggested; things like asking him to clean his room or change out the cages where he kept his critters in the garage; but this was different. He was angry and spiteful towards us all at the same time.

He threatened to drop out of school and run away, and was heading into a dark place that we were barred from. That's when I talked to my sister, Cynthia, about the possibility of sending him down to The Valley, hoping a change in environment would bring him out of whatever it was that was dragging him down. It was a last resort, and one we hoped would do the trick.

He left during the summer, and Cynthia enrolled him in Holtville High School. He was finally out of the house, and life slowly settled into a new kind of normal. As much as I hated to admit it, his absence brought a sense of relief—and even Vaso seemed lighter, somehow changed. Plus, it was nice not dealing with bugs and snakes in the house and grease on the driveway. Once we cleaned his room, the smell of teenage boys eventually dissipated, and our housekeeper finally went back in there.

I talked with Cynthia at least once every other day, and she'd bring me up to date on how Alex was doing. We bought him an old truck so he wouldn't be a burden to them, and he was always fixing it up. He and Eddie had really bonded, and he gladly helped with chores around the farm. Every week I'd send him a quick note telling him what we were doing, and sometimes I sent photos. Even though I knew how he was doing, I always asked what he'd been up to, and I made sure to tell him we loved and missed him. He rarely wrote back.

Cynthia and Eddie loved having Alex stay with them, and if hard pressed, I'd have to have admitted I was envious of their relationship. I knew we were taking a back seat to someone their child admired, and sometimes when I lay there in bed, I'd listen to Nick snore and silently wipe the tears that slipped from my eyes.

Eventually, Alex graduated, and Nick, Vaso, and I went down to be there for the ceremony. I was hoping he'd come back up with us then, but he said he wanted to wait until the end of summer. We'd planned a trip to Europe, hoping that being back with the family would make him realize what he'd been missing, but when I told him he just said, "Fine. I'll be back before we go."

One reason we were going was for years, Nick had wanted to visit the village of his childhood. Another couple with two daughters close in age to our children wanted to go with us. Alex was eighteen and Vaso was fourteen when we flew to New York to board a ship to take us to Lisbon, Portugal, and around the Mediterranean. Alex slept through most of the cruise, even missing the ship's fire drill. We were hoping he'd appreciate his first opportunity to travel, but before we left, Alex met a girl he was interested in, and he was eager to get back home.

Vaso loved the ship, the food, and the ports we visited. She was our 'romantic' and she fell in love with young men on shipboard and in every port. We bought her a gold and pearl charm bracelet, and she loved picking out charms everywhere we went. There was a gold Eiffel Tower, the Colosseum, the Leaning Tower of Pisa, a matador from Spain, and I can't recall what we bought in Portugal. She also found some gold rings with "diamonds," but we were never sure they were authentic.

We had to keep an eye on her, for she looked far more mature than her age, and boys ogled her.

Within a couple of months of our return, Alex told us his girlfriend was pregnant and that they wanted to get married. She was only seventeen!

Most parents feel the mate their children have chosen is not good enough for them, and that's how I felt from the moment he told me. I didn't judge her because she got pregnant; that could have happened to anyone. In retrospect, knowing Alex's temperament, I think I knew she was going to be as good as he was ever going to get. Not that he wasn't handsome; he was. But even *he* would say years later, he was just never a happy person. And eventually, I respected Jean for staying with Alex while he gallivanted off into his own dream world. Eventually, she put her foot down and moved on without him.

They married quietly in a small chapel, and then we shared dinner with her parents. They were kind, yet distant, and I could tell from the start we'd never bridge the gap between us. Her mother had lived through divorce; her father had adopted Jean and her sister long ago—reminders that every family harbors its own shadows.

Alex wanted to go into the service, so he enlisted. It was the second time he'd left me feeling hollow, and if I was honest, I resented him. I'd had to smile through everything—his graduation, the wedding and his deployment to Oahu. But this was where our granddaughter, Chloe, was born, and her arrival brought about a change in me that I welcomed.

Maybe this was a chance to maybe get it right with someone who needed me in a different way.

Nick, Vaso and I went to Hawaii twice to see them in their tiny one-bedroom apartment, and even though Nick and I had started out with no money, I wasn't sure how Alex and Jean would survive.

The Vietnam War was raging at that time, and I prayed Alex would never have to fight, but I'd heard him tell someone he was ready to kill those bastards if he could. I knew there was something inside him that would have welcomed the opportunity.

I didn't know how to express my happiness when Alex's enlistment ended and they came back home. We loaned them the money for a down payment on a house in Long Beach, and he came back to work for us in the construction company, but I knew in my heart he would never really return home to me.

CHAPTER THIRTY FOUR

KATE

By this time, Vaso had grown into a beautiful young woman. She'd always been a good child, but I spoiled her—thankfully, she had never been a brat. I knew I'd tried to compensate for always working, and I'd tried to make up for anything I might have missed with Alex. She did well in school, and having grown up around our business, she learned at an early age to talk to people, and was responsible enough even at a young age to answer the phones and take good messages.

By the time she was in eighth grade, I knew she was bored with private school, even though it was a wonderful opportunity for her to learn languages and to study subjects not taught in public school. By the ninth grade, she'd pestered us so much she finally talked us into letting her go back to the public school system. That's when she changed.

She'd been seeing a new young man for a while when I grew concerned about her sexual activity. She'd always kept a monthly calendar, and I started checking it regularly. By the time she was seventeen, her behavior started changing. There wasn't much we could control about that, but I knew I could do something to avoid an unwanted pregnancy. I never told Nick, but I made an appointment with our family doctor, and we put her on the pill.

We let her keep the car we won at the Lion's Club fair. It relieved me of making sure she got to school, but the false sense of freedom it created for her, along with getting involved with the wrong crowd of people at school, propelled her into her own form of a downhill spiral. She was never angry like Alex was, but almost overnight, she started challenging our rules, and we soon realized we'd lost our little girl.

Nick and I both smoked, so it wasn't surprising when Vaso picked up the habit, too. Neither of us had ever been around drugs, so it took us a while to recognize she was getting high on something. It was the late 1960s, when drugs like marijuana and LSD were constantly being written about in the newspaper or talked about on the news. One thing we were grateful for was that Woodstock was nowhere near us in California, or I'm sure she would have been there.

In her senior year, Vaso was caught ditching school, and at her principal's suggestion, we agreed she needed to get out of her surroundings. She graduated early from high school and enrolled in community college to get away from her "friends," as she called them. We hoped this was going to expose her to more mature people and get her to stop seeing the people who were encouraging her destructive behavior. But the total college experience never happened; only a couple of months after she began classes, she got bored and dropped out.

So that we'd know where she was, we had her start coming to work at the office. She rebelled at first, but when she got her first paycheck, her attitude changed a little. She still stayed out late, but at least she was focusing on something other than cruising around the school all day.

We worried she'd end up killing herself by overdosing or drinking and driving, and when we'd ask her anything, she'd deny everything.

"Don't worry," she'd say. "I can take care of myself."

Nick and I were relentless when it came to her. When one of us was ready to give up, the other would dig in, pushing even harder to get her back on track. But the final blow came in June—the day she was supposed to walk with her graduating class. She left the house in her cap and gown just before my mother arrived so we could head to the ceremony together. My mother had dressed to the nines, as always—wearing a tailored knit dress, her signature mink collar, and a hat with a delicate veil.

It was unusually warm that day, and we sat in the crowd waiting for the principal to call her name. But we never heard it, and we never saw her. We kept scanning the program, thinking maybe they'd made a mistake, but they hadn't. The mistake was believing Vaso had finally turned a corner.

I was beyond angry—I was humiliated. My mother, to her credit, didn't say a word, but I could see the storm behind her silence. If any of us had pulled something like that when we were young, she'd have dragged us out by the hair and made sure we felt a switch across our bare backsides.

When we got home, we found her gifts unwrapped and a note in their place. That was it—the last straw. Still, my mother just sat there, listening while Nick and I volleyed our frustration back and forth, our words heavy with hurt and disbelief. Nick looked gutted. I was livid.

Finally, he threw up his hands and said, "That's it. I've had enough."

I wasn't sure exactly what that meant, so I said nothing. All I could think about was how Vaso had been such a sweet child and how she'd given so much of herself to others as she was growing up. When she was ten and eleven, she volunteered at the United Way and took the bus downtown, where she typed and stuffed envelopes asking for donations. She was the youngest volunteer they'd had. She went to the Poor Farm at Rancho Los Amigos for Christmas with her school and had wrapped small gifts like tissues, socks and slippers to give to residents for Christmas. She was one of the most generous young people I knew, and somehow she'd taken a wrong turn and instead of being the leader she could have been, she was following the wrong people.

I was sorry for the time I wasn't able to devote to either of my children, and I wondered if I was partially to blame for her behavior. For the first time, I wondered if we'd be able to figure out what to do with her.

I was mortified when my mother ended up telling Stavros about the graduation disaster, and a few days later he called and said, "You know, one of my clients is sending their son on a trip you might be interested in. He's going away to gain a better perspective on life."

"I think I have the answer," I told Nick later that night. He blanched when I told him how much it would cost, but I also reminded him it included a semester of college.

He said, "This will be the last thing I will do to make her figure out what she needs to do to get her life together."

I didn't want him to tell her that, because I didn't want to send her away thinking we didn't love her. But I didn't argue with him, for I knew he was at the end of his rope. It was my turn to be the one who believed Vaso would figure it out.

I missed her more than I had expected while she was gone. Nick did too. And as much as we cared about her, we both admitted there was a strange relief in not constantly worrying about her coming and going. Of course, that relief quickly turned into a different kind of worry—wondering how she was managing out there on her own. Still, we held on to the hope that time away might give her perspective, that she'd see how others lived and maybe, just maybe, come back with a deeper sense of gratitude.

I wrote to her every day and sent Polaroids of what was happening at home. I also wired money when she called from Japan, telling me she'd already spent her allowance. I never told Nick, for I knew he'd tell me I wasn't teaching her to live within her means, but when she told me the types of things she was spending the money on, I felt these weren't frivolous purchases. And while I wanted her to think about her life, I also wanted to see her take advantage of a wonderful opportunity to see the world.

When I saw her wave to us as the ship docked back in Los Angeles, even from afar, I could tell she was a different person. More mature, more lovely. Maybe our prayers had been answered. To say I was shocked to see how much she brought home was an understatement. Alex had to bring a truck to bring everything home.

Time would tell if we'd done the right thing.

PART TWO

CHAPTER THIRTY FIVE

VASO

I was almost nineteen when I answered a help-wanted ad for a job at Capitol Records in Hollywood. Just the idea of working at a famous company seemed glamorous to me, and I couldn't believe my good luck when they hired me on the spot.

I had a prestigious title, Manufacturing and Procurement, which really meant I typed up purchase orders for album covers. My claim to fame there was that I ordered all the Beetles' *Sgt. Pepper's Lonely Hearts Club Band* album covers for the United States. On the cover were, of course the Beetles, with images of other famous people surrounding them. It was the first album I'd seen that included the lyrics on the back, and when I read some of them, like *"Lucy in the Sky With Diamonds,"* in my infinite wisdom, I predicted the album would never sell.

Thankfully, I never shared my opinion with anyone—the album sold over thirty-two million copies.

Around this time, I started dating a man named Bill who was unlike anyone I'd known. He was in his late twenties, tall, and muscular. And it didn't hurt that he drove a Corvette.

He told me how his ex had cheated on him, and how devastated he'd been—he also told me he thought I could be the best thing to come his way in a long time. He introduced me to jazz music, and we spent weekends at the Lighthouse Café in Hermosa Beach, and afterward, we'd go to his apartment and make love. I'd never felt so wanted and adored.

We were always home a little after midnight, and I could tell my parents thought that although he was a little old for me, I'd finally turned a corner, bringing home someone who wasn't a derelict.

Our relationship moved quickly. I was awestruck by having someone so mature be interested in me, and after only a few weeks, he told me he was in love with me—that I was his soul mate, and that he'd never met anyone like me before.

Once I'd fallen, he began making subtle suggestions about my appearance. He told me he thought I should quit smoking, and I agreed—it was a healthy choice, so I did. Not long after that, he told me I had such a pretty face, and that I'd look amazing if I lost a little weight. Other than Stavros commenting on my weight when I was growing up, I hadn't thought of myself that way now, but I took his comment to heart and started dieting.

I still had a terrible habit of picking at my cuticles, which he made clear he found unappealing. On the surface, his suggestions sounded thoughtful—even caring. But each one landed like a quiet critique, chipping away at me. And when I stepped back, I couldn't shake the feeling that he wasn't in love with who I was, but was slowly and carefully trying to turn me into someone else.

If I ordered something indulgent at dinner, I'd notice his quiet judgment. I began second-guessing everything—was my skirt too short? Too long? Did this outfit hug my body too tightly? And when I asked if we could talk about how I felt, he'd suddenly disappear—no calls, no visits for days, sometimes a full week. Then, just as quickly, he'd be back with his charming smile and a bouquet of flowers, as if nothing had happened.

And then came the night I wore a new dress. He said nothing when he picked me up, but as I got into the car, he told me he didn't care for what I was wearing. The comment embarrassed me—and it hurt. When I reacted, he accused me of being overly sensitive and dismissed my feelings entirely, which only deepened the sting. For the rest of the evening, I couldn't shake the heaviness I felt. When I wasn't enthusiastic about ending the night in bed with him, he said I was overreacting. He didn't force himself on me, but I felt emotionally guarded and withdrawn—and that clearly disappointed him, too.

I felt like I was living on a seesaw, constantly off balance—always wondering what version of him I'd get next. It was an emotional roller coaster, and I was losing my grip.

About a month later, I was listening to a radio talk show on my way to work, and a psychologist was describing narcissistic behavior in men, and the light bulb went on. There'd been so many red flags that I'd missed, but I'd never had an actual boyfriend . . . I felt so stupid; I'd never seen the signs.

I'd been a fool to fall for someone like that.

I began not answering his calls, and then when I was ready, I told him to go find someone else to torment. Not knowing how aggressive he would be, I worried he might stalk me, or worse. I couldn't tell my parents how he was making me feel, so I just told them he found someone else.

It took me a while to lick my wounds, and for a few months, thoughts of him haunted me; remembering how loving he was before he changed. I knew I'd made the right decision to stop seeing him, but that didn't make the heartache go away.

While I was feeling sorry for myself, there was an executive at Capitol Records who expressed an interest in seeing me outside of work. I'd joined him for lunch a few times, but always with a group of others, and he'd done nothing inappropriate.

He was probably around forty, and there was something undeniably flattering about having the attention of another older man in a position of power. I found myself wondering: if I dated him, would that be the start of some glamorous, exciting life? Or would I be just another passing interest, replaced the moment someone younger or newer walked through the door? He had a polished, distinguished look—always in tailored suits and bright, confident ties. But I knew bringing someone like him home would definitely raise eyebrows with my parents. I was also beginning to notice a pattern. Why was it that I kept gravitating toward older men? And what did that say about the kind of attention I seemed to need?

I never did go out with him; in fact, I quit my job after being there for only six months. I didn't see myself becoming a music executive, and the drive was wearing on me.

Maybe I was starting to use my brain a little.

My parents were very supportive when I told them I was quitting; they'd worried about me driving all that distance every day, and were proud of me for doing what I did. The problem was I was still not interested in going to college, and there was nothing else I wanted to do. They suggested I work in their office in the interim, which was now twice the size it had been when they worked from home. I'd always liked clerical work, and I'd been around the business my whole life, so it seemed like a perfectly good stepping stone until I found something else.

I'd moved on from the dive bars I used to frequent to a nightclub, where I met some gals who took me under their wing. They were a little older than me, and their mission was to keep introducing me to eligible men until I found someone I liked. I'd cut back on my drinking, and would sometimes only have one beer before I switched to Coke.

One Friday night, they invited me to go to Irvine Park for a picnic on Saturday. I'd never been there before, and they said I could ride with them.

"Wear something nice," one of them said. "Mr. Right just might be there."

"I wish," I said.

That Saturday morning, I finally chose a lightweight striped sweater and dark pants. I didn't know why, but I was a little nervous, wondering what everyone else would be wearing.

It was mid-May, and while the weather in Long Beach was still a little cool, it felt like it was going to be a nice day. We drove about twenty-five miles inland on a freeway system that only took us so far—and from there, we drove another twenty minutes through orange groves and oak trees to the lake and park. We laid out our blankets and set our baskets of food in the center so we could all share when we were ready to eat.

I sat and watched as everyone else either joined in a game of football or stood on the sidelines and cheered. I didn't know anyone, and I hesitated mingling; I had to remind myself I was there to meet people, not hide on the outskirts. I began to feel conspicuous as I sat there by myself, so I finally got up and walked toward a tree, where I could continue to watch without bringing any attention to myself.

And that's when I saw him.

As if he saw me watching him, he sauntered over, and the strangest feeling came over me. He wasn't very tall; maybe five foot eight, slender, with light brown hair and amber eyes. He wasn't particularly handsome in the pretty sense of the word, but I found him very attractive. His nose was on the larger side, and even from a distance, I could tell he used hairspray to keep his neatly combed hair in place. He was clean-shaven and had fine lines around his eyes. He wore a striped long-sleeved shirt with an open collar and jeans.

My stomach flipped, and I realized I was looking at the man I'd marry.

He walked with a casual gait, and rolled his shirtsleeves up as he came closer, making me wonder if he was coming in for the kill.

"Are you here with someone?" he asked, looking around.

"Just the girls," I said, tilting my head toward where they were.

"I'm Thomas."

"I'm Vaso."

He cocked his head in thought, and then said, "That's an interesting name."

"I'm Greek. It's short for Vasiliki."

Thomas nodded, as if that made perfect sense.

He wasn't into the football, so we made our way to the blanket. I opened the cooler and took out two beers.

"Are you old enough to drink?" he asked with an easy smile.

"I'm old enough to do whatever I want," I answered, a little annoyed.

His smile was disarming.

There was something about the way he studied my face, looking from my eyes, down to my lips, and then slowly back up. I instantly knew what he was thinking, and I wasn't opposed to the idea.

Thomas drove me to his apartment, and we spent the afternoon in his bed. He wasn't what I would have called an exceptional lover, but other than Bill, I hadn't had any satisfying relationships to compare him to. When he asked if he could see me again, I said yes.

After a quick dinner, he brought me home, but I didn't have him come in. I wasn't certain I was ready for my parents to meet him yet. Over the next week, we saw each other every night, and I was struck by how grounded and emotionally mature he was—it pulled me in.

Thomas was an engineer in the aerospace industry and had traveled from site to site when one government contract expired and another was won. Even though he tried several times to explain exactly what he did, I never really understood, and quit asking.

He admitted after his daughter was born, he didn't want more children, so he had a vasectomy. I was a little surprised at that, but then I reasoned he was entitled to his own convictions. He told me he wanted me to know that before our relationship got serious. Thomas divorced his wife eight years later when he found out she'd been seeing someone else. His wife kept the house and all the furnishings, and he'd walked away with very little. His daughter wasn't much younger than I was, and instead of seeing that as a problem, I saw it as an opportunity for a ready-made family.

When I talked about myself, I left out most of the sordid details about the last few years of my life, fearing he would think me terribly immature and be disappointed in me. We talked instead about my family and the construction business. I did tell him I tried my hand at college, but it just wasn't for me, and I found when I talked about working with my parents, I was describing something I liked doing.

We dated for only a few more weeks before we talked about getting married, and when I introduced him to my parents, my father was furious with me.

"You're still very young," he said. "You're not pregnant, are you?" he added.

"No, and I love him," I said. "Besides, he can't have more children."

Until now, I hadn't thought about how my parents would feel about having no more grandchildren.

My father raised his eyebrows in surprise.

My mother's eyes widened.

"He is a little older than we would have preferred," my mother said, trying to diffuse the situation. "And we've only just met him."

"He's only nine years younger than I am," my father repeated as he stormed off. "You're too young."

"It'll be okay," my mother said. "I'll talk to him."

I knew my parents weren't happy, but I couldn't see any reason marrying Thomas was such a bad idea. I still lived at home, and I needed to explore the possibilities of the world on my own. I'd never had a relationship with anyone I even remotely wanted to live with, and while I didn't know it then, getting married was the best decision I ever made.

My mother sat me down and gave me an encouraging smile, and I thanked God it wasn't the same gritted-teeth smile she used when hearing about Alex and Jean. She was always the diplomatic one when it came to the family. She was the problem solver and the peacekeeper, as most mothers are.

"Your father will come around. You're his little girl, don't forget, and he wants only the best for you. You know that, and so do I." She sat for a minute in thought, and then said, "Now, what are your plans?"

Six weeks after I met Thomas, we were married. By then, my father had accepted the inevitable, and he'd warmed a little to the idea. I understood that he was doing his best, and I knew he didn't dislike Thomas. . .he was more concerned with our age difference. On my wedding day, he came into my bedroom, where I was putting the finishing touches on my hair, and he put a coin in my shoe. He looked so handsome in his suit and my heart swelled. He'd never actually told me he loved me, but I'd never doubted it for a minute.

"I love you too," I said to his unspoken words. "And we'll be fine."

"Well, let's get going," he said, turning to leave. "We don't want to be late."

"Dad?"

"Yes?"

"Thanks," I said, then pulled him to me so I could give him a big hug.

We had a small wedding with just our parents there. My brother Alex and his wife Jean stood up for us. I still don't understand why I asked him to be in my wedding, except I didn't have any close friends, and Thomas's best friend had been killed in an automobile accident the year before.

My parents still had the house in Palm Springs and now an apartment in South Laguna, and they let us use both for our honeymoon.

Marriage was what I needed. I blossomed. We rented an apartment, and for the first time in my life, I wasn't homesick. Being married suited me.

I'd been a young woman with an adventurous spirit, and I found happiness in marriage and settling down—not by abandoning who I was, but by discovering a new kind of adventure—one rooted in intimacy, growth, and shared dreams.

I loved building a life together, and in creating a home that reflected both our personalities. Each decision, from choosing a paint color to decorating, became part of a shared journey. With him, I had a new kind of freedom—one to dream, to try new things, because I thought he believed in me.

I continued working with my parents in their construction company, and I ran our flooring division. By the time I was twenty-one, we'd saved enough money to buy our first house, and I was in seventh heaven. I cooked, gardened, and when we added a family room, I loved the process of remodeling. I had a house to decorate, and I welcomed the responsibilities that came with it. I enjoyed my job, and I loved being married.

I did crafts and had boutiques in our backyard, and I donated time to the United Way Charity—just as I'd done when I was young—typing up and stuffing hundreds of donation requests and dropping boxes of them back off to be mailed.

I loved entertaining, and we danced to Creedence Clearwater Revival when we hosted parties with Thomas's car club buddies and their wives. We'd talked about having pets, and one day, Thomas surprised me with a Siamese kitten that I named Kimi. I loved my house, and my grown-up life was as perfect as it could be.

CHAPTER THIRTY SIX

VASO

Jobs within the aerospace industry were always hanging by a thread. Thomas was transferred twice in the first few years we were married. If a contract ran over budget, engineers were laid off. If a new project hadn't been approved, they were laid off again, or moved to an entirely different facility.

One day, Thomas came home in an unusually bad mood and told me he was going to be one of a handful without a job. We were looking for an estimator in my division of the business, and I didn't see why Thomas couldn't learn to go see jobs. I talked with my father, and he agreed it was worth a shot. A week later, we bought Thomas a new Ford Ranchero for all his samples, and he learned to become a flooring estimator. We worked well together, and it was a relief for him to finally have a secure job and paycheck. I handled the office and ran the jobs, and he had the freedom to make appointments, write up his estimates and come and go.

Thomas's mother passed away about five years after we were married. She had multiple myeloma—a white blood cell cancer in the bone marrow. She was such a petite, lovely woman, and when I noticed her gradual weight loss, I asked Thomas if she was unwell. She'd never said anything to us until she was almost on her deathbed, and it took us completely by surprise. Looking back, I understood then why, around six months earlier, she told me she could die knowing Thomas had finally settled down and she was glad he had someone like me in his life.

The loss devastated my father-in-law, and while Thomas wasn't what I'd call a demonstrative man, I could tell he felt her loss, too. His daughter, Carolyn, didn't want to go with us to the funeral, so her mother dropped her off. I knew when we got married, Thomas and his daughter weren't close, and as much as I tried to encourage her to come see us, she preferred being with her mother. She sat with us at the funeral, but each time I saw her, I was reminded of the hope I'd carried into my marriage to Thomas—that somehow, we'd become closer. And the truth was, it had never happened.

I wished Thomas would have seen this opportunity to reach out to touch her hand or do something to acknowledge he understood her sadness at losing her grandmother. But he didn't.

After the service, Thomas and I stood outside with his father, saying goodbye to the small group of mourners, and we both saw his former wife get out of the car to greet Carolyn.

"My god, she's gained weight," Thomas said to no one.

There was no way she could have heard him, but she looked up at him at that exact moment, and I found myself embarrassed for her. I quickly took my father-in-law by the arm and led him back to our car, all the while thinking about his ex-wife. She was definitely a bit chubby, but I could tell she weighed less than I did. I couldn't help but wonder—what, then, did Thomas think of me?

We'd been married for about seven years when I started to feel the quiet shift in our relationship. There were no big arguments, no dramatic fights—but a slow-growing distance had crept in. Intimacy had become rare, and our evenings followed a routine that kept us in separate worlds—the minute we got home from work, he'd head straight to the family room to watch TV while I stayed in the kitchen preparing dinner. He'd held on to a 1932 Ford Phaeton sedan after his divorce from his first wife, and now that it was fully restored, he was deeply involved with his hot rod club, attending events and going to car shows. Meanwhile, I still found comfort in different things—needlepoint, volunteering, and reading. We were living parallel lives, and the space between us kept growing.

Being married was what had settled me down, but somehow, I realized I'd begun to outgrow Thomas. He was still the same person he was when we got married, and I realized that was the problem. Even now, he had that same youthful gait, and his disarming smile hadn't faded, but I felt I'd matured more than he had in some ways. He was forty-two to my twenty-six, and his mannerisms were those of a much younger person—plus he still liked to party.

On one Tuesday car-club night, I got a call around midnight from one of his friends; they'd been drinking, and Thomas had been arrested for exhibition of speed as he was leaving a bar's parking lot. I'd spun out in water myself, but part of me was angry that he'd been reckless after drinking, and had put himself in that position. I had no choice but to go down to the station and bail him out of jail. It was late. But beneath the frustration was a gnawing worry. No matter how upset I was, I still cared about him. So I threw on some clothes, grabbed my wallet, and headed out into the night to get him.

He told me there were no DUI charges filed against him, and I had no reason to question it—so I believed him. But years later, the friend who had called me that night let it slip that Thomas had actually been released on bail and had gone to court without my knowing it.

Throughout our marriage, my weight fluctuated, and most of the time I felt healthy and comfortable in my body. But I could tell Thomas began to see me differently. He was of the same slender build as when I met him and could still eat anything he wanted to—and his comments, subtle or not, made it clear he thought I should be thinner.

Even though I'd always taken pride in choosing clothing that suited me, I could still see it in his eyes whenever I wore something he didn't think was quite flattering enough. Like his comments about his ex-wife at his mother's funeral, I knew he felt the same about me. And every comment chipped away at my confidence and I became self-conscious around him.

Thomas had never been a passionate lover, and in recent years, intimacy between us had become completely one-sided. I started finding excuses to avoid it—headaches, long days, anything that might sound believable. One night, when I simply said I was tired, he responded with, "I guess I'll have to start looking for it elsewhere."

It wasn't the first time he'd made a comment like that, but for some reason, this one cut deeper. It wasn't loud, it wasn't cruel in tone—but it was cruel in meaning. Like my value had come down to whether or not I was available to him. I felt small, ashamed, and suddenly so alone. Part of me wanted to fight back, to say something sharp. But another part said, "Do what you want to, but just don't do it in front of our friends."

Once I said it out loud, I knew there was no turning back—we'd reached the point of no return in our marriage. Marrying Thomas had helped me discover who I was, but now I saw that it wasn't enough. The romance between us had faded. I still cared deeply for him, but I was no longer in love. I think the hardest thing for me to come to terms with was the fact that our marriage had failed.

I'd had this imaginary belief that I'd get married and live happily ever after. It took me years to understand that Thomas had always kept a part of himself hidden from me. And looking back, I see now that I never truly knew him.

Since we still worked together in my family's construction business, I knew I could never ask him for a divorce; but I also knew I needed something else in my life.

I went on Weight Watchers and lost twenty-five pounds. I found the person inside me that I'd forgotten. I began noticing men paying attention to me, and I loved it. I realized I now enjoyed buying new clothes, and I'd catch myself walking past a store window admiring the new me.

And then I bought that yellow Corvette.

On the nights Thomas went out with his friends, I started going out too—at first with a girlfriend, then once I felt comfortable at this one nightclub, I began going alone. I always told anyone who asked that I was married—it was my shield, a way to keep men at a distance. But even as I said it, I recognized the contradiction. Why go to a place full of singles if, deep down, you weren't hoping to be noticed?

I played into the mystique—I was slim and stylish, I smoked colored cigarettes, and I had a way of tying a colorful scarf around my head with a certain flair. And as I watched the sparks between the dancers on the floor, it hit me just how much I longed for that kind of excitement and connection. Eventually, I came to the perfect conclusion: I'd stay married, but I'd find a boyfriend.

It didn't take me long before I totally complicated my life. I met Steven.

CHAPTER THIRTY SEVEN

VASO

On a Tuesday night out, a man with a quiet confidence sat down beside me at the bar.

"I'm Mark," he said, watching me closely.

"Vaso," I replied, not offering more than that.

He tilted his head slightly. "I think I know you."

I didn't answer, just met his gaze.

"You're Vaso Pappas, aren't you?"

I raised an eyebrow, unsure whether to be amused or wary.

"Your father used to come into the flower shop where I worked," he said. "You were just a kid back then. Big eyes. Always quiet."

He ordered a scotch on the rocks, then turned back to me. "Can I get you something?"

"Coke," I said. "And I should mention—I'm married."

He gave a small shrug. "So, what brings you here?"

I took a sip before answering. "Let's just say my husband goes out on Tuesdays. And lately, I've found I prefer not to stay home waiting."

Before I could say more, another man appeared beside me and asked me to dance.

Even in the dim light of the club, I could tell he had the palest of blue eyes, a pleasant smile, and a full beard. I was somewhere else in my mind—half in the past, and half wondering what I was really doing there. It had been years since someone had asked me to dance, and I didn't want to be rude to Mark, so I thanked him, but said no.

I told Mark, "I think I might have hurt his feelings when I said no thank you."

"Nah. That's just Steven. He'll find someone to dance with."

For the rest of the evening, we talked about everything; his old boss, my father and mother, my marriage, his divorce, and every so often, I'd catch Steven glancing in my direction. I returned his look with a polite smile, careful not to send the wrong message. I'd already told Mark I wasn't looking for anything more than just this—whatever this was.

Around eleven, I was ready to go home, and while I said I was there just to get out of the house, I casually looked around the bar to see if Steven was there. A twinge of disappointment surprised me when I didn't see him. It was just as well.

I did this for about two months, not really sure what I was trying to prove, and every Tuesday, Steven and Mark would be there. And every Tuesday, Steven would ask me to dance. Eventually, I gave in, and the moment he held me, I felt a charge between us; a magnetism that stunned me.

I knew then I could be headed for trouble if I wasn't careful.

This went on for a couple more weeks—where we'd dance once or twice, and then I'd leave. But I'd catch myself thinking about him while I was at work, and comparing how I felt around him versus how I felt about Thomas. Looking back on it all, while I was off daydreaming, Thomas didn't seem to notice. In fact, he was in a world all of his own.

The following week, Steven and I danced a few times, and each time we did, I felt we had a connection, an instinctive natural rhythm as we moved effortlessly around the dance floor. Things were getting a little complicated. He gave me a quick hug before walking me back to my seat at the bar.

By then, an older gentleman who'd been drinking too much had taken the seat next to mine, and we struck up a conversation. He was a sales manager for a car dealership around the corner, and he began trying to convince me he'd be perfect for me in all ways. I tried to tell him kindly I wasn't interested, but he was quite persistent. He wasn't taking 'no' for an answer.

I finally looked up across the bar, and there Steven sat. Apparently, he'd found this exchange entertaining, for he raised one eyebrow at me. I smiled slightly and just stared back at him.

I knew beyond a shadow of any doubt I was opening a door that I wasn't sure I wanted to go through, but I made a decision. I was a damsel in distress. With my eyes, I said to him, "Rescue me."

And he did. He got up from his barstool and came around to where I sat and said, "May I have this dance?"

The moment he held me in his arms again, I could feel that same electricity between us, and I knew everything was going to change.

"You're obviously not happy at home if you're in here every week," he said. "I'd love to see you if you're ready."

It was just after Christmas, and I couldn't believe it, but we made arrangements to see each other on New Year's Eve.

"My husband will be out of town," I said without hesitating. What was I thinking? Then he kissed me and I melted.

It was getting late, so we got ready to leave.

"I'll walk you to your car," he said.

Outside, the fresh air should have brought me to my senses, but it didn't. I hadn't felt this way in years. At my car, Steven reached down to kiss me again, and just then, I recognized my husband's car slowly driving toward us. He knew where I went on Tuesdays, and apparently curiosity had gotten the best of him.

When Thomas saw me, he smiled with an exaggerated grin, and then, as he passed us, he gave a slight wave.

And I froze!

"Oh, my God—that was my husband," I said through clenched teeth. I was frozen in place, my stomach flipping as if it had turned inside out.

In an instant, my recklessness dissolved, and I felt like someone had kicked my legs out from under me. I'd been caught in a dangerous game. Obviously, he'd seen my Corvette, so he knew I was there. And now he'd caught me on the verge of being unfaithful.

"I need to go," I said clumsily.

"Will you call me tomorrow? I need to know you're all right," Steven said frantically.

"Yes."

All the way home, I kept rehearsing what I could say to Thomas; how I could give him a reasonable explanation of what I was doing there. Why hadn't he gotten out of his car and confronted us? I had no idea what I was going to do. When I got home, all the lights were out. I quietly made my way through the house and up to our bedroom, and then I saw he was already in bed and his back was to me. When I crawled in beside him, he didn't say a word.

He hadn't even waited for me to get home so he could accuse me face to face of cheating on him.

I don't know how I slept.

The next morning, I lay in bed for a few minutes expecting some sort of confrontation, but there was none. Just like nothing had happened, we got ready for work, and somehow we spent that week going through the motions, never bringing up the fact he'd seen me with another man. New Year's Eve was on a Saturday that year, and on Thursday, Thomas packed a bag for his guys' trip and left.

Clearly, we were broken.

On Saturday, I pulled out all the stops. When the doorbell rang, I answered it with only my bathrobe on, open just enough to give Steven an idea of what I was expecting.

"I'll be ready in a minute," I said after inviting him in.

Being with Steven set my world on fire. It was the stuff movies were made of, and I knew immediately I could not have him in my life if I was still married.

Then, a hundred things happened.

I told Thomas we were beyond repair.

He told me he had a girlfriend.

I suggested we get a divorce.

We made a list of what we each wanted to keep.

I wanted the house.

I told my parents we were splitting up.

And Thomas quit his job. There would be no way we could get a divorce and continue to work together.

Later, my mother told me, "I could see it in you, and I didn't know how to tell you. I knew you were unhappy."

And my father said, "The one good thing about your marriage was that at least I knew where you were at night."

Being with Steven brought me warmth and tenderness I'd only dreamed of. He was the kindest and gentlest man I'd ever met. We spent hours just talking about our lives; how I began to realize my marriage was what settled me down, but there had been something missing, and it was passion.

We talked about my recklessness when I was younger, and how I was so fortunate to have finally grown up. I'd seen for myself how men were generally the ones who lost most everything in a divorce, and Steven had fared worse; he lost his house, their car, and walked away with only an old van, which was sometimes where he slept. He talked about how he almost drank himself to death after his divorce. A former neighbor, who found him sitting in his van outside his old house, finally convinced him he was only hurting himself and that at the rate he was going, he'd never be good for anyone. Truthfully, I was surprised he was willing to open his heart to another woman.

"I fell in love with you the first time you danced with me," he said when we talked about moving in together. "But I knew I'd have to wait for the right time to ask you to be a part of my life."

A year later, we were planning our wedding. My neighbor's son was a jeweler, and he designed a ring for me. I wanted a large stone, but we couldn't afford a diamond, so he designed something with a cubic zirconia, and it was perfect. For years, I used to feel somewhat guilty having a stone so large that when people commented on it, I'd often tell them what it was. I wasn't trying to pass myself off as being wealthy when I wasn't.

On Memorial Weekend 1978, Steven and I were married in the Greek church my grandparents helped build in 1949. The same priest they'd brought to America performed the service, and when he looked me up in the baptismal records, he told me I was the last child to have been baptized that first year.

Except for my parents and eventually Cynthia and Eddie, none of the children had had traditional weddings, and since my first wedding to Thomas was in a chapel, I wanted everything to be different with Steven. When planning the wedding, Yia´ Yia told me we had to work around the Greek calendar. The first two weeks of August were devoted to the Virgin Mary. Lent, the forty days before Easter, was not a good time. August 29 marked the death of Saint John the Baptist. September 14 was the celebration of the Exaltation of the Holy Cross, and anytime in the forty days leading up to Christmas was out. When she told me this, I asked her to come up with a date that would work and let me know when we could marry; we'd make sure we were available.

Steven had to be baptized, and I'll never forget his expression when I told him he'd have to sit naked in the baptismal so the priest could check that he was fit to service his wife. His face flushed crimson, and I struggled not to laugh. I told him if he didn't believe me, he could always ask my grandmother.

"You'd better believe I will," he said.

Somehow, I talked Yia´ Yia into going along with the story, and when she saw the look on Steven's face, she winked at him. It was only then that he finally relaxed.

Uncle Eddie, who'd also been baptized in the church, stood up with us. Steven's girls, Holly and Tara, along with my brother's daughters, Chloe and Alexandria, were flower girls. We wore my grandparents' Stefana—the white wedding crowns joined by a ribbon, symbolizing the bond of two lives becoming one. The kumbaro, our best man, placed them on our heads, exchanging them back and forth three times before we circled the altar together. Each step marked the beginning of our new life as husband and wife.

The service was in both Greek and English, which meant it lasted twice as long—and by the end, my feet were aching. The reception took place right there at the church, and as usual, Yia Yia's lady friends prepared a feast fit for a village: leg of lamb, Greek rice, roasted potatoes, salad, and just about every Greek pastry you could imagine. When the band struck up, my feet hurt so much I had to slip off my shoes just to dance.

I teased my grandmother when I said, "If this is what it's like to have a Greek wedding, I'd hate to see a Greek divorce."

She didn't say a word, but her raised eyebrow said plenty.

CHAPTER THIRTY EIGHT

VASO

Like Thomas, Steven had once been a design engineer in the unstable aerospace industry. But when his divorce hit him out of nowhere, he abandoned it all and went to work for his uncle, servicing gas stations. I'd never really noticed gas pumps before, but through him I learned how they ticked—the fuel flowing through little mechanical computers that spun and added up gallons and cost in real time.

Steven's parents owned a mechanical computer service in Paramount, where he'd been born and raised. They refurbished the old machines that came back after being replaced. When his parents were ready to retire, we bought both their house and the shop down the street. Steven left his uncle's business and stepped into the family business. He loved being his own boss, and before long, he'd nearly doubled sales. But things changed when Chevron started phasing out the mechanical systems in favor of electronic ones. For the customers who still relied on the old models, obsolescence was no longer just a threat—it was inevitable.

When Chevron approached Steven to design a test cart that could retrofit the old pumps with digital technology, he built a prototype—but the contract was awarded to someone else. Within six months, his business had nearly ground to a halt. The young men, who'd been with his parents for years, had learning disabilities, and they counted on him for work. Suddenly, they were at risk of losing their jobs. We were desperate, scrambling to find a way to keep them employed.

Steven bought a lawn service. Despite purchasing equipment and adding new customers, we just couldn't make enough money to keep going, and we projected that our business would not survive another year.

It felt like déjà vu when I approached my parents to see if there might be a place for Steven in the construction business—and to my surprise, there was. He started working out in the field and quickly moved up to a superintendent role. Not long after, my parents sat us down and told us they wanted us to take over the flooring division I had managed for years. They even loaned us enough money to put a small down payment on a property in Paramount that we could renovate and eventually call our own.

We found a new tenant for the old computer business property, and one for the portion of our building we weren't using, and suddenly we owned three pieces of property and had five tenants.

It was several years later that Uncle Eddie was diagnosed with prostate cancer. He and Aunt Cynthia still lived down in the Valley, and after the portrait on the porch, I never saw him again. Once we got the grim diagnosis, my brother Alex made the trip back down to see him before he died.

Uncle Eddie was cremated, and for years Aunt Cynthia kept his ashes in the original container on the fireplace mantel. When she was finally ready to let him go, she called Alex.

CHAPTER THIRTY NINE

ALEX

By the time Uncle Eddie died, I was knee-deep in hog shit. With over twenty pigs to feed and clean up after twice a day, I could barely keep ahead of it. Linda helped as much as she could, but she couldn't handle it alone for more than a couple of days, which meant I was tied to the farm. Both of us being gone at once was impossible. I didn't have a steady helper I could call on for backup. And with the slaughtering rig I'd built in the bed of my old Chevy, I was busy with customers ready to have their livestock butchered and turned into dinner. Once the killing was done, there was no waiting around—the carcasses had to be dealt with right away.

I'd built a shop outside the camper trailer and room, and put in a walk-in refrigerator and freezer. I'd learned from when I built the first house that I needed to build it to code in case the building department came by. But what I never expected was that the Food Safety and Inspection Service (FSIS) sons of bitches would come down on me like a lightning bolt. I had to fill out paperwork until I thought my fingers would fall off just to keep my business going!

Now, I've always kept a clean working area, but those damned inspectors would drop in unannounced, and more than once, I thought about telling them to F-off. But I had a going business, and when hunting season started, men brought me their kill. When that happened, I took care of my regular customers first, and had to turn some hunters away.

I never made it down for Eddie's funeral dinner, but I'd talked with my aunt and I knew she understood. I told her Eddie had been like a dad to me. He taught me how to work the land, how to harvest and bale alfalfa, and how to man up when things weren't going my way.

I told her he was the only person I told when I found out about my dad not being my dad, and I knew she knew. Of course, she'd known the whole time.

"We only did what your parents wanted, which was to make sure you always felt like you were just as important to them as Vaso," she said.

"I get it, but it's still hard to forgive them."

"And it would break their hearts if you ever said anything to them."

"I'm sorry I'm not there. Is there anything I can do?"

"Actually, there is," she said, still referring to him as William. "William wanted his ashes scattered," she said.

"I'll do it," I said without hesitation.

"I'm not ready just yet; maybe in a few months?"

"You just need to let me know, and I'll take care of it."

Six months later, she called and said it was time. I knew when I saw her, she was goin' downhill. Her walkin' was stiff and awkward. She held on to every table in the house as she shuffled by. I said nothing, but she gave me that look that warned me to keep my mouth shut.

How're you doin'?" I asked anyway.

She knew I wasn't talkin' about spreading Uncle Eddie's ashes.

"I worry I'm getting a little forgetful," she finally confessed.

Aunt Cynthia was afraid to go up in a small plane, or in any plane, for that matter. So Kaylee and I made the arrangements to say our last goodbyes, and Eddie Jr., who was still a Navy SEAL, flew in from somewhere to be there. Now, spreading someone's ashes like that is against the law, but the pilot was a friend of Eddie's, so he didn't give a damn if we were breaking the law or not. We figured no one would ever be the wiser.

We flew over a few of places we thought Eddie would be pleased with, and at the last drop, as we tipped the container it accidentally went overboard along with Uncle Eddie's identification information.

We figured no one would ever find it, but the local sheriff did, and he gave it back to Aunt Cynthia with a warning that what we'd done was against the law. But since he was one of Eddie's drinking buddies, he'd tossed the tube and looked the other way.

CHAPTER FORTY

KATE

When Eddie died, a big part of Cynthia's life ended, too. Eddie had been her rock. She often told me how there wasn't a day she didn't love him more for sacrificing everything for her, and even then, she always felt she'd become, in her words, "one half of a physically able woman." So when he died, I prayed she'd be able to handle her new world without him. The kids were gone, and even though someone worked the land, it and the little house were too much for her to care for. She was adamant she didn't want to move back to Long Beach; instead, she sold the farm and bought a house in town.

I spent a week with her as we packed up the farmhouse; mostly it was me packing and Cynthia telling me what to keep and what to donate. I hired a couple of their farmhands to move it all to the new house, and the first thing she did was find a place for Eddie's ashes on the fireplace.

Since I had to get back to Long Beach, Kaylee came down and helped unpack and put everything away. After she was settled, Kaylee brought her and Eddie's ashes up to Long Beach for his celebration of life.

While cooking for all of us was becoming harder for my mother, she insisted on preparing the meal. Stavros was there with a new girlfriend; Vaso and Steven were there, as were Cynthia's two children and her grandchildren. Before we ate, Stavros gave a toast.

"To Eddie," he said, raising his glass.

"To Eddie," we all said together.

Two days later, Kaylee drove Cynthia back home and stayed with her for a few days. Even though his ashes were still in the original container, the first thing Cynthia did was to put Eddie back up on the mantel.

I made Cynthia promise to call me if she needed anything, since she'd be living by herself now, relying solely on some good friends. I called her once a week when I visited my mother so they could talk and get caught up.

Although it was gradual, I could tell Cynthia was starting to struggle physically, and her voice was getting weaker. When I asked her, of course, she denied it, and told me she'd let me know when she needed help. I could also tell she'd begun drinking more, and I wasn't sure if that was complicating her Multiple Sclerosis. I was never flippant about her health, but I began to feel she was getting to a point that it really didn't make any difference what vices she kept.

CHAPTER FORTY ONE

VASO

One day out of nowhere, Holly and Tara told us their mother was getting remarried and planned to move to Tennessee to be near her new husband's family. The girls, just starting high school, were old enough to think for themselves, and though they loved their mother, they didn't want to leave everything they knew behind.

Our two-bedroom house in Long Beach was perfect for Steven and me, but it was too small for the four of us. So when my sister-in-law Jean mentioned they were selling their ranch-style home and moving up to Hayfork, a crazy idea sparked. Maybe we could buy their house. I never truly loved it, but I didn't hate it either—it had four bedrooms, and all we needed was enough money to pay off their small loan. They would carry the balance. We could keep the original Long Beach house and rent it out.

The girls resisted at first, pointing out they'd still be leaving their friends behind. But after showing them the property and promising they could decorate their rooms however they wanted, they reluctantly agreed.

True to form, I wasn't content to leave things as they were. I talked Steven into remodeling the master suite by combining two bedrooms into one large room with space for a sofa and a TV. We turned the old laundry room into a third bathroom, stacking the washer and dryer to make space for a toilet and sink. The kitchen was outdated, but it had a rustic charm, and instead of remodeling it, we added a family room onto the back of the house.

We spent months clearing the property of rocks and junk my brother had left behind—twenty trips to the dump before we could even think about a lawn. I watered constantly, bringing dead patches of lawn back to life. We kept the barn Alex had built and the surrounding pens, which added to the rural feel.

Every weekend, I made huge breakfasts—eggs, pancakes, bacon, and fresh orange juice—for anyone who came to help. Over time, our family grew in ways I hadn't expected: three dogs, thirteen cats (the result of forgetting to spay three strays), ducks, geese, a rabbit colony, and a turkey that tragically drowned the first afternoon we had it. We even had a wild rooster that attacked me twice before Steven finally shot him.

I'd never imagined becoming a full-time parent, but I found myself up for the challenge. Steven loved his daughters, and I was determined to do my best for all of us. We eventually found a rhythm, and while we certainly had our moments, we built a new life together.

When the house next door came up for sale, I didn't waste any time—I picked up the phone and called my dad. I told him I thought it was a smart investment. Sure, it needed a lot of work—more than a little, honestly—but I could see the potential. Once it was fixed up, it would easily be worth more than what they were asking. I figured he'd jump at the chance. But instead, he kind of chuckled and said, "I don't want to take on another project right now." Then, without missing a beat, he added, "But if you really believe in it, I'll give you the money and you can buy it."

That was just the kind of thing my parents did for me. I never asked them for money, and I certainly never expected it—but when something felt like a once-in-a-lifetime opportunity, they were always there to support me. This house was one of those moments, and I knew I couldn't let it slip by.

As soon as escrow closed, we got to work. The previous owner had four dogs, and the place reeked—it was overwhelming the second you walked in. But once we tore out the old, musty carpet, painted every room, and put in new floors, the transformation was incredible. It didn't even look like the same house. The guesthouse out back was in better shape—it just needed some cosmetic updates to freshen it up, and it came right back to life.

Even before we were finished with the renovations, I put an ad in the paper and stuck a "For Rent" sign out front. Within a week, we had tenants lined up—and just like that, we added two more units.

I understood why my brother had loved it out there—it really did feel like country living, even with all the new developments popping up around us. We ended up staying almost eight years, but the long commute—twenty-five miles each way—started to wear us down. And after the girls moved out, we found ourselves wondering what was keeping us there anymore.

The truth was, despite everything we did to the house, I had never fully claimed it as my own. I still referred to it as "my brother's house," and deep down, I knew it would never be mine. One night, lying in bed, I realized it was time to move on. I suggested it to Steven, and he agreed without hesitation.

By then, we had been married almost ten years. Steven had proved his unconditional love over and over again—supporting me, respecting my opinions, and never once criticizing me, no matter how impulsive I could be.

We put both of the houses up for sale and started looking for something back in Long Beach. I fell in love with a Cape Cod house in Park Estates, an affluent neighborhood in Long Beach, known for its peace, spacious homes, and well-rated public schools. Although it only had two bedrooms and a one-car garage, it was so charming, we bought it. Six months later, our youngest, Tara, chose our backyard for her wedding reception.

Steven never mentioned his ex-wife without anger. It was like a switch flipped the moment her name came up. That was the only time I ever saw a darker side of my otherwise gentle husband. Even after all those years, the sting of what she had done to him hadn't faded.

"I hate that she's coming out," he admitted when we talked about the wedding.

I hesitated telling him I understood, for not only did I not want to add any fuel to the fire, I hated the thought too. For years she'd intruded into our lives, even from miles away, and now we were expected to welcome her into our home—and I would have to pretend it was okay.

"It'll only be one day," I said, hoping to calm both of us down.

The day before the wedding, Tara picked her up at the airport and, thankfully, she avoided bringing her to the house, knowing how her father felt. On the night of the rehearsal dinner, his ex-wife made a point of talking to everyone, telling them how wonderful her new life was, and she made sure they knew how well her new husband was doing.

She smiled as she spoke, but I saw how her eyes told a different story. The first glass of wine had softened her, the second blurred the edges, and by the third, something inside her seemed to give way. She started talking too much—about nothing and everything—her words slightly slurred. She laughed at the wrong moments, and then fell quiet just as quickly, her gaze drifting somewhere far away.

She wasn't loud or dramatic—just acting like people do when they begin to unravel. Thankfully, we had a reprieve when dinner was served, and by the end of the evening, it was almost as if she had gone into her shell as a tortoise would.

I could hardly wait until the evening was over.

It was a beautiful summer day for the wedding, and Steven and I greeted people as they filled the church. I knew the protocol—the mother walked down the aisle before the stepmother, and I accepted it as the tradition and the expected order of things. I understood it, and prepared myself for it, and at the rehearsal in the empty church, it didn't hit me. But once the pews were full, and I saw everyone turn to look at Steven's ex-wife walking down the aisle before me, I didn't expect it to hit me as hard as it did. It didn't matter that she was supposed to be there—after all, she was the girls' mother, but she was Steven's ex-wife.

She basked in the honor, and something in me crumpled. It was as if the years I'd spent loving the girls and keeping our family together didn't matter.

At the reception, I was busy, and Steven mingled with our friends. I reminded myself the day was for the bride and groom, and I realized our friends didn't care to take sides. I watched as she lingered near the edge of the crowd, smiling too hard, while most guests simply nodded and moved on. Hardly anyone stopped to chat with her. And to my own surprise, my bitterness gave way to something softer. I actually felt sorry for her.

Not long after, fate stepped in again. A neighbor across the street from my old Long Beach neighborhood called to tell me her daughter was selling her Georgian Colonial—the very house I'd admired at twenty-one, certain it was forever out of reach. I told Steven I had to see it. He thought I was crazy, but we made an appointment to see it anyway. The moment we pulled up, I knew I was in love.

Built in the late 1930s, it was a wonderful older Georgian Colonial home on a mature tree-lined street, its wood and stucco painted off-white with black shutters. While the interior needed updating, it was even more enchanting than when I'd seen it so many years before.

We bought it, even though it meant moving again after only eighteen months. We were short a few thousand dollars for the down payment, but my neighbor offered to loan us the money. It was an opportunity we couldn't pass up. It was 1988, the height of the real estate boom—we sold high and bought high. We camped out in the small guesthouse above the garage while we refinished the floors and painted inside.

This was it—our forever home.

Our first daughter, Holly, loved it too. She chose to have her wedding in the backyard a few years later. I had lost twenty pounds by then, but still felt self-conscious about finding a dress I liked. But when I was dressing for the day, Steven he looked at me with such honest affection and said, "You look beautiful."

I believed him, and that was all the affirmation I needed.

His ex-wife returned for the wedding, recently divorced and looking like an entirely different person than the last time we'd seen her. Her once-beautiful hair was dyed stark black, her makeup was heavy, and her dress clung too tightly, as if trying to hold on to something already gone. I thought I'd be able to handle having her in my home differently than I had before, but I caught myself judging her—this was not her day, and I felt strangely protective of it.

The same feelings of resentment filled me, and I hated the thought of her having the freedom of our house. I couldn't help but think about how much she'd hurt Steven, and when she sat next to my mother-in-law, I wanted to scratch her eyes out. But I could tell Steven's mother was only trying to be polite as they spoke.

The issue of being second down the aisle was solved when only the groom and his best man made their way down the brick walkway to the ivy-covered gazebo in the backyard and turned to wait. No one escorted either "mom." Steven walked Holly down the aisle, moving in step to the soft music of the live band, and I tried to blink away the tears when I also turned to see the guests rising. Once Steven handed Holly over to her future husband, I saw him wipe his own eyes as he came back to sit by me.

After the ceremony, the minute the band started playing, the bride and groom danced the first dance. Steven and my father made sure everyone had their dance, except for Steven's ex-wife. She remained seated at her table, holding her empty wine glass up for someone to fill it. Again, wedding guests passed by without stopping, their conversations drifting elsewhere. No one approached her, and most didn't even know who she was. No one asked her to dance, and she sat alone, watching the celebration from the sidelines, like someone who'd arrived too late for a life she no longer belonged to.

As I watched her, the bitterness I'd been carrying again quietly slipped away. For the first time, I saw her not as the woman from Steven's past, but as someone completely alone in a world that had moved on without her. And in that moment, I didn't feel anger and resentment anymore—just a quiet kind of compassion.

Steven, ever perceptive, squeezed my hand and said quietly, "She'll be gone soon, and then we can go back to normal."

And in that moment, I felt a wave of gratitude wash over me—for the life we had built together, for the man who stood beside me, and for the home that truly felt like mine.

CHAPTER FORTY TWO

VASO
MEMORIES OF MY PARENTS

My father's dream had always been to live by the water. After selling the house on Magnolia Avenue where I was raised, my parents moved into an apartment building they purchased right on the ocean, overlooking the Queen Mary. They combined two back units facing the beach and converted them into a penthouse. It became their home until they retired and began scaling back their investments. That's when they bought property on the Peninsula to build a new house.

The lot was right on the sand, facing the bay. Because of the small lot sizes, construction focused on size and height. They hired a well-known Long Beach architect to design the home. Since construction called for steel beams set into the sand, they hired an experienced building contractor to manage the project. Watching the house take shape was exciting, and my mother documented the entire process with photos.

Three months in—just after the foundation had been poured—my father suffered a heart attack and underwent quadruple bypass surgery. In his sixties, he seemed too young, and I still carried the illusion that my parents were invincible. My mother, as always during a crisis, reassured me that everything would be fine and pressed on with the building project.

I helped where I could, joining her to select plumbing fixtures, countertops, cabinetry, limestone flooring, and carpeting. I also sat in when she met with the designer to choose furniture styles and fabrics.

"Yippee," my mother joked. "I can finally get rid of my early Sears furniture."

We laughed about keeping the true costs of it all a secret from my father, and even though some choices stretched her comfort zone, she was determined to get exactly what she wanted.

As construction neared completion, I helped my mother sort through their belongings, pack what she wanted to bring, and arrange for movers. I helped her plan the furniture layout at the new house with the designer, and when the move-in date finally came, her housekeeper assisted with unpacking boxes.

"I can always move things around if it doesn't work once we're settled," she said.

The house was stunning—a contemporary, three-story, six thousand square foot masterpiece. People walking by often mistook it for an apartment building. On the ground floor, there was a four-car garage and a two-bedroom apartment built for Yia´ Yia if she ever needed it. The second floor had an en suite bedroom, a large atrium, the living and dining rooms, a powder room, and a galley kitchen complete with two refrigerators, a bar area, a warming drawer, and two ovens. The pantry alone was about ten by twelve feet. The third floor was home to the master bedroom suite, complete with two bathrooms (one for each of my parents), a massive dressing room and closet, and another en suite bedroom.

A spiral staircase led up to a rooftop deck, a favorite spot for the grandchildren, and there was an elevator for easy access to every floor.

Except for one piece of art, my father left all the decorating to my mother and the designer. One day he brought me a torn magazine page showing a limited-edition pastel orchid by a Hawaiian artist.

"Can you get this for me?" he asked.

"Did you get approval?" I teased.

"I don't need it. I'm paying the bills," he said, smiling.

"I'll take care of it," I promised.

I ordered the print and had it framed. I made him wait until the house was finished before revealing it, and we hung it in the stairwell leading up from the entryway where it remained until they eventually moved.

By the time the house was complete, my father had recovered well. I helped my mother host a housewarming party that all their friends attended. True to form, she avoided the spotlight by constantly bustling between the buffet and the kitchen, while my father, who basked in the attention, proudly showed off the new house.

"I told the decorator to hold her down to what she wanted," he joked.

Later, as we cleaned up, he stood gazing across the bay.

"Look at that view. I'll never get tired of those lights," he said. "I wasn't sure I'd live to see this. I've come a long way since being a peanut vendor."

"Yes, you have," my mother said, giving him a hug. "And, more importantly, you're still here with us."

"I couldn't have done it without you," he said, giving her a kiss.

"You're right about that," I added.

No one mentioned the glaring fact that my brother hadn't bothered to come for my father's surgery or to celebrate the new house.

Later, Stavros married his fourth wife at the beach house, as we called it.

I overheard my father say to my mother, "I can't believe he's doing it again with that track record of his."

"Be nice," my mother scolded gently. She always looked for the good in people. "If this is what he wants, then he should do it."

My father just shook his head.

It was a small, intimate wedding officiated again by one of Stavros' judge friends. His new wife, Jane, was a sweet woman about my age—a law clerk for the very judge who married them. Jane was very different from Stavros' previous wives. She was a Southern woman—conservative and well-dressed, with minimal makeup, slender like the others, but exceptionally polite and genuine. Despite their twenty-year age difference, and being totally opposite in appearance, we all agreed she was his best match yet, and secretly we gave this marriage the highest chance of lasting.

My parents spent some good years in that house, and I knew how much they loved it. Steven and I spent at least one night a week with them, having dinner, and then watching my father's favorite television programs upstairs in their TV room just off the master bedroom. They had this enormous house and yet felt most comfortable in the room where my mother sewed, and my father read the paper. It had a kitchenette with a full-sized refrigerator, a microwave and toaster oven, and if we didn't come over, that's where they had their meals.

For my father's seventieth birthday, I created a video to celebrate his life. It took months of work just to organize everything before handing it over to a videographer. I started by researching major events that took place during his lifetime, finding images to accompany my narration. Then I sifted through boxes of family photos, arranging them both chronologically and by theme.

The video began with a look back at the turning points that shaped the last seventy years. . .the medical advances, space travel and revisiting the past. . .and then showing my father as a young boy in Greece. I carefully selected music to match each section: Bette Midler's "Boogie Woogie Bugle Boy" for his years in the service, "Do You Want to Dance" for the dancing photos, and Nat King Cole's "Unforgettable" for moments with my mother. Crosby, Stills & Nash's "Our House" accompanied the images of their homes, and Bette Midler's "You've Got to Have Friends" played over photos of him with his friends. For pictures of me growing up, I chose "The Wind Beneath My Wings," also by Bette Midler. I included photos of Alex and me as children, and then moved into images of the grandchildren, each of us sharing messages of love for him.

The tribute ended with Frank Sinatra's "My Way."

In my heart, I knew it was the best gift I could ever have given him. I'll never forget the moment we sat together in their living room, watching it on their big television. By the time it ended, I was sobbing. But he knew—he truly knew—how deeply I loved him.

Alex wasn't there that day either, so I sent him his own copy of the video. And as I sit and write this now, I realize I can't even remember which song I had chosen for his life.

CHAPTER FORTY THREE

VASO

"Are you sure you're as old as you say you are?" I teased my grandmother one Saturday afternoon during a visit. It was before Cynthia had moved up to Long Beach, and my mother was taking a break from sorting bills to chat with her on the phone.

"Well, I think I am," my grandmother said with a playful wink. "You know, back when I was young, my age changed depending on what my parents needed it to be—so now, I figure I can be whatever age I want."

She was in her early nineties by then, and still as sharp and quick-witted as ever.

After talking with Cynthia, she'd make coffee for her and my mother. Before we left, I lit the Livani (lee-von-ē) a fragrant incense blend of frankincense, myrrh, balsam spice, patchouli, and sandalwood. In the Greek Orthodox religious tradition, it's used in sacred rituals and symbolizes a connection to the divine. Outside the church, it's also believed to purify spaces and ward off negative energies. I'd gently wave the smoke over to grandmother, my mother, and myself, cleansing each of us, and then I'd carry it from room to room. At some point, I had decided that that was my new role now: the keeper of the Livani offering.

On this one visit, I remember my mother talking to Yia´ Yia about cemetery plots. She'd just purchased one for her and my father, and one for Yia´ Yia herself. She was considering moving my grandfather and her brother Michael from the cemetery in Inglewood to one closer to home in Long Beach. Some people might have found it strange to relocate the dead, but I thought it was a wonderful idea. The old cemetery was too far away, had fallen into disrepair, and no one really went there anymore. In fact, I couldn't recall ever having visited it myself.

Maybe I was on the same "death wavelength" as my mother, because it got me thinking about the end of my own life—and where I wanted to be buried. I'd never seriously considered burying my parents; I think part of me still believed they'd always be there. But the more I thought about it, the more melancholy I became, haunted by the idea of someday being without them.

Steven caught me that night flipping through a cemetery brochure. He looked at me, puzzled. I explained what my mother was doing and admitted that I'd been thinking about us, too.

"Do you ever think about dying?" I asked.

Familiar with my odd questions, he simply raised an eyebrow before answering.

"I try not to," he said, "but I know it's inevitable. What's on your mind?"

"I think I'd like to be buried next to my parents."

"Well. . . I don't have a problem with that," he said thoughtfully, then grinned. "As long as I can go with you."

"Perfect. I'll tell my mother," I said, setting the brochure aside.

One of the things I loved most about Steven was that he never made me feel silly for the things that mattered to me. He always supported me, often in ways I wondered if he even realized.

"You're going to think I'm crazy," I said to my mother the next day, "but all this talk about moving everyone has got me thinking . . . and I'd really like to be buried next to you and Dad. Is that silly?"

"Of course not," she said immediately. "I think it's wonderful. Your father would too. Do you want me to take care of it?"

"Are you sure?"

"Yes, I'll talk to the woman helping me and handle it tomorrow."

There was a beat of silence before I added, "Mother?"

"Yes?"

"I'm sorry for all the dumb stuff I did when I was younger."

She sighed. "My god, Vaso, you've been apologizing for almost thirty years. Stop already."

"I just want you to know how much I love you and Dad."

"We know, honey. Stop thinking about it."

True to her word, my mother called the next day to say everything was arranged. She had purchased a plot for Steven and me across the walk from theirs.

"It's my gift to you," she said seriously. "And it's not silly at all. I want to be near my parents, and I think it's wonderful you'll be near us too."

The next time I saw my father, I joked, "You'll never be able to get rid of me now."

He just rolled his eyes, but I knew in his heart I was still his little girl.

When Cynthia died, she was cremated, but she'd asked to be buried with our family. She hadn't wanted any fuss after her passing, but Yia´Yia insisted on a church service, and my mother took care of everything. Since none of us hadn't attended church in years, my parents made a generous donation—not just for her service, but to atone for the years we'd all been away.

At the church, we lit candles and made the Stavro—the sign of the cross—as we entered. Few people came: my cousin Kaylee with her daughter and granddaughter, Eddie Jr. with five of his eight children, Uncle Stavros and Jane, my parents, Steven, and me.

Alex was a no-show. He was in the middle of hunting season, and his walk-in refrigerator was packed with carcasses.

After the service, my father drove Yia´ Yia to the beach house where Steven and I were finishing up setting out the buffet. Kaylee, now very heavy, wore a black, flowing caftan and was visibly perspiring. She had recently come out to the family as being a Wiccan, and four of her friends—also dressed in black, wearing amulets, rings, and bracelets— had already gathered at the house.

Kaylee set up a small altar with a photo of Cynthia, surrounded by crystals, charms, and a smudge stick, much like the Livani I would later use. She and her friends took their positions: Earth to the North (holding a rock), Air to the East (holding a feather), Fire to the South (holding a candle), and Water to the West (holding a cup). They quietly called upon the powers of the four directions to watch over Cynthia.

It was a pleasant ceremony, but strange. Stavros was the only one who made it obvious he didn't appreciate the service, but once everyone was seated for the meal, he lifted his glass.

"To Cynthia," he said.

"To Cynthia," we echoed.

"And to those who are no longer with us—or who couldn't be here today," he added.

I meant to look up Wicca later when I got home, but I never did.

CHAPTER FORTY FOUR

KATE

Before her burial, I set Cynthia's urn on my coffee table, where every time I passed it, it called up little things that made me think of her.

She had always been strong-willed, even as a child. Once she figured out how to pick up a fork or spoon, she didn't want anyone to help her eat. She potty trained herself early after seeing Michael and me use the toilet. I remember my mother thanking heaven for the reprieve of washing out dirty diapers.

Thankfully, she grew out of having tantrums and stomping her feet if something didn't go her way, but she always had a presence about her, almost like royalty, that made people do as she wished.

She adapted to her new unglamorous life on a small farm, but she always dressed like Lana Turner or Jayne Mansfield, with tight pants and sweaters that accentuated her statuesque figure. Until she died, she certainly commanded attention.

I remembered when we were very young, and a man with a pony came to our neighborhood to see if any of the children wanted their photos taken. Of course, Cynthia did. She pushed Stavros off the horse so she could go first. She ignored his crying and climbed up onto the stool to mount the pony. My mother grabbed her by the arm and pulled her down. She tried to sit Stavros back into the saddle, but his ear-piercing cries made the man put his hands up to his ears.

"If you don't stop this, I'll move on," he said brusquely.

She hated to lose at anything and if things didn't go her way while playing a game of marbles, she'd stomp the dirt messing up the game, or she'd wipe out the lines for hopscotch if she didn't throw the chain in the right square.

Cynthia was an average student, more interested in boys than in studies. She'd sneak out at night and make me promise to tell no one. But she also had a great sense of humor and would tell me something dumb she'd done and laugh at herself. However, she would never admit *anything* if she were caught doing something she wasn't supposed to be doing. And any criticism of her was not accepted, regardless if it was accurate or helpful. Her standard reply was, "Whatever you say, Kate." Then she'd walk away.

Once she moved away, she would never have taken what she referred to as 'charity' from me, but she was delighted when I sent her a care package, often filled with non-essentials like a book, nail polish or her favorite lipstick.

She was there for me when we needed to do something to get Alex to turn his anger around; I told her I feared he knew about being adopted. She and Eddie just took him in, and they straightened him out. I could never repay her for that.

I couldn't make her do anything she didn't want to do, so I had to be satisfied that I'd at least done my best to be a good sister to her. I loved her, and she knew it.

Although we didn't see each other a lot as adults, we always spoke, and she was forever in my heart. I was going to miss her. I could tell her death greatly affected my mother as well. It was almost as if a light went out in her, and she lost her zest for life. Mother had always thought of Cynthia as the child who needed her the most, and now that child was gone.

Kaylee told me she'd go through the few boxes of family photos and the old Johnny Mathis albums. She told me she'd sort through the pictures and the next time she saw her brother Eddie, she'd give him a box. I saw her wearing her parents' wedding rings on a chain the day of the service, and I was glad she'd kept them.

CHAPTER FORTY FIVE

YIA´ YIA/EFFIMIA

I sat stiffly in the pew, my hands folded over a handkerchief I hadn't used yet, but I knew I would. I still marveled at the new church, although it had been years since the day the doors opened. I'd purposely stayed away during construction, not wanting to give any misunderstanding that I approved of any part of it.

My husband, Petros, and I had been godparents of the old church—a title that once carried weight, which surely had to mean something to someone. But here, in this new place, I was just one of the few remaining faithful, and suddenly I felt small. As if the old ways no longer had a home. As if all that we gave, all we sacrificed to help build that church, had already been quietly forgotten. I'd dressed in my hand-knitted dress, with my mink stole resting gently across my shoulders. Petros bought it for me for our fifth anniversary, when he still went to our building in downtown Los Angeles, and I knew today would be the last time I would wear it.

I forced myself to concentrate on Cynthia's service, but my mind continued to drift—despite their best efforts, the last few priests hadn't been able to restore what had been lost.

Once the liturgy was over, Kate helped me from the church, and other than our family, only two old women who used to help me cook came out.

"Sillipitiria" (sill-i-pi-tir´ ia) they said. Condolences.

We went first to the cemetery and watched as the men put Cynthia's urn on top of Michael's grave. I thought for sure it would topple over as they started shoveling the dirt in, but it didn't. I did my Stavro, and then Stavros, ever the man who wanted to be in control spoke.

"I wasn't sure I should say anything, but she was my sister. That's not something you just ignore. Growing up, we didn't always see eye to eye, but she filled a room and she'll leave a space behind that no one else quite fits into. I hope she's finally found peace. That's all I've got."

Nick drove us in silence to their house on the beach. Kaylee had warned me she was going to set up something for her mother, and I just knew it was going to be against everything I believed in. But I couldn't stop her.

At the house, I sat at the round table in the corner and just watched as people talked to one another, and suddenly I was exhausted, a kind of tiredness that even sleep couldn't fix.

"Do you want to stay here tonight?" Kate asked, breaking my train of thought.

"No, I'd like to be at home. But thank you, my dear." I said.

Once everyone left, Kate drove me home and helped me undress. I could tell she was reluctant to leave me alone, but she respected my wish to be by myself. Without Cynthia sitting at the dining room table, the house seemed empty. And even though I heard every sound the house made that night, I managed to eventually fall asleep.

The next morning, I woke up to the sun. I dressed in my housecoat and made myself a cup of Greek coffee. I sat at the dining room table, next to where Cynthia would have sat if she was still here. I hadn't emptied her last ashtray, and it smelled terrible, but I couldn't bring myself to do it yet.

Most days, that's all I did. Kate brought over food, and every day she sat there until I ate something, but my life as I'd known it was over, and I was waiting for the courage to tell her.

I had plenty of time to think, with no one but me in the house. I tried to watch my soaps, but I found it hard to concentrate or to remember who was who. They reminded me a little of my family, although maybe not so dramatic. I was happy for my children; I had suffered with them and, hopefully, I had rejoiced with them, too. I accepted both the decisions and choices they made; after all, I knew there was nothing I could do. I felt their joy at adding a new child, and their disappointment at the loss of a mate, whether by death or divorce.

I hope I was always there for them either way.

I couldn't stop the passage of time, of everyone living in the present, when the parents no longer spoke Greek if they didn't want their children to know something. Stavros and Cynthia hadn't even married Greeks. And now the grandchildren didn't learn Greek—unless you counted the bad words.

I've come to accept that all our customs will die with me.

Lately, I've been missing my husband, Petros, or Peter—his American name. I was determined to marry someone I loved, and he was certainly that person. We worked side by side, unlike most traditional Greek families; usually it was the husband who worked, and the wife who took care of the household. While Petros believed that we should share the responsibilities, I ended up with the children. I was better with them than he was.

I never *did* see my childhood friend, Thalia, again. We wrote for many years, but eventually we both lost track of time and each other. She ended up marrying the man her parents chose for her, and I often wondered if she'd eventually found the love she was so desperately seeking.

I would have told her, even though my parents were gone, I also eventually marrying the man my parents thought of when we were back in Greece. His name was Yanni, and it was a terrible mistake. I ended up telling him to leave—there was no way I was going to live the rest of my life unhappy.

I've lived a full life and have carried the burdens God gave me. Apparently, he thought I could handle them.

And now I was tired.

I waited almost six months, and then I told Kate it was time for me to go home.

CHAPTER FORTY SIX

VASO

Cynthia's death had drained my grandmother of her life. I was still visiting her weekly, and it was shocking to see how quickly she'd gone downhill. For her age, she had very few wrinkles, but her face, which was once healthy and pink, had turned gaunt, and her cheeks seemed to sink more with each passing week. Her eyes, which were once keen, were now emotionless.

I could see death settling into her, but I clung to the hope she would stay with us a while longer. Then one day, she simply took to her bed—and that was it. My mother and I took turns sitting with her, and even if it sounded morbid, I wanted to be there when she passed. I wanted to witness her spirit leave her body.

She drifted in and out of consciousness for several days, and at one point, she asked for the priest, who came to administer her last rites. Speaking to him in Greek, she told him she had seen her father, her mother, and her husband. She spoke of the children she had lost, too, their faces appearing to her as she slipped between worlds.

Kaylee was there toward the end. One afternoon, as Yia´ Yia drifted off, Kaylee gently touched her feet to let her know she was nearby. Yia´ Yia startled awake, lifted her head slightly, and muttered sharply, *"You always were a troublemaker!"*

The words caught us both off guard. We froze, unsure what to say or do, until my grandmother's head sank back onto her pillow and she let out a long sigh. I noticed the tears filling Kaylee's eyes.

"I just wanted to tell her I loved her," she whispered, beginning to cry in earnest.

"She didn't mean it," I said gently, trying to comfort her.

I knew better than to touch my grandmother now. If she was ready to go, she needed to be free to leave without us clinging to her.

I stepped away briefly to call my mother. From the way Yia´ Yia's breathing had changed, I knew the end was near, and I wanted my mother to be there. When I returned to the room, the floor creaked under the carpet as I moved toward her bed. I worried the sound would wake her, but it was too late. Her skin had taken on a sickly gray hue, and I knew she was gone.

Kaylee came back into the room, her eyes red and swollen, and by the look on my face, she understood. She hesitated at the doorway, too afraid to come closer.

"I know you'll always remember what she said," I told her, "but it's over now. When your mother was so sick, I didn't know it at the time, and she was so grumpy. The last thing I said to her was cruel because I thought she was just being difficult. I've had to live with that. But you didn't hurt Yia´ Yia. Touch her now," I urged. "She won't snap at you this time."

Kaylee looked at me uncertainly, and then somehow we both started giggling—half from grief, half from hysteria—until we couldn't stop, much like we'd done as children.

When we finally calmed down, I reached for Yia´ Yia's hand. It was cold. I knew she was in a better place, but the loss hit me deeper than tears, and I stood there in silence, wrestling with the guilt that I had left her for just a few minutes. I was angry at myself—for missing the moment I had so desperately wanted to witness—I'd hoped to see her spirit lift free, to glimpse the aura people often spoke of with death. It was selfish, but it was the truth.

And in that moment, I realized: I never wanted to be there when my parents died.

My mother arrived not long after.

Still trembling, I called the mortuary.

CHAPTER FORTY SEVEN

STAVROS

I was drowning in mounds of depositions when Kate called about Mother. We'd all been anticipating this moment, so it wasn't as though I hadn't expected it. I just didn't need it to happen right at this moment.

I recalled the time when my father died. He was at home too, and his casket sat on a tall stand in the living room until it was time to take him to the church. I was in my early teens, but I had never seen a dead body before. I knew I was being irrational, but even as a young man, when I looked at his face, I felt as if he could still see me. I had been quietly defiant for years, and just like I felt with my brother Michael's photo in my parents' room, whenever I had to pass through the living room, I would hurry past, afraid my father might somehow wake up and scold me.

Kate said Vaso called the mortuary—I knew they'd take care of it all, and I was grateful I wasn't going to have to be involved with all that.

In my file cabinet, I found the folder with Mother's name on it; inside was all the pertinent information I'd need to take care of the death certificates and settle the estate. There was the house where she now lay, and some investments. The property in Los Angeles, which was initially worth an incredible amount, was now worth almost nothing, and we'd sold it several years back. Kate had all of that paperwork, and I wouldn't need it.

I dialed my secretary and let her know I'd be leaving the office. I just needed to make some quick notes, so I'd be able to pick up where I left off. As I left, I asked her to let my client know there'd been a family emergency, and I'd need a day or so to get back with him.

"And will you call Jane and let her know?" I asked.

I was accustomed to attending funerals where there was standing room only, and at first, I was surprised that there weren't a lot of mourners that day; only the family and a few old women dressed in black. But then, when I thought about it, most of my mother's philos, or friends, were already gone. And then I recalled it had been the same when Cynthia died. Even in death, my family didn't draw large crowds.

As we left church, I spotted my ex-wife Kelli out of the corner of my eye. Dressed appropriately in a black dress, she wore her grief well. Instinctively, my jaw tightened, and Jane touched my hand, reminding me to unclench my fist. When Kate saw her, I could tell she was happy to see Kelli, and although she had every right to be here, my stomach soured.

This was a day for the family, and not for her. I harrumphed in annoyance as I passed her by.

I thought it was rather peculiar when Kate made arrangements for my father and brother to be moved to the cemetery near us, but now that Mother was gone, it made perfect sense for her to be buried with him.

At the gravesite, the new priest performed another ceremony, and eventually the casket was lowered into the ground. Kate said she'd take care of adding her name to the gravestone later.

We agreed to rent out the house on Loma and keep her cash in investments. Nick's brother George still lived in the back house with his third wife, Tommie, and even I didn't feel it was necessary to uproot him—plus the rents could be split quarterly and the property would appreciate until then. (When he died two years later, we sold the house, and my plan was to divide everything between Kate and me. That wasn't *her* plan, however, as she felt Cynthia's children should receive *something* from the estate.)

Neither Kaylee nor Eddie Jr. had much to speak of, so I finally agreed, and we split everything three ways.

I could have used the money.

CHAPTER FORTY EIGHT

ALEX

I'd been out on a 'kill' job when my mother called about Yia´ Yia. She'd left two messages. The first one was cryptic and not specific, and in the second one she told me Yia´ Yia had passed away. I always hated the phrase 'passed away.' People *died*.

I wasn't really surprised. Yia´ Yia was what? In her mid-nineties? I hadn't made it down to Cynthia's or Eddie's services, but I knew they'd forgiven me. She and Uncle Eddie knew me better than most people, and it wasn't the ceremony that counted; it was the thoughts inside that made the difference.

I'd have to figure out how to get down there for Yia Yia's service, though. Shit, I hated it down there.

When I actually talked with my mom, she said she'd have to call me back with the date of the service so I could make arrangements to take the time off.

"Yeah, I'll have someone come take care of the animals for me. Thankfully, I don't have anything hanging in the walk-in."

"Of course," she said. I recognized that tone of voice, and I knew she wasn't happy with me. But what was I supposed to do?

"And Alex? Please wear something nice."

Eff, if I would. I'd wear what I always wore, and Yia´ Yia wouldn't care.

I brought down clean overalls and one of my newer hats. Besides the family, there were very few other people in the church; mostly it was old women. The service took forever because it was in Greek and English. When it finally ended, we went to the cemetery, then back to my parent's house on the bay for lunch. Because the house was down by the beach, parking was a bitch, so I rode with my parents. The Greek ladies didn't come to the house, which was fine by me. I'd worn my new desert boots, but I had a bunion on my left little toe, and my feet were killing me. The first thing I did was sneak into the bedroom and change into my comfortable work boots. No one said anything, and I didn't really care if anyone did.

My cousin Kaylee and some friends set up some sort of voodoo table, which was annoying. I'd heard she'd done the same when her mother died. Personally, I didn't care what she believed in, but I didn't think she should bring that stuff to Yia´ Yia's funeral service. Whatever. No one else seemed to care.

Stavros and his third or fourth wife, Jane, were there. I couldn't keep track of them all. She was helping to get the food out. My sister Vaso did her Livani stuff, and she acted like she was in charge of the kitchen when she started gathering empty plates and bringing them in to rinse and put in the dishwasher.

Then, Uncle Stavros clinked his glass to get everyone's attention, and raised it to make a toast.

"To Mother," he said. "And to those who are no longer with us, or couldn't be here."

"To Yia´ Yia."

"To Mother."

I had a lot to do at the ranch, so I left the next day.

CHAPTER FORTY NINE

KATE

Even when you expect someone to die, it's different when they're actually gone. That's the way it was with my mother. I'd prepared myself for the inevitable, but it still surprised me how I felt about the emptiness of not having her there.

I no longer had to call her every night to make sure she was okay. And it took me a while to adjust to that. I remembered giving Stavros a pillow once that said, "Call Your Mother" because he rarely did. His wives did it for him. What was he going to do with it now?

"Let me get that," Jane said to me as we were setting out the food. We had platters of roast beef and turkey, shrimp cocktail, chips and dips and several plates of cookies. One of Stavros' daughters made spanako-pita (spa-knee-co´-pee-ta), which is spinach and feta cheese layered in filo dough. My mother had taught her how to make it, and it was deli-cious, but very time-consuming. Vaso and Jane placed all these on the buffet table surrounded by Mother's favorite flowers: white gardenias.

We'd asked for no flowers, but friends who didn't attend Mother's service at the church had sent four large arrangements that now gave off an almost overpowering fragrance in the living room.

Stavros had expressed his dismay that Kaylee had set up her altar again, but I told him to leave her alone; it was her way of honoring Mother.

My mother had come to America, like so many other immigrants, to find a better way of life. She was independent, and I knew where Cynthia got that trait. Instead of marrying the old man her parents wanted her to, she went to Chicago with her cousin and then to Los Angeles, where she met my father. I could only imagine them as they were in the old photos I'd set out for her memorial. One was her by herself, with her long hair parted down the center and pulled back into a bun. She had on a white blouse with a large collar, and she was standing next to a basket of flowers sitting on a pedestal. Her black skirt hit her ankles, and she was wearing fancy closed black shoes.

In the second photo, she and my father both wore long black coats, hats and mittens. They must have been somewhere other than California, for our weather here never got cold enough to dress that way. My father was very handsome, and Mother had her hair pulled back as usual, but she was wearing a flower tucked behind her left ear. Her dark hat, with its wide brim, partially covered it.

My mother was not an especially complicated woman; she did her best to care for her family, and somehow she endured the loss of her husband and six of her children. I believed her death was the only way she could accept losing Cynthia.

I'm not sure why I thought of it now, or when I learned my father had syphilis. He'd contracted it in WWI; he'd been treated for it, but I always wondered if that was one reason so many of his children died. My mother suffered no symptoms to my knowledge, but I later learned the bacteria could be passed from mother to child during fetal development. If my parents would have known, I'm certain they would have never tried to have more children. It wasn't something I felt comfortable discussing with anyone, even my doctors, but I knew some complications from syphilis were its effect on the brain, heart, blood vessels and liver. That was just to name a few. His official cause of death had been listed as a heart attack.

My father died at the age of fifty-two, which was around the same time Nick lost his father. We'd just finished dinner with my parents, and he said he was tired and was going to lie down on the sofa. He closed his eyes and never woke up.

My mother was only in her mid-fifties. By today's standards, she still had a second life she could have lived if she'd chosen to. Most of her widowed friends never remarried, but I always wondered if it was because they never loved their husbands and felt another loveless marriage would be just an extension of the first. If their marriages had been arranged, possibly the thought of true love never entered their minds. But my mother *had* married someone she loved, so she might have thought there was no way anyone could have taken my father's place.

She never talked about it.

Whenever I felt a need to go to her about something, she was always very philosophical. I'm sure that's where I got that trait. She'd always have a different way of looking at something, and rarely did I feel she judged me. I knew she did what she had to, to keep her family intact, and I never resented her for choosing Stavros over me for an education.

When we built Nick's dream house down on the bay, we included enough room in the plans for a ground-level two-bedroom apartment where she could stay if she ever needed to move from the house on Loma. Thankfully for her, she never did, and when she died, I couldn't help but think she'd gone the way most of us would prefer—quietly and at home. When she died, she had six grandchildren, sixteen great-grandchildren, and one great-great-grandchild.

We buried her where my father was now buried, and next to where Cynthia and my brother Michael were. Nick and I would be buried next to her, and Vaso and Steven would end up across the narrow sidewalk. In death, we'd all be together.

That is, with the exception of Alex. He'd probably want to be cremated and scattered somewhere in the mountains.

CHAPTER FIFTY

VASO

I always thought I had time to ask Yia´ Yia more about her life, but I never did. Over the years since her death, I've wished I'd asked her more. Sometimes on our Saturday afternoon visits, she'd feed me little tidbits.

As she grew older, she started wearing a housecoat during the day. Years before, she'd broken her wrist after tripping on the steps of her front porch, and for some reason, the bone never healed properly, making the housecoat easier to slip in and out of. But she always dressed for the occasion if she was going out, and never wore the traditional black widow's attire.

She never swore, and she always looked for the best in everyone. When she and my grandfather came to America with the rest of the Greek immigrants, they were proud to learn English and to become citizens. It was what one did in those days. You became an American, and you didn't expect America to become you.

After going through her photographs, I saw one of the man she married some years after Papou died. His name was John. He was a creepy little man, and I could never understand why she did that, except my mother told me he was the man her parents had wanted her to marry so many years ago. I could tell by my mother's 'fake smile' that she didn't care for him, either.

"Let's pay him off and get rid of him," I'd overhead Stavros say to my mother one day.

Yia´ Yia divorced him about a year after she married him, and we were all glad to see him out of her life.

Before Yia´ Yia died, she'd shown me a small shell collection she'd kept since she was a young girl. It was with her jewelry, and she told me when she was very young, her family had gone to the coast and she collected shells and rocks to bring back home. When she and her parents came to America, she obviously couldn't bring everything with her, so she gave her rock collection to her friend, Thalia. But she'd hidden these few shell pieces in her suitcase and had kept them in a safe place for over eighty years.

When she died, I asked my mother if I could have them, and I now keep them in my own jewelry box, in a silk jewelry bag, along with the large gold tree of life charm my mother had made for her years ago.

Whenever there was a lull in the conversation, Yia´ Yia would say, "Afta eneh," which loosely translated into something like "and so. . ." And half the time when she called me by name, she would get Kaylee's name mixed up with mine and call me "Ka-Vaso."

While she was still driving, my grandmother would take her church ladies to services every Sunday until, one by one, the group dwindled down to only a few of them. In the early 1990s, the construction of a larger, more impressive church in East Long Beach led to the sale of the old Greek Church where Steven and I were married.

As a family, we made it a point to bring my grandmother to the annual Labor Day Greek Festival every September, and it was usually the hottest weekend of the year. For years, she'd make sheets of cookies to donate to the bake sale, and then, when she turned ninety, she said, "I'm done. I've done enough." And she quit. "Let the younger ones do it now."

My parents, Steven, and I would pick her up, and as we passed the men grilling the chicken and souvlaki, she'd say, "I remember Papou doing this many years ago."

When we watched the young Greek dancers, she'd tap her feet and ask me, "Do you remember when you danced?"

I had. Around the age of ten, I joined the Greek folk dancers at our church. Since I hadn't developed a figure yet and they were always short on boys, I made the perfect stand-in for a young Evzone. My hair was still cut short in those days, which only helped me pass as one of the boys. I was a pretty good dancer, too. I could jump and twirl and still keep in step with the dance, but when I started showing my girlish figure, there were no female dance positions available, so I had to stop dancing.

Usually after we had already eaten, Stavros would show up with whichever woman he was dating at the time, acting like he'd been there from the start. He'd act all important and ask if anyone needed anything while he was up getting their food, but we'd all just shake our heads and say no. He'd leave his date at the table, and an awkward silence would settle over us until my mother, who was a pro at this, would jump in and start a conversation.

His children were adults then, and they'd sometimes meet us there. It was nice to see them since we usually only got together a couple of times a year as a family, and it gave us a chance to get caught up. Whoever Stavros brought, she'd try to pretend she felt comfortable and would try to get them to talk to her. I think they felt the way we all did; whoever it was, she was just temporary.

Each year, Yia´ Yia would tell us the same story: "We used to have to travel to the next town over to attend the festival every year when I was growing up. Our village was too small to have its own festival. People came from all over, and we'd set up a booth and sold the olive oil and cheese that we didn't need."

Sometimes I felt like we all treated her like the little old lady she was, for we'd nod in response, and then one of us would ask her if she needed anything just to keep the conversation going.

One summer, my grandmother said, "I don't care to go now anymore. I don't know anyone. Everyone has died."

I understood how she felt. The last few times we'd gone, there were fewer and fewer Greeks, young and old. Where it used to feel like stepping into a piece of our heritage, the old families grew older, their children drifted away and the heart of it all thinned out. The booths now sold souvenirs and trinkets appealing to tourists. It felt like we were trying to keep a memory alive.

We still wanted to support the church, so Steven and I would pick up dinner and bring it back to Yia´ Yia's house, where we'd meet my parents and eat with her.

After Yia´ Yia died, when I asked my parents if they wanted us to take them to the festival, they admitted they too were done, so Steven and I stopped going as well.

People often asked if I cooked Greek food, and I'd just give them a look like, "Me? Cook?" Eventually, I asked my grandmother to teach me how to make a few of my favorite dishes. She was always bustling around in her kitchen, and I thought it would be smart to write down some of her recipes.

We started with spanakopita (spawn-knee-ko´-pee-ta) and, while it turned out delicious, I quickly realized it was way too much work to make on a regular basis. That was probably for the best, because it was very fattening.

After that, we tried fermenting olives, which was even more of a project. First, we picked them off her trees, rinsed them, and carefully sliced each one so the brine could soak in. Then we soaked them in cold water for about a week, changing the water twice a day. Once the bitterness was gone, we submerged them in a saltwater solution for another few weeks, again refreshing the brine weekly. Since I couldn't be there every day, poor Yia´ Yia ended up doing most of the work.

Then came the final brining, which meant draining and re-soaking the olives every week for a month. I loved Kalamata olives, but after seeing how much work it took, I decided I'd stick to buying them from the store. Our batch lasted almost a year—and I was done. We never made them again.

Our last "cooking class" was baking my favorite cookie: Koulourakia, the Greek Easter cookies. Thankfully, they didn't take as long as the spanakopita, but after rolling, twisting, and baking tray after tray, I decided they also were too much trouble, and they too were fattening. I made sure to leave the whole batch at Yia´ Yia's so I wouldn't be tempted to eat them all myself.

I had already figured out a long time ago that some women genuinely loved to cook, and I just wasn't one of them. Trying my hand at traditional Greek recipes only confirmed it. I tucked the recipes away in my old Spice Islands cookbook, never to be seen again.

"You never knew your Papou," Yia´ Yia said one afternoon while we were playing cards. "He was a very smart man."

"Of course he was," I said. "He married you."

"Well, there's that—but when I met him, he was the most handsome man I'd ever seen. I lived in downtown Los Angeles then and worked as a seamstress. One afternoon, on my way home, I noticed this man standing next to his fruit cart, and he had a snake wrapped around his waist!

"I dared to stop and talk to him, of course worrying the snake would bite me," she said. "But he said, 'Don't worry, the snake doesn't bite.' Then I asked, 'Why do you wear it then?' He replied, 'Because I always have cash in my pocket and I don't want anyone robbing me.'"

"His name was Peter. I made a point of stopping to talk with him every time I saw him and pretended I only wanted to buy an apple. He knew what I was doing, and he always had one ready for me. And he never charged me."

She paused and smiled. "I knew he was the man I wanted to marry."

"That's so romantic," I said, and I meant it.

"We were married in 1922," she said wistfully.

My grandfather died when I was only two and a half. My grandmother lived for over sixty years without him.

"Tell me about him buying the building," I said. I knew the story, but I also knew my grandmother loved to tell it.

"Well, your grandfather had that cart right outside a dry goods store in Los Angeles, and when he had to go to the toilet, he'd go inside and use the bathroom. They eventually tired of him and one day they told him he'd have to find somewhere else to go. So, he showed them. He bought the building! We had that thing for years, and when we moved to Long Beach, the store that moved in signed a fifty-year lease." Even after telling that story so many times, she still shook her head in wonder.

I'd remembered my mother and Stavros talking about that lease not so long ago. Back in those days, it was unheard of to be so creative with such a long-term lease. However, my grandfather never took into consideration inflation, and eventually they were stuck with a rent income that never kept up with the times. Once the lease was up, Stavros and my mother finally convinced my grandmother to sell the building just to get rid of it. By then, it was in a neighborhood that had become so rundown that most of the buildings were either vandalized or vacant. The company who'd leased the property had moved out several years before, figuring it was cheaper to just pay the rent than it was to keep the business going.

One afternoon, I finally gathered the courage to ask her about my brother. We were sitting at her dining room table after my mother had already left, and I knew I was going to ask her to reveal a family secret, but something inside me just needed to know.

"Was my mother married before?"

She paused for a moment, as if weighing whether to go against my parents' wishes, then, as casually as she could, she answered, "Yes."

That was enough to answer the biggest question that had been on my mind. Alex was not my father's child

"What happened? Did he die in the war?"

She sighed. "No, he did something that made your mother angry."

She must have understood how I'd come to ask these questions, assuming I had seen the photo of Alex standing next to my father at my parents' wedding. I could have asked more, and she likely would have told me, but something told me I already knew enough.

I made a promise to myself then—never to betray her trust again, but years later, I still wished I'd asked her more. I also finally understood why my parents never celebrated their wedding anniversary. It was August 15, and whenever I'd ask my mother how many years they'd been married, she'd simply say, "Oh, it's been such a long time ago. I haven't even kept track."

CHAPTER FIFTY ONE

VASO

It was five years after Yia´ Yia's funeral when we lost Kaylee. She had grown terribly obese and was now housebound. She still lived in Grandma Bessie's own-your-own. The complex resembled a one-story motel with a courtyard from the 1930s. My parents had updated the kitchen for her, and Kaylee's friends tore out the old carpet to reveal the hardwood floors beneath. But the job was left unfinished—the staple holes were never filled, leaving tiny black dots scattered across the floor and tracing the baseboards where the tack strips had once been.

My mother started checking in on her and was the one who initially told me Kaylee was not doing very well. Mother asked me to order her a chair that had a motorized lift so she could get in and out of it easier, and that's where she sat all day, every day, with her black cat, Merlin.

Now and then I'd call her, and I'd announce myself by saying her name in a drawn-out voice like a game show announcer, "Kayyleee?"

She'd answer in that same drawl, "Vaasso?"

One day, I called and asked her if she'd be interested in doing some part-time work from home. I was working on a multi-piece mailing for our remodeling business, and I thought she'd be a perfect person to sit and apply the labels.

I dropped them off one afternoon, and we got to talking.

Merlin sat on her lap while we talked, and I could hear Kaylee's labored breathing. She'd always had asthma, and it brought back memories of her years ago having to stop and catch her breath if we were outside running or playing.

Kaylee was two years older than I was, and her face was smooth and full, with very few wrinkles.

She said, "Remember the time we stayed at Yia´ Yia's and she made us soft-boiled eggs? She cut our toast up into strips so we could dip them into the egg?"

"No, but I remember her making us sugar toast. Now *that* was good. Do you remember the song *Sixteen Tons* by Tennessee Ernie Ford?" I asked, then went into my own rendition of it.

"And the night we were trying to get spitballs to stick on the walls?" she asked.

"And we were cracking up so hard, Yia´ Yia came into the room waving her slipper and told us if we didn't stop it and go to sleep she was going to come back in and let us have it."

"Yia´ Yia had on her long sleeping gown, and all we could do was laugh more at the thought of her trying to catch us," Kaylee said, giggling. "She gave up. Shook her head and turned to close the bedroom door behind her. . .do you remember going through all her old photos?"

I instantly thought of that day and how we'd looked at the wedding photos of my parents, and there my brother was, standing beside my father. I wanted to change the subject.

"You *do know* what that means, don't you?" she'd asked.

"Unfortunately, I do."

"Have you ever asked your mom?"

"No," I said quickly, and changed the subject. "Well, I'd better get going. Let me know when these are ready and I'll come by and pick them up."

I brought her a few more mailings, but then I had no more projects after that, so I quit calling her. My mother called me one day a couple of months later and told me Kaylee was in the hospital. I knew she'd been suffering from leg ulcers that weren't healing, but I hadn't expected her to never come home. The cause of her death was listed as morbid obesity.

She was cremated, and there was no funeral. Her Wiccan friends did a private ceremony and then scattered her ashes somewhere. After they packed up her house, my mother put it up for sale. Eddie Jr. was now the only remaining heir, so Stavros sent the proceeds to him in Hawaii.

One of her friends took Merlin and cared for him until he died a year later.

Over the years, I've thought about Kaylee, and something I said to her after I'd lost weight. Steven and I were still dating, and we attended Stavros' wedding to Kelli in Palm Springs. I wore my long hair down with a bejeweled scarf tied around my head, and I also wore my favorite bracelet, a scorpion embedded in resin.

I was hot—in my eyes—and there Kaylee was, over a hundred pounds overweight and still married to her second husband, who looked like a biker. During a conversation with her, I said something I thought would inspire her to do something about her appearance.

"You really ought to take that weight off. . .for your own sake, and out of respect for your husband."

The words had slipped out of me, sharp and thoughtless, and only years later did the irony land with full force—when I was the one who had gained all my weight back and more. I kept replaying that moment, wondering why she hadn't snapped back at me. Perhaps she was far kinder than I ever gave her credit for. I've carried regret for saying that to her ever since—just as I've carried the regret of the careless thing I once said to her mother before she died.

Now, with both of them gone, I'd never have the chance to tell either of them how sorry I was. The apology lives only in my head, and that's a kind of punishment I probably deserve.

CHAPTER FIFTY TWO

VASO

If I were to look back on it, I started noticing minor changes in my mother when she was in her mid-seventies. Some things were more obvious than others; we all sometimes forgot little details, or some words didn't come to mind when we wanted them to. She drove her white Cadillac to our business every day while my father golfed. She would often hand me a stack of customer files and ask detailed questions—not to challenge our work, but to do what she did every day in their construction business; ensure everything was billed correctly and the profit margins were where they needed to be. It was less about oversight and more about staying aligned on the numbers.

She had her own office where my accountant's assistant would come every week to do our sales tax and payroll. My mother was the queen of the office, and everyone loved her.

"She's so cute," a friend would say when I brought her to lunch. Or if someone I knew came by the office, they'd say, "You're so lucky to have her."

Almost like clockwork, Steven would come back into the office after seeing jobs, and we'd have lunch. Mother would automatically hand him her credit card, even though she and I would normally split a meal. She loved Steven and would only have to mention something that needed to be done, and he took care of whatever it was.

She made me take the time to walk with her, saying she needed to get up and move more often, which I knew was her way to get *me* up and moving. At first, we walked only a block, and then, once our stamina increased, she would say, "Let's go a little farther." I think we got up to almost a mile.

"I miss walks with Abby," she'd say. "We used to go for walks after lunch."

"I know."

In the early 1960s, Abby arrived in California straight out of secretarial school in South Dakota, carrying herself just as she'd been taught. Poised for her interview with my mother, she was properly dressed with her white gloves, nylons, respectable pumps, a hat, and she carried a small white purse. I can still picture the formality of it, as if she'd stepped right out of a training manual and into our lives.

I was around thirteen, and she was almost twenty. My mother hired her right on the spot, and it took her a few months to feel comfortable dressing down; she ended up working for my parents for over forty years.

I don't remember now why my mother and I stopped walking. I think my lower back went out, and I struggled just to walk around the office. Then we both forgot.

When my office manager began mentioning she was having a hard time finding some files my mother had filed, neither of us thought much of it. I'd lost more paperwork on my own desk than I ever cared to admit.

"What if you try an old trick; look at the letters before and after what you need and see if that helps?" I suggested.

It worked. She'd find the files she'd been looking for.

Mother still repaired and hemmed her own clothes, but she'd comment on how difficult it was getting for her to see the thread when she threaded a needle. I could understand that also; without my glasses, I had the same problem.

They'd been in their beach house for almost ten years before my mother mentioned how nice it would be if we lived closer to them. I think they would have welcomed Steven and me into the house; there was plenty of room, but we had cats, and my father didn't want pets. And parking on the Peninsula was tight. I knew they always wanted to remain in their home if the day ever came that they needed care, and I had given little thought about them making any major changes in their lives until she said that.

People always gave my father, Nick, the credit for the success he and my mother built together. But anyone who truly knew them understood it was my mother who carried his ideas across the finish line, who quietly made sure his dreams became reality. She was content to let him shine, the silent partner in their shared endeavors. Now and then, I'd nudge her, telling her she ought to stand her ground when she had an idea of her own that didn't match his. But she rarely did.

My father was never the overbearing Greek husband stereotype—he never belittled her, only praised her. And through it all, there was never a doubt in my mind that they adored one another.

My mother was always a very private person. She rarely said anything unkind about anyone, but I knew how to read her. Not just the look on her face if something or someone bothered her, but it was as if she could telegraph her thoughts. Sometimes she'd just look at me, and I knew what she was thinking; like that forced smile she produced the time Alex told her he was going to marry Jean, and in *her* mind, ruin his life.

But as her cognitive impairment worsened, she'd sometimes comment aloud. "He's really tall," or "That outfit looks terrible on her." Sometimes it was embarrassing, and I'd have to put my finger to my lips to remind her not to say those types of things aloud.

She hated sharing personal information with anyone. She waited until a few days before she was scheduled to have her hysterectomy before telling her office she was going to be off work for a while. Even I hadn't known she'd been having issues. And she did the same thing when she had her bladder lifted. Only Abby knew, which I always thought was silly. But Abby honored my mother's requests to keep her secrets.

Years later, when she lay in the ICU, I knew in my heart my mother wouldn't have wanted anyone to see her that way. By then, there was hardly anyone left—just me, Alex, Abby, and Stavros. Abby was back in South Dakota, Alex was too consumed with his pig farm, and in the end, it was only Stavros and me who came to sit by her side before she died.

When I was little, I adored the way she smelled on nights when she and my father were heading out. She'd bend down to kiss me goodnight, and I'd breathe in the soft, familiar fragrance of her favorite perfume—Avon Cotillion. I still keep an empty bottle of it tucked away in my dresser drawer. Every so often, while looking for something else, I stumble across it, and the memories come rushing back. That moment—her perfume, her kiss, watching her getting ready—felt as if it belonged in a magazine ad.

And sometimes when I get in bed at night and pull the sheet and blanket over my head so I can fold it down across my chest, I think of when I used to climb under the blanket on my bed and pretend I was sinking down into my mattress so deeply that no one could see me—like young children do when they cover their eyes and think no one can see them. My mother would come to my doorway and say, "I wonder where Vaso is?" I'd try not to giggle and let her know I was there.

Looking back, I know my mother regretted not spending more time with Alex and me while we were growing up. She did her best to be everything to us while also chasing everything she wanted for herself. She once told me she had promised herself she'd make the time for Alex's children, and she was true to her word. They grew up adoring her. Though she and my father still worked seven days a week, she always carved out time to see them. She'd take them shopping and then to the park near their house by the ocean, where she'd sit and watch them play. I knew she would have done the same for me if I'd had children of my own, and I never felt anything but admiration for her.

One time I teased her and said, "I don't remember you ever taking *me* to the park."

And before she could say anything, Steven, who was always so quiet, said, "She did. You just kept finding your way back home."

Looking back, I still think it was the funniest thing he's ever said. We laughed until our sides ached, and every now and then, I have the opportunity to tell someone that story.

I loved to see Mother's face light up when she told me funny things the grandchildren did.

"When Nik was about three," she said one time, "he was in the tub playing with some toys. He looked at me and pointed to his little penis and said, 'Look, Yia´ Yia. It schloats.'"

Another time she told me that when the children were spending the night in their penthouse, Nik was running around and being noisy. My mother shushed him and said, "You need to be quiet. There are people living below us, and they'll hear you." My nephew stopped short and quickly looked under the bed and declared, "There's no one under there."

My mother also promised herself she'd make sure Alex's children had the opportunity to either go to college or attend a trade school after they graduated from high school. When she told Alex that Chloe, the eldest, wanted to go to cosmetology school, he said no.

"Let her earn it," he said.

Despite him, my mother had Chloe come down and stay with them while she started beauty school. Chloe eventually decided that being a beautician wasn't what she wanted to do after all, but being the pragmatic woman my mother was, she was satisfied she'd given her the opportunity to give it a try.

When his middle daughter, Alexandria, wanted to become a medical assistant, Alex said no again, but my mother sent her to school, anyway.

My mother once told me she never regretted doing what she wanted for the girls, no matter how Alex felt. When Nik mentioned he wanted to learn to operate heavy equipment, Alex told her he could pay for it himself if he wanted to go to school, she was weary of arguing and simply stepped back. Nik ended up finding a job and paying for his own trade school. Looking back, she said, she had always wished she had trusted herself and followed her own instincts.

Mother had always adored young children, and as her cognitive decline became more noticeable, her affection for babies seemed to grow even stronger. Whenever we were in a restaurant and she spotted a baby, she couldn't help but pause and admire the child, often stopping at the table to say how darling they were. She was never intrusive, but occasionally she'd catch parents off guard by lingering nearby, quietly enchanted. Once they realized her sweet intent, though, they always smiled—sometimes even beamed—touched by her genuine warmth.

I often think of her while I'm doing the simplest tasks, like changing the sheets. I can still see the way she'd flick the top sheet into the air, letting it float down perfectly onto the bed, as if by magic. Or when she dried the dishes, how she'd flip each piece of silverware into its rightful place in the drawer with swift, practiced precision. She had a way of cutting a perfect hole in a head of lettuce to rinse it twice before using it. And the way she sliced carrots—so fast, so sure—I was convinced that if I tried to do it the same way, I'd lose a finger. Through my young eyes, it was as if she pulled off quiet, death-defying feats every day.

She had the most contagious laugh, and sometimes we'd laugh hysterically at the stupidest things. When the Sit n' Sleep commercial would come on and Larry would declare, "If we can't beat anyone's mattress price, your mattress is free," we'd sing "your mattress is fwee!" and laugh so hard we couldn't stop.

"I have to pee," she'd announce, and we'd burst into laughter again. If my father was nearby, he'd just shake his head at us, but the glint in his eyes always gave him away—he loved my mother and he loved me, and he was just as amused as we were.

Mother and I were both avid readers, and she'd give me her credit card when I went to Barnes and Noble to buy books.

"When you're finished with them, pass them along to me," she'd said.

The next time I saw her, I'd always ask where she was in the latest book, and she'd happily bring me up to speed. She kept reading well into her later years, though eventually she began forgetting her place and had to reread sections. I'd done the same myself after leaving a book untouched for a while, so at first, it didn't strike me as unusual. But over time, when I noticed a book left unfinished, she would simply say, "Oh, I keep getting sidetracked."

I'd been overweight most of my adult life, and sometimes I'd look at photos of Mother and me, and I felt like I was twice her size. It didn't help that she was a very petite woman; I used to joke and tell her she made me look bad. I don't think she ever weighed more than a hundred and twenty-five pounds. Ever. She had always loved sewing, so when she finally had her sewing room at the beach house, she took some classes in dressmaking. By this time she could afford whatever she wanted in equipment, so she had several high end sewing machines, a professional dress form, and a custom sewing center built in the TV room, complete with eight foot high cabinets to store all her fabrics in.

We once had a color consultant help us figure out our best shades—I had no idea everyone was considered a "season." Based on your skin tone, hair, and eye color, they could determine which palette suited you best. With our dark hair and eyes, we were classified as Winters. After that, my mother designed a dress pattern that flattered my body shape and began sewing dresses for me using only fabrics in my seasonal colors. They were among the most beautiful clothes I've ever worn.

Eventually, she found a dressmaker she liked and had her make my dresses. Mother gave me eight to ten dresses a year. They were perfect for work, and no matter where I was going, I always felt I looked the best I could.

She never once told me I was eating too much or that I needed to exercise more—she was always unconditionally supportive. My father, on the other hand, would occasionally glance at my plate and shake his head in disapproval. Whenever he did, my stubborn, childish streak kicked in—I'd flash him a cheeky grin and take an exaggerated bite, just to make a point.

I idolized my father, but my mother was my hero. There was never a doubt in my mind that she loved me and would do anything she could to help me accomplish what I wanted to do. She was very philosophical, which I'm proud to say is a trait I inherited. She was also my best friend. If I told her something didn't work out the way I'd planned it, she said something like, "Things have a way of working themselves out, and you'll just try to do it differently next time." Or if I was discouraged because after I'd done a lot of research, I decided not to undertake a project, she'd say, "Look at what you learned and you've made the best decision not to pursue it." When I made so many mistakes running my business, she'd always told me, "Just think of it as your college education."

Never, ever, ever, did she say, "I told you so." I could talk to her about anything and she'd figure out a way to help me solve my problem.

Mother had embraced both Thomas and Steven, as well as their children, into our lives with open arms. I knew she saw them not only as important parts of my life, but as positive, grounding influences that brought something meaningful to my world. I don't remember her having any unkind thoughts, although I'm sure she saw things she didn't approve of. She never brought up my past, although for years after I settled down, I thought about how I'd hurt her and my father by being such an inconsiderate idiot.

We soon spent at least three nights a week with them at the house on the bay, and my parents had dinner ready for us when we got there. Most nights, I'd find my father looking out their large window to the north, where all the houses were lit.

"Isn't this just something?" he'd say.

I'd help Mother clean up while Steven and my father sat at the table and talked about nothing and everything. When we were finished, we'd go upstairs to their TV room, where the men would sit in the recliners and watch TV and Mother and I would sit behind them at the small table they ate at when they didn't have company.

I'd do their pills, and every time Mother and I would start talking, my father would turn to us and say, "Now don't go talking to her while she's doing the pills."

Mother just stuck her tongue out at him and laughed.

If Mother wanted to shop for anything, whether for the grandchildren or for herself, she'd always find something I needed and tell me to put it in the cart. One time when we were at Target, I wanted to get a new set of sheets, and she said, "Get them." That was the way my parents were with me, and my mother would never let me pay her back. When I mentioned we should get Alex a gift card to be fair, she said, "Whatever you want."

But when I sent it to him, he said, "Why are you having Mother buy you anything? And I don't want an effing gift card."

I don't recall his ever having sent it back.

I knew my parents were getting closer to where they'd eventually need some help, and I wondered if they'd take the basement office and make it in to the two-bedroom apartment they planned on building out for my grandmother so someone could stay with them if that time came. I also started thinking about the possibility of us moving in with them if that's what they'd want.

There was an older couple who lived on the corner across from us. Before they passed away, their adult son, Larry, returned home to care for them. He and Steven often chatted, and as we got to know him, we discovered they shared a common love of old cameras. One day, while showing Steven his collection, the son casually mentioned that he didn't think he could afford to stay in the house for long. His sister wanted to sell everything and divide it up. When Steven told me this, I went along with him one afternoon to take a look at the house.

Built in the late forties, it needed one of everything. We were in the right business to remodel the house, and we told Larry to let us know if and when it would go on the market. I mentioned it to my parents the next time we saw them, and my mother's face lit up when I suggested they might move across the street from us.

My father's response was, "Over my dead body."

CHAPTER FIFTY THREE

KATE

I knew the changes in me hadn't happened overnight. As we age, we all start the process—some differently than others. For me, it was quietly, like forgetting words in the middle of a sentence, or driving a familiar road that suddenly felt unfamiliar. At first, it was easy to brush off, or to laugh, to say you're tired, distracted, getting older. But then it keeps happening, again and again.

There's a slow, creeping unease in realizing that something inside you is shifting. You forget why you walked into a room. You stare at a friend's face and it takes a beat too long to place them. Emotions, once sharp and certain, begin to dull or tilt unexpectedly—things that used to move you deeply now feel distant, or worse, things you never dwelled on suddenly sting.

My brain is forgetting how to function. First it was doing our pills, then it was reading, and what I've missed most of all is my sewing. I look at my fabrics and I can see something beautiful in them, but then I do not know how to start. I'd finally found a passion other than our business, and I only had a few years to work in my sewing room.

I knew it sounded corny to say it aloud, but there wasn't a day that passed that I didn't realize how lucky I was to have had Nick in my life. Even though he's gotten crotchety in his old age, he's been a wonderful husband and father. He had all the ideas about how to better our lives, and of course, it took a lot of work on my part to make it all work out, but we've been a perfect couple.

I'm not blind; I realize we aren't aging at the same pace. Nick seems to have a better grasp on the world as it is today, but he's had the most medical problems.

I find I can't keep up with the things I used to do every day. I used to be concerned about which of us would die first. If it were Nick, I'd be able to take care of myself for a while, but now I wonder. If it were me, I didn't know what Nick would do. Of course, we'd always have Vaso and Steven. He's such a dear, and he would do anything for us.

And thank god for Abby, who still does my bookkeeping and keeps me on track. When she retired, Vaso started taking care of some of my paperwork. And Tim, my other bookkeeper, still comes in every week to help me enter everything into the computer and write checks. We had so many accounts I could sometimes hardly keep everything straight.

I've given up reading. It was always another passion I had. I loved the stories and characters, yet sometimes I found I was upset at the decisions they made. The print got smaller too, and I could not read for more than a few minutes at a time. Most times I had to make a list of the characters, even if there were only two or three. I seemed to forget who they were. And I hated that I had to go back and reread something I read yesterday, because I couldn't remember where I left off.

I never told Vaso this, and I still let her buy books for us; she has the credit card. She is such a beautiful girl, and I am so proud of her. When I look at her, memories of her childhood flood back...mostly as snapshots held together by love and time.

I remember the softness of her hair after a bath, and the way she hated it when I combed out the tangles of her curly hair. I remember how she used to hold my hand tightly when she was very young, and then looser, until one day she didn't reach for it anymore.

There were always bedtime stories and stuffed animals that she kept until her teens. How she didn't like to sleep in the dark, and how she sucked her thumb for years past the time when some children quit. She hated being dropped off at school or sleeping over at a friend's house. And I can still see her sitting on Nick's lap, and him calling her one of his pet names. I also remember the slammed doors and how, for a while, we thought we might lose her to all the poor decisions she made as a teenager.

If I go back even further, I remember holding her as a beautiful new baby, and how Nick looked at her with a mixture of awe and disbelief, as though she were fragile and perfect. And of course she was both.

I don't remember when Nick bought it for me, but I want her to have my diamond ring. I think about it when I'm sitting and watching television with Vaso and Steven, but I keep forgetting to tell her about it. I need to make myself a note.

I've been grateful for so many things. I know I didn't always make the best decisions, but who has? I've learned to live with the consequences of what I decided was best at the time.

I've begun wondering to myself, and I may have even said it aloud, that it would be perfect if Vaso and Steven lived closer to us. There's plenty of room in our house for us all, but they have cats, and Nick doesn't like animals roaming around the house. It's not that they live so far away. It's only a few miles, but it's so congested down on the peninsula it wouldn't be possible for all of us to park.

I know Vaso would be the one taking care of us.

I need to remember to talk to Nick about all this.

CHAPTER FIFTY FOUR

VASO

It was 2008, and the real estate market was going through a downward phase. Once we told the neighbor, Larry, that we were interested in buying the house for my parents, they had us at a distinct disadvantage. There was no negotiating, and my parents paid the asking price for the one chance they had to live across the street from us. But they were optimistic when they put the Beach House up for sale, and right away a movie producer offered to buy it.

We ended up stripping the new house down to the studs and took out unnecessary walls to open it up to resemble the Beach House's open floor plan. We took out the laundry room, which gave us a gigantic kitchen, where we put in a second refrigerator and bar area just like at the old house. My father got his warming drawer, and we added a stove and a second oven.

There was a step down from the living room to the rest of the house, and when we installed African mahogany wood floors, we built a ramp with wood banisters and railings so that it looked like it was a natural feature of the house.

Since my parents were used to having their own bathrooms, we extended the back of the house so we could build two toilet rooms and two vanities. We also widened the doorways and made the shower on the same level as the bathroom floor to accommodate a wheelchair if and when the time came. There was a guest house in the backyard, and we tore it down to the walls also, replacing the kitchen, bathroom and heater. With its painted paneling and open-beamed ceiling, it looked just like a cottage.

While we were making roofing selections, my father said, "Why don't we put a new roof on your house while we're at it?" And when we installed iron railing on their small porch, he insisted we add railing up the steps to our front door.

"Are you sure?" I asked.

"In case I ever want to come over," he said with a wink.

Unfortunately, the buyer for the Beach House couldn't get his financing in order, and the sale fell through. We were in the middle of a recession, and property prices continued to go down. A new buyer stepped up, but the selling price dropped.

Mother and I combed through every corner of the Beach House, deciding piece by piece what to keep and what to let go. With my housekeeper and her sister helping, we worked one room at a time, sorting everything into three piles: what would move with us, what my housekeeper could use, and what we would donate. Since my mother no longer spent time in her sewing room, we carefully packed up her supplies and passed them along to a cousin who loved to sew. The greatest task, though, was the basement office. Steven and I spent over a month clearing it out, shredding box after box of old paperwork until it finally felt manageable.

I did a floor plan for the new house, so we knew exactly what would fit and where it would go, and it was amazing how, despite the new house being much smaller, there was room for almost everything but one guest bedroom. By the time both house projects were finished, we were all exhausted.

My mother loved the new house.

My father accepted it and then grew fond of it. On the interior, it was as close to their Beach House as I could come—just without the bay view and sailboats. And although he never said it, I knew he understood this was what he needed to do to make sure I was there for my mother.

A few years later, my father felt a pulsating lump in his abdomen, and when his doctor did an ultrasound, they found he had an abdominal aortic aneurysm. Not only was my father lucky in gambling, but he was lucky the surgery was completed with minimal invasion. During his recovery, every morning, Steven and I had breakfast with them before we left for work, and we brought dinner home every night.

I said nothing about how grateful I was that they were across the street, and when my mother said, "See, Nick? Wasn't this a good idea, after all?"

My father just curled his upper lip the way he did when he wanted to pretend he didn't like something.

CHAPTER FIFTY FIVE

NICK

I've attained more in my lifetime than I ever thought possible. Someone was looking out for me when I met Kate on that beach so many years ago, and with her by my side, we worked hard to be where we are today. Sometimes I'd let memories of my childhood cloud my way, like when I thought I wasn't good enough to join the country club, or when my friends were men who either had more education or money than I did. I always tried to surround myself with people who knew more than me; that was how I learned. I had the personality to cover up my background and lack of schooling, but I also had street smarts. I'd pick people's brains. I'd try to take the best of someone I knew and apply that philosophy to myself. What I didn't like, I tossed.

I made a lot of mistakes along the way, but who hasn't? A few of our investments went sour, and we lost money, but most of them made us money. We'd sell something to buy something better; a better location, a better investment.

I had a saying, and I truly believed it. "Don't go by what it costs you; go by what it makes you." And I wasn't afraid to take a well thought out gamble.

I also made a promise to myself and to Kate that I would accept Alex into my life and raise him as my own son. I knew what it felt like to live with a parent who treated you differently. Plus, there's something about a two-year-old that tugs at your heartstrings, and I had no problem loving him.

I worried about not telling him the truth. Everyone knew; of course, Kate's family and my family. In those days, there were a lot of family secrets. Most of them were much worse than ours. But I promised her I'd never say anything, and I didn't.

When he grew older, he became quite a handful. He had a lot of friends in the neighborhood, and there was always someone in the garage with him while he worked on bikes or took care of his snakes—people were attracted to him. I admired that because when I was growing up, I never felt that I had anything to offer anyone. I was always working to help support my family, plus I didn't start out speaking English.

Alex was sixteen when he showed me the photo.

"What the hell is this?" he'd demanded.

"Alex," was all I could say.

"I've known it for a while. I'm not sure why it makes a difference now, but just so you know, the minute I can, I'm out of here. You can tell Mother or not."

He was so angry his entire body shook. I tried to talk to him, but he turned his back on me.

Alex never asked who his real father was, and I didn't tell him. I also never told Kate about our conversation. I couldn't bear to break her heart. He stopped talking to us, and the abrupt difference in his behavior was alarming. Whenever Kate tried to ask him what was going on, he turned and walked away from her. Aside from losing her father, I'd never seen Kate in tears, but for weeks, I'd wake knowing she'd been crying. That's when she asked Cynthia to take him in so he'd at least graduate.

Many years have passed since then, and time seemed to take care of most of his hard feelings. I couldn't show it, but for years I was angry with him for hurting his mother. Kate seemed to take it all in stride, chalking it up to teenage rebellion.

We don't see him often, but he calls us. I usually answer the phone, and we talk—or I should say, *he* talks. I don't know how he can talk about so many unimportant things, like how he needed to replace the ball bearings on something, or how he and his wife went to the store. If Kate came into the room to see who'd called, I'd hold the phone away from my ear for a moment and she'd recognize it was Alex. He didn't know how to tell the short version of anything and while what he talked about was generally interesting, it went on way too long—and it was always about him.

His wife would constantly talk in the background, which was even more annoying, and when she wanted to talk to Kate, Kate would just shake her head.

"Love you, son," I'd always said as I handed the phone to her.

I loved Alex, but I wondered where all his anger came from—it certainly wasn't from Kate. I'd tried not to show favoritism, for I remembered what it felt like when I was growing up. George and I were never treated the same as my stepmother's children.

Vaso was just the opposite. Growing up, she was studious, liked to cook surprise meals for us, and loved to entertain us through the doorway to the living room. She'd stand there like it was her stage and either do something silly, or sing off key, but then she'd always curtsy and bow for her applause. When she was young, I thought she'd never stop sucking her thumb and biting her nails, for of course, I wanted her to be perfect. All fathers want their boys to grow up strong, and their daughters to be beautiful young ladies. I always saw her as a sweet and beautiful child, and I called her my princess.

When we moved to the apartments in Long Beach, I used to love standing on our balcony and looking out at the Queen Mary. But when we built our beach house, I could stand in our dining room and look at all the lights from the houses across the bay. For hours, I could watch the people on the sand who laid out their blankets in front of our house; some would have young children who played in the water, and others would just sit and read a book. We had one group who would come every week and have a barbecue with friends.

I didn't like the sand itself, so I never went down to the beach at either house, but I loved watching the water. I never thought we would live anywhere else. Even with the heart attack I had while we were under construction, we'd built our dream house, and this was where I wanted to be for the rest of my life.

I always referred to my stepbrother Chuck as my brother, although I never would have said that in front of my brother George. Chuck and I had the same political views, and we'd remained friends until he died. We rarely spoke about life with my father and his mother, but once he told me he was sorry I had to grow up the way I did. He admitted his mother wasn't the fairest when it came to me and George, and he apologized.

"Pops had it pretty rough too," he laughed, referring to my father.

When we got the call that his lovely wife had died, Steven and Vaso drove Kate and me up to Marin for her funeral. I hadn't seen my half-sister or other stepbrother in years, and when I saw them, I told Kate I wished I would have made the time to call them all more often.

"You were a good son," she said to me. "And it's not too late to do a better job going forward."

She was also so positive and philosophical.

When Kate started forgetting things, it was so gradual I didn't give it much thought. We were both in our seventies, and I was already keeping a calendar of my many doctor's appointments—cardiologist, urologist, nephrologist for my kidney disease, podiatrist, proctologist. Kate's job was to keep track of our medications, and then Abby typed up lists for her—what to take, which times during the day—and it made her job simpler.

I had a pretty good idea what my pills were, and when I started noticing a missed pill here and there, I'd ask Kate about it. It would take her a few minutes, but she'd figure out she'd forgotten to put one in the pillbox. But then she started doing other things, like forgetting which drawer the silverware went in, and she'd sometimes ask me the same question more than once.

Now, I'm not saying I didn't end up doing that towards the end of my life either; it's just she never used to be like that, and it was becoming obvious she needed some help. That's when I asked Vaso to start doing our pills when she and Steven came over for dinner. Kate would sit there while Vaso counted everything out. If she'd talk to Vaso, I'd said, "Now, Kate, leave her alone while she does the pills." She'd mostly wrinkle her face or stick her tongue out at me and then keep talking.

Sometimes they'd get the giggles, and their laughter was contagious. Even though Steven and I didn't know what they were laughing about, we couldn't help but look at each other and shake our heads—we were always smiling, though.

I always helped Kate do most of the cooking, but our meals were simple. When Vaso and Steven came over, Kate wanted to add vegetables and Jell-O. One time, she forgot to put the Jell-O in the refrigerator to cool, and then got upset with me for not reminding her.

When I could see it was just too much work for her to coordinate meals for the four of us, Vaso started bringing over either Greek food from a restaurant we all liked, or Kentucky Fried Chicken. Vaso already had our credit card with her.

A few years later, Kate started talking to me about how nice it would be to live closer to Vaso, but I reminded her we were only a mile and a half away now.

"Yes, but it's not the same as living across the street from her," she said one day. "That house is for sale."

It felt like the floor just moved under me, and I knew then I'd lose any battle to stay where we were.

We bought that house, and as it turned out, I adjusted to life without my water view. Parking was a lot easier, and getting in and out of our new neighborhood was a breeze. I still went to lunch at the club, and Kate would drive to Vaso's office to do her bookwork. I could see immediately that Kate felt relieved to have Vaso so close to us, and I had to admit that having Steven around to fix things or watch football with was a pleasure. He was there no matter what we needed, and he never made me feel like I was imposing, even when I had the simplest of projects for him. Over the years, he'd grown used to my personality, which I knew could be strong.

"Will work for food," I used to tease him, because he loved to eat.

By then, they were with us probably five nights a week and for breakfast, too. I watched as Vaso combed Kate's hair, and I loved watching them together. Vaso would tease her about something, and Kate would laugh. Sometimes when they started giggling, I saw the innocence in Kate's eyes, and it made me realize again that Kate had been right in having us make this move. I would have done anything to make her happy.

Sometimes I caught myself getting impatient with her for forgetting to do things that in the past had been second nature to her—like putting the right amount of coffee in the coffeemaker, or bringing me my water without spilling it. A few times when she did something that frustrated me, I even said, "Goddammit," but she never gave me any indication she even noticed. I did that once when Vaso was there, and she immediately called out, "*Hey*!"

For that, I am sorry.

What am I proud of?

Kate and I helped many people over the years. We gave a lot of young people their first jobs; for some, we were just a stepping stone to something else, but it gave them work experience. For others, we taught them to become skilled as painters and carpenters, and they worked for us for years.

I provided for my wife and children and gave them every comfort in life.

I tried to repay my family in Greece by sending them money, and I sponsored my cousin Dimitrios and his family, hoping to bring him to the States so they could have a better life. We spent several years working with an immigration attorney, but nothing we did worked.

Although we never went to church, we donated freely to the Greek Church, and I used to laugh when I told Yia´ Yia we were buying our way into heaven. She used to say, "Kako Nico." Bad Nick, but I always got a smile out of her.

I did everything I could think of to get ahead, and yet, one of my rules was that I would never step on anyone else along the way. Sometimes it meant I didn't win, but in my heart I knew I always did.

And what do I regret?

I don't think I supported my father enough. I'm not just talking about money. I did everything I could for him and my stepmother, but I always wondered if I could have been there for him more. I know he made tremendous sacrifices to make sure my brother George and I had a future, and he was so proud when he became an American citizen. He never got to go back home again to see his mother and his aunt before they died. He made me promise I would go there one day, and I did. My grandmother was gone by then, but I still have a photo we took of my aunt, who helped raise me. In it, she's dressed in all black and bent at the waist from osteoporosis. I remembered her being a vibrant young woman, and to see how she'd ended up was unsettling.

I should have spent more time with Vaso and Alex, preparing them for all the trials and tribulations life had to offer. I should have supervised them more when they needed it. I was so busy providing for us all, I couldn't fit everything in. I watched them struggle, and yet I knew that even if I would have tried to talk to them, they wouldn't have listened to me.

Kate and I gave them everything they wanted and needed, and I knew even before Vaso went through her teenage years, I should have been stricter with her. She was like me, though, adventuresome and fearless, and she didn't always make the best decisions. But she came out of it and turned into a wonderful and caring woman, just like her mother.

When my buddies from the club would talk about life and our regrets, I'd tell them I wished I'd joined the club sooner. They'd talk about their kids and complain about something one of them did, and I would think of mine. When they asked me, I'd tell them how proud I was of both of them, even though I had to admit it was Vaso who grabbed the opportunities presented to her, and who wasn't afraid to risk and fail. And it was Vaso and Steven who had stepped up to be there for us.

It was never Alex. I'll be forever thankful that Kate kind of forgot about him until he called.

In the end, Vaso and Steven were enough for us.

CHAPTER FIFTY SIX

VASO

I used to tell my parents they were aging in dog years—every week seemed to bring some new reminder of their advancing age. My father still took his daily walks, but one morning he lost his balance and fell into a bush. A passing neighbor heard him struggling to get up and helped him to his feet. After that, he started walking with a cane.

"That damned dog down the street hears my cane hit the pavement and starts barking from a block away," he grumbled one day.

"Bark back," I said, giving him a hard time.

He kept his own calendar, and it filled quickly with medical appointments. One week, it was blood work to monitor his Coumadin—another week, a check on his kidney function. Then there were regular podiatrist visits for his toenails, and routine check-ins with his cardiologist.

My mother, on the other hand, was physically strong. Aside from her memory loss, she was healthy as a horse and rarely needed to see a doctor.

Over the years, Steven and my father had grown incredibly close. Steven often said he wished he'd had a relationship like that with his own dad. My father leaned on him for everything from changing light bulbs to fixing things around the house, cashing checks, and driving him around to settle football pool bets. They'd watch every game together, placing small wagers—not just on who would win, but on every obscure point combination. Sometimes, my father would slip Steven a hundred-dollar bill—just because.

Years ago, my father had added Steven to their checking account. Steven had already taken over their banking—making deposits and withdrawals—and years earlier he had hand-delivered the paperwork when the beach house sold.

"Take *this* to the bank," my father said, handing Steven the check for two million dollars.

Steven once shared with me three things my father had said to him that he never forgot.

"You've been a good husband to Vaso. It's clear you love her—but try to get her to stop eating so much," he'd said with a shrug.

"I know I fought the move here, but I need you to look out for Kate. That's the best way I know how to help her now."

And finally: "We lost Alex a long time ago. But Vaso brought us you."

Steven never said it outright, but I knew he loved my parents deeply. It's hard not to love people who make space for you, who show their love in the quiet, steady ways. Our fathers weren't big on affection or praise, but my father never criticized Steven or made him feel small. When asked about his own upbringing, Steven would say, "I never got into trouble—I didn't want to face my dad."

In the mornings, my father made oatmeal for all of us before work. I'd comb my mother's hair, pull it back into a ponytail, and she'd sit at the counter while I cleaned the kitchen. Steven and my father would be in the other room watching Fox News. Eventually, we convinced my mother to let us drive her to and from work. Her car sat in front of their house for a couple of months before she finally agreed to sell it.

I handled their basic bookkeeping and prepped everything for Tim, our accountant. He was endlessly patient with my mother. At first, he sat with her as she entered everything into the computer, reminding her where she needed to post something, but when she could no longer follow him, I gently suggested she change places with him and watch him as he worked. Eventually, I suggested we let Tim do the computer entry while we went into the family room and watched *House Hunters* together.

The one thing she never lost was her ability to laugh. Sometimes it was over the silliest things, but her laughter cut through the fog of memory loss—and in those moments, I found I could laugh with her, and forgot everything else.

CHAPTER FIFTY SEVEN

VASO

On April 15, 2011, my father died.

Had I not left my sunglasses on the newel post, my father wouldn't have knocked them over. And if they hadn't fallen to the floor, he wouldn't have reached down to pick them up. And if he hadn't done that, he wouldn't have lost his balance. In slow motion, I watched him fall backward and hit his head on the hardwood flooring.

"*Fuck!*" I cried.

"*Where are you?*" he called, his voice warped and disoriented.

There was something in his eyes—open and glassy—that told me he was already somewhere else.

I cradled his head. Blood pooled where his skull had struck. My hands were shaking so violently I couldn't think straight. My mother sat frozen on her side of the couch, her expression vacant, like she wasn't seeing what I was seeing

"*Where are you?*" he asked again, not knowing I was right there.

In my mind, I heard the thud of his head hitting the floor again.

"I'm right here."

I tried to think, but my hands were shaking so badly I picked up their phone and dialed 411. The minute I realized what I'd done, I hung up and dialed 911. And then I ran next door to get our neighbor, who was a nurse. She came over right away, and we put a towel under my father's head. She stayed with us until the ambulance arrived.

They didn't take him to the local ER. It wasn't equipped for what had just happened. Instead, the ambulance took us to a trauma center farther away, as if more distance might offer more hope. The minute I saw my father on the gurney, I knew he would not make it. The ER doctor confirmed my suspicion when he said, "Your father is never leaving this hospital as you knew him."

I could see it on her face—my mother was still in shock.

I called my brother and told him to get down here. And then I called Stavros, and within the hour, he was there.

Reaching the curtained room, we found him intubated; the incessant clicking and beeping of medical machines created an unwelcome and unsettling rhythm.

As soon as I saw him lying there, I knew.

The light in him had faded. Just the shell of my father, held upright by tubes and wires. The man I knew was already gone. This was just his body, waiting for us to catch up.

They'd put cold presses on his eyes to keep them moist—reminding me of getting a facial at the spa—and suddenly I was afraid to go to him. I glanced at the empty bed next to him, which should have been curtained off. But with the bloody bedding and the quantity of blood still pooled on the floor, whoever they brought in before us couldn't have lived either. From the neighborhood we were in, I assumed the blood was from a gunshot wound victim.

It was too late for me to un-see the mess. The minute the doctor came in, he closed the curtain.

Next, I called Abby.

"He's going to die," I said.

In the private waiting room, Steven and I sat on either side of my mother, and Stavros took a separate chair across from us, already settling into some imagined position of decision-maker. I could see his brain turning. We listened to the doctor tell us there was no way they could help my father. He had intracranial hemorrhaging, caused by the blood thinner he'd been taking. His brain was bleeding and was swollen enough to push it to one side of his skull.

I don't know if Mother fully grasped what he meant. Maybe she did, and maybe she just couldn't bear it yet.

"I think we shouldn't let him live this way," I said carefully.

"*I* think we need to wait," Stavros said. By the tone in his voice, I could tell he was trying to assume the new role of head of the family, which he wasn't.

'*Why?*' I wanted to shout. '*And who are you? You're not in charge of this family. We know what's going to happen. He's going to die.*' But I didn't. I just looked at him and said nothing.

Alex wouldn't be there until the next morning, and even though it was only prolonging the inevitable, I understood I couldn't make that decision on my own. My mother still didn't seem to understand what had happened, which in a way I was grateful for.

The next morning, Alex called for directions—although my parents had lived in the new house for five years, he'd never been down to see them. I couldn't believe they'd brought their two little dogs down with them, but they claimed there was no one in town that could take care of them while they were gone. Before we left for the hospital, I had a few minutes to talk to Alex about what the doctor had said. I think it was the first time we'd had a normal conversation and agreed on anything in years. They left the dogs in the guest house and propped the door open so they could go in and out if they needed to.

My father's Lexus wasn't large enough for all of us, so Alex and Linda followed us to pick Abby up at the airport on the way to the hospital. The whole time, I still wasn't sure my mother comprehended what was going on; we were going to tell the doctor to take my father off life support.

When we got to the hospital, we crowded into the elevator, and the sudden heat of all our bodies was claustrophobic. When the door opened, I felt a rush of cold air, but it didn't make me feel any better. Alex went in first to see my father, and when he came out, he appeared almost detached, as though he wasn't facing a life-or-death situation. I didn't go in, choosing instead to take my mother into the relative's waiting room where we were the night before. I couldn't help but think about the hundreds of other families who'd sat there before us, waiting to discuss the fate of their loved one—asking themselves, *what do we do now?* Abby had seen my father, and she eventually joined us, visibly shaken, and wiping her eyes with a tissue.

When Stavros got there, he took on the pompous role that came so easily to him.

"I don't want to make any hasty decisions today," he said, greeting no one. He then looked at Abby and said, "You're not family."

Mother shot him a dark look, but he didn't notice, and she didn't say anything. I wanted her to tell him to go to hell.

"We've decided to remove my father from life support," I volunteered.

I looked at my mother to see if she was able to process what I was saying, and I couldn't tell *what* she was thinking.

"I think we need to wait for the doctor," Stavros said, as if he were the one who would decide.

As if on cue, the doctor came in and reiterated what he'd told us the day before.

"We can't get the swelling to go down, and in plain English, that means your father has suffered a traumatic brain injury. Nothing has changed since yesterday," he said.

He went on to tell us what happens with this kind of injury, and I let my mind wander as he spoke. I knew what he was saying—my father was going to die. We were just keeping his body company.

I went in to say goodbye to him first. His skin was pasty, and his hand was icy when I reached out for it. Technically, he was already dead. Part of me wanted to be there when they turned off the life support, but I was afraid he would jerk or do something that might make me feel he was still alive. If that happened, I knew I'd carry that memory with me forever. It was already bad enough to remember the way he fell.

"Where are you?"

It still played over and over in my mind.

If only I hadn't put my sunglasses on the newel post.

On April 15, the Titanic sank, killing 1,514 people, Abraham Lincoln was assassinated, and my father died.

Regretting my past behavior so many years ago, I'd made myself a promise that I would always be there for my parents, no matter what. They would come first, and that's what I'd made sure of. I'd started years before, with the little things I did, but it was time now to ramp it up. Now, I would be fulfilling that promise even more.

I appreciated everything my parents did for me over the years, and they'd given me a tremendous amount of opportunities. My father would tuck a couple hundred dollars in my hand whenever Steven and I went on a vacation, or when I commented our washer and dryer were getting old, my mother bought us a new set. They were very generous to my brother and me, and the grandchildren for our birthdays and Christmas, and yet I never felt I took advantage of them. My mother spoiled me and Steven the most.

When Steven decided it was time to get hearing aids, she paid for them—not because we said we needed the help, but because it was something they wanted to do. For our tenth anniversary, they gave us a thousand dollars to spend on a cruise to Mexico. They gave us the money to purchase the house next door to the Tustin house when it came up for sale, and when we sold it, they didn't want the money back. When we bought the second building in Los Alamitos, they gave me the money for the down payment.

I know they would have done the same for my brother if he were down here and wasn't so stubborn. Instead, they gave it to him in round-about ways; they offered to pay for the education of my nieces and nephew; my mother did major clothes shopping when they came down here and took the two girls with them on cruises.

My father used to tease me about paying him back for everything he'd done for us, although he'd always say, "Nah. I'm glad we could help you out."

And I'd say, "I'll pay you back, Dad. When you go to heaven, I'll write you a check and put it in your casket."

"Great! I'll never get to spend it!" he'd said and laughed.

Abby stayed home with my mother and the dogs and called the cemetery while Alex, Linda, and I went to the mortuary. Linda's incessant talking was already getting on my nerves, and I tried to pretend she wasn't there. Somehow, I thought this would be a perfect time to bond with my brother again, and I didn't want her as a distraction.

When we got in the car, I asked Alex if he wanted to go shopping for something for the funeral.

"Nope," he said. "I'm good."

Elevator music, massive floral arrangements and the sound of a water fountain greeted us as we opened the door to the mortuary, and within seconds, someone came to greet us. I told them who we were, and they had us come into a nicely decorated room so we could discuss the details of the funeral in private.

Alex sat there in his bib overalls and twirled his grubby hat in his hands while I tried to focus on what we needed to do. Linda reached out to touch his hand, whether it was to still his hands or comfort him, but he shrugged her off.

"What do you think?" I'd ask Alex when we had choices to make.

"I don't care. Pick out what you want," he said.

I sighed.

In the past, I'd asked my parents what they'd had in mind when the time came for their funerals, and somehow we never came up with anything definitive. We were not religious, and they never talked about wanting a big to-do.

So I chose the casket and the flowers and then filled in the paperwork for the death certificate. I'd decided in advance to have a service at the Greek Orthodox Church before going to the gravesite, and I made myself the primary contact.

"See, now that wasn't so bad," Linda said to Alex as we left.

"I'll be right back," I said, as I went back inside.

I found the man who'd been helping us and said, "Can you be sure to put this in his casket?"

When I handed him the check—one million dollars, made out to Nick Pappas—he looked at me like he couldn't quite believe it. But I meant it. It was more than money. It was the promise I'd made to my father, and this was me keeping it.

At first I hadn't seen her, but as we exited the church, I saw Stavros' former wife Kelli sitting in the last row. She'd always loved my parents, and they felt the same about her. She'd been crying, and she gave my mother a big hug.

"Hello, dear," my mother said, hugging her back.

Stavros stood by with a raised eyebrow, but Kelli waited until my mother turned to leave before sticking her tongue out at him. My niece Chloe and nephew Nik went to stand by the car so they could light a cigarette. The only other person who should have been there was my brother's middle daughter, who apparently found it too distressing to come up from Murrieta.

"I have no idea what her problem is," Alex said, full well knowing the reason she didn't show up was because he'd told her she couldn't bring his ex-wife Jean, and they all disliked his new wife. "We haven't talked for several years. I told her if she didn't like the way I was living my life, it was tough shit. She could do what she wanted."

My mother sighed. "I don't understand," she said.

"I think she didn't feel well and was really upset about Dad's death," I said to her as an explanation, and she shrugged her shoulders with acceptance.

When we went to the gravesite, I led the impromptu eulogy, and I tried not to cry when I started talking about my father.

"My parents were always the best. My father was always a very generous man and never stepped on anyone's toes to get where he was. He had a wonderful sense of humor and always made everyone laugh." I started crying then. "I used to wonder how I was going to pay him back for everything he did for me while he was alive, and I hope I can be half as good a person as he was when I grow up."

I stopped for a few moments. "So I loved him, and I'll miss him terribly. I was there for my parents when they moved across the street from us, and when I said goodbye to him, I promised him I'd take care of my mother."

I'd chosen my words carefully, leaving my brother out altogether. In my opinion, he hadn't gone out of his way to be anything to them over the years, and I felt my sentiments were my own.

I waited for a few minutes to see if anyone else wanted to say anything, but no one rushed up. Then, our youngest daughter Tara got up. She stood by me and unfolded a piece of paper.

"Nick," she started. "N could be a letter for normal. But Pops wasn't that."

Everyone chuckled.

"N is for nonstop, notable, and nutty." Again laughter. "Negotiable, nervy and never-failing.

"I is for incredible, intelligent and always interesting. Plus, irreplaceable.

"C is for clever, constant, caring, compassionate and charming.

"K is for sometimes kissable but always kindhearted, and always kickass!

"The letters I didn't find in his name were G for grandfather and P for Pops to me and my sister, and always for being generous. You sometimes didn't know where you stood with him, especially when you were just getting to know him. But the glimmer in his eye if he caught you off guard told you he was making a joke. I'll really miss him."

When she finished, I gave her a big hug. "I love you, and I think you should start working on all the letters of my name for my day!"

We had lunch at a restaurant near the house, and our table was ready when we got there.

Stavros said, "I'll sit at the head."

"No," I said. "Mother will sit at the head."

"Oh," he said, jerking his head back in surprise. "Then I'll sit at the other end near my daughters."

When it came time for a toast, I started it.

"To my father. I can never thank him enough for everything he did for me."

"Ahem," Stavros said, standing. "To Nick. The best brother-in-law I could have. And here's to those who went before him, and those who couldn't be with us today."

When I lay there in bed that night, unable to sleep, I couldn't quite tell if I'd acted vindictively or just bitchy about Alex. Either way, it had been intentional.

CHAPTER FIFTY EIGHT

VASO

My nephew Nik and his wife left after the luncheon, hoping to make it home to Northern California by midnight. My mother was concerned he'd taken two days off work to come down, and she had me write him a check for five hundred dollars before we left for the funeral. After she signed it, she said, "Don't say anything to Alex. He's such a cheapskate."

It always amazed me how she could cling to certain thoughts, yet let others vanish in an instant.

Thankfully, Stavros decided not to go back to the house. The idea of him walking through that door and taking over—it was too much. I didn't have the strength to pretend I could tolerate it. However, the thought of everyone trailing back to the house also felt overwhelming. As it was, my brother and his wife, their two dogs, my niece and Eddie Jr. were already more company than I could manage, and when we were all there at one time, they sucked all the air out of the room. It reminded me of the chaos of getting ready for the family portrait so many years ago. And if I were being honest, I resented their presence. Abby was different—I considered her more of an extension of my family, and besides me, she was the only one Mother wanted to be with. I longed for silence, for space—I just wanted to be alone with my mother, to sit with her even if we didn't speak. Losing my father was already almost more than I could stand.

For the next few days, I stayed at my parents' house with my mother, though it hardly felt like their home anymore. Too many bodies filled the space, and although everyone tried to feel useful, it was too much. They talked and laughed as though we weren't in mourning, but instead, at a family reunion. Alex entertained everyone with his stories about how he made some part for a piece of equipment that wasn't working properly. And then he went on to tell everyone about all the drug dealers who lived right up the mountain from them and how helicopters constantly flew over spying on them.

He talked about killing and dressing animals for his customers, and since it was getting close to hunting season, he was expecting over a hundred deer and elk to come through his doors.

"I couldn't do it all without this lady," he said, pointing to his wife Linda, who sat like a lump on my side of the sofa, their two dogs asleep on her lap.

What amazed me was that people were actually interested in what he was saying. It reminded me of when the neighborhood boys would gather around him in the garage on Magnolia Avenue, and how I longed for the friends he had. I'd idolized him then, but not now. I think this was when I understood just how much I despised him.

My mother seemed to diminish in front of my eyes, like she might just suddenly disappear. I wanted to clear the room, tell everyone to go— just *go*—but I didn't. I couldn't. So instead, she escaped when she could, slipping away into Abby's room, which had become a quiet harbor.

For the next few nights, I climbed into my parents' bed beside her. The room still smelled faintly of my father's aftershave, the ghost of him lingering on the pillowcases. I lay there beside my mother, listening to her breathing. There were moments I wanted to reach for her hand, but I didn't want to remind her she was now alone. I couldn't imagine how she would go on, and I didn't know how I would either.

On the third morning, I went across the street to our house to shower and then left for work. I preferred my office staff to the chaos in my mother's house.

Everyone but Alex, Linda and Abby left while I was gone, and when I saw my mother sitting on the sofa with Abby, I sat next to her and, for the first time, had the courage to ask her how she was doing.

"I'm all right. It's hard, but I'm getting by," she said. "I wish this wouldn't have happened. And I'm glad everyone's gone," she said.

I was feeling territorial, and honestly, I wanted my mother to myself. I spent two more nights sleeping in my parent's bedroom with her. I'd washed the sheets and the mattress cover of his bed, but I could still smell my father on the pillow; and every time I turned over, his scent woke me. My mother got up a few times in the night to use the bathroom, but other than that, her snoring told me she'd slept okay. I wondered how she did it—how she didn't cry, and how she didn't talk about him. I decided it was because she wasn't thinking clearly. And I thanked god for that blessing.

Alex and his wife were still at the house, along with their two yapping dogs. I loved animals, but these dogs weren't cute, and their constant barking grated on me. I knew I was being petty, but it also irked me that Linda had made herself comfortable in the spot on the sofa where I always sat. She'd seen me there every time she came in, yet for some reason, she thought it was fine to claim that spot as her own. I was being childish, but I promised myself that the next time I saw her there, I was going to say something. Instead, I shot her a look, and I could tell Abby noticed. She was fully aware of the tension between Linda and my mother and me, and I could see how she tried to keep our conversations neutral, careful not to make things worse.

"Okay then," Abby said.

Since we didn't have any groceries in the house, I suggested we go out to dinner that night. Alex wanted to cook instead, so I asked if he and Linda wanted to go to the grocery store.

"Get whatever you want," I said, handing him Mother's credit card.

He eyed it, and then asked, "Whose card is this?"

"It's Mother's."

His mouth thinned with displeasure, and then he said, "Nah, I'll get it."

For the first few days after my father died, I was grateful my mother was where she was with her cognitive issues, but she'd become listless and lethargic. I was hoping this wouldn't be the new marker for her in her decline. I made an appointment with my doctor, and she ordered a series of blood tests.

"She's dehydrated," the doctor said. "Make sure she drinks more water, and let's start her on some vitamins. I'm sure she'll be all right."

"I've started working on the estate paperwork," Abby said when I returned with my mother. She was at the dining room table.

Alex was sitting in my father's chair, and I hated seeing him there like he owned the room. He had on his old sweaty hat, and I could only imagine how it smelled. When he took it off to wipe his head, I noticed his forehead had turned blue from all the silver he regularly ingested. He believed it could cure everything from the common cold to cancer.

But here he was still wearing the new bib overalls he'd brought down; I didn't remember him ever washing them. And he had on the same plaid shirt he'd worn to my father's funeral. His fine salt and pepper curly hair was braided in a ponytail, and it looked as though it hadn't been combed out since he'd been here.

He was disgusting, and suddenly something snapped in my brain. It was everything I could do not to blurt out that Alex had molested me! There was no logical reason for me to do it, but I wanted to.

I went to sit at the dining room table by Abby instead.

"She told me she misses him," Abby said.

"What else has she said?"

"Nothing. Just that he was a good husband, and she misses him."

I let my head fall to one side like I were stretching my neck, and I closed my eyes.

"I'm glad she's said something to someone." I took a deep breath, and then I said, "I wish they would leave. I think she'd prefer the silence."

"We should meet with the attorney before he goes."

"We need to keep her distracted enough so that she won't think of him all the time. And it's awful to say," I said, "but of the two of them, it was probably better that my father went first. She's a little insulated."

I could tell Abby was a little surprised I'd said that, but then she nodded. "I agree." She went back into the office, and I followed her. "I'd like to keep working," she said.

She'd made a list of what she needed to do; she'd already contacted the CPA, and we'd agreed to meet with the attorney Stavros recommended. Since my father's death, I felt he'd tried to be the one in control. I, for one, couldn't stand his attitude, and I felt he was too close to the situation. He'd been my parent's attorney and had drawn up their trusts, but he strutted around acting like he was in charge of everything.

That next day we took my mother to meet the new attorney so they could verify she could communicate her wishes and while she couldn't remember their names afterward, the three of us, Alex, Abby and I felt she'd been clear she wanted us to handle everything.

It also gave the attorney the opportunity to meet all of us to see exactly what she was going to be dealing with. Abby remained the neutral party, for she wasn't an heir, and she was who the attorney could expect to get financial information from.

"We're from a small town in Northern California called Hayfork," Alex said when they asked where he lived. "There's no stoplight in town."

I couldn't help but wonder what they thought of his saying something so brainless.

When I looked at him, all I saw was someone rough around the edges—unkempt, out of place, and painfully unaware of how he came across.

"Where do we start?" Abby asked.

My parents' original trust stated that upon their deaths, everything would pass to the surviving spouse. In the initial review, the attorneys discovered Stavros had somehow neglected to include an apartment building in the trust, so they had to transfer it in, which required several county recordings. We had to have their properties appraised as of my father's death. Abby gathered all the bank accounts, life insurance policies, annuities, and stock portfolios. She notified Social Security and the DMV.

By the time we were finished with what was called The Exemption Trust, we'd spent close to fifty thousand dollars between attorneys and accountants, not to mention Abby's and Tim's time.

Abby had already gone home when the death certificates finally arrived, and I began processing everything in the folder Abby had left. It felt good to be able to check off some items on her list.

Mother still came to work with us every day, and we started eating breakfast on our way in instead of making something at home. Steven ordered a full meal, and my mother and I shared; she ate like a bird, nibbling on her wheat toast and bacon. We were used to bringing dinner home for my parents every night, so we started eating on our way home from the office, which eliminated my having to heat everything up and then do dishes.

We'd stay with my mother until around nine when she started getting tired, and then she'd get ready for bed. I gave her her evening pills, and then she walked us to the door and said, "Get a good night," before she locked it behind us.

The next morning, I could hear clothes in the dryer, and she was dressed and ready to start another day. After my father's death, her universe changed, but we quickly settled into a comfortable routine.

I never asked for compensation, but Stavros determined it would be fair to pay me to watch Mother, so he established a two thousand dollar monthly budget. He came by most Sundays to visit her, and since I was always with her, he'd make idle conversation with me while watching the Golf Channel.

Because I'd never experienced the death of a parent or the inner workings of estate planning, I usually had general questions for him; if I called the Exemption Trust the Survivor's Trust, he'd dryly correct me. "The Exemption Trust is your father's, and the Survivor's trust is, guess whose? Your mother's."

"Do we need to report her income separately?"

"No."

Tim continued to come every week, and he'd post and write checks to pay any bills. I signed the checks and put them in the mail. I emailed Abby copies of accounts she worked on, and since she worked remotely from her home in South Dakota, I could sit at Mother's desk and watch as she made journal entries or updated what I'd sent over.

"How does the accountant know what to do with everything Abby sends her?" I asked one Sunday as Stavros helped himself to some cookies.

This is when I'd usually get a deep sigh, like I was the dumbest person on earth.

"The accountant knows what to do with what Abby sends her," he said in that infuriating tone he used when he thought I didn't understand.

Then I'd give up for the day.

My mother would sit there the entire time and look from me to Stavros like she understood what we were saying.

"Does that make sense?" I'd asked her.

"Yes," she'd said.

Sometimes a week or two would go by where I didn't have questions, but then something Abby or Tim worked on would generate a question, and I wrote it down for the next time he came over. And then I'd have more questions.

It was clear he was growing weary of me, for one Sunday, after asking a simple question, he got up and without a word, he stomped out and slammed the door behind him. I had clearly pushed him too far—he'd reached his limit, and his silence said everything.

"What was that about?" my mother asked.

"I'm not sure. But I think it's me."

"Well, what did you do?"

"I think I've asked him too many questions."

"Well, how does he expect you to know what's going on? Or how to learn anything if you can't ask him questions. *What's wrong with him?*" She looked disgusted, and then asked me to turn our TV program back on.

Looking back on it now, I came to understand Stavros must have thought I was more interested in what I'd receive from the trust, rather than just having natural questions about how it all worked. He'd also disapproved of my asking about anything in front of my mother.

A little over a month after my father died, I found the video I'd made for his seventieth birthday and had it updated. I added images of the sun glinting off the coffin as it was being removed from the hearse and then as it was being lowered into the ground. I chose Josh Groban's "You Raise Me Up" as the soundtrack, and I've never been able to describe what that song does to me. It's not just emotional; it's spiritual. And even now, years later, when I hear it, my eyes fill with tears, and I turn the volume up.

I sent revised copies to Alex, his children, and Abby. I knew it was being childish, but I didn't send one to Stavros.

CHAPTER FIFTY NINE

VASO

Sometimes my mother would catch me by surprise with random thoughts that floated into her mind and she needed to say them out loud.

She'd said before, "I want you to have this house."

"I know you do, and I'd love to have it. But it'll all take care of itself one day."

"But I want to tell someone I want you to have this house."

"Okay, I'll tell the attorney the next time we meet," knowing I would never say something like that to the attorney. No matter how true it was, it would sound as though I'd come up with the idea myself. I also knew that when my mother passed away, Alex and I would split everything up by value.

One time she said, "I don't remember what it was your father used to do to Yia´ Yia, but I can hear her tell him, 'Kakos Nikos.' She'd call him 'Bad Nick', but he never was bad. She loved him."

"I know she did. You've told me that was her way of teasing him when he would sneak up on her and give her a hug. She'd always have a kiss for him when she called him that," I said. "He used to tell her she was the best mother-in-law he ever had."

"Yes. . . " she said thoughtfully. "Although she was his only one. I miss them both."

"So do I, Mother. They were both wonderful people."

"You know, you were Yia´ Yia's best granddaughter."

"What?"

"You were her best. You were the one who came to see her, and you never asked her for anything. You played cards with her."

"You're right about the cards. And you went to see her then too. So you were a wonderful daughter," I said. "You'd bring her stamps and pay her bills. You made sure she had enough food to warm up and eat. And you took her to the doctor when she didn't drive."

"I did?"

"Of course you did. You were a wonderful daughter."

I don't know what made me think of it then, but I asked her, "Did Yia´ Yia ever poke you with her hatpin when you were young?"

I should have prefaced that with something like, "Do you remember your childhood?" for she looked at me like I was nuts.

"Yia´ Yia always used to tell Kaylee and me that if we were bad, she'd poke us with her hatpin. She never did, not that we didn't deserve it, but did she ever do that to anyone? Or was that just a threat?"

My mother tilted her head in thought, like children often do when trying to think of something, then finally said. "I don't think so. I don't remember that."

"That's fine. It doesn't really matter. And I don't know why I even thought about it."

"My goodness," she said. "She's been dead a long time."

"Yes. It's been a while."

"And I can't remember when your dad died—was it just last month?"

I was sorry I'd started this conversation.

"Dad's been gone for almost four years now."

"Oh, he has? I see him every time I look at your beautiful face."

My stomach sank.

"And sometimes I still cry at night."

"Why haven't you told me this sooner?"

"I forget. But it's okay. I'll see him one day."

"Yes, you will."

Alex still called her once a week, and when he did, I'd usually leave her and run across the street so she could have some privacy. I think in some respects this was something I should have kept a better eye on, for Alex started asking me about going to dinner or getting frozen yogurt like we did almost every night. He asked about the credit card statements and wanted to see them.

"What for?" I asked. "Nothing has changed. Tim still posts them, and Abby still sees them every month."

"I don't care. I still think I should start seeing everything."

I wasn't sure how to respond to him. He'd never been interested in my parent's affairs, and nothing had changed since my father died. I wasn't sure how to respond when he said things like that. In fact, over the years he'd said he didn't want anything from them. I hung up the phone unsettled, but the longer I sat with his words, the more the unease gave way to anger. I felt completely baffled. The only explanation I could come up with was that somehow he no longer trusted me. Did he really think I was mismanaging Mother's money—or worse, helping myself to it?

It didn't make any sense until Abby pointed out what I hadn't seen: this was the first time Alex had any real awareness of how much money our parents actually had. And Linda—his ever-present wife—was always chiming in on his calls, her voice just loud enough in the background to steer his doubts.

After that, it felt like nothing I did was ever good enough. Every decision, every effort—I felt watched, second-guessed, diminished.

CHAPTER SIXTY

VASO

The guesthouse had rarely been used over the years, and no one had stayed there since my father's funeral, so when our daughter Holly told me she was coming into town to meet with a client, it seemed like the perfect place for her to stay. I mentioned it to Alex, thinking it was a simple courtesy—just letting him know—but I wasn't asking his permission.

"I think we need to charge her rent," he said flatly. There was something in his tone—tight, watchful—that made it clear he didn't trust my intentions. As if he thought I was trying to slip something past him.

This was Steven's daughter, and she'd be there for a night or two, not moving in. And yet there was this wedge of suspicion, subtle but sharp. "Are you kidding?"

"No rent—she doesn't stay there."

I was so embarrassed when I told her; I couldn't think of anything else to tell her but the truth, and I offered her the guest bedroom at our house. I understood when she said she'd make life easier and just bill her company for a hotel.

Not long after that, Steven bought a 1947 Cadillac, a beautiful beast of a car that was too long to fit into our garage. We thought it made perfect sense to store it at Mother's—her garage had been sitting empty since my father died. Since I still felt the sting of Alex's reaction to Holly staying in the guest house, I decided to run it by him first. I barely got the words out before he cut in with, "He needs to pay rent."

It was like I'd crossed some invisible line I didn't know was there. I didn't realize I should have known better than to even suggest something so simple. I suddenly felt foolish for even thinking we could talk about something so straightforward. With my parents, this would never have been an issue. I hadn't realized how much control my brother had over me, and it wasn't just what he said, but how he said it.

I understood I was not on the same footing with him—not even close.

We bought a cabin up in Lake Arrowhead, and when Alex found out, he and his wife Linda must have Googled me, for when he discovered I had also opened a small store selling cabin décor and antiques, he had a hundred questions for me.

"How are you paying for your inventory?"

"What?"

"How are you paying for your inventory?"

Of course, the first thing I did was get defensive. "Are you kidding me? What are you really asking?"

"Are you using Mother's credit card?"

"Where is this coming from?"

Then I recalled a few times when Stavros had come over and I was at Mother's, I was pricing merchandise to take up to the store. He must have been talking to Alex.

"No, I'm not using Mother's credit card for my store."

I hung up on him.

In a rare moment of goodwill toward Stavros, I invited him to join us for Sunday breakfast at our favorite restaurant. We sat at our usual spot in our favorite waitress's section. Steven brought the newspaper, as he always did, and had just opened it when Stavros said sharply, "I hope you're not planning on reading that at the table."

Steven froze, startled. His face flushed red. Reading the paper at breakfast was our quiet routine, but without a word, he folded it up and set it aside.

My mother looked at Stavros, puzzled.

We made small talk while waiting for our food. Mother asked Stavros how his girls were doing. When she referred to people loosely, I knew from experience she'd forgotten their names. She did that with almost everyone's children now, except Alex's daughter Chloe, who still called her regularly. I was grateful Stavros didn't notice, for he went on and on about the girls and his granddaughters.

When the pancakes came, I reached for the butter.

"You know, that's a lot of calories," Stavros said flatly.

"Yum," I replied, stuffing a piece of bacon into my mouth. He had a way of pulling the worst out of me, like I was twelve again.

"Mind your business," my mother said sharply.

Good for her, I thought.

"I'm just saying," he muttered.

When the bill came, Steven reached for my mother's credit card to pay. Stavros looked at him as if he'd just pulled out a loaded weapon.

"What?" I asked.

"Is that Mother's card?"

"Yes. Do you have a problem with that?"

"Well, I just don't think Steven should be walking around with your mother's credit card. I'll pay for myself."

I wanted to call him out for what he was being—a jerk—but I bit my tongue. Steven, meanwhile, looked genuinely hurt.

My mother turned toward Stavros again, clearly confused. I silently pleaded with her: 'Say something.' But she didn't. Not a word in Steven's defense.

"Are you serious right now?" I said. "What is your problem?"

"Nothing. I just think he should be accountable for what he uses her card for."

"Oh, come on, Stavros," I snapped. "Dad never had a problem with it, and Steven's been helping with their banking for years."

His eyes narrowed, and I realized I'd just stepped on a landmine.

"Well, your father's not alive anymore, is he?" he said coldly, folding his napkin. Then, looking straight at me, he added, "Steven needs to be taken off all the accounts."

I turned to my mother, willing her to step in. But she sat there stunned, offering nothing.

Steven nudged me. I slid out of the booth so he could get up. My heart broke for him. After everything he'd done for my parents, he was being treated like a thief.

As Stavros walked off, my mother finally spoke. "I don't understand what he's so upset about. I want Steven to have my card."

"I know, Mother. He's just being an ass."

"Where's Steven?"

"He's probably outside. Stavros really hurt his feelings."

"I could see that. I'll tell him I'm sorry."

By the time we stepped outside, she'd already forgotten exactly what had happened—but not enough to forget to apologize.

"For whatever he did," she told Steven. "He can be such an ass."

"I'm sorry," I told Steven on the drive home. "I'll call Abby. And the attorney."

"No need," he said quietly. "I get it. He thinks I'm stealing your parents' money."

I turned around to my mother in the backseat. "Why didn't you say anything? Stavros wants you to take Steven off the accounts. He needed to hear that you didn't agree."

"Well, I don't," she said.

My voice was sharper than I had meant it to be . "He needed to hear that from *you*."

"I'm so sorry," she said quietly. "I didn't understand what he was really doing."

I let out a long sigh. I didn't want to be angry at her, but I was.

I called Abby the minute we got back to Mother's, and she was puzzled.

"The only explanation I can come up with is that, like me, Steven isn't technically family—and if he weren't who he is, someone in his position could easily take advantage of your mother and drain your parents' money."

"You've got to be kidding," I said, getting angrier.

"Call the attorney, and I'm sure they'll tell you the same thing. Stavros can be quite a jerk when he wants to, and he should have explained the reasoning behind his comment," Abby said.

"Even if that's true, it really hurt Steven's feelings."

"Was Mom with you?"

Abby always called her that when she talked about her.

"Yes, and she didn't know what to say."

"I'm so sorry. Call the attorney, and tell Steven to consider the source, which I know will be hard for him to do."

We hung up, and on Monday I put a call in to the attorney.

The attorney said, "Technically, Stavros is correct. Even though your parents added him to their accounts, now that your father has passed away, he wants to protect your mother. You'd be surprised at some of the things we hear relatives do, and I know that's why he did it. I have to admit, he could have been a little more diplomatic about it, and at least you now understand the fiduciary responsibilities."

I was disgusted, and Steven couldn't even talk about it. I knew he was humiliated, and yet there was nothing I could do.

Although I was terribly embarrassed, I went to the bank the next morning and had Steven's name deleted from my parent's bank accounts.

"My father died, and our attorney suggested it," I said, as if I needed any explanation.

"Yup," the banker said. "It's all part of the game."

It turned out my mother didn't care for it up in the mountains. She didn't like the drive up, or how she felt walking on the uneven ground. So we started having someone we knew watch her from Friday morning until Sunday afternoon. If I went up with a girlfriend to work in the store, Steven would take over staying with her.

After Alex questioned whether I was using Mother's credit card for personal expenses, I started to feel both uneasy and oddly guilty for leaving her. I wasn't trying to hide anything from him—far from it. I just wanted to be transparent, especially so he'd know who would be with Mother if something came up. If we'd had a more trusting, normal relationship, it probably wouldn't have mattered. And in the beginning, it didn't.

One Sunday afternoon when I was home with Mother, Alex called and I eavesdropped on her conversation with him. I watched as she held the receiver away from her ear for a minute, like my father used to do, and she mimicked talking with her hands. Alex must have been telling her about something she wasn't interested in. She gave me a wicked smile, and I realized my mother was still with it, even if it was only for the moment.

"I see," she said. She held the phone away from her ear again. "That sounds like a wonderful opportunity for you," she then said.

When she finally hung up, I asked what "opportunity" Alex was going on about. First, she said, "His wife is always in the background yipping, and it drives me crazy."

Then she mentioned his neighbor was thinking of selling the ten acres next door—Alex had always wanted to buy it and finally have the whole thirty acres to himself. He'd talked about that for years, along with how much he loathed that neighbor.

I surprised myself by calling him back. For the next twenty minutes, Alex ranted about the guy next door and how badly he wanted him gone. He was looking into getting a loan to buy the property.

"How much is the land?" I asked.

"Three hundred thousand," he said.

"Oh," I said, taken aback—that was more than I expected.

"There's a double-wide on the property. Linda and I could fix it up and actually live there," he added. "Right now, we're still crammed in our one room with the camper, and all her craft stuff is taking over."

I couldn't believe I cared, but an idea started to form. "I'll call you back."

Turning to my mother, I said, "I have a crazy idea. Do you remember Alex just telling you about the land next door being for sale?"

She nodded.

"Well, what if we gave him some of the money he's already going to inherit? If he doesn't need a loan, the sale could go quickly, and he'd finally have a house."

She barely paused before saying, "I think that would be wonderful for him. Let's do it."

So I called him back, asked for the paperwork, and cleared it with Abby where to withdraw the money from. When I told Steven, I could see it all over his face—he thought I'd lost my mind.

"After everything he's done to you?"

"I know. But I can set that aside right now. This is a real opportunity for him, and I want to help."

It felt good to do something generous, even for him. My mother might not remember the conversation, but I knew it was the kind of thing she and my father would've done without hesitation. For a brief moment, Alex and I were friendly again—though that wasn't the point.

Alex must have told Stavros, who exploded.

"What made you think you could do something like that without talking to me? There are two trusts involved. Of course you asked your mother, but she'd agree to anything you suggested. You've opened Pandora's box."

Later, I asked my mother how she felt about helping Alex. She admitted she didn't remember the earlier conversation, but she said she still thought it was a good idea, and that was good enough for me.

That was the thing about her. She didn't always remember details, but if you asked how she *felt*, her answer was consistent. I never believed I was taking advantage of her—no matter what Stavros or Alex thought.

CHAPTER SIXTY ONE

VASO

When my father was still alive, I took my mother to see a neurologist, who enrolled her in a clinical trial. I sat in on her first appointment, instinctively jumping in to answer questions for her when she hesitated.

"Who's the vice president of the United States?

"What's today's date?"

I quickly realized they were trying to make a note of her answers, and eventually let her attend the sessions alone. The clinic staff never shared any results with me—not that I expected they would, and my father and I understood the trial wouldn't cure her, but was for research.

From her neurologist, we *did* learn one thing: she didn't have Alzheimer's. He called it a cognitive disorder. He recommended a few supplements and prescribed a patch—while it wouldn't stop the decline, it might slow it down.

Each evening, I'd apply it to her chest. Sometimes I'd hold it up and gently ask, "Where does this go?" She'd smile and touch the top of her head, or her ear. The innocence of it—so childlike—was almost too much to bear.

"No, it goes here," I'd say softly, guiding her hand to her chest.

Around this time, I started having the same unsettling dreams. In them, I'd walk into a massive shopping center or a big building, and when it was time to leave, I couldn't find my car. No matter how many times I clicked the key fob, nothing happened. The parking lot didn't look the same anymore. I was disoriented and always woke up just as panic set in.

Then came the creeping fear that maybe I was losing my grip, too. Every time I forgot something or made a simple mistake with my bookkeeping, I'd spiral down, wondering if I was experiencing early signs of cognitive decline. I started asking friends if they ever forgot names or did absentminded things.

"Are you kidding?" one of them said. "I can't remember what I had for breakfast!"

It made me feel a little less alone—but not enough to quiet the fear. I didn't fully trust their reassurance. Or myself.

Eventually, I began taking the same supplements my mother was on. The more I thought about how alike we were—same shaped face, same little moles on our chins and upper lips—the harder it was to ignore the dread. I couldn't shake the thought: maybe I was looking at my own future.

Every day, I missed the mother I'd known. I used to be able to talk to her about anything, and she'd follow my conversation, but now I was confusing her if I talked about anything that had a lot of detail. When she'd cock her head and get that look on her face like she was asking, *"What?"* it was clear I was the cause of her confusion. I eventually stopped talking to her about multidimensional subjects. I began telling myself, 'For god's sake, Vaso, you're in your sixties and old enough to make your own decisions! Quit asking your mother.'

Since my mother was on her own after nine each night until the morning when we came for her, I often found myself wondering whether she was actually sleeping through the night. She never gave me any reason to think otherwise, but that didn't mean much—she could be waking up at two in the morning, getting fully dressed, turning on the television, and waiting for us to show up hours later. I began to question whether she was still showering regularly or brushing her teeth. I could ask her, of course, but I knew she'd instinctively say yes, whether it was true or not.

The idea of a baby monitor or a discreet camera in her room crossed my mind—something I could keep by my bedside to alert me if she was up during the night. I even started researching options that would notify me of movement or unusual activity. In the past, I would've just bought it without hesitation, but this time I decided to check in with Alex first.

He wasn't on board. He said it felt invasive, like spying. While he didn't directly address the cost, my mention of the price gave me a sinking feeling that his concern might be financial, and not about privacy. I'd assumed he'd share my concern for her safety, but apparently, he didn't.

To avoid another disagreement, I dropped the idea. Instead, I started quietly checking for signs that she was sticking to her routine—if the shower floor was damp, if her toothbrush was wet. She still ran a load of laundry every day, including a towel, but that didn't mean she wasn't just washing the same clothes over and over.

Out of nowhere, Alex started showing a sudden interest in the day-to-day details of Mother's finances. As a trustee, he was technically within his rights to ask for the reports he wanted, but the constant requests made me furious. It felt accusatory—like he didn't trust me—and I struggled to keep from internalizing it. The only way I felt I could push back without outright refusing him was to say that if he needed more detailed documentation, we'd have to involve Abby or Tim and pay them for their time. I figured that would discourage him, but it didn't.

Since Tim still came by once a week, I asked if he could take over sending the reports. I hated spending more money from the trust, but I hated even more the feeling that I was under Alex's scrutiny.

"I can do it," Tim said. "But what's going on with him?"

"I don't know," I admitted. "All I know is that every time he asks me for something, it feels like he's accusing me of cheating, and I can't stand it."

I was well aware that I was being sensitive—maybe even overreacting—but the more he pushed, the more I resented him. Thankfully, Tim took over, and each week he sent Alex printouts detailing what we'd done.

When I mentioned it to Abby later, she was surprised. "That's just going to cost the estate more money," she said. "Is Alex talking to Stavros?"

"I don't know. Maybe. All I know is it hurts. And it makes me feel like I'm doing something wrong, even when I know I'm not."

"I'm sorry you're dealing with this," she said gently. "You've already got enough on your plate taking care of Mom and working."

Somehow, in the mounds of paperwork being emailed around, Stavros found Steven had signed a credit card transaction from the drugstore, and he hit the roof.

"Under no circumstances should Steven be involved in *any* financial matters. I've already told you that. His name absolutely has to be removed from everything. What else is there I should know about?"

"But he's been involved with my parents' dealings for years. He's not doing anything wrong." Although I kept my voice even, I was seething inside, and I despised him too.

"I've already told you, a non-family member can't be involved in your parent's finances. You need to address this immediately."

I was livid, and I was sure that if I said *anything* to him, I'd sound like a petulant, spoiled child. But how dare he even continue to suggest there was any impropriety! Steven had been a trusted member of our family for over thirty years! And how did Stavros even get a copy of anything I sent to Alex? I hung up on him.

I felt like a child crying to Abby, and she was not happy.

"I think Stavros is overreacting, but I also think you have to work with this as objectively as you can," she suggested. "I'm really sorry you're going through this. I don't know what's gotten into Alex *or* Stavros."

"I'm sure he's seen terrible things relatives have done involving his clients, but that's not the case here at all. You've seen almost everything Steven's done, and I can't help feeling like suddenly I'm under a microscope. I can't just pretend I'll offer to sign a receipt—do you know how hurt he's going to be when I tell him?"

I was not wrong—he was shattered again.

"Are you kidding me? I feel like I've just been socked in the stomach. Again." He was insulted, and so was I. "We're doing everything we can to take care of your mother," he said.

"I know. I hate them both," I said, referring to Stavros and my brother.

In the meantime, my mother still came to work with us, but she set her clerical work aside. I rearranged my office and made a space where we could put her extra recliner, and we bought her a small television. I knew plunking a person with cognitive issues in front of a TV all day was not the best stimulation, but I was still running my business and I needed to have her near me. I felt guilty, like I was the parent who gives their child a cell phone or tablet so they'll be quiet while they get something done.

As I watched her, she turned into a gentler, more beautiful person. I took her everywhere with me. Wherever we went, she waited patiently, always smiling, and sometimes asking questions.

I wanted my mother for as long as she could be with me.

I tried to keep my anger with Alex and Stavros away from my mother, for I knew it hurt her to see me upset, but one day at work, I'd had three scathing emails from my brother, and I started crying. Actually, my brother didn't know how to use the computer or send emails, so his wife Linda did it for him, and her illiteracy irritated me even more.

I, Linda, am typing this for Alex
CVS/Pharmacy...Oct. 14, 2014...Total Amount $70.49. I need to know what was bought and who it was bought for???

My reply:

Receipt for $70.49 is a prescription. Based on the receipt, I can't tell which one; however, I'm having CVS give me a printout of mother's prescriptions filled for the year. This is all I can do going backwards. As I mentioned in a previous email, I'll begin making copies of the actual prescription envelope, which should show the date and what the medication was.

I, Linda, am typing this for Alex
CVS/Pharmacy...Oct. 16, 2014...Total Amount 41.78. Need to know what was bought and who it was bought for???

My reply was the same:

Receipt for $41.78 is also a prescription. Based on the receipt, I can't tell which one; however, I'm having CVS give me a printout of mother's prescriptions filled for the year. This is all I can do going backwards. As I mentioned in a previous email, I'll begin making copies of the actual prescription envelope, which should show the date and what the medication was.

I knew duplicating my reply would annoy Alex, but it was something I could do to make the obligation of complying with him less aggravating for me.

I, Linda, am typing this for Alex

Vaso, I received some receipts from you. Some were on my list, others were not. The two (2) receipts you sent on the list below had no description nor was it stated who it was for which I sent back to you to answer on those two. I still need to know what the other charges are, and who it was for. Apparently you did not read the email stating I would like to know what the CVS purchase is and who it is for. I am resending this request to you below. I want answers to my questions below now. Alex.

In October, I sent them a receipt from Smart & Final and this is the reply I sent to their questions:

You're funny. The Charms Mini Pops are candy to give out at Mother's on Halloween. We have trick or treaters down here. I wouldn't touch them myself. The Soft Bath is toilet paper. The Triskets are what Mother and I have for lunch when we have tuna and cottage cheese.

He replied:

Vaso, you need to pay for your own stuff. Mom pays for her own. The Trust should not be reimbursing for snacks etc.

So, in order to keep my sanity, I started photocopying *all* credit card charges, whether prescriptions or cough drops, and I automatically emailed Alex, Abby, and Stavros a copy, along with a description. I was hoping the paperwork would make him crazier than he was.

At the end of the year, I received the annual Citizen of The Year award from Cerritos Community College for all the community service Steven and I had done over the years. I mistakenly assumed it would be all right for Mother to buy our tax-deductible tickets to the event, as I knew she'd enjoy going with us.

"Let's buy you something new to wear," she said when I told her about the event.

When Alex found out about it, the shit hit the fan.

I, Linda, am typing this for Alex, Vaso.

Congratulations on your award, but I think if you take Mother, she doesn't need to pay for your tickets! Everyone should pay for their own. And I don't think she should pay for you to have a new outfit. Either pay for it yourself, or wear something you already have. Alex.

I got an email from Abby congratulating me on the award, and she cc'd a note to Alex that he should be proud of me for the work I'd done. It was her way of telling him to back off without actually saying so.

Alex hadn't come down for Christmas for over twenty years, and if he had, he'd have known that Steven and I, the girls and our grandchildren, celebrated the evening with my parents. Steven and my father used to barbecue New York steaks, and we'd make Greek Spaghetti to go with them. After he died, we kept up the tradition, and Steven gladly took on the role of head chef. Our youngest, Tara, made the spaghetti, and Holly would usually bring her famous cheesecake.

In years past, Stavros used to bring his daughters to celebrate Christmas with us, and even after they'd grown and moved out, he would still occasionally join us for dinner. But this year was different—he didn't show up like he used to when my father was alive, and truthfully, no one seemed to notice he was missing.

My parents had always covered the cost of our holiday meals, so when we made our annual trip to Costco to buy the steaks, I naturally sent the receipt to Alex—who, true to form, responded almost immediately.

I, Linda, am typing this for Alex

Hello Everyone, It does not matter how many bring something for dinner, it would still be nice to treat Mom to a Christmas Dinner that you pay for or everyone can pay for their own meals. Alex

Instead of telling him to 'F off' I just didn't respond. I never told Steven or Mother about that email and instead decided it was time I learned to stop getting so offended by the things Alex and Stavros did.

That same Christmas, I forgot to send Christmas cards to Alex and his family, so the next time Tim came in, we wrote their checks. I wrote a quick note about running out of time, and no one but Alex even commented.

I, Linda, am typing this for Alex,

Vaso, I'm assuming you wrote your family's checks on time, but sent my family's cards out late?

In January, I had an idea that was a little crazy. I emailed Abby to run it by her.

"I'm thinking of sending everyone their birthday cards at one time. Like this month, regardless of when their actual date is. That way I don't have to calendar fifteen cards throughout the year. I'll put a note in the card and explain what I'm doing."

"Sounds good to me," she said. "Anything that will save you time. You have enough going on."

So I went down my list and wrote out everyone's checks and put them in the mail with my explanation, and everyone got a kick out of it. Everyone, except Alex.

I Linda is typing this for Alex.

Vaso, What are you doing? You can't send out everyone's card at one time. The cards should go out on their birthdays. They'll cash the checks.

My reply:

Well, they're going to cash them anyway, so what's the difference? I'm the one who is stuck remembering everyone's birthday, mostly your family's. And this will save me and Tim time in the long run. I ran it by Abby and she thought it was a clever idea.

Abby? Who told you you could ask Abby? She's not even a trustee. She can't make any decisions.

I felt like Alex had now suddenly turned on Abby. She'd been the one who worked tirelessly to get all my parents' affairs in order, and we would have been lost without her. We could never repay her for everything she'd done for us, and it was all from her heart. She loved my parents.

Since my mother was now slowing down physically as well as mentally, I asked her doctor to prescribe physical therapy. I knew it couldn't hurt her to go through some basic routines, and it was interesting watching them put her through some exercises that hopefully would make her feel more stable. I filmed her walking on a large flat treadmill, strapped into a harness so she could improve her balance. I sent Abby a copy of the video, and in her reply email, she was happy I'd started taking her. Realizing I had something I could keep to myself, I childishly decided not to send Alex or Stavros the video. I would continue to keep my mother to myself whenever I could.

We went two times a week, and as I sat and watched her go through her routine, it broke my heart to see my sweet mother rely on the therapist to guide her through the exercises.

We were still heading up to the mountains on weekends so I could work in our store. A woman named Lupe was our waitress where we had breakfast most mornings, and she just loved my mother. I asked her if she'd be interested in a part-time job. We'd known her for years, and she had a warmth and attentiveness that felt right. After checking in with Abby, we agreed to pay her fourteen dollars an hour for two twelve-hour days. Lupe made sure my mother had her meals and took her on short walks every day. She even offered to help clean, but we still had the housekeeper from the beach house, so that part wasn't necessary.

I knew I should've mentioned it to Alex first. But at that point, I was tired of asking for permission, tired of defending every single choice I made, and tired of feeling like I was always on trial. So I didn't ask. I just decided I knew was right for my mother—and then I told him afterward.

CHAPTER SIXTY TWO

ALEX

I started calling Stavros after my dad died. He'd sometimes cut me off, like the prick he is, but I'd just keep talking. He'd ask me things about Vaso, and I told him. When I told him about buying the property, he went through the roof. But I didn't care. My parents had the money, and there wasn't any reason I couldn't do what I wanted to now and not wait until Mom died. Even though she was going downhill, it could take forever.

For years I'd had to share the bridge onto our properties with my neighbor Sam, who was a total jerk. He'd complain that he had to look at all the stuff on my land, like my old truck parts and farm equipment that lined the dirt road to my house. I told him it was *my* land and I could do anything I wanted with it, though he wasn't the only one to tell me it looked like I lived in a junkyard. Linda had gotten on my case about it too.

When he told me he was ready to give it up, I couldn't believe the opportunity had finally come, but then I'd have to get a loan. I hated the thought of doing paperwork; everyone would know my business. So when Vaso said Mom would give me the money now, I thought, *why not?*

I asked Mom the next time I called if this was something she wanted to do, even though I'd already told Vaso I'd take the money—and I had to remind her what it was she'd agreed to.

"I think that's a great idea," she said.

I'd complained about my neighbor over the years—when I talked to my dad—but sometimes, I wondered if they even listened to me. I was never sure what to say to them other than to ask them how they were doing. It was always the same.

"We're fine," my dad would say.

So then I'd talk about anything that I was doing, going into gory detail just to pass the time.

That was the thing about my mom now; you could ask her something and she would give you a logical answer. If you asked her later if she remembered what you asked her, she'd admit she couldn't; but if you asked her the same question again, she'd give you the same answer. I've wondered what really went on in her mind.

I think Vaso asks her to do stuff that suits Vaso, and Mom just says yes. When I call and ask if she told Vaso to do something, she doesn't remember. I think Vaso is taking advantage of Mom. The money she spends is outrageous. They don't need to be going out to dinner. And Vaso should pay her own way.

Without asking me, Vaso has had someone come stay with my mom on Saturdays and Sundays when she and Steven take off for the mountains. Someone needs to be with her, but I'm not happy with the arrangement. One day when I called down there, Lupe answered the phone, and I started asking her some questions. She told me she'd known Steven and Vaso for several years and really enjoyed spending time with my mom. I asked her what she did for work during the week, and she told me she was a waitress!

I asked my mom if she liked Lupe, and of course she told me she did. What else could she say when the woman was probably standing right there?

And now, Stavros has made me wonder if Vaso was trying to throw me off when she came up with the idea of giving me money to buy my neighbor's land and house. He said we've opened up an opportunity for her to start taking money from the estates.

I told Linda to go to the post office every day until that check came. It couldn't be soon enough to get rid of Sam.

CHAPTER SIXTY THREE

STAVROS

I've sometimes wanted to cut Vaso down to the quick. I always thought Nick and Kate spoiled her, and I resented the fact she never earned everything they gave her. I didn't have numbers to back me up, but I just knew. And now, since her father died, she's been a pain in the ass. Her questions about the trust have driven me crazy; in fact, if it weren't for the fact my sister has shown more signs of dementia, I would stop going over there. Vaso is always there, making me feel like she's watching over everything. It's made me realize she is looking forward to Kate's death so she can get her fair share of the estate.

I knew technically I wasn't in a position to ask for financial information about the trust, but Alex was a willing accomplice. He'd started calling me after Nick died, and at first, I wanted to be there for him, but he's also gotten on my nerves. He talks about things I'm really not interested in, and it only gets good when he tells me things Vaso has done.

I know I hurt his feelings when I asked him how he could be so foolish as to have Vaso write him a check for that property next door.

"Now you've left the door open for your sister to ask for something," I'd said.

"She gets enough as it is," Alex said, but he cut our conversation short.

I didn't think I'd have the opportunity to ask Kate if she approved of giving the money to Alex if Vaso was there when I came to visit, so I called her.

"It's Stavros," I said when she picked up the phone. I didn't know if she'd recognize my voice.

"I know who it is, dear. I'm not totally brain dead."

For a moment, I was speechless.

"Since we don't talk much on the phone, I wasn't sure you'd recognize me."

"What do you want?"

"Ah, I just wanted to check in."

"I'm fine."

"Is anyone there with you?"

"You mean Vaso?"

I wasn't certain how to react to her abruptness, so I said, "Well, I was just checking in. I won't be coming by."

"That's fine. I'm good," she said again.

"Okay, well then. I wanted to know how you felt about Alex buying the property next door." There, I'd said it.

"What?"

"The property next door to Alex. How do you feel about him buying it?"

"I think he's always wanted it, so I'm glad. I think it has a house on it."

"Well, yes, it does."

She sounded totally lucid.

"Well then. You're by yourself?"

"Yes, Vaso went across the street. I told you that. I'm fine. Glad you called."

And she hung up.

'Well, that doesn't mean she knows what she's doing,' I said aloud.

"What was that, dear?" my wife Jane said as she came into the room.

"Oh, nothing," I said. "Kate knew who I was."

"Well, of course she would, Stavros. You're her brother."

CHAPTER SIXTY FOUR

VASO

One day, I received a package from Ameriprise Investments. Since I'd already received my distribution from my father's trust, I wasn't sure why they'd sent it. I emailed Laura, our account manager, asking about it, and I received this email back from Alex.

> *I, Linda typing this for Alex Pappas* (this is verbatim)
>
> *Vaso, I am not sure what you are doing. You turn this over to me a month ago and I have been in contact with Ameriprise. I explain this to Laura the last time we talk on the phone.*
>
> *Reading the emails below makes me think your interference is confusing everyone. I definitely did not realize your involvement concerning my half since you turn it over to me a month ago. Like the email stated below, you already received your half any more of your involvement is confusing **it does not** concern you.*
>
> *Would **you please stay out of this** let me work with Ameriprise alone. I do not need your interference.*
>
> *Alex*

I didn't waste my time with a reply, but the next day, I received this email, which was sent to Abby in South Dakota and cc'd to me.

I, Linda, writing this for Alex

1. ***Steven petty cash*** *(250.00 + or - month) needs to be close down. This comes out of the Trust it was never approve by the Trustees Vaso started this before Dad pass on. Claiming there are things they have to pay cash for. I was against this from the beginning.*

2. ***Double-dipping***
    Vaso is paid $2,000.00 a month to take care of Mom. Plus Vaso has the "Trust" pay for individuals to take care of Mom when Vaso takes off the weekends or when ever. The Trust never agreed to pay for these individuals and Vaso refuse to take out of her $2,000.00, Lupe receives $337.50 + or - ***every weekend*** *depending on the hours she receives. Lupe is not a certify health-care giver actually her employment as a waitress Lupe told me. At time Vaso pays other individuals out of the Trust to help take care of mom. This did not receive unanimous approval.*

3. ***Food***
    Steven and Vaso needs to cuts back on eating out they are unnecessary spending way to much money $2,500.00 + each month on food. When ever there is a special occasion on Steven side of the family they take them out to eat on Mom credit card pays for everyone meals. Better yet Steven and Vaso should do the right thing pay for their own meals charge to their own credit card. On mom credit card should be only charges for mom meals and expenses.

4. ***Nickel and dime the Trust*** *it has come to my attention asking question on the expenses that Vaso will combine their items with Mom having the Trust pay for all. Vaso and Abby commented when I brought this up that I was being petty stating for all the things Vaso does for Mom, Vaso is owed this. The Trust pays Vaso to take care of Mom.*

5. ***Guest and Travels*** *when ever family (especially family and close friends) come down to visit mom. Vaso hands over the*

credit card tells them to go shopping, provides a car for their own personal use. Yes we all been guilty of this. It is now time for everyone pay their own travel expense. (A hidden gifting that has not been discuss) which can run up to $1,000.00 + for each guest.

6. ***Guest House*** *- Instead of giving Steven daughter a free lodging it is time to have her pay rent for the use of the guest house she uses when she comes down to visit the Company she works for, better yet she can use a motel/hotel take it off as a business expense.*

7. ***Garage****—Steven stores his prize car in mom garage with alarm service parking mom car out on the curb. It is time for Steven to either start paying storage rent or take his car out put mom car back in the garage where it belongs.*

8. ***Credit Cards*** *- it has come to my attention upon asking what the CVS charges were for. My question was "what are these charges and who are they for?" I am always being told mom in such good health. I was flooded with unnecessary amount of emails mostly not answering the questions, when the answer could have been sent in one (1) email. I sent my request in one (1) email. Anyway, it turns out that Vaso will combine her charges with Mom have the Trust pay it doesn't matter how small or large the Trust does not owe Steven and Vaso they need to pay for their own items with their own credit cards.*

9. ***Reimbursements*** *- Vaso is turning in receipts stating the Trust needs to reimburse her for items she bought for the Trust combine with her items she bought for herself. Being Trustee's I was under the impression Trustees are not to received gifts and reimbursements.*

10. ***Abby $500.00*** *- each month Abby received $500.00 when I originally ask about this Vaso told me it was a life time gifting from Mom. This was something that Mom wanted to do for Abby. Abby receive a wage from both Trusts and should not be gifted $500.00 a month which she is still receiving. I want*

> *to know why the $500.00 a month is continuing and what it is for? Here is the November info: dated 11/11/2014, check #1384, account Personal Expenses, Memo #47, $500.00.*

> **11. VasoOffice -** *a while back Vaso ask Uncle Stavros and me about moving her office into mom office. We both said no unless she want to pay rent, no reply. Knowing Vaso she has already done this. Which leads to doubts when ever the Trust is bill for Computer service and expenses who is it really for? Vaso needs to verify she did not did it anyway without Trustee's approval.*

When I read his email, my blood pressure skyrocketed. I could feel my heart pounding in my chest and my stomach turning. I had to close my eyes and sit still for a few minutes, just to breathe. My first thought was simple and searing: I hated my brother's fucking guts.

My second thought was: *How the hell do I respond to this?*

And then, unexpectedly, I laughed at Linda's mangled attempt at English. She was an idiot. A clueless, half-witted idiot.

But the truth was, no response I could write would ever satisfy Alex. Anything I said would come across as defensive. And that's what made me so furious—because I had nothing to defend.

The garage? The only car that had ever been stored there was our father's before he died. Mother's car had always been parked out front. After she stopped driving, Abby used it when she came into town—mostly to visit her son in Perris, or to attend meetings with the accountant and the attorney. And whenever she was at the house, even before my father died, she joined us for meals. That was how it had always been—my parents were generous with everyone. Grandchildren, nieces, nephews. Visitors. They gave freely. Even Alex accepted their money when he came down for Dad's funeral.

Before my mother died, *she* was the one who wanted to do something for Abby. After nearly fifty years together, she suggested the lifetime gift. It was her idea—not mine.

As for using Mother's office—it had made sense. I had an office across the street, but after I retired, it was easier for both of us if I did my bookkeeping and writing at her place. It was more comfortable for her. But now, Alex had the nerve to accuse me of updating Mother's computer for *my* benefit? As if Tim's work on it had been some scheme?

I'd even done the math once. Based on the hours I spent—twelve a day, seven days a week—it worked out to over 360 hours a month. That was about $5.50 an hour. If I were billing the trust what I could have, it would've been nearly $5,500 a month. But I never thought of it that way. I wanted to be there. I chose it. Steven too, though unpaid, was there beside me, taking on the responsibility. We were not ripping anyone off.

I had the answers to all their accusations. But none of them would matter to Alex or Stavros. They didn't want answers. They wanted someone to intimidate and control.

I was livid. And he'd pushed me too far.

So I did the one thing I knew I probably shouldn't: I called Alex.

As I waited for him to answer, I glanced over and saw my mother dozing in her chair. My heart pounded with rage. When he picked up, I didn't even think—the words just rushed out.

"You're a fucking asshole," I said. "And I still remember you and Richard Bice sitting in the family room sofa bed, smelling like cigarette smoke and body odor—and you molested me. I was twelve years old, for God's sake."

There was a long, stunned silence on the line.

"Fuck you, Vaso. I never did any such thing!"

"Why would I say that if it weren't true?"

"Because women always say things like that."

"I fucking hate you," I said, and I hung up.

I stared at the phone, shaking. *Did he actually believe what he had just said?* Had he never thought about it? Never wondered if I'd tell someone? I should've told my father. He would've killed him. Or at the very least, disowned him.

But what would that have done to the family?

Sometimes I thought about telling his children. But what good would that have done? They would be just three more people with even more wreckage in their lives.

Instead, I told my mother.

I watched her face as the words registered. She stood up and came toward me.

"I'm so sorry. I'm so sorry," she said, crying. "Why didn't you ever say something?"

I couldn't believe I'd said it. Why now? Why *this* moment?

"I'm fine, Mother," I said, hugging her. "I don't know why I told you."

"But you did," she said softly. "And he's an awful person. I'm glad he moved away. He's not my son anymore."

"I'm so sorry," I whispered. "I didn't let it ruin my life."

But deep down, I felt I'd done something even worse than telling Alex or Stavros's families—I'd told my sweet, aging mother a truth she never should have had to carry. I prayed she'd forget. That she'd drift back to sleep and let the memory slide away.

Eventually, she returned to her chair and nodded off. I sat watching her soft, rhythmic breathing, hoping she'd wake with peace instead of pain. And maybe that's what happened, because she never mentioned it again.

When I told Steven, he didn't judge me, but I knew he wasn't entirely okay with my hasty decision.

"Do you think she remembers?" he asked.

"She didn't seem to," I said.

Steven had hated Alex since I told him what had happened over thirty years ago. He tolerated him for the sake of keeping the peace, but he'd always said, "I have no use for him." And from then on, I tried not to tell Steven every cruel thing Alex said, because I knew it would only upset him more.

But he always knew—when I got that look, when I came unglued— he knew something new had happened.

For days, I worried my mother would bring it up again. I wished I could take it all back. I started to believe I *was* the bad person they made me out to be.

But she never said a word.

A couple of weeks later, I took another risk. I knew the truth, but never wanted to embarrass her by asking outright. So when the moment felt natural, I tested the waters.

"My father really looked after Alex, didn't he?" I said once.

"Yes, he did."

"He was a good father to both of us."

"Yes," she said. "He was."

That should have been enough.

But I couldn't stop.

"My father wasn't Alex's father, was he?"

She didn't flinch. "No," she said, without drama. Then she turned back to her program.

And that was that.

After that, I let it all rest. I didn't press her again. I wanted her to have peace. There were no more secrets left between us.

And from that moment on, I started referring to my father as *my father* whenever I spoke to Alex. It was a small twist of the knife—but it was mine.

CHAPTER SIXTY FIVE

VASO

More than once, I've wondered if I was losing my mind to bitterness. Not my memory, but my actual mind. Resentment had eaten away at me, and I wanted to turn back the clock to when I wasn't so angry. But I was growing more intolerant every day. I hated myself for feeling the way I did, but I'd felt I'd come close to being pushed over the edge. I didn't want to feel that way, but it seemed each new day brought some sort of dilemma. Alex and Stavros constantly made me feel like I was taking advantage of my mother, which, sadly, would be easy to do if that was my plan. And no matter what I could say to defend myself, I believe it would have just made everything worse. I needed to be more careful. I saw now that any time I'd disagreed with them, it made me look guilty.

What has surprised me most is that if I could step back and see everything from an objective point of view, I think I'd almost understand it all. But Alex and Stavros were going about it all the wrong way. More than once, I wondered if my parents had told him things I was doing in my teens—I knew my parents had forgiven me years ago, but was he still holding my stupid actions against me?

I haven't been able to control my thoughts about them, and I'm tired of being so angry. If I told my mother, she'd only become upset. If I talk to Steven about it, he'll fight to defend me. Neither is good. I've learned to keep a brave face around them.

I know Stavros has gotten copies of Alex's emails and my responses. I can tell because he's asked me questions about things he'd only know about if he'd been privy to the information I sent to my brother.

Retaliation is a word that's come to mind lately. I've thought about telling Stavros' children about his illegitimate child, and that he adopted Emma. I know Sophie was sent away to have a child and put it up for adoption; something her rebelliousness told me she'd never forgiven him for, and something we all knew. He has lied all these years, and I want to humiliate him.

What if I told Alex's children what he did to me when I was young—they probably wouldn't believe it. Or maybe they would, since he's such a radical asshole. He already has one daughter he hasn't spoken with in years, so he wouldn't care if she knew. But how would he feel if I told my other niece and nephew? From what they'd told me over the years, neither is close to him.

I'd never held a grudge against my brother for what he did to me, even though images of two naked teenagers on the sofa bed have flashed into my mind over the years. And I'd chastised myself for being so stupid as to have let them touch me. But I'd never let it affect my life before. Now, suddenly, I wanted to punish Alex. There weren't many ways I could do that, but telling his children was one.

I'd always known these things, and I'd still thought about saying something. I knew if I said something now, I wouldn't be hurting either of them, though—I'd just be hurting their children. And there was a possibility no one would believe me. These two facts have kept me from saying anything.

Just keeping it in my arsenal made me feel more powerful.

I've contacted an attorney to see what the statute of limitations was for reporting an assault. I knew before I even spoke with him I'd never be able to prove anything, and it would be a long and drawn-out ordeal. That was not going to be the way to deal with it.

I needed to keep balancing it all—caring for my mother, running our business and managing Mother's household and ours. Our business was constantly pulling me in all directions, and I was grateful our daughter Tara works with us. She and Steven run all the jobs.

Some days I've just leaned back in my desk chair and tried to breathe. Tears stung my eyes, and I've just wiped them away. I've just taken another breath and gone back to my work.

CHAPTER SIXTY SIX

KATE

More and more, I've felt things slipping—memories, routines, the order of my days. I know my husband is gone, but I can't remember how long it's been. I reach for him at night, still expecting to find him beside me. Sometimes I wake up because I don't hear him snoring. His clothes are still in the closet, but the house is too quiet. I know he fell, but I don't remember what happened after that.

Vaso and Steven have taken care of me. She's my strength, my darling girl. Sometimes I've forgotten Steven's name, but he's kind and always calls me Mother, just like Vaso does. When they come in each morning, I try to be ready—showered, with a load of laundry done, the news on. I forget things, though. My sweater, where the brain patch goes, and the names of people I used to know well.

I don't drive anymore, although I vaguely remember Vaso selling my car but not how she convinced me. It doesn't matter. I've forgotten how to write in a straight line, and my handwriting is shrinking. I've tried to make notes, but by the time I've found a pen, I've forgotten what I wanted to say. I used to be so organized.

The memories I do have are odd—my mother's friend with chin hairs like mine, and the typical widow's black dress. When my brother visits, he bores me. I want to tell him to stop being so critical, but I forget what I mean to say. I don't like how he talks to Vaso. He makes her upset, and that upsets me. I've never really liked him—he's always had his nose in my business.

And my son . . . he's worse. I know he does things that hurt Vaso, but I can't remember what. I want to protect her, but I don't know how anymore. I hear her and Alex arguing about the emails, and I wish it would stop. I just want peace.

Lately, she's been asking about her father. I think she knows. I never meant to tell anyone, not even Alex. But Vaso must know the truth. Nick loved him like his own. We planned for him the same way we did for her. She deserves everything we can give her.

Alex asks me confusing questions: Do I want to go out for breakfast? Dinner? I don't know. I just say whatever comes to mind. He moved away. Vaso stayed. She's here every day, holding everything together. She should have this house. She made it beautiful again.

She told me what Alex did to her when she was a young girl. I didn't want to believe it, but why would she lie? I remember that. I wish I didn't. I thank God Nick never knew—he would've been devastated. I think about that often, even if I don't say it.

I sit in her office now, watching the news, dozing off, and waking up when someone comes in. Just being near her comforts me. I can see her house from my window at home, and that brings me peace.

But deep down, I wish Alex and Stavros would just go away. I know I shouldn't think that—I'm their mother and sister. But I do. I want to tell them to stop whatever it is they're doing. I just can't remember what it is, and I hate feeling like this.

CHAPTER SIXTY SEVEN

VASO

I hadn't seen it coming, and the truth was, I should have. Afterward, I realized there had been changes—subtle at first—things I chalked up to aging. She was moving a little slower and was more forgetful than normal. She held her back when she walked, and when I asked about it, she told me it ached. I assumed it was because she'd become so sedentary, sitting in her recliner all day. Even when she sometimes didn't finish her second piece of toast at breakfast, I kept brushing it off, reassuring myself it was nothing serious. It hadn't been that long since we'd done her annual blood work. Looking back, the signs were there like breadcrumbs—I just didn't follow them.

In November, we took Mother to Hof's Hut for our usual early Thanksgiving dinner, and afterward, we drove up to the mountains so I could be in the store for our weekend sale. Lupe offered to spend the weekend, and I appreciated it. On Sunday, the moment I walked through the front door, I knew something was wrong. Mother was slumped on the sofa, leaning against Lupe, her eyes barely open. She could hardly lift her head. She looked at me briefly and then rested her head back down again.

"How long has she been like this?" I asked, rushing over, trying to keep the panic out of my voice.

"She was fine this afternoon. This started about an hour ago."

I kneeled in front of her. "Mother? Can you hear me?"

She stared at me blankly. I immediately called 911, and when the paramedics arrived, they asked her simple questions she couldn't answer.

"What's your name?"

"Do you have any pain?"

They checked her vital signs.

"Is she always like this?" one asked. I knew what they were thinking—just another confused old woman.

'No,' I wanted to scream. 'She's *not* always like this!

"She was alert earlier," I said. "Something's wrong."

Our next-door neighbor came over when she saw the ambulance, and she stood with me as they loaded my mother into the back. "She'll be okay," she said, trying to reassure me. She'd said that when my father fell and hit his head.

Steven and I followed them to the hospital, and while he parked, I ran in. They rushed her into the ER, hooked her up to fluids, took more vitals, and drew blood.

I couldn't shake the guilt of having left her behind.

"Once we run the labs, we'll know more," the nurse said.

After a short wait, a doctor came in. "She has systemic inflammation, or what we call a serious urinary tract infection."

"How did this happen?" I asked.

"It's more common than you think, especially in older women. Is she allergic to any antibiotics?"

I had no idea.

"Not that I know of."

They started with IV antibiotics and around 2 a.m., a nurse told us she was stable enough to go home.

"Are you sure?" I asked. She still looked so tiny and fragile in the bed.

"She's hydrated now and medicated. She'll rest better at home."

The early morning air was frigid, and we quickly bundled my mother up and got her into the car. It took a few minutes for the heater to kick in, and I immediately regretted putting her in the back seat where the warmth didn't reach her quickly. By the time we got home, she was shaking uncontrollably. I didn't even change her clothes—I just got her into bed and layered her with blankets. Then I climbed in next to her, trying to warm her with my own body heat. After an hour, the shivering stopped, and she slept.

Each day, she got a little better. I called Abby to bring her up to date, but I avoided Alex. Instead, I emailed him, simply stating we took her to the ER, and she had a UTI. It was the first civil response I'd received in months: *"Thanks for letting me know."*

With Christmas approaching, I considered heading to the mountains to work in the store, but my conscience wouldn't let me. My store manager told me everything was under control and encouraged me to stay home with my mother.

The next day, we were back in the ER. Mother couldn't urinate, and her belly was distended. Two nurses tried to insert a catheter but failed. Eventually, a urologist made a small incision under her belly button and inserted a catheter. The next day, the hospital transferred her to a convalescent facility for round-the-clock care and physical therapy. The first day she was there, she slept, and it was heartbreaking to see her in a place I knew she'd hate when she woke up—but she needed to be there.

I had to tell Alex where she was, and every time I spoke with him, his wife Linda chimed in with advice. My patience was hanging by a thread, and every word out of her mouth made it worse. I finally snapped. "I don't want her talking in the background when we speak," I told Alex.

That backfired spectacularly.

The next morning, he sent a typo-riddled group email:

I have a problem with Vaso. She made it quite clear my wife is not family. My wife and I are a team. She will speak in the background, to your face, and be part of all decisions. Vaso, where is Mom now?

I didn't respond to his tantrum. Instead, I sent an update to Alex and Stavros:

Mother is improving. She's receiving daily physical therapy in bed. I met with the case managers, and I'm satisfied with her care. She'll be released when she's stronger. Abby came out to visit, and I called Alex's kids so Mother could talk to them—she enjoyed that. She doesn't have a phone in her room, but the facility can bring her one for calls. They're reviewing whether she needs to resume blood pressure meds.

She's ready to get up for PT and needs something to wear, so I'll get some sweats and write her name in them, like summer camp. She really wants to come home.

Alex replied:

I have a problem right now with Vaso, she does not want my wife to be involve who helps me tremendously nor does she want my wife to speak. made it quiet clearly My wife is not family. I do not know how this is going to work, all of you must understand, especially you Vaso, my wife and I are a team, my secretary and she will speak to your face and in the background when I am on the phone and when I am talking I will refer to my wife in the conversation. When a final decision is made it is I (Alex) and you Vaso together that makes the final decision. Does everyone understand this? Vaso we all need an update where mom is now?

I didn't reply to that email, but I sent a new one to Alex and Stavros.

I met with the case managers, a physical therapist, and two other women to go over Mother's care. So far, I'm pleased with the care she's getting. She's scheduled for physical therapy, first in her bed, then today in a wheelchair, and that will continue Monday through Friday.

I did already mention this, but she does have a doctor from the facility that looks in on her and other patients. So far, so good. I have an appointment with a urologist, and they will transport Mother and me to the appointment. She won't be released from the facility until they feel she's strong enough to get up and I agree. And she's really doing a lot better!

Abby made a trip out to see her and visited her on Monday.

They're calling Mother's cardiologist to see if he wants her back on her blood pressure meds; apparently she hasn't been taking anything since she went into the hospital and yet her blood pressure is really good.

I stopped at Kohl's and got her 3 sets of sweats so I can wash them. I put her name in them, just like going to camp! I'll have to get a laundry bag too, since they don't have any.

She's really doing well, and can hardly wait to get home! I don't blame her.

V.

Alex responded:

Not that it is anyone business, my sister is being a perfect ass, I would like everyone to know that I personal let my children know that mom was ill and in the hospital from the beginning keeping them updated.

I've not talked with my other daughter in over 20 years, I do not have her phone number I left it up to the other two kids to let her know. They choose not to say anything to their sister because of all the drama she causes, frankly they did not want to put up with it especially with the issue that she had with Pops funeral all the drama she cause then and choose not to come to the funeral without her mom, my ex-wife who she lives with still to this day being 47 some years old showing disrespect for me and my wife

We need to stick to Trust Business leave our dirty laundry in the hamper even when updating everyone on Mom condition.

Alex

I couldn't believe how much I hated my brother!

CHAPTER SIXTY EIGHT

VASO

Mother kept improving, and she kept begging to come home. I talked with Abby, and after ten days, and against the facility's advice, I brought her back home. I was newly retired and could care for her during the day. Lupe stayed overnight in the office on the pull-out couch.

A nurse came daily to check the catheter, and a physical therapist helped with her mobility. Everything seemed manageable. Still, Alex and Stavros insisted I hire a licensed agency. Worried about fiduciary liability and tired of the criticism, I found several services and hired a caregiver at $25/hour. I moved all her valuables across the street to my house, and for a crazy moment, I thought about photographing everything I gathered to document what I'd done. In defiance, I took the photos, but kept them on my phone.

Ten days in, Mother stopped getting out of bed. I'd lie down in her other bed so I could be with her in case she needed me. She'd had both catheters removed and was, until then, going to the bathroom on her own. We'd moved her toilet chair next to her bed, and every three hours, she'd wake up and try to go to the bathroom. Most of the time, she couldn't. She was obviously having a relapse of some sort.

Back at the ER, they gave her something so strong it left her agitated, thrashing in her bed. Within moments she became incoherent, and I called for a nurse. They tried another medication to calm her.

"She's ready to go home," one of them said not long after.

"Absolutely not," I shot back. "Look at her."

Only then did they finally admit her. Through tears, I asked if it could be a bad reaction to the antibiotics, but no one could say for sure.

When she was finally settled in her room, Steven and I went in to see her. Seeing my tiny mother lying there, dwarfed by the hospital bed, I first thought I was in the wrong room. The frail old woman I saw was not my mother. My eyes stung, but I still took her hand and squeezed it. When there was no reaction, I dragged the hospital chair closer to the bed so I could sit close to her. Even though Steven brought the other one over and sat by me, I still felt alone.

She was dying of acute renal failure and never became lucid again.

I called Abby first. She booked a flight for the next morning. And then I called Alex.

"She's dying," I said.

"I can't come now."

"*Are you kidding me?*"

"I'll come for the funeral."

"*You're fucking kidding me,*" I said, low and shaking. "*Get down here. She's fucking dying.*"

He mumbled something about coming soon, but I was hanging up.

It wasn't only anger that blinded me; it was fear, grief and exhaustion all twisted together until I couldn't separate one from the other.

"If he was here now, I'd rip his fucking face off," I said as I came back into the room.

Steven just sat there processing my fury in stunned silence.

Stavros arrived within the hour. "I'd like to be with my sister," he said.

I didn't move.

Later, the hospice team asked if I wanted them to let her go.

My mother always hated sympathy.

"I want her comfortable," I said, meaning yes.

Mother's cardiologist was on call and had come to see her. Like us, he was Greek and had treated her for years. He hesitated when I said this, clearly emotional.

"We need to let her go," I said softly.

He nodded, and I left him to visit with her alone.

That night, I sat beside her, brushing her hair into a ponytail. Her breathing was shallow and uneven. Her face looked peaceful but sunken, with circles under her eyes and tiny hairs on her chin—they seemed to have grown overnight. When was the last time I'd plucked them for her? She would hate for anyone to see her like that, so I asked the nurse if she had a pair of tweezers.

I held her hand, marveling at her soft skin. I tried to remember her as she was before all this, but it was hard. Guilt crept in. I had missed all the signs. It didn't make any difference that I had no idea how serious a UTI could be.

I remembered telling her what Alex had done to me, and how she'd said only, "I'm so sorry." And now, I wondered if I'd burdened her with something she couldn't fix.

I leaned in close. "It's okay to go, Mother. Go find Dad. It's okay." I said it again and again.

Her breathing slowed, then stopped. And then started again.

I called the nurse. By the time she came, Mother was breathing again. She picked up her chart, then gave me a weak smile.

"I'll be just outside if you need me," she said, leaving us alone with her.

It felt like we'd been living in slow motion, watching her slip away inch by inch. And yet, somehow, it was only three months—the length of a single season. I'd watched my mother disappear in fragments. Her decline hadn't come in a dramatic crash but in a gradual decline of confusion replacing clarity and silence where conversation used to be.

I'd watched the woman who raised me, who once bustled with energy and sharp opinions, become someone I held like a child, someone whose breaths I now counted to make sure she was still here.

I'd always feared the day would come when she wouldn't recognize me. In the end, I couldn't tell if she even knew I was there, but there was a small comfort in that—I'd never have to wonder whether the look in her eyes meant she remembered me or not.

I remembered missing my father when he died. I ultimately hadn't wanted to be there, and now, I didn't want to see my mother die, either. I didn't need signs or souls or closure—I just needed to let her go. I'd been there for her as long as I could be.

Steven took my hand, and we said goodbye. A few hours later, I got the call she was gone.

CHAPTER SIXTY NINE

ALEX

I knew even before Vaso called me, my mom wasn't going to make it much longer. When I talked with her on the phone at the rehab center, she didn't understand what I was talking about. I tried to keep her up to date on how my season was going and how I'd been remodeling the mobile home. But she couldn't follow me.

"*Get down here. She's fucking dying,*" Vaso said when she called me.

Something in the tone of her voice set me off. I hated the way she talked to me about our parents, like she was the know-it-all, and I was just a thick slug.

"I'll have to come down for the funeral," I'd said stupidly.

The line was silent for just a few seconds.

I could feel the hatred through the phone, and then she hung up.

I knew I should have reacted differently. If my mother *was* dying, I knew I should be there, but it was short notice to find someone to watch the animals, and I'd have to bring the dogs down. I couldn't just up and leave. Vaso was just being dramatic, but my mom wasn't long for this world. I couldn't see spending thirteen hours driving down for a few days, and then going back when there was a funeral later.

It was too bad. My mom was a good woman.

I had to get some cutting done before I could leave. I couldn't have my customer's meat spoil. I figured it'd take me a day, and then Linda and I would get on the road. Vaso would want to be in control anyway, so I didn't really need to be there to pick out a casket and make all the arrangements. We'd disagreed on everything for my dad's funeral, so I didn't want to go through that again.

My day ended up being productive, so I cleared out the truck to leave in the morning.

I let my two kids know, and figured they could tell their sister if they wanted to. When my dad died, Vaso gave the kids money to help pay for their expenses to come down, and I wasn't going to agree with that again. Let them pay their own way. They'd no doubt be getting something once the estate was settled. They could work for it.

"Got the dogs?" I said to Linda when I was ready.

"We're ready to go," she said, putting both of them in the front seat with us.

"We have about thirteen hours ahead of us. Did you bring something to eat?"

"Yup." She kissed the dogs, then fastened her seat belt.

All the way down there, Linda kept asking me questions about my mother's estate, and hell, I didn't know what was going to happen. Stavros and the attorneys could figure it out. What I did know was that I didn't want Vaso wasting any more of my mom's money.

"I'm dreading having to deal with your sister," she said. "She can be really bitchy towards me, and I don't think I deserve to be treated that way."

"Are you pouting?" I asked.

"A little. I wish you'd stand up for me when she disrespects me."

"Ah, Goddammit, Linda, let's just get down there and get this over with. I don't want to deal with her either, but I'm stuck with it, aren't I?"

"We need to make sure she doesn't keep all Mom's things."

"Stop it. We'll figure it out when we get there."

"Did you bring a clean shirt?"

"What do you think?"

"And your newer hat? I know how everyone feels about the way you dressed at Dad's service."

"Do I act like I give a shit?"

"Ok. Just axing."

I hated it when she said that word.

CHAPTER SEVENTY

STAVROS

I'm the only one left now. And Kate's death couldn't have come at a worse time. I'm in the middle of a major negotiation for some property for a client, and I have to go out of town for a few days. I've also just started working on a divorce for another big client, and it's going to be a doozy. They had a pre-nup that specifically stated that if either of them had an extramarital affair, the client's assets were up for grabs. So what does my client do? He screws around and gets caught.

And then the lease for my office space is coming up for renewal, and I've been trying to decide whether to downsize and find a new space, or retire.

On top of all that, this means we'll have to start all over again with Kate's trust, and I'll have to deal with a hundred questions from Vaso.

I'll also have to see everyone at least once before her service, and they all get on my nerves. My wife, Jane, has already asked me if she can do anything.

"Just let them decide what to do," I finally said.

I'd have to unbury the trusts and review them. I felt everything was in pretty good shape now and hoped to close it down fairly quickly. Then there was Vaso and Alex. What a pain they'd become. They were just like all the other heirs I've dealt with over the years, but Vaso has had too much freedom in her life. She's been spoiled, and I think I need to look into that.

I feel this is going to be a long process.

Crap.

CHAPTER SEVENTY ONE

VASO

I picked Abby up at the airport, and just seeing her red, swollen eyes brought tears to mine. The last thing she'd said to me when I called her was, "I hope I make it before she's gone."

But that didn't happen.

She hadn't had breakfast, so we stopped at Hof's Hut and shared an order of pancakes.

"When's Alex due in?" she asked.

"Anytime."

"Does he have a key to the house?"

"No." I quickly changed the subject. "Will you go with me to the mortuary?"

"Of course I will. I can't believe both of them are gone," she said, her eyes filling with tears again. "I'll find the paperwork and we can call this morning."

Alex and Linda were sitting in their truck in front of the house when we drove up.

"Oh, dear. I wonder how long they've been here?" I said innocently.

"You're terrible," Abby said, seeing right through me.

"Any time I can be."

"You could have left me a key," Alex grumbled as he got out of the truck.

The dogs were running around in the front yard, and one of them pooped.

"The key to the guest house is hanging on the hook," I said as I helped Abby with her luggage. "We're going to the mortuary this morning if you want to come."

"Nah, you two can take care of it. I drove all night, so I'm going to take a nap."

"Suit yourself," I said. "And clean up the dog shit."

When we returned later, I set the mortuary packet on the counter and said, "Now all you have to do is to be there for the service. She'll be buried with my dad."

"Well, don't you want to know what they picked for your mother?" Linda asked as she came into the kitchen.

"It's done," was all he said.

I gave myself a victorious grin.

I'd already started sorting Mother's jewelry on the dining room table. I assumed this would be the only time I'd see my brother and his family again, and I thought the grandkids would like to have something to remember her by. As I was finishing, Steven pointed out something of my father's he'd like to have. He picked up a gold money clip.

"Take it. You've earned it." I said.

Mother had already given me her large diamond, and we'd had it reset a few years ago. Since no one ever noticed, I didn't say anything. Alex looked at everything displayed on the table, and I wondered if I should have done an inventory to make sure he and his wife didn't help themselves to something they felt entitled to. When my niece showed up, she went directly to the table and set aside several items she was interested in.

"Just in case I have a choice," she said sheepishly.

"We can wait until your brother gets here, and then we can split everything up," I said. My niece was very close to my mother, and I knew she'd cherish whatever she got to keep.

My nephew came in later that afternoon, and we started the "pick."

"I'd like this of Dad's," Alex said, picking up a coin.

"I'd like my dad's peanut," I said, picking up a silver box shaped like a peanut. It always reminded him of when he had been a peanut seller in Detroit.

Steven picked up something else he wanted, and then Linda found one of Mother's necklaces. Chloe and Nik found something, and then we did a second round. I'd already kept Mother's ruby ring when we removed it from her finger in the hospital. When I saw Abby standing in the background, I realized that if anyone should have something of my mother's, it should be her. She'd been a loyal friend and employee for so many years.

"Find something you'd like," I said, calling her over to the table. I could tell she didn't want to impose, but she came over anyway and saw a gold cross necklace.

"I'd love to have this," she said softly.

"Is that it?" I asked. "What about this?" I said, picking up a small ring.

"Are you sure?"

"Absolutely. Enjoy them."

I decided to just have a graveside service for my mother. We didn't go to the church, and I didn't even call the priest. It wasn't that I cared less for my mother than I did my father, but I knew it wasn't that important to her. It's what *I* wanted when it was my time.

The mortuary brought her casket, and she was placed on top of my father in the grave. As I talked about her, I cried.

"I promised my father I would take care of my mother when he died—and that's what Steven and I did. I was able to be with her every day, and while I hated seeing them both age, I cannot tell you how honored I felt that they both knew I was there for them."

I hadn't prepared a speech, and I hadn't intended to say it was all about me and my time with them, but I really was there for my parents. "I made sure I was there for them when they needed me. Not everyone can say that, and I fulfilled the promise I made."

Our daughter Tara had prepared something and got up to speak. She'd spelled my mother's name out with words of love, just like she'd done for my father.

"K is for being the kindest person I've ever known. She was also the most knowledgeable person I've known, and she was a knockout even into her eighties.

"A is for being adorable, affectionate, and always an angel.

"T is for being the most thoughtful person I've known. She was tactful but not always talkative; she was tenacious but tender.

"E is for being enchanting, enthusiastic and easy. E also stands for elderly."

Everyone chuckled.

"What I didn't find when I was looking up the letters in her name, were words to describe my grandmother as I want to remember her. She was loving to me and my sister, and every day, even when we weren't at the office, I could see how much she loved my parents for being there for her. I'll miss her."

Abby had prepared something too and stood next.

"I hope I can make it through this." She cleared her throat. "When Kate died, a big part of me died with her. I spent over forty-five years with her and Nick, and she was my mentor, my confidante, and my role model."

She used a tissue to wipe away a tear.

"No matter what was happening in my life, her words of wisdom always saw me through. I was just off the bus from Spearfish, South Dakota, after taking a secretarial course that I hoped would prepare me for a job in Southern California. I was nineteen, and I showed up dressed in what my school recommended, which turned out to be overkill. Kate took a picture of me that day after she offered me the job. 'You don't mind dogs, do you?' she asked as their dog greeted me. 'His name is Metaxa, but we call him Tax.'

"I'll miss you and Nick."

I'd arranged for lunch at the small Italian restaurant where we met after my father's burial, and after everyone had their drink, I quickly stood and thanked them for coming.

"Here's to my mother," I said, raising a toast to her.

I thought Stavros was going to knock his chair over trying to get up to beat me to the punch. He had his glass in his hand and gave me a dirty look. One point for me.

"To my sister," he said, just to get a toast in. "To those who couldn't make it, and to those who are no longer with us."

I used Mother's credit card and, of course, kept the receipt to send later to Alex and Stavros. I didn't care what they thought.

That night, I stood in the great room and looked at my brother's family. Linda was sitting in my spot on the sofa talking to one of my cousins, giggling her stupid giggle, and my brother was sitting in my father's recliner with one of their dogs on his lap. The other dog was running back and forth trying to decide where to sit, and finally, she decided Linda's lap was going to work for her.

"Stavros and I still think Mother should have come home to die," Alex said out of the blue.

"What?" I asked.

"Mom and Dad both wanted to stay in their own home until they died," he said.

I looked at Abby, dumbfounded.

"Are you kidding me? You're thinking of this now? You *did* see my father in the hospital, didn't you? He was in no condition to come home," I said.

Alex turned to look at me then, and his eyes narrowed.

"And Mother was also in no shape to come home. There wasn't enough time for me to arrange for a hospital bed and a twenty-four-hour nurse to be with her. And she was hooked up to machines—and if you'd have had the decency to come down to *see* her while she was dying, you'd know that. So fuck off, Alex."

The room had gone silent, and I didn't care. Alex looked at me like I'd lost my mind, and I didn't care about that either. He was a dick.

My brother hadn't changed out of his 'Sunday go-to-meeting bib overalls' from the burial, and I resented him because he didn't really care what people thought of him. He looked dirty, his beard was too long, and when he took off his solid sweaty hat, his bald head and thin braid looked ridiculous. His fingernails were dirty, his bib overalls accentuated his big belly, and I found him repulsive. Everyone but Alex and Abby were planning on leaving in the morning, and that wasn't soon enough for me.

I told Alex I was going to write checks to the kids and our cousin, who'd flown in from Hawaii for the funeral.

"Mother did it when my dad died," I said. Of course, I hoped he picked up on the reference to my father being *mine,* and not his.

"Well, absolutely not. They don't need checks. It's their responsibility to pay their own way. There will be no checks."

I looked at Abby, who just shook her head.

"Fuck you," I said under my breath as I went into the office and wrote the checks, anyway.

Alex was anxious to get back home, but we needed to set up an appointment with the attorney.

"You'll have to come back down if you don't stay now," I said, annoyed.

"*Fine*," he said, picking up one of his dogs. "Hi, little girl," he said, kissing her.

My parent's original trusts were set up so that Alex and I could live off the estates and then, when we both died, everything would go to his children since I had no natural children of my own. We'd both known that.

With my father's death, his trust, the exemption trust, was transferred to my mother, so now there were two trusts. Hers was the survivor's trust. When she died, the plan was to combine both trusts. However, a couple of things had happened that made us all rethink this.

One was that my brother, in a tantrum in front of the attorney and Stavros, declared he would not give anything to his children, especially the one daughter he hadn't spoken to in over twenty years. Plus, he was concerned his wife wouldn't have access to his part of the inheritance if he died before her.

A red flag went up. We weren't sure if Alex was just letting off steam, or if he was serious.

The second thing was that Alex and I didn't seem to be able to have a civil conversation about anything. His emails to me were becoming more hurtful, and he still wanted every penny of the estate accounted for. He insisted on having an attorney up in his hometown review everything, which took longer and cost the remaining estate more money.

The third thing, and the most significant, was that Stavros and Alex had asked for an accounting of *every* dollar my parents had either given or loaned me over the last thirty years.

My mother, being a detailed bookkeeper, had kept just about everything ever posted to my account in her general ledger, so even if we wanted to, we wouldn't have been able to delete anything.

"Your parents never expected you to pay that back," Abby said. "And I know that. But I don't know what I can do about it if Stavros wants to press the issue."

"I know. And I understand. And I hate to admit that I can see how someone else might look at this. I'm sure Stavros sees it all the time, but I'm not like everyone else."

When Stavros said something before my mother died, I told her, and she'd said, "I don't even know why I kept all that. It was just an easy way to post things. I wish I'd never done that," she'd said.

My parents never intended for me to pay them back for anything they'd given me. And now there was no way to back out any numbers; it was all there for them to see. There was a small balance from remodeling my first building over twenty years ago, and a first trust deed they took on a house we purchased for an investment. They'd told me not to worry about making payments until they let me know. My new roof and the handrails my father wanted installed had been posted to the new house remodel as was the landscaping. Everything else was in there, and even Abby couldn't back me up without it looking like she was favoring me.

"What about the truck they bought for Alex?" I asked, suddenly combative.

I instantly realized that was a weakness on my part, and I frantically tried to come up with other things my parents had done for him over the years.

"I don't see it here," Stavros said, looking at the reports.

"I'm sure they did other things for him over these same thirty years." I kept my voice calm, although inside, I was trying to mask my hostility. I felt that if I pursued it further, I would appear even more defensive.

I knew my brother had had the same opportunities as I did, but he never wanted to make the most of anything. And if it ever came up in the few times we actually spoke to each other, he'd always said, "I don't care what you do. Go for it."

Well, now that he realized how much he could lose, he wanted it paid back.

I just looked at the attorney, and she didn't say a word.

So, in order to separate everything, we all agreed to change the trust, and take my "already received" share out. Alex and I agreed that at this point there was no way we could be partners in anything.

His children would each receive fifty thousand dollars, and we would split everything else.

In retrospect, this was fair, but at the time, I felt everything was so imbalanced. I really never thought I should end up with more than my brother did, but I also knew I was the only one who had taken care of our parents. I was their caregiver. I helped them move. I took care of their personal needs. I'd been part of their lives after he'd moved away and done whatever he'd wanted to.

After Alex left the meeting, I asked the attorney if other families had similar problems. I wanted someone to tell me every family was a little broken, and she said, "You'd be surprised. I've seen families quit speaking to each other over who got the piano."

Abby tried to remind me to look at it objectively. She said, "Think about it this way if you can. You'll both have plenty of money and focus on what your parents were able to give you. Try to think of it that way."

Logically, that made sense, but emotionally, I was devastated.

CHAPTER SEVENTY TWO

VASO

Abby stayed for two weeks so she could start working on my mother's estate.

"This time, it should go a lot smoother," she said confidently.

I figured while she was there, we could start going through old accounting records and start destroying them. I packed up boxes of records we needed to keep, along with a 'destroy date'. When they moved from the Beach House, we'd moved Mother's tall storage cabinets into the garage, and I cleared them out and put everything we needed to keep in there. Everything else would go to a shredding company once we finished. We had records we hadn't gone through from the old house dating back thirty years. I knew what I could toss, and I was relentless.

As I started going through all the photos my mother had saved, I was overwhelmed. I separated those that I'd send to Alex's children, and when I came across some of Alex, my first thought was to burn them. Instead, I added them to my niece's box and thought she could do with them as she wished. When I came across the picture of Alex with the American flag attached to the back of one of his motorcycles, I recalled the day it was taken. We were in the parking lot of the office in Bixby Knolls. He was wearing a bandana on his head, and he looked like a Hell's Angel. I remember sometimes showing people photos of him and laughing.

"That's your brother?" they'd ask.

We were such opposites.

"Crazy, isn't it?" I said. "I'm obviously the pretty one."

I wondered now if, in a way, I also laughed with him, and if there was still a little bit of pride in me at the rebel in him.

I selfishly kept the photos of my parents and grandparents for myself; I'd never thought of them being young and full of passion and dreams. To me, they'd just been parents and grandparents. Old. Although all of my brother's family photos had been lost when his house burned down, I still wouldn't make a box to send to him. I moved everything across the street, where it all sat in my living room until I had time to package it up and send it off.

I gathered the birthday and Mother's Day cards my mother had kept, my father's discharge papers, and their marriage license, still bearing her first married name, and added them to the drawer in my dresser where I stored my photographs and keepsakes.

"How long have you known?" I asked Abby.

"For years."

"You were very loyal to my parents."

"I loved them, Vaso."

After Abby left, an eerie silence greeted me when I had to go across the street into my parent's house. I couldn't stop myself from looking at the area on the floor where my father had fallen four years earlier. I could still picture him lying there and calling out, "*Where are you?*" I closed my eyes and whispered, "I'm here."

Collecting the mail from the basket under the mail slot, I quickly sorted it while I stood there. At Mother's desk, I finished the task of shredding what we didn't need and setting aside what needed a change of address. I'd already started sending change of address notices out for anything important, and I added to the pile of accounts I could close.

Now that they were both gone, I needed to start throwing away things that were no longer useful. Like my mother's medication, her toothbrush, and her cleansing cream. I found her brush still in the kitchen, where I used to do her hair before we left for the office in the morning, and I set it aside to bring it home. I'd never told anyone about guarding my role of taking care of my mother, and when Abby would ask if she could comb her hair, I'd hesitate, then reluctantly give her the brush. She adored my mother—I knew that—but something in me didn't want to share her. It was selfish, and I knew it, but I couldn't help it.

I couldn't help but think back to when I would trim her long pony-tail. I'd make exaggerated snipping sounds, and make a big deal about whacking off a couple of inches, inevitably making her laugh.

I was her person. I was the one she depended on for everything from making sure the sweater she wore every day was washed, to which pills she took.

I began the task of cleaning out the kitchen cabinets, and when I saw bags of dry cereal from before my father died, it brought to mind one morning when my mother still made their coffee. She poured cereal into her coffee cup. When she did things like that, I wanted to ask out of curiosity, "Where is your mind right now?" Or "What are you thinking?" But I never did, and I wasn't sure she'd even be able to tell me.

I couldn't stay focused on one area to sort through, so I left the kitchen and went into the master bedroom. Mother's toilet chair was still sitting in the corner, and when I'd pass it, I couldn't help but see her standing over it, struggling to go to the bathroom.

It made sense that the last memories you have of someone you've lost are the first images that come to mind when you think of them. And even though they might fade with time, no matter how much you try, you can never erase them completely.

I turned and looked in their closet and immediately closed the door. I didn't want to deal with anything else. I checked the refrigerators again to make sure there was nothing in them that could spoil, and then I locked the front door behind me as I left.

I wanted everything to go back to when my parents were still alive.

A woman in our neighborhood organized estate sales, but before I contacted her, I emptied my mother's cabinets of all her nice serving pieces and pots and pans. I hadn't entertained in years and I had no use for any of it, so our two daughters came over to see if there was anything they wanted to keep. My mother had always believed that if your serving dishes were white, they'd go with any color or pattern of china you were using, and she was right. The girls cleared out quite a bit, and I was glad to see them take things they thought they could use.

I'd thrown away underwear and socks, and I had my housekeeper come by with her sister to see if there was any clothing they might want before the sale. I told them to feel comfortable taking everything they wanted, and while they left with large bags of both men's and women's clothing, it hardly made a dent in their closet. They also took all the pots and pans, and the canned and packaged food from the pantry.

The estate gal suggested I put a Post-it note on any furniture I wanted to keep, and to then take everything else I wanted out of the house. She warned me that once it was sold, I'd never get it back. I marked my mother's contemporary mahogany and chrome coffee table, not that I had any idea where it was going to go in my traditional home, and the two large wicker chairs and an ottoman from the guest house. I took the hand-colored photo of Mother's younger brother Michael and hung it in my upstairs guest bedroom.

Our oldest daughter took the contemporary art pieces she wanted, and Abby had her son, who still lived locally, come and pick up some furniture he could use. Even though I'd told the estate gal not to sell the cleaning supplies, after the sale, I saw they were all gone. The day after the sale, a truck pulled up in front of the house, and an older gentleman and his son took all the miscellaneous things that hadn't sold.

That left us with the oversized custom buffet that was originally built for the beach house but had still somehow fit into the new house; I was going to leave it there, hoping a new tenant could use it. The only other thing that didn't sell was their large dining room table with ten chairs. We ended up moving it across the street into our living room, where it would sit for over a year until I could decide what to do with it.

Except for the wicker basket that sat on the floor under the mail slot, the house was now empty. It had taken only a week to dispose of my parents' personal possessions, and it certainly put things into perspective.

I was left alone with Mother's bookkeeping. Abby could work remotely, and Tim still came by once a week to pay whatever needed to be paid. I'd stepped back from anything involving money, except for signing checks that Alex and Stavros got reports for.

I thought Alex's emails would taper off once he had copies of everything he wanted, but he never seemed to grasp the full picture of the estate process. He had no issue approving the recording of properties that went to him, but when a bill came through for a property I inherited—including recording fees tied to the trust—he fired off an email accusing me of trying to make the estate cover my personal expenses.

I tried to laugh about it, so I wouldn't want to kill him, so I responded with, "You're so funny. Did you even read the email I sent? I told you I was breaking it down, and that I'd pay my portion."

His reply was, "Vaso, this is your bill. Pay it."

And then another bill from the attorney had something to do with transferring the properties from a parent to a child. Technically, the trust should have paid for the entire bill, but I knew Alex wouldn't understand, so I offered to pay for what related to the properties I'd inherited. I figured Alex would pay his portion, so I sent him the bill along with the explanation of why we had to deal with the county assessor's office again, but after thirty days, I received a past due invoice for what should have come from him.

I emailed, "Just received this from the attorney and I need to know what your plans are for paying this, or if I should make other arrangements." Why I opened that door on that one, I didn't know, for his email response said, "Make other arrangements."

I paid the bill personally.

The straw that broke the camel's back was when we needed to decide what to do about a lemon ranch my parents had owned with Stavros. Per the trust, he would keep his half of the property, and Alex and I would each keep a quarter interest.

"I'd like to give Stavros my quarter," Alex said.

He'd come down for one final meeting with the attorneys, and along with Stavros, we sat at the large table in the conference room.

"I'd like to keep mine," I'd answered.

Stavros just sat there with a smug look on his face, and I wondered if they had discussed something prior to the meeting. If I fought it, we'd be doing this forever—if I agreed, I'd be admitting defeat. I looked to the attorney for some type of guidance, even if it was silent, but the way she looked at me, I knew I'd lose.

Alex said, "I will trade property for property if Vaso gifts her portion of the lemon ranch to Uncle Stavros. All other assets are to be split down the middle. If Vaso says no, then re-appraise all the properties. Vaso, which way do you want it?"

We'd never appraised the ranch at the time of my father's death, so I wasn't sure what it was even worth. I really didn't want to be partners with either of them, but when Alex and Stavros gave me an ultimatum— that either I signed my portion over or they would stop the separation of the trusts and have all the property appraised again—I saw no other option than to let it go.

I wanted this whole thing to go away, and the only way that was going to happen was if I gave in.

Even to my own ears, my voice had gone tight and thin. "Fine," was all I said.

The attorney grimaced slightly, and her eyes darted towards me.

When we left the attorney's office that day, cold wind rushed in the minute we opened the door to the outside. The sky had turned ominous, and it seemed to mirror the way I felt right then. On the way to my car, I felt a drop of rain on my cheek. Or had it been a tear?

Since my father died, it felt like every decision, every expense, and every act of care was met with a raised eyebrow, as if I was scheming rather than surviving. They didn't say it outright, but the message was clear: I was too close to the money, too involved, too comfortable. As if loving my mother disqualified me from being trusted.

I hated Alex, but I especially hated Stavros, who gladly accepted the gift of the ranch from us. His later email to the attorney said, "Thank you. I appreciate the generosity of Alex and Vaso. Please bill me for any costs relative to transferring the property into my LLC account. No trustee fees will be due to me on this. Stavros."

Of course, he appreciated our "gifts". They were probably worth fifty thousand dollars each. And was I resentful? Of course I was.

Abby came out one more time so she could finish closing the estate. She stayed with her son, who lived about an hour away, and she used my father's Lexus. She was the only one who drove it, and when she went back home, I put it up for sale.

Almost two months later, the updated grave marker was set. I purposely hadn't consulted with Alex when I ordered it—I couldn't risk him meddling with something so personal to me—or turning it into another power play. And as it turned out, he was on to other things, and couldn't have cared less.

My father's inscription said, "Everybody Night Night," his signature way of letting everyone know it was time to clear out so he could go to bed. And my Mother's said, "Get a Good Night," her parting words to us when we left them at night. I texted Abby, Holly, and Tara the photo and told them, "I said hello for you."

They all texted right back with, "Thank you."

I didn't send the photo to Alex or Stavros—not because I was angry, but because I simply didn't have to. They'd see it if they ever chose to visit the grave.

CHAPTER SEVENTY THREE

STAVROS

I should have done this before Kate died, but I need to do it now. I've loved my wife, Jane, the most. Of all my wives, she was the sincerest, never needing attention like the others. She was levelheaded and had a way about her that could calm me down when I was upset. And I've realized that with age, I've lost some of my ability to control my anger. A good attorney always has a poker face, even if they're seething inside. You never show your emotions. You let no one get the best of you. But that ability has somehow vanished.

I need to end our marriage before it's too late. I have to set her free. I am almost eighty, and she is barely sixty. She's never made me feel like I was an old man who just wanted to stay home—we still meet friends once a week for dinner, but most nights I'm in bed around eight. I don't sleep well, and I've always risen around five so I can read the paper in silence. Not that our home is noisy, but it is my 'alone' time.

We have cats now; I can't believe we have two. They want to sit on my lap when I try to read—talk about annoying. I've never been a pet person, so it's surprised me how much I care for them. Jane does the litter box, and she feeds them, so they mostly stick with her. One has even clawed my leather chair, and I can live with that; when they're gone, I'll have it reupholstered.

I need to set her free—there is no way I will let her take care of me when I'm no longer able to get to the bathroom. All I can picture is my sister lying in that hospital bed waiting to die. Someone had to change her diaper and wash her.

It only makes sense unless there's a freak accident, I'll be the first to go.

I told her tonight after dinner—I knew neither of us would have been able to eat if I had done it before. As it was, I barely picked at my food, and Jane asked if I was alright.

I didn't realize she'd take it so hard.

"You can't just shut me out now," she'd said. She began crying. "I knew when I signed up for this what I was in for, and I want to be there for you. I want to have you for as long as I can. Please don't do this."

I hate seeing women cry, and I'd never seen Jane so distressed.

"I've made up my mind—I've already bought you a condo. It'll close escrow in a week. I'll stay somewhere and leave you here so you can pack your things without seeing me."

I'd done it, and not for the first time in my life, I felt like a real shit. I knew I was setting free the one person who'd truly loved me. If it was the best thing to do, then why did I feel so empty?

Next, I needed to close down my law practice. I had only two clients left—both my friends from college. I gave them some names of younger attorneys who could take over, and I had my secretary help me pack up their files so a courier could deliver them. She only worked a couple of days a week now, and that was about all the stamina I had, so we began the process of either shredding old account files or packing them up for old clients if they wanted them.

It was an exhausting process. I'd had both rotator cuffs repaired, but my shoulders still hurt, and I was sure I'd torn something lifting boxes. I constantly shuffled because I was so bent over from osteoporosis, and my poor posture over the years had caused me to hunch my shoulders. I've wondered if I was going to break my back, but I'd take an Advil and try to stretch my shoulders backwards every so often.

I'm thinking of taking up smoking my Dunhills again. I'd finally quit about a year ago, but I've missed them terribly. I've decided that starting up again wasn't going to shorten my life at this point, anyway.

I've transferred ownership of the lemon ranch to my name. Thank God that the entire process went as well as it did. I felt Alex pressured Vaso into giving me her twenty-five percent, but I truly felt I had it coming to me. I detested her sense of entitlement. I had to work hard for everything I had—had to learn to live like the wealthy, how to eat, how to act. And Vaso just did what she wanted. It was so obvious she was Nick's favorite.

I did so many things for Nick and Kate over the years, and they compensated me—they gave me twenty-five thousand dollars from the sale of the beach house. And they paid me lump sums over the years. But I never received any compensation for handling both of their trusts. That was the one thing I detested about being the family attorney for Alex and Vaso; I was expected to be there for them, but I couldn't expect to get paid. On top of that, I had to deal with their constant bickering.

The last thing on my list is to make sure my wills are complete. No one but my attorney knows that I have two. I needed to keep my children separate. The thought has crossed my mind more than once that I should have told them about their brother. But I always felt it was best to leave things as they were. And what's done is done; and after that, I'll be ready to go.

I must stop this incessant rambling.

PART THREE

HOW IT ALL ENDS

CHAPTER SEVENTY FOUR

VASO

It's been five years since my mother died, and today she would have been eighty-nine. Steven and I picked up a bouquet of flowers for her birthday—I wondered if she was disappointed that I hadn't visited her more often. Before she died, we'd taken her to see my grandmother and Aunt Cynthia a couple of times, and she once reminded me that the frequency of her visits hadn't meant she didn't think of them often. I tried to think of that now.

Years before, our youngest daughter, Tara, had ordered the water container that was now overgrown with grass. We cleared away the weeds so we could get the container out, and Steven filled it at the nearest spigot while I took the flowers out of the plastic and broke off the stems before rearranging them. I should have remembered that two bouquets would have been better than just the one we'd brought. I kept adjusting them until I stuffed the plastic into the vase to hold them tall and balanced. As I stood to check my work, a white dove flew by and landed on the lawn across from where I stood. I listened in silence as it cooed before it took back off

When I turned back to their graves, I almost heard her say, "That's my sister and brother. And look over there; it's my parents."

My heart broke. What did she feel when she thought about them—about my father, especially? I watched as she fumbled to open her purse and pull out a tissue to wipe her eyes. We still rarely talked about my father's death, but I wondered if I should have made more of an effort to talk to her about him.

Finally, she said, "You know, I miss him. He was such a good husband."

All I could say was, "I know you do. I do too."

There was no grave marker there where that dove had landed, but I knew it was where Steven and I would eventually be buried. I never said anything to Steven, knowing he would think even for me it sounded a little eccentric, but over the years, every time we visited my parents, I'd glance over to our patch of ground, just to make sure no one else had been buried there by mistake.

Time has dimmed a lot of the painful memories of my parents' deaths; the ones that used to cut me like a sharp knife. Eventually, I quit thinking about everything every day; how I detested my brother and uncle, or how I missed my mother. I loved both my parents equally, and I would have missed them with the same intensity, but I often wondered why I hadn't missed my dear father as much after he died. Then one day I realized I'd had to set aside the grieving for him to take care of my mother. Now when I think of him, it's when I think of things he used to say or how he used to feel.

"My father would have hated this—,"I say when the lights in a restaurant were too dim to read the menu or when a restaurant was too loud.

Whenever he talked about aging and making the most of the things he loved, one of his favorite things to say was, "I only have so many good summers left. . ." or when he joked about his age, he'd say, "I don't buy green bananas anymore."

Whenever we ate out, he'd instinctively touch his plate. "Warm food on a warm plate. Cold food on a cold plate," he'd say—echoing the stories he often shared from his days working in a Detroit hotel. If the plate temperature wasn't right, he'd give a subtle shake of his head, disappointed the restaurant hadn't lived up to the standard he never forgot.

He hated it when football players forgot sportsmanship and turned a touchdown into a self-congratulatory performance, or a one-man show. He'd say, "Ama deh" (ama´deh), meaning an ignorant person like an old Greek countryman, and wave them away. When I was doing something annoying, he'd wave his hand in the air and say it to mean "knock it off."

He shows up in my conversations more often than I expect. I can still hear him say, with that glint in his eye, "I remember when I was a

Greek god—now I'm just a goddamn Greek." And whenever we're stuck waiting too long for food or dealing with poor service, I can't help but laugh and say, "My father would've looked around and said, 'This would be a great place to open a restaurant.'" He had a way of turning frustration into a punch line—and I miss that more than I can say.

And when you did something dumb, he'd call you a ding shit.

Where my father was always the funny man, my mother was the quiet one, but the glue that held us together. I still find myself surprised when I think of something I would have shared with her: she was always my first call. . .the one I turned to with news, worries or just to chat. I used to forget she was gone, and I still think, "I should tell her this." It was a habit formed over a lifetime, going back to when I'd sit at her desk and tell her about my day. Letting go was harder than I thought. ..

She still comes to mind at the most unexpected moments—like when I'd instinctively reapply my lipstick without a mirror, she'd marvel, "I don't know how you do that." I've kept the little mirror she always carried in her purse, and I use it almost every day at my desk. And sometimes, without thinking, I catch myself using her words—"You're a doll"— whenever someone shows me a kindness, just like she used to say to me.

I also remember the quiet strength she showed in grief or hardship, and the way she always encouraged me to pick myself up and start again. Her parting words when I was leaving on a trip—a mother's words that you knew just came with the territory—were "Call me when you get there" or "Drive carefully."

I never needed a pillbox until I began taking more medication and supplements, and now I have one, just like my parents. It keeps me on track and every week when I "do my pills" I think about sitting with my mother, using the list Abby typed up, and hearing my father say, "Don't talk to her while she's doing the pills."

I had Tim transfer all the accounting to my home computer, so I'd have access to everything I needed. Every morning when I log in, I have to enter her password, and it's Pappas spelled backwards. Sappap. Her name, Kate, still pops up as I open a program, and for some reason, it still surprises me. I look at it this way: in a way, she's still with me throughout my day.

I still feel a pang of guilt when I think about the times she offered to help me price new inventory for our cabin store. She always wanted to be part of it, to feel helpful, but more often than not, it was easier and faster if I did it myself. If I wasn't in a hurry, I'd ask her to unpack a box of ornaments while I made out price tags, and I'd hand them to her one at a time so she could stick them on. But when I was in a hurry, which was often, I'd tell her I was almost finished, even when I wasn't, just to speed things up. I'd thank her anyway and watch her smile as if she'd done more. Those moments didn't seem like much at the time, but now they feel like missed chances and small kindnesses I could have let her give me.

There were times I felt frustrated with my father when he lost patience with my mother—but after he was gone, I began to see how sometimes that same impatience crept into my own voice. I caught myself doing the very same thing. My mother never let it show, but I wondered how many times I'd brushed her off without realizing I might have hurt her feelings.

I recalled how my mother would occasionally jot down the names of characters in a new book to keep them straight. Just the other day, I found myself starting a book with so many characters and nicknames that I had to do the same. I flipped back to the beginning, sorted out who was who, made a note, and slipped it into the book as a makeshift bookmark. It wasn't a big deal, really, but for a moment, I found myself wondering—is this how the decline starts?

And then I remember my father's head hitting the hardwood floor and him calling out to me, "Where are you?"

When I thought about all these things, I admitted I'd become a sentimental soul, sometimes walking through my life with one foot in the past.

In 2021, I had been experiencing some pelvic discomfort, and my doctor suggested having an ultrasound. I was diagnosed with ovarian cancer—the silent killer. After the affected ovary was removed, tests showed the cancer hadn't spread, but my gynecological oncologist and surgeon highly recommended chemotherapy.

"If you don't do it, I'll shake you by the shoulders. . ." he told me.

I listened to my inner voice, and when I knew I would not die, I agreed. It wasn't the treatment I dreaded so much as the thought of losing all my long curly hair. I wasn't willing to bare my head in public, and not keen on wearing a wig, I wore brightly colored scarves tied around my head like I'd worn when I met Steven over forty years ago.

I had six treatments every three weeks, and my primary side effect was being tired and having no stamina. I told every woman I met that an early diagnosis was critical to survival.

"If you feel discomfort in your abdomen, you need to have an ultrasound," I'd say.

When you have no hair, you have nothing to draw the eye away from your other features, like bags and wrinkles, so I made sure I had makeup and lipstick on even if I was staying at home. I thought about covering my mirrors, but that signified death, and I wasn't going there. Instead, I tried to keep a smile on my face, and smiled to make my face look more cheerful.

While in treatment, I asked my oncologist about eating better, and his thought was to eat what I wanted to eat, and not worry about it. His belief was that eating to "cure" cancer, and taking supplements at this point could actually hinder the chemo process. I went with his opinion.

On my last day of chemo, the nurses surrounded me, their bells ringing in unison. It was one of the few moments during the entire journey that brought tears to my eyes.

Once my hair grew long enough to look like I intentionally had short hair, I quit wearing scarves. I thought about brushing all the curls out and wearing it like I did as a young girl, but I hated that look. Using hair products, I left it curly. I went about my life, and when I could eventually twist my hair up in a clip, I never thought about my hair again.

It was several years later, when I hadn't heard from my niece Chloe for a while, just as I thought about texting her, she called. We still got caught up three or four times a year, and she wondered if I'd heard from Alex lately.

"No, nothing's changed," I said, referring to our nonexistent relationship."

But a flicker of unease stirred in me, unsure of what might follow.

"Well, you didn't hear it from me, but he's had a really terrible stroke."

One part of me heard her words, while another struggled to fully grasp their meaning. . .

First came the petty satisfaction. . ."Well, look at that," I said to myself. Life finally caught up with him. There was a bitter part of me that felt like justice had quietly slipped in the back door.

Then, the moral conscience hit me like a ton of bricks. What kind of person thinks that way? No matter what he did, he was still a human being.

And finally, I felt a hollow sadness. . .not for him exactly, but for the finality of it all. . . for the things that would never be said, and the damage that would never be undone.

"When?" I asked.

"A little over a month ago. And he's not doing well."

Neither of us spoke. I couldn't help but wonder what was going on in her mind. I didn't sense that she'd been crying, or that she was even upset. I thought for a few moments, and then said, "I really appreciate you calling me."

"He won't let anyone come visit him," she said. "He's such a jerk. He just sits there with his oxygen. I'll send you a photo. Hey, can I ask you something? Are you going to call him?"

"No."

"That's too bad."

"You're right. It is. But he did a lot of things to hurt me and—well, let's just leave it at that."

"I miss Yia´ Yia," she said, changing the subject.

"I do too."

We talked for a few more minutes, and then she said, "Okay, gotta get ready for work. I'll talk to you later. Love you," she said.

"Love you, honey," I said.

I don't know why, but after I hung up, I thought about the wedding photo of my brother standing next to my father at my parents' reception. I couldn't help but think he was the cause of all our problems, and my ambivalence towards him now surprised me. I wasn't really sure just how I felt about him.

My niece was the only one of the grandchildren who ever called my mother and father every week when they were alive. She loved my mother, and I could still remember her as a small child waving down to us from their apartment balcony in Hawaii. She was a precious little girl.

I've thought about her often, but I didn't always take the time to pick up the phone and call her. I knew the phone worked both ways, and I vowed to do a better job of staying in touch.

Once we hung up, as much as I tried, damn me, I couldn't get vindication out of my mind. I tried to only let it simmer for a minute or two before I willed myself to think about something else. But he was getting paid back. Then I realized that living the rest of your life disabled like that was maybe too harsh a sentence, even for him. I found I didn't care about him as my brother, but as a person and a stranger; someone I saw trying to make his way down the street in a wheelchair. I think the biggest part of me felt sorry for him. He finally had a house after thirty years, and all the money in the world; but he didn't have a life to live it in. That's what was truly sad.

When Steven got home, I told him about the call.

"Now I need to tell you something, but you have to promise to keep any bad thoughts to yourself. Can you do that?"

"Probably not," he said. "Just tell me."

"Well, Alex has had a pretty serious stroke."

I could see the glimmer of a wicked smile in his eyes.

"Are you going to call him?" he finally asked.

"No. But I think I feel sorry for him."

"Well, I don't," Steven said with a shrug. "Do you think he'll leave anything for his children when he dies?"

"To be honest, I really don't know. Linda told Chloe they have a young family up there they've 'adopted'," I said, making air quotes. "I'm not sure what that means."

Later that night I went on Google and looked up the friend who was there that day with Alex. There were a few listings for a Richard Bice in the right age group, but there was no way I would have ever recognized him from over fifty years ago. I wondered, though, if he ever thought that what he and my brother did to me was wrong. If confronted, would he have said the same thing Alex did? That I was making it up?

I would never find out, for I had no intention of ever finding him. It wouldn't have done either of us any good.

Over the years, I've had my share of urinary tract infections, and each time I called my doctor, I couldn't help but wonder if I'd missed something with my mother. She used to say, "I'll just use the restroom before we go," and I'd ask, "Do you want to go or need to go?" Now, I wonder if she suffered from frequent infections that I never knew about or if she simply forgot to tell me how they made her feel. It's one of those thoughts that keep circling in my mind. If I'd known the symptoms, would her last infection have been so deadly? I'd sometimes wonder if there were other things I missed. Had she been allergic to antibiotics? And was that final dose what ultimately killed her?

Now, I live with the ache of hindsight—the weight of all the things I didn't see until it was far too late.

CHAPTER SEVENTY FIVE

VASO

I always thought being a good person meant you were good all the time. But I've learned that just isn't so. I'm a good person, but I've had a lot of bad thoughts. I'd also heard that if you can understand where a person is coming from, or why they did what they did, you can forgive them more easily.

I think both are true.

I will never forget how my brother and my uncle hurt me, but I can now understand why they acted the way they did. Stavros had spent his entire life looking at everything through critical eyes. He doubted everyone's intentions, and he questioned everyone's motives. He witnessed families torn apart by what was fair and what wasn't.

He once told me about a very wealthy friend of his who married a bleached-blonde cocktail waitress with two children. His friend had never been married, and he wanted an heir, so they had a daughter who turned out to be totally spoiled. They sent her to one of the best colleges, bought her cars, and paid for her to live in Paris for a year. I think he thought of me in that context; that I was just a spoiled child who would never grow up and assume responsibility.

I realize now that when I asked him annoying questions about my parent's estates, he thought I was asking about the money itself, when I was really only asking because I'd never experienced handling an estate before. If he would have taken the time to explain more to me and Alex, I, for one, would have understood more.

Although he had his children, he died a lonely old man. And despite everything that had happened, I had actually thought about caring for him after he divorced Jane. I'm grateful I never had to make that decision.

Alex, on the other hand, hadn't been as easy to pinpoint. He was just different. I realized he'd felt cheated in some way. I never asked him if he knew the truth about my father; instinct told me he did.

Even when my parents were still alive, I fended off calls from realtors asking if their apartments on Ocean Avenue were for sale. Recently, I'd received a call from someone asking where he could reach Alex regarding the property.

"I don't know," I said. "We don't really speak anymore." There was that good person in me saying bad things. I could have just said I didn't know.

"Oh. Well, I just sold a building similar to his for two million dollars, and I wondered if he might be interested in selling."

"I don't think he'd be interested. And can you take his name and this phone number off your list for me? Thanks."

I hung up.

Two million dollars? He was already receiving around fourteen thousand dollars a month in net rents. Was I resentful? You bet I was!

My blood boiled.

Two years later, at eighty-five, Stavros died. I didn't hear it from either of his daughters, but from Eddie Jr.'s son a month later. What a roundabout way of finding out *that* was. I called his daughter, Emma, and asked her why she hadn't told me.

"I knew you had hard feelings about my father," she said.

Hard feelings didn't come close to how I felt, and I said, "But he was still family. And family comes first. You should have let me know."

"Well, I'm sorry," was all she said. "I didn't think you'd care."

Care? What I wanted to say was, "You're right. I don't really care. Your father and my brother treated me like shit when my parents died, and they wouldn't close my mother's estate unless I signed over my quarter percent of the lemon ranch to your father. Which I'd like you to think about when you go to sell it. That was my money."

I wish I could say, for once, I didn't say what I thought.

But I *did* say it. And then I hung up.

For a long time, I couldn't shake that conversation from my mind. I had hoped that telling Emma what I thought, would bring some relief—maybe even a sense of vindication—but it rarely works out that way. I'd spoken my mind to at least three family members who have since died, and those words were impossible to take back. I've often regretted not having the strength to be the better person in those moments, but I suppose that's part of being human—we all lapse, we all stumble, and sometimes we let frustration or hurt get the better of us. It's a hard truth to accept, but it reminds me kindness and forgiveness aren't only meant for others—they're something we owe ourselves as well.

At the beginning of summer, Eddie Jr.'s son called to let me know Eddie had died of complications of Alzheimer's and a stroke. I hadn't seen him since my mother's funeral, and it struck me with some sadness that we'd never really been close. Growing up, I'd idolized his sister Kaylee, while Eddie Jr.'s hero was Alex. Quite a few years earlier, he'd relocated to Hawaii, and had retired as a warehouse manager for Costco.

There would be no services—Eddie wanted his ashes to be spread in the lush jungle behind his house.

After we hung up, I couldn't help but think that it was only Alex and me now—the last two standing, yet still worlds apart. The family ties that once bound us had unraveled years ago, and it felt as though we were playing a game of Russian roulette. Even with his deteriorating health, it was only a matter of time before one of us would be next.

CHAPTER SEVENTY SIX

VASO

On my mother's ninety-fourth birthday, I brought fresh flowers to the cemetery and sent texts to Tara, Holly and my niece Chloe.

Tara called first, and I said, "It's my mother's birthday."

"Yes, it is," she said.

"Will you come visit me when I die?"

"Most likely."

"Okay, I feel better. Love you."

"Love you too," she said.

Holly, who'd remarried and moved out of state, texted, "Wish I was there. I still can't believe she's gone."

My niece Chloe called right after that.

"I wanted to send you a picture of my dad," she said.

I checked my phone, and there was Alex with gray scraggly hair and an oxygen tube in his nose. He didn't have his cowboy hat on, and his forehead still had that weird silver blue look to it. He was actually smiling.

"I can't believe that's him," I said.

"Yeah. It is. I went to see him, and he actually let me in. Did I tell you I sent him a blanket for his birthday?"

"No."

"Well, I had one made up with photos of him and Linda, some of the dogs, a few of me, and he sent it back."

"What?"

"He told me not to send him anything, and he sent it back without even opening it."

"What a jerk," I said.

"He's an ass," she said.

"I'm sorry. I know it's hard to have a dad like that. But he's the one who has a problem, not you."

"That's what my sponsor says."

"Try to remember that."

"I've been sober a year now. Yia´ Yia would have been proud."

"That's wonderful, honey, and yes, she would have. Keep up the good work."

"It's one day at a time."

"Yes, it is. Hey, can I ask you something? If my dad dies before Linda, which will most likely happen, do you think she'll keep all the money?"

I sighed.

"I hope your dad does what he promised he'd do, but I can't answer that."

"I don't really care, but I was just curious."

"Only time will tell," I said.

"You're right. Love you," she said.

"Love you, too."

I called Abby when we hung up. The last time we'd talked, she'd asked if I'd heard from Alex recently. She said she'd left him several messages, but he never called back.

"That makes sense then, why he hasn't called. We used to talk a couple of times a year, and I've been trying to remember how long it's actually been."

She admitted she never quite knew where he stood after my parents passed away. And she shared that when he and Stavros told her she wasn't 'family,' she considered not reaching out to him again—but that just wasn't in her nature.

I told her I'd found one of my mother's old notebooks from when she took her sewing classes.

"Let me read this," I said. "Waist elastic twenty-seven inches, wrist eight and a half. And there are tiny swatches of fabric, but they don't look like anything she would have worn. Her writing was always so small and concise. Do you remember later when we could hardly read what she'd written?"

"Her writing had gotten so small," Abby agreed.

"I keep it with all my old photos in my dresser. One day when I'm gone, Tara will most likely be the one to go through my photos and decide what to keep and what to toss."

We talked about the weather in South Dakota, and then she said, "I miss your folks."

"I know. So do I."

CHAPTER SEVENTY SEVEN

VASO

In December, my niece Chloe called and said, "I've been trying to decide whether or not to tell you this."

My heart skipped thinking something was wrong with her.

"Just tell me," I said, preparing for the worst.

"My dad died."

"Oh my god," I said. I knew he'd gone downhill after his stroke, but I was dumbstruck.

"He had a massive heart attack."

"When?"

Two months ago.

I waited to be flooded by emotion, to instantly feel the loss of someone I loved—but that didn't happen. Nothing happened, and I wasn't sure what to do about that.

"Did everyone get together and decide not to call Aunt Vaso?" I wanted to know where I stood.

"No, in fact, I didn't even go up to see him. Linda said it was better we leave everything the way it was while he was alive."

Which I took to mean no visitors and no interest in talking with Chloe.

I hadn't even thought to ask if he was he buried or cremated? Knowing Alex, he would have wanted to have his ashes spread across his land. And the biggest question was what was going to happen with my parents' money? Even when we were in the middle of the ruination of our relationship, we both agreed we wanted our spouses to have access to the money if we died first, and that's why the trusts were split.

I was hoping Linda wouldn't turn her back on my brother's children—but all signs pointed in that direction. There was no way I would ever know.

When Steven came in from the garage and asked me if I was all right, I sadly said I was. To me, my brother had become just a person I knew; actually worse than that. I'd grieved more when I lost a friend. It wasn't until the next day, when Alex came to mind, that I felt my first tear brewing. It wasn't because I loved him—it was because I felt so sorry for him.

If Linda had called me when it happened, I'd like to think I would have told her how, even though we hadn't kept in touch, I was genuinely sorry for her.

I'd told myself I'd never make the trip to northern California to say goodbye if he died before me, and I was spared that choice. I didn't respect him, and when I told a friend how I felt about him, she said, "you're indifferent," and I liked that word better than saying I didn't care.

I hadn't needed to worry about it. Linda never did call.

Over the years, I've tried to remember if Alex and I were ever truly friends, and honestly, there were very few times I could think of. When I was six, I wet my pants in class. The next day on the playground, when the other kids started teasing me, he stepped in and told them he'd beat them up if they didn't quit. For all his bluster, it was clear he didn't hate me back then. For years, I'd craved his attention and approval more than I realized. I would have done anything for him to spend time with me or to just see me as a person. Even after what he'd done, I still included him in my life. Even standing up for us when I married Thomas. And I helped him buy the land with the mobile home on it.

The other day, I passed the trash truck on my morning walk, and suddenly Alex came to mind. I remembered something he told my mother when he was young. "I want to be a trash collector when I grow up," he'd said to her. "That way, I'd only have to work one day a week."

After he died, on my birthday, he crossed my mind again. For years, we had this silly tradition of sending each other the same reproduction ten-thousand-dollar bill in the same card on our birthdays. It was like a thread that said, 'I'm still here.' We passed it back and forth each year, then for whatever reason, somewhere along the way, one of us stopped sending it. I don't remember who let it go first. It was before my parents died, and already the space between us had grown too wide.

In the fall of that year, I got a call from someone I'd grown close to when she worked with me in my parent's office. We used to hide snacks in our desk drawers, and laugh if we didn't get caught eating them during the day. Now and then, she'd call just to catch up. She had been divorced with three children when she married a kind and loving man, and whenever I thought of her, I couldn't help but feel so happy for her. We hadn't talked for years, and I remembered her grandmother being my mother's favorite weekend bookkeeping clients so many years ago.

I told her about Alex, and the line went silent for a few seconds.

"You know, I always knew," she said quietly.

It took me a moment for her comment to register, and then I said, "How come you never said anything to me?"

"Your mother talked with Grannie Marie about it, and she swore me to secrecy."

"Oh my god," I said. "You've kept that a secret for almost fifty years!"

It wasn't long after that that her husband called to tell me she'd died, and I apologized to him for not doing a better job of keeping in touch. Her husband was now in his mid-eighties, and their oldest daughter had just moved into their house to help take care of him.

I couldn't help but wonder how someone could have kept such a secret for so many years. . .

In the time since my parents have been gone, just when I think I've finished with all the nonsense of it all, sadness and bitterness creep in. Sadness because I still miss my parents. I wondered if they would have been disappointed in me when we sold their house across the street, and ours, and moved away. While I was packing up our house, I came across my old Evzone costumes from over fifty years ago, and I donated them to the Greek Church.

There are still moments when a wave of bitterness catches me off guard. And when it does, I try to remember what my mother said to me, more than once.

"Alex was the one who moved away. And when he did so, it broke my heart, for I knew he'd never come back. But in the end, I got you instead."

When the bitterness crept in, I reminded myself of the one truth that grounded me: I was the one who stayed. I was the one who held my parents' hands at the end, and that wasn't just a victory—it was a bond no one else could claim.

AUTHOR'S NOTES

I got the idea for *Family Portrait* when I was sorting through old family photos after my parents passed away. When I came across the portrait, the one and only one of my family as a group on my grandmother's porch, I realized everyone had their own story to tell. This is a fictionalized memoir, and while I drew from my own observations from life, it is a work of fiction.

I always dedicate my books to my wonderful husband, Larry, who is the most supportive person I know. Whenever I have a doubt about my work, he always tells me to just write what I feel like writing. And it's the one time I always take his advice. He truly is "the wind beneath my wings."

I never want to forget to thank my dear original readers, Myrt Perisho, Pat Aldridge and Susan Denley, who gave me encouragement to begin my writing journey. Sue Jorgenson tries to find my typos, and I can't thank Diane Streich and journalism student Jaclyn Rodriguez enough for reading my author's proof copy before I give my publisher the go-ahead to print.

I've met some wonderful readers on my writer's journey, and I can't thank you all enough for not only reading my books, but for the emails you send. Please keep it up. You can always contact me at chrysteenbraun@gmail.com. If you haven't done so already, go to my website, www.chrysteenbraun.com, and check out my bookmarks and notepads; if you'd like either, just let me know and I'll send them out to you.

Chrysteen

BACKGROUND FOR THE NOVEL

Both sets of my grandparents were born and raised in Greece, and they came to America in the early 1900s. My parents were born here in America. If I don't do an ancestry test, I'm a hundred percent Greek. I say that because over the centuries, so many cultures have intermarried, I could be Scandinavian and Portuguese. LOL.

Along with most immigrants coming to the U.S., Greeks were discriminated against, and were not able to get jobs in some industries. The largest Greek communities in America are located in Queens, NY, Chicago and Detroit.

Greek is one of the richest languages in the world; over a hundred and fifty thousand words of English are derived from Greek words.

On a more serious note, while this book is a work of fiction, it is based on my life and things that happened to me.

My brother, who has now passed away, *did* touch me inappropriately when I was twelve, and somehow I was able to compartmentalize this, and I didn't allow the experience to scar me throughout my life. As an adult, when I confronted him, he denied it, and told me women made things like this up, just as he did in the book. After my parents died, I often wondered what would have happened to our family if I had told them—and I'm certain it would have torn us apart. There were times when I wondered if I should have said something, even understanding that.

Molestation is officially the crime of engaging in sexual acts with minors, including touching of private parts, exposure of genitalia, taking pornographic pictures, rape, and inducement of sexual acts. Often, it's denied or never reported.

According to the *Crimes Against Children Research Center, University of New Hampshire*, 1 in 5 girls and 1 in 20 boys are victims of child sexual abuse. Over 20% of adults recall a childhood sexual assault. Over the course of their lifetime, 28% of U.S. youth have been sexually victimized; most vulnerable are children between the ages of 7 and 13.

And approximately 63% of women have reported sexual abuse by a family member.

If you have been a victim of sexual abuse, or know of a child in need of help, contact the Rape, Abuse & Incest National Network (RAIN) hotline at 1-800-656-4673.

Sibling conflicts and eventual estrangement often arise as a painful consequence of the complexities involved in settling a trust or will. Inheritance disputes can be incredibly stressful and emotionally draining for all involved, potentially damaging family relationships beyond repair.

Unfortunately, my brother and I were perfect examples of that. When my brother moved away to break free of the rat race, as he called it, my parents felt he was no longer pivotal to their lives. I lived the closest to my parents, and for over twenty years, my husband and I were the only ones they could rely on. When their health began to fail, I was the designated caregiver, and suddenly my life was complicated by insinuations and accusations that I was taking advantage of my parents.

In the end, my brother and I didn't speak for over ten years, and then he died of a massive heart attack. It was interesting to note that this type of estrangement is also not an uncommon outcome for families after the death of a parent. In fact, over 60% of siblings disputed a will, claiming the outcome of their parent's death(s) was unfair, but only about 12% of estate disputes have reported no lasting damage to their family relationships. "Unfair" division of land and property ranked highest in arguments.

HOW TO LEAVE A REVIEW

If you enjoy my books, please take a moment to leave a review. It's a wonderful way to let other readers learn about new authors and books.

Amazon.com

1. Go to the product detail page for the book
2. Select Review this Product
3. Write a product review in the Customer Reviews section
4. Select a Star Rating (4 or 5 stars)
5. A green check mark shows you've successfully submitted your review
6. Follow my profile to keep up to date with my new books

BookBub.com

1. Click on the book to go to its BookBub Page
2. From this page, select Reviews to give the book a star rating or to leave a review
3. Afterward, if you'd like to share your review, visit the book's page on BookBub and scroll down until you see your review
4. Follow my profile to keep up to date with my new books

Goodreads.com

1. Click on the book to go to its Goodreads page
2. Write your review in the Give Feedback form
3. Leave a Star Rating (4 or 5 stars)
4. Check the "Post Review to Goodreads"
5. Submit your review
6. Follow my profile to keep up to date with my new books

THE MAN IN CABIN NUMBER FIVE, BOOK ONE

When Annie Parker discovers her husband's infidelity, she doesn't let it destroy her. She packs her bags and heads to Lake Arrowhead, California, the mountainside town where her family used to summer. Immersing herself in the restoration of seven 1920s-era cabins, Annie begins to put the pieces of her life back together. But starting over is never easy.

Alyce Murphy needs closure. When she discovers her father did not die from a heart attack, as she's been led to believe for the last 30 years, but in a murder/suicide, she is determined to uncover the truth of his death. But when she visits the cabin where her father ended his life, Alyce has to accept she may never know the true story.

Annie is looking toward her future while Alyce needs to put the past to rest. In parallel stories, both women are drawn to the rustic mountainside cabins as they search for the missing pieces—but they soon discover that the cabins have their own stories to tell.

THE GIRLS IN CABIN NUMBER THREE, BOOK TWO

In book two of the Guest Book Trilogy, eighty-one-year-old Annie Parker recounts taking on, against the wishes of her new love Noah, an out-of-town design project that leads her down a path that is more than she bargained for.

Back in Lake Arrowhead, California, a long-awaited mystery is buried in Cabin Number Three. Annie meets Carrie Davis who wants to update her childhood home on the lake and feels a tie to Annie's cabins. Apparently, Carrie's parents stayed here during the Roaring '20s when Bugsy Siegel ran an underground speakeasy and distillery. Unconvinced, Annie decides to investigate and finds their names in the old guest books—Elizabeth Davis and Thomas Meyer. As exciting as that sounds, it's only the start of a winding tale that Carrie and the new man in her life uncover. The pair unravel a family history filled with gangsters, working girls, and a surprising twist to a family tree.

The Girls in Cabin Number Three combines women's fiction with romance, cozy noir mystery, and suspense—all wrapped up in the majestic environs of this lovely lakeside haven.

THE STARLET IN CABIN NUMBER SEVEN, BOOK THREE

Return to picturesque 1980s Lake Arrowhead, California where another cozy cabin sheltered amongst the sweeping pine-lined vistas holds a long-buried secret, waiting to be divulged.

In this third installment of The Guest Book Trilogy, a young Annie Parker is struggling to overcome her grief over the recent loss of her sister, when a childhood friend unexpectedly turns up seeking refuge from an ill-fated marriage. It would have been easy for Annie to sink deeper into sadness, but when she learns her newest design client, Hudson Fisher, is the son of the late film actress Celeste Williams, her curiosity is peaked. As it turns out, the Roaring 20s starlet was no stranger to the Lake Arrowhead cabins—and this revelation sparks the unraveling of a scandalous story from Hollywood's bygone era. Did an illicit romance between this leading lady and her dashing costar take place in Cabin No. 7? What really went on behind-the-scenes during the filming of that silent picture? Will discovering a piece of the past bring closure to Annie's present?

A heartwarming tale of friendships, forgiveness, and a touch of old Hollywood glamour, *The Starlet in Cabin Number Seven* will have readers captivated from beginning to end.

THE MAIDSERVANT IN CABIN NUMBER ONE THE BEGINNING, BOOK FOUR

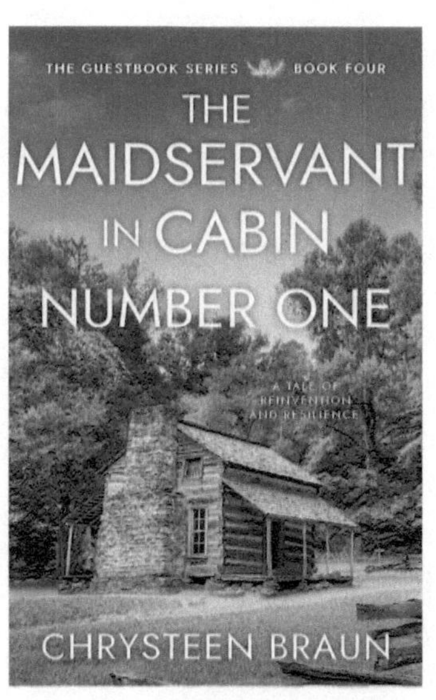

After her father's death in 1923, when Ruth Ann Landry is just ten, she joins her mother as a maidservant for a wealthy Seattle family. The hours are long, the rules are strict, but she and her mother desperately need her wages to survive.

By the time she's seventeen, they've moved into the house, and she's become a mistress to her employer. While accompanying the family on vacation, she sees an opportunity to start a new life, and leaves. Ruth eventually finds solace in the mountain town of Lake Arrowhead, California, where she stays in one of the cabins owned by a man who becomes part of her future.

The Maidservant in Cabin Number One is the beginning of the story of The Guest Book Trilogy, and of Annie Parker who eventually comes to own the cabins where Ruth Landry stayed.

DEAR NOAH: THE CONCLUSION, BOOK FIVE

Now in her mid-eighties, Annie Parker reflects on a life shaped both by heartbreak and healing. Her journey began with a life-altering decision to start anew, dedicating herself to restoring a collection of 1920s-era cabins, each rich with its own story. Through this labor of love, she wove together the memoires of her past with the promise of her future.

In *Dear Noah*, Annie reflects on her passionate love affair with Noah Chambers, a relationship filled with joy and laughter but overshadowed by an ominous prophecy from an Indian fortune teller. As their love story unfolds, the prophecy casts a long shadow, leaving Annie alone and mourning.

Seeking refuge from her sorrow, Annie moves to Prescott, California, hoping for a new beginning near her mother. There, she meets Phillip, the charming owner of the local antique shop, who help her navigate the complexities of love, loss, and second chances. Through the stories embedded in the cabins and her evolving relationships, Annie discovers that life still holds surprises, and that healing is possible at any stage.

Dear Noah: The Conclusion is a tale of love, loss, and the rediscovery of hope in life's later years. It offers a poignant exploration of resilience and the enduring strength of the human spirit, reminding readers that it's never too late to embrace hope and love.

WHEN THE DAFFODILS BLOOM: CHARLOTTE'S STORY, BOOK SIX

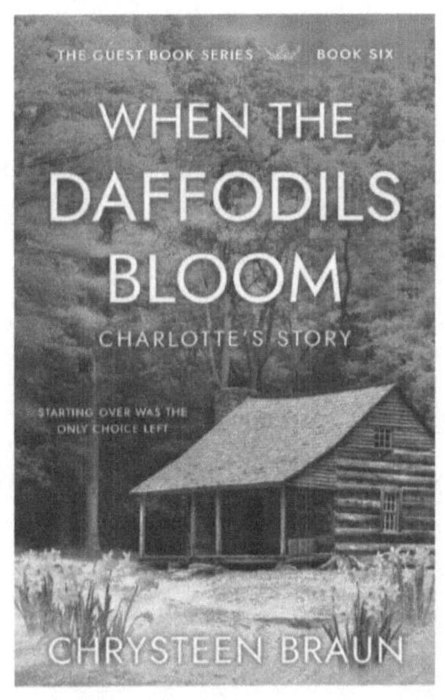

Another story of love, friendships, and new beginnings with a touch of mystery for fans of The Guest Book Series. All books can be read as stand-alones.

In the 1920s, Charlotte Hayes grew up in a small, dusty Texas town where she and her mother dreamed of one day opening a diner; a place filled with warmth, laughter, and home-cooked meals. When her mother dies, Charlotte carries that dream with her to California, determined to find a new beginning.

A housekeeper in a luxurious hotel by day, at night she sings in the smoky lounge to make ends meet. She falls in love but is pulled into a web of mobsters, and when she witnesses a killing in one of the hotel suites, she knows staying in Los Angeles isn't an option.

She flees to the quiet refuge of the Lake Arrowhead Mountains, to her friend Ruth Landry, (*The Maidservant in Cabin Number One*) and while rebuilding her life, she takes a detour when she reluctantly marries a man with ties to the Tudor House and Bugsy Siegel. After his death, she's alone again, but discovers he's left her with a shoebox filled with his memories and money.

With grit and determination, she restores a fire-damaged building in town and opens her diner. The only thing she's missing now is love. Her heart still waits for it to find her.